Tell the Truth;
The Devil Won't

Tell the Truth; The Devil Won't

Colette R. Harrell

Urban Books, LLC
97 N18th Street
Wyandanch, NY 11798

Tell the Truth; The Devil Won't

ISBN 13: 978-1-62286-819-3
ISBN 10: 1-62286-819-6

First Trade Paperback Printing November 2015
Printed in the United States of America

10 9 8 7 6 5 4 3 2 1

Distributed by Kensington Publishing Corp.
Submit Orders to:
Customer Service
400 Hahn Road
Westminster, MD 21157-4627
Phone: 1-800-733-3000
Fax: 1-800-659-2436

Dedication

To my mother Dorothy, because she shines bright.

Acknowledgments

Every road is unique. Still, God can! I had, and still have, big dreams. And my age doesn't matter, thank you very much. I only have to pull up Amazon to see how many other authors are working just as hard to make it. We all are in a stage of perpetual hope.

This is my sophomore project. No longer a neophyte, I still feel brand-new. In the last year, I've learned some things. For every person that leaves your life, God has others ready to step in. For every person who lets you down, God has fashioned someone else to hold you up. These thanks are for those who never stopped praying, encouraging, and providing help along the way. You are stars shining bright; darkness cannot comprehend you.

You always have to thank the one who has seen you at your best—and worst—and still calls you Baby. Thank you, Larry. To my children, Langston and Melissa—keep going, it's all good. To Asia and my new grandson, welcome to the family. I promise to love you forever.

There are family members that work the dream with you. My daughter Melissa, my worker bee, and encourager. Best friends are sisters too. Jackie is always on the other side of my husband helping to make it all happen. Whatever is needed, she's there. To my sister, Marcia, you're awesome. If you know her, then you have probably bought a book from her. My cousin Faye, more than a state away, but she called on everyone she knew to buy a book and promoted me everywhere she went. And, thank you to Dianne and Paul, Richard and Joyce, Angela and Aunt Dorothy. Also, cousin Cynthia, and Melanie. Y'all are truly ride-and-die family. To all the Harrells, you've been so supportive and your hearts have been in the right place.

I have a group of people who are so confident in their own abilities that they were able to champion mine. They are the cream that rises to the top. So secure in their own abilities that they were able to stand and applaud me. This group is golden. They are my Dream Runners: Pam, Rita, Jackie C., David, Fredrina, Gregory, Janet, Khalila, Latonya, and Cathy. You have no idea how each of them helped me. Special shout-out to Carolyn and Celeste, much love for your leadership! My book launch party posse: Langston, Breyanna, Keonna, Karlos, Keisha, Z, Luanda, Martina, Tchaka, and Vincent. And Evangelist Earline is in a class of her own. To all of you, your continued diligence in making me shine was amazing. I am humbled.

Then there are those who promise to support you and do. Thank you to Alyncia. Shout-out to all the SIVAD book club members. Thank you to the First Ladies who championed me, First Lady Sheila at Eagle Rock, Elder Sondra Graham, First Lady Delrita and to People's Community Church in Detroit, and the awesome members of Kingdom Christian Center in Columbus. To Victoria Christopher Murray and Joylynn Ross (EN.Joy), your mentorship continues to be invaluable.

Thank you, Toni, Todd, Adia, and Alice for your contributions. Along the way I have met some great people that have inspired and supported me: Ella, LaSheera, Orsayor, and LaShaundra. Their encouraging words and deeds kept me amazed. Kathy, Kevin, Lance, and Prophetess Joanne . . . Lord knows you've prayed me through; much love!

I do my own book covers, and it's never without amazing help. Thank you to the photographer; Karlos of Fulton Enterprises; model, Takeiciou; makeup artist, Melrose; and SIVAD Boutique for the jewelry.

There are people who knew you way back when . . . and they remember. Thank you, Sandra and Annette, you went the extra mile. To Southwest Detroit, they closed down our school but not our hearts.

Prologue

In The Beginning
2007

Now war arose in heaven, Michael and his angels fighting against the dragon. And the dragon and his angels fought back, but he was defeated, and there was no longer any place for them in heaven. And the great dragon was thrown down, that ancient serpent, who is called the devil and Satan, the deceiver of the whole world—he was thrown down to the earth, and his angels were thrown down with him (Revelation 12:7-9, ESV).

Thunder, lightning, and rain streaked across the hemisphere. Ominous swirls of rapier tails materialized, forked tongues snapped, and fangs gnashed in the darkness. A battle was raging. It was a war of infinite proportions. Brilliant light streaked across the dark where clashes of midnight scaly wings met their match as they engaged wings powered by truth and justice.

Michael's angels were of superior supernatural strength. Lessons were being taught, mettle tested as Archangel Michael rose to the forefront wielding the sword of the Spirit. With one swinging arc of his arm, eerie cries and shrieks trailed behind fallen demons. There were no triumphant cries in response, just silent blinding light—then nothing.

One battle down.

Michael's legion of angels took flight to return home.

Swiftly they flew through softly perfumed clouds that floated through the firmament. A collective sigh of satisfaction echoed in their wake. This was the first heaven. The battle took place directly below it, but there was no evidence or residue here of the skirmish. The foulness of demon debris was too close to the glory of God not to burn into nothingness. Expectant, the angels flew higher.

The second realm of heaven twinkled with stars, and a crescent moon glowed. On the other side, the sun shone, marking the way to paradise.

Michael soared, stretching his torso to its full capacity; his wingspan filled the area around him. Elation filled his being, and it reverberated throughout his legion. They were almost there.

They burst into the last realm, freely gliding through the air, their wings humming in harmonic joy. No other place held the majesty of it. No human mind could imagine its splendor. The gates were made of one solid pearl, and its jewel-encrusted walls were so pure that they resembled the most delicate of hand-blown glass.

Angels stood guard before the gates. This was the New Jerusalem scheduled to descend into the earth realm on the command of God Himself. Like a nuclear missile aimed for the devastation of mankind, the Holy City would descend for those who held out against the mark of the beast, but were graced for eternal peace. Michael continued southward to meet his brother, Archangel Gabriel, the holy messenger.

The two met. They were mission-bound, determined, and fierce. Gabriel's second in command was Zadkiel, a dominion-class angel. Zadkiel's assignment was important to the greater good. Evil was creeping into an area where it was once defeated. It was their collective divine purpose to destroy its stronghold.

A short flutter of activity announced their guest's arrival. Dominion angel Zadkiel had reported to council.

Zadkiel gestured to the guards at the gates. "The Seraphim's glow brings such warmth that each day, I am loath to leave." He spread his wings upward and tilted them to absorb the light force's maximum portion.

Attuned, Michael's wings spread wide before him, and the armor of his coat shined metallic in the jeweled wall's reflection. "But leave you must. It is a just cause. It's one that will help to prepare many of God's children for war. Without our help they will perish."

Zadkiel twirled up into the air, dipped, and sailed next to Gabriel, who shook his head at his antics and said, "This is serious business, and you play?"

Zadkiel's expression was patient. Michael almost smiled. Gabriel's fierce countenance looked alien on his face. It was Michael who was the warrior. Yet, Gabriel panted in exasperation at Zadkiel's antics.

Zadkiel moved forward. "I am not at play. The earth is filled with broken humans. It is necessary for me to fill my own cup to overflow, so that I may fill theirs, to do His will. The healed are overrun by the magnitude of acts committed by the misled. They are getting weary in well doing. As a dominion angel I am charged to cover the guardian angels on their assignments. Some hold earthly devotion for their charges and have become glorified babysitters. There is slack in their ranks. 'For whom He loves, He chastens.'"

Faster than mortal beings could measure, Michael faced Zadkiel. He leaned forward a hair's breadth away. His eyes glowed, fervent in his message. "There are many who were healed, but lost faith. As a result, they became entangled again. Evil is restless, and never slumbers. It stalks its prey, searching through the mirrors of the soul to see if the Holy Spirit dwells within.

Man is confused. He turns away those with a tarnished history. But, it is those who have stumbled that God can use mightily for His Kingdom. They were bold, cunning, and confident creatures of the dark one. We need their kind to turn once again from their wicked ways and embrace holiness. Do not be afraid of the damaged. Once they are healed; they are our greatest warriors."

Gabriel nodded in agreement at his brother's wisdom. He then addressed Zadkiel. "Remember that love counters all. Agape love is the greatest, but there are other forms the Great I Am has created. Some run from it, ignore it, abuse it, and misuse it. No matter how they act, let love rule."

Zadkiel twirled one last time up into the heavens, sailing over the cherubim, whose four faces and four wings were filled with eyes glowing with wisdom and protecting God's glory. He was filling his cup, his chest glowed bright from the connection with their illumination.

Michael's voice reverberated through his mind, and Gabriel's command resonated throughout his being, "Go, daybreak cometh."

They watched as Zadkiel descended swiftly. He passed angelic forces relieved of their nighttime duty, and upon return, were rising into their heavenly homes. Simultaneously, legions of angels assigned to the daytime descended with Zadkiel for their assignments.

Michael the warrior smiled as he shared the telepathic link of Zadkiel's final message to his commander in chief. "I shall not fail. Let love move every mountain."

Chapter One

It was dead cold. The air crackled with the sound of ice-covered tree branches crashing onto cement sidewalks; it was an unnatural arctic day, even for Harlem. There were motorists stranded on every major highway as an epic ice storm settled over the length of New York City. And while the air over those highways was filled with road rage, explicit language, and hunger pains, the contrasting hush of the opulent brownstones on 132nd Street was shattered by an eerie scream that filled the bitter air.

Monica Hawthorne, the ex-Mrs. Briggs Stokes, stood shaking uncontrollably. Her beloved, risked-everything-she-had-to-have-him husband of one month, Randall, lay in a pool of blood on their imported Brazilian cherry kitchen floor. If Randall could, he would have stood up and told her for the tenth time that ten thousand dollars for a floor was too much, and just because she could buy it didn't mean she had to.

But Randall couldn't utter a word. She watched horrified as his blood seeped into the natural grooves of the wood, giving credence to the fact that maybe the cost was too much.

Monica blinked, but he wasn't getting up or giving her advice about her newly acquired wealth, because standing over him was his newly divorced wife, the ex-Mrs. Meredith Hawthorne. This She-Spawn-from-the-Pits, with her six hundred-dollar hairdo mussed, her designer clothes askew, and her chest heaving in spastic breaths, clutched the knife that once protruded from Randall's chest. Words of explanation weren't necessary; the vivid picture painted its own morbid story.

Monica was spellbound. She was in her own home. The ordeal of leaving one husband to claim another's was behind her. The guilt had been laid aside. The shame stamped down, at least temporarily. It was Randall and her against the world. But it had all just changed drastically.

Snapping to, Monica shrieked, "Oh sweet Jesus! What have you done? You crazy—!" Her cries were halted by the demented gleam in the ex-Mrs. Hawthorne's eyes. The maniac's focus switched from Randall to her, then back to Randall.

Mrs. Hawthorne had gone mad, crazy, bonkers, cray-cray.

Monica's head hurt at the thought that she was still addressing this woman by what was rightfully her new name. It bore psychological study that she could only think of the witch as Mrs. Hawthorne. For over three years the woman had railed it at her, negating Monica's right to ever wear the title. She'd stood in haughty arrogance and promised in divorce court that she would never relinquish it. At the time, Monica didn't care; she felt Mrs. Hawthorne could keep the last name, as long as she had the man. Now she felt she had been short-sighted. If in the middle of a bloody rampage, she thought of her that way, then who was she?

The murderous interloper looked on in glee as blood bubbled out of Randall's mouth. Monica observed her spiteful approval as Randall's hand feebly stretched over his wound, but failed in mustering the strength to staunch the flow of his river of life. His eyelids fluttered—pausing, fighting to focus as he scanned beyond Mrs. Hawthorne's face. His eyes settled on Monica's outstretched hands.

"Randall," Monica whispered. She swayed in agony. Time was grinding to a stop, like an old-fashioned watch discarded in a moth-eaten hope chest, it would soon end, and Randall would be done. She needed a way to get close to him, but Mrs. Hawthorne stood as she had for the last three years, directly in her path.

Always . . . in my way.

Rage bubbled into a go-for-broke moment. Monica launched forward and charged Mrs. Hawthorne with a Joan of Arc warrior's roar. The sound of the impact and responding grunt was dulled by the body that crumpled to the floor. Monica gambled . . . and lost. Her body fell inches from Randall's.

Her hands bloodied, Mrs. Hawthorne rocked in despair. She had meant to take her time with the slut, but her offensive attack had taken her by surprise. Then . . . Monica moved. What she was witnessing had Mrs. Hawthorne's keening wail ricochet throughout the spacious brownstone. She glowered in anguish, howling as Monica's fingers inched toward Randall's, and they entwined even in their near-death status.

She watched in ghoulish repulsion as the almost loving tableau played out before her. Her eyebrows arched as she made out Monica's pleading words, "Jesus, help us."

A rattle of air descended from Randall . . . and then stillness.

In slow motion, Mrs. Hawthorne turned in robotic movements away from the scene. Her steps faltered when she heard Monica's fading voice, "Father, why hast thou forsaken me?"

The prophetic words washed over her as she stood in cold resolution. Shaking it off, she strutted away from the two people who had humiliated her in public and had caused her heart to bleed dry for three unbearable years.

Randall had won his freedom, imprisoning her in her own madness in the process.

She had sworn to Randall's dying mother, there would be no divorce. Tears gathered at the end of her hawkish nose, dribbling onto her twice-a-week, spa-waxed upper lip, then streamed down her cosmetic-tightened neck. She was Mrs. Meredith Hawthorne, of the Hawthornes, and failure was foreign to her.

In agony, she backtracked, and stumbled, tumbling over the bodies. Blindly, Meredith wiped her eyes, reared back, and spit in Monica's face. Still feeling empty and unfulfilled, she stared, craving the ability to wake Monica and kill her again.

Rising, she noted Randall's discarded, prized Civil War-era, matching pearl- and jewel-handled knives. She blew a kiss at him, and left the knives there. It was only fitting Randall have ownership of what he demanded in the divorce decree. What better way to deliver his bounty, then to use it as the method of obliteration for both he and his tramp?

Mrs. Hawthorne reached into her purse and pulled out her derringer. Acting as a lover whose desire is close to fulfillment, she caressed it.

Her insides churning, she panted, taking one last glance at the co-conspirators to her destruction. She could answer Monica's final question. God had forsaken Monica because she was a Delilah home wrecker. What Mrs. Hawthorne wanted to know, was why He had forsaken her.

She lay the letters for her children—who never called— on the solid mahogany credenza, then her purse. All she'd had was the facade of a happy life. She'd paid for it in an avalanche of tears as she played dumb blonde to Randall's neglect and numerous indiscretions over the years, anything to keep him home.

And how had he repaid her? By falling for a nasty, ashy-prone, ghetto rat. The slut's resulting pregnancy, and his request for a divorce, "so he could be happy" was the Joker's wild card. How many wrongs was she expected to endure?

She looked around and hiccupped laughter—a great-granddaughter of the Confederacy ending up in a brownstone in Harlem?

Well, rise up every long-buried plantation owner and move over. I'm coming in, and from this gaudy, overpriced slum.

In the middle of her cynical chuckle, she bit her lip. She was stalling and knew it. The gun shook in her hands as she placed the barrel to her temple; lips pressed together, she focused on the brightness of the moon, brilliant against the frigid dark sky.

The trigger was pulled, and the gun clattered to the ground. Once again blood seeped into the Brazilian cherry hardwood floor.

It should now have been quiet in the apartment. Instead, after the booming sound of the gunshot, you could hear through the intercom three things: the startled cries of a newborn, a phone ringing, and a feeble whimper.

The air was clear and sweet with the aroma of citrus floral and the essence of myrrh. Large winged inhabitants fluttered about on missions of supreme purpose. Above, two hovered in midflight, one apparently holding the other from takeoff.

"Why do you hold me, Zadkiel? I must go. Did you not hear Monica scream? I am hers, and she is mine. Monica thinks that God has forsaken her. I am here," he bemoaned. What the guardian saw split him in two. He could not linger.

Zadkiel pulled the guardian angel back, his wings clutched, and held him firm through the struggle. "Stand down. She cries out in fear, not faith. We are not charged to react to tears, but we are rewarders of faith. What is occurring is heartbreaking, but you have not been given leave to interfere."

The guardian wanted to push at Zadkiel's wings, but that would have been disrespectful. "Oh, why do the humans act this way? Must they torment and cause such pain to each other? They have left a child and though Monica has not been innocent for many years, her screams of pain bring too many hurtful emotions to the forefront. How can you float above it all?"

"I am not above anything, but we must be obedient to our Lord of Hosts. He has not given us permission to intervene; a greater good must be coming." Zadkiel then telepathically shared with him how he kept the sounds of Randall's and Monica's pain in the background of his thoughts. "I am empathetic to your feelings. I have learned that our God knows all and His will is the only way. He did not create this mess, but He will make a way out for the innocent babe. Go sing a song of praise. It will ease your soul."

Large expansive wings flapped in decisive strokes as a voice of power and beauty soared over majestic heads. As other voices joined in song, the angelic choir trumpeted the holiness and sovereignty of God. Contrary to the chaos, He continued to reign.

In another realm, the gates of hell rattled in anticipation of the eventual capture and consumption of the new souls. It was a two-course meal: adulterer and murderer, their favorites.

Chapter Two

In Atlanta, Georgia, the winter had stilled any lingering smells of magnolias floating through gauze-covered windows. The night air was crisp and cool. Briggs Stokes, the ex-husband of Monica Hawthorne, finally had an opportunity to put his feet up and open his mail. It had been a hectic day. Having primary custody of his son made most days hectic.

His laptop open, he did his usual evening ritual of reviewing his e-mails and reading the few letters that still came from the U.S. post office. His brow furrowed when he saw a thicker envelope postmarked by the same lawyers that represented Monica in their divorce. Briggs's heart thudded as he slit the envelope open and began to read. Within minutes his evening was ruined.

"When Hades freezes over!" Briggs shouted, slamming down the letter from Monica and Randall's attorneys demanding primary custody of his son. "You leave me, and now you want my son?"

Briggs picked up the subpoena and read it again. Initially, Monica's desertion had devastated him. Later he realized that he had invested in a life with someone who had never made a deposit into his. Now, this summons was launching him backward in time to a place he had fought like a chained junkyard dog to gnaw his way out of. He couldn't and wouldn't let this throw him back into a world of darkness and fog.

Two years before, ten months after Monica left, he'd hit his lowest point. But the revelation for his comeback came with a knock on the door, in the form of his father, the world renowned televangelist, The Honorable Bishop Stokes.

The day care staff looked askance as a scruffy, unkempt Briggs dropped his three-year-old son at the child care center. He ignored them and left. His intentions were to drag himself home and into bed, an unproductive habit he had been performing for months.

A half hour later, mission accomplished. Briggs stumbled out of his jeans and into his unmade bed—a siren luring him closer. He sighed and sank into its peace. Then a loud knock at his door disturbed him. Sleepwalking into his living room, over papers and fast-food bags, he snatched open the offending door. His father, his image thirty years in the future, glowered at him.

Bishop Stokes eyeballed a hole into Briggs's disheveled appearance. He stepped past him, his eyes recording Briggs's stained shirt, spotty goatee, and uncombed hair. He sneered at his sagging boxers. "Son, I'm sorry for your pain, but this can't go on. I have members everywhere, and I don't need my phone ringing from day care staff who are worried about Briggs Jr.'s daddy."

"So, you worried about what people are saying? Of course you are," *Briggs snorted, as his father took a seat.* "Stupid of me to think you came here for me."

Bishop Stokes stood abruptly, his actions dislodging his Kangol cap. "Son, I raised you to respect your elders." *He picked up his hat and hit it against his thigh.* "But it sounds like you buried a bone, and it ain't dead yet, 'cause the taste of it is still in your mouth." *The bishop waited for Briggs to say something. When he took the Fifth and remained silent, Bishop Stokes growled.* "It's

Monica you're still angry with, and she's not here, but I am. So make yourself happy."

Briggs spewed years of frustration. "How come you have wisdom for everyone but me? Where's my prophetic, 'God's going to turn things around' word? I need an appointment with one of your fifty assistant ministers? Should I call your hotline for prayer? Tell me, Daddy, how do I get in touch with the Honorable Bishop Stokes?" Briggs held his father's incredulous stare.

Bishop Stokes flopped down, shaking his head. "You rattling my cage? That girl leaving you has made you slip and bump your head. Her abandonment has you believing you been neglected? Boy, we were inseparable right up until you entered college. You were entering manhood; it was time to allow you to walk all the talk—time to let you make some new mistakes. Why make ones I had already made? Those lessons were already taught and learned. It was time to let you make a new sin that needs a different repentance, to become the teacher for someone else."

Briggs clapped his hands. "And the award for father of the year goes to—"

"I will pull off this belt and old school you. Better yet, I will meet you outside in the yard with some boxing gloves. Forget what LL Cool J said, 'Daddy gonna knock you out,'" Bishop Stokes stood to leave. "Where are you coming from to disrespect me like this? I love you, son. But I am not the punching bag to absorb your pain." His lined face was creased with agony. "Is this the coping lesson you're teaching Briggs Jr.?"

Briggs heard the break in his father's voice and saw his contorted face. He realized he had attempted to share his pain, instead of his heart. Shaking his head, he murmured, "I can't do this. We should talk some other time."

"No, you've been wallowing for months. We'll talk now. Can I tell you what I've observed over the years?"

"Could I stop you?" Briggs gave a short fake laugh.

His father gripped his shoulder. "Honor thy mother and thy father, Briggs, and your days will be long. You gon' fool around and shorten your days anytime now. You ready to give me some honor and listen?"

A chastened Briggs straightened his posture. "Yes, sir."

"God didn't make this storm, but He can navigate you through it. You at the altar crying about God letting Monica leave you when you should be at the altar asking Him to show you your next level." His grip on Briggs's shoulder turned into a supportive squeeze. "Y'all created what I call false intimacy. It wasn't real; but it sounded right. You had a baby together, so it looked right. But it wasn't. Like those scripted reality shows. You don't know those people. It's all smoke and mirrors. You and Monica had your own reality show. You were the only fan in your real-world fantasy."

Briggs attempted to defend their relationship. "Well, the pain is real. And—"

Bishop held up his hand. "Shush, let me finish. She wasn't the first person you ran to with your triumphs or your failures. When you got the new church you called me and your mama. Told us you would tell her later."

Red-faced, Briggs said, "She wasn't at home at the time."

Bishop paced impatiently. "Neither were we. Boy, we don't live with you. You called us on your mama's cell just like you could have called Monica."

"You're really making me feel better," Briggs said. His sarcastic tone wasn't lost on his father.

Flat-footed, Bishop glared. "Oh, is that why I came—to make you feel better for a little while? Or was it to help *you see that you have your whole future ahead of you? There is a woman out there who will love and pray for you so much, you will have a Peter experience and receive healing whenever her shadow passes over you."*

Briggs blinked and mumbled, "Esther."

"What's that, son?"

Briggs shook his head as though clearing it from a barrage of distorted memories. "I hadn't thought of anything I might be gaining. I couldn't see past the loss." He then buried his face in his hands and breathed.

"I think . . . No, I know I felt that I had been obedient to God in staying with Monica when I wanted to divorce her right before I learned she was pregnant. Her leaving feels like a slap in the face of my sacrifice."

"I remember, son, but scripture says obedience is better than sacrifice. Your answers lie with you. Did you hear from God before you up and stayed with a woman who had already left you long before your thoughts of leaving her?"

Briggs sought to clarify his and Monica's timetable for his father. "She hadn't left me back then, Dad. We were still together."

"Oh, she had left you. Did she listen to your dreams? Did she support your goals?" Bishop Stokes said, fingering down an invisible list.

Briggs had to shake his head.

Bishop Stokes nodded. "Okay. She wasn't employed outside of the house so did she cook your meals, wash your clothes, handle paying the bills? Make love to you as only a wife can? Share her dreams, her goals, and her needs?"

Briggs hung his head in defeat. "Well, for a minute, and then . . . Uh, no."

He slapped Briggs lightly with his hat. "Then, she had already left you; you just didn't know it."

Briggs clutched his stomach as though he had been punched in the gut.

"Son, back then you called me, and I tried to counsel you on making good choices. You thought that meant staying with Monica. When you said you and Monica were reconciling, I didn't have the heart to tell you that sometimes what looks right is just that—appearance."

Briggs's head swiveled around. "Staying was a bad decision?"

"As pastors, we want to send our members the right message. You stayed with Monica all these years because you thought your sacrifice made you a better man of God. Now, there are those Christians who believe marriage is forever, even if it turns bad or dangerous. But you're the only one who knows what God spoke to your heart."

"I felt that no matter what, I had to give my marriage all I had to try to make it work," *Briggs said, brushing his fingers over his fuzzy hair.*

His father's voice was sympathetic. "And now she's gone. She had the courage to do what you only thought about. This is your blessing, a season to begin again. It doesn't look like it, but it is. Don't try to hold on to what's letting go of you."

Briggs's cloudy eyes became clear and focused.

"Maybe Monica did do me a favor, both of us just going along, day to day." *Briggs spoke with final resignation.* "She didn't go about it right. She could have done it better—" *Overcome he said softly,* "I got a great son out of the marriage."

"He's the best. You've done the pity party, now get your Holy Ghost dance going. Pray your way through this. Ask God for your next steps." *Bishop Stokes wrapped Briggs in a fierce hug. He then marched to the front door, then turned to face him.* "Forgive her and move on.

It's okay to fall, son. A man standing before me with a history of falling also has a history of getting up."

Briggs's smile was genuine. *"Yes, leaning, but I'm up. More proof I'm now in my right mind. I'll take Mama's offer to help out."*

"Troubled halved can make you whole." Bishop Stokes stepped outside and called over his shoulder never looking back. *"Get reacquainted with some soap and water, son. You liked to scorch the hairs in my nostrils."*

Intent on the present, Briggs shuffled through the legal document and heaved a sigh. He had pulled himself together after his father's visit. The next week, he had stepped down from the small church he was pastoring and took a sabbatical. For months, his mother came over daily and helped him stabilize Briggs Jr.'s days. She even gave him the nickname BJ and it stuck.

When Monica's guilt had subsided enough to ask him for weekend visitation, he reluctantly allowed it. As long as Randall was not sleeping at her place when BJ was there, he agreed. At that point BJ was four years old, and he just wanted his mama.

Their arrangement started out fine. While Briggs had retreated from his relationship with Monica quietly, Randall's wife had fought, with spite, hatred, and bitter revenge. Her weapons were carnal, persistent, and ugly. She'd even had Briggs hauled down to the courthouse to be disposed and drawn into her and Randall's divorce proceedings.

He'd told his truth, to shame the devil. Only the devil has no shame, only more devastation.

He'd tried to help; felt it was his Christian duty to caution Meredith Hawthorne to look up and live. But as spittle ran down her chin, she tried emasculating him by labeling him weak and ineffective, blaming him for not being able to keep Monica under control.

On that day, Briggs knew Meredith was losing it, and he had warned Monica.

Then, Monica got pregnant by Randall after two years of Randall fighting to get a divorce.

The pregnancy caused the volcano to erupt between Randall and Meredith, and when the cinders were sifted through, Randall won the divorce, but lost his social standing in Atlanta. Last month, Monica married him, and relocated to Harlem. She hadn't seen BJ since. Briggs thought a new marriage, baby, and city were keeping her busy. Not an elaborate plan to steal his son.

The day before, he had received the best news of his life next to his son's birth. Love Zion, his first church assignment, wanted him back. Reverend Gregory, whom he had subbed for as interim pastor over six years before, wanted to retire. He was asking Briggs to take over his legacy.

The cherry on top of life's ultimate sundae? Briggs's college sweetheart Esther, the woman he almost walked away from his marriage for was now available. Briggs had made the decision he was going for it all: the job, the woman, and the joy. His current circumstance had been short on passion. He wanted—no, needed—that in his life.

Briggs rolled up the papers, hitting them on the desk. "Now this man is about to make me put up my clergy collar and wring his neck." He sighed, then straightened out the document. He leafed through it looking for Monica's stamp on it. He knew her methods and couldn't see her usual maneuvers played out on it.

Could Randall be doing this on his own as some grand gesture of his love for Monica? Old wealth has long arms of influence.

Briggs vowed to get to the bottom of things and though it was after midnight, he phoned Monica. The phone rang numerous times before finally going to voice mail.

"Monica, I can't believe you would pull this stunt. Call me," he yelled.

The next morning after two more attempts during the night to reach Monica, his phone rang. It wasn't Monica returning his call, but the New York Police Department, 32nd Precinct, Harlem.

Chunks of ice melted from Briggs's Cole Haan wing-tipped oxfords. They left a muddy puddle on the pristine floor of New York Presbyterian Hospital's ICU. A normally considerate person, he didn't care. His thoughts were consumed by the comatose woman reclining in the bed. Briggs stared at the tubing connected to Monica's throat providing her only means of breathing.

She cannot be dead. I've wanted to kill her. I saw it in my dreams. But not this.

Shaky hands tentatively touched her. He exhaled feeling her warmth. "It will be okay. You're so headstrong. Fight, Monica. Fight to live!"

An authoritative voice filled the room. "Briggs Stokes? Of Atlanta, Georgia?"

Briggs spun around, his gaze made hazy with unshed tears. The doorway was blocked by a balding, medium-height man, with a pad and pen in his hand. He was rocking back on his rubber-soled heels.

"And you are?" Briggs asked curtly, offended by the man's tone and apparent disregard for common courtesy.

In response, the man arched his brow and gave a curt reply. "I'm Detective Edward McWilliams. We spoke on the phone."

His eyes scanning Monica's still form, Briggs rubbed his cheek and exhaled. "Thank you for calling me. But my family and I just got here. I came straight from the airport. Can your questions wait?"

Detective McWilliams moved a toothpick around the corner of his mouth. "Mr. Stokes, you were called to town for a reason. I know your parents and son are at the station taking custody of the baby. I like to close my cases as fast and efficiently as possible. I'd also like to go home to my family. Your cooperation is appreciated concerning this murder-suicide case."

Briggs didn't want to argue or have this conversation in Monica's presence. Hadn't he read somewhere that comatose patients heard what went on around them?

Gesturing that they step outside of the room, Briggs walked briskly down the hall with the detective on his heels. He needed caffeine. Reaching the vending machines and taking change out of his pocket, Briggs bought coffee, then sat on the nearest bench.

"What do you want to know?" Briggs sipped, then scowled that his caffeine was barely lukewarm.

Detective McWilliams flipped through his notepad. "Were you acquainted with Ms. Meredith Hawthorne? Were you aware of the tensions surrounding this new marriage, of your ex and Randall Hawthorne?"

Head hung low, Briggs remembered Meredith's facial features contorted in unbridled fury at the court deposition she dragged him into. "Meredith couldn't let go. The last time I saw her, she was in naked agony, and it was hurtful to witness."

Briggs looked up at the detective with haunted eyes. "Randall and Monica started a new life, had a baby, and it seemed that every smile they wore broke Meredith a little more. She was deranged with it." He rubbed his eyes in weary sorrow. Turning the cup up and draining his coffee, he crushed it with reddened knuckles. "I warned Monica that they should not dismiss Meredith's malice, but they continued to underestimate her wrath."

Chewing on the end of his pencil, Detective McWilliams asked, "You called several times last night, each voice mail you left was more agitated than the last. Were you in a custody dispute with the couple?"

Briggs fingered his collar, loosening the top button before giving an answer.

"Not really. I had just gotten a letter from Randall and Monica's attorney saying they wanted custody of my son. He's been in my care since the separation and subsequent divorce, over two and a half years ago. I wasn't going to allow that to happen."

Briggs leaned forward making direct eye contact. "My son loves his mother, Detective. This is a nightmare. Ironically, I will now have their daughter while she recuperates. Monica has no one else with the exception of some distant relatives in Jamaica. If there's nothing else, I need to get back. I was waiting to speak to her doctors."

Closing his notepad, Detective McWilliams nodded. "Thank you for your time. You're a good man for stepping in. Your account of the situation lines up with everyone else's, including the newspaper clippings about the divorce battle, and even Randall and Meredith's adult children said she wouldn't let go."

Briggs had one parting shot before he walked away. "No, her suicide proves she finally let go. What she couldn't figure out was how to forgive."

Two ominous figures sat in quiet contemplation. The larger one's head was gargantuan in nature, and foul droplets of acidic mucus fell from his protruding fangs.

The smaller one stood sixteen feet tall, and his rapier tail was wrapped protectively around his middle. He sat as still as cold, hard stone. His sinister eyes were yellow-rimmed and telegraphed evil cunning. He was known as The Leader.

Their silhouettes cast eerie shadows against the backdrop of the smoke-filled flames that spewed from the lake of fire. They had been here before. This place, this type of meeting. It was The Leader's least favorite venue, not because of the atmosphere, but because it was where "he" liked to meet. The Leader hated The High Master. For him, only humans equaled this type of loathing.

A thunderous voice filled the dark void, its hiss deep and unending.

"There is a barrage of angelic activity. I can smell the stench of their perfumed presence everywhere I ascend. We are losing battles. The angel, Michael, and his legion are formidable opponents. You must be vigilant. You have failed with this group before, and you begged for a second chance. It's an inane request at best, but I felt you may know the weaknesses of these disposables, and that may give us the upper hand."

The Leader sat as he always did in the presence of The High Master—silent. He wanted to wrap his tail in a protective manner around his middle, but The High Master hated signs of vulnerability. His stomach bore the signs of the last time he was bound in red-hot chains while liquid fire was poured through the gash in his middle. He had failed his assignment to destroy Mother Reed and all who were close to her. He had paid the price in guts and tears.

Mother Reed was an old human, long headed for the boneyard. Yet, she lived and raised devastation in their ranks. More than one imp had perished at the hands of her intercessory prayer. She had shaken many a demon to the core with her worship. She had to be stopped.

The High Master slithered over to him. His close proximity made The Leader visibly convulse. "Are you repulsed, toad? If you fail to complete this mission for darkness' sake, I shall personally see to your demise one century at a time. It will never end, and you will never know peace."

The Leader wanted to respond, needed to tell The High Master that he had never known peace. But eternal death was better served cold. He simply nodded his head and held his own counsel.

The High Master continued. "Randall and Meredith are surely headed here. He bought into the notion that if it feels good, let the games begin. And Meredith allowed hate and bitterness to be the travel agent for her destination staycation. Monica is the joker card in this deck. We must win her soul." He then raked his claws across The Leader's stomach. "A reminder of the penalty for failure. Do not fail me!" he screeched.

The Leader's tail inched toward his middle—an automatic reaction to his wound—but fell away when The High Master's raised eyebrows spoke of contempt for his show of fragility. His scaled back straightened into a ramrod stance, and not tears, but an angry small rivet of pus-filled muck oozed from the corners of his yellow-rimmed eyes.

The High Master chortled. He took his index claw and ripped down his own face. Gushes of membranes and slime rolled down his endless frame. "Pain is good, get pissed off. Get enraged at me, but use it against the humans. I want their carcasses strewn from dimension to dimension starting with all who are close to the old hag. Call out the spirits of pride, lustful perversions, and slothfulness." He then swayed back and forth inches from The Leader's visage. "Now get outta my face."

The Leader pivoted in the opposite direction, plotting as he slithered along. Only the small trail of slime he left behind indicated he had ever been there.

Chapter Three

Six months later

Briggs Stokes stood on the rise at the Woodlawn Cemetery in Detroit, Michigan. He stretched and inhaled. It was a clear sunny Friday, and no factory stench infused or clouded the air. His view reached beyond the manicured graves and narrowed to look down at the woman of his dreams, his yesteryears. She was cheerfully planting flowers and of all things having an animated conversation with a grave. Sighing his satisfaction, he leaned back on his car in repose.

Esther Wiley Redding looked good. Her cheeks were flushed from the mild September wind, and her short, spiked hair fluttered attractively around her oval face. She was a lush woman, with curves that called to the baser nature of man. Her caramel skin glowed with health, and his first instinct was to reach out and touch her. He couldn't see her eyes, but he remembered their luminous glow when she was happy. He wanted to see that glow again, and often. It had been seven years, and he felt as though he had walked through fire, staggering over burning, red-tinged coals to come to this moment.

He had been faithful to God, he had been obedient, and he had stayed the course. Surely she was his double reward. He wanted to run and shout her name. Since college, she was his oxygen, like blood pumping through his veins. His head tipped back, remembering her strutting across campus in her skintight jeans and bubble gum lip gloss. Years and people had gotten between them. Now it was all lining up; he just needed to believe and act on it.

His mouth opened, but he remained silent. *Esther, I'm here. It's our time.*

He gave a self-effacing grimace. He had promised himself he would be cool, but he was like a heathen in the church house. He couldn't sit still.

He had come out to the cemetery to pay his respects to Reverend Gregory, his mentor for many years. He would miss him.

Reverend Gregory had written and requested he take over Love Zion Church when he retired. But everything went wrong six months before, and Briggs was delayed. He couldn't believe that instead of taking over for Reverend Gregory's retirement, he was standing over his grave. Monica's attack and hospitalization had caused him to miss the funeral. But he'd finally been able to come to the cemetery to pay his respects.

Coming here, and accidentally seeing Esther was his sign that soon they would connect. However, he was sure that the graveside she sat at belonged to her late husband, Lawton. And, while a brother was smooth, the grave of a widow's husband was the last place he could plead his case. What would he say? *Excuse me, but I noticed that this brother has been lying down on the job. Can an alive-and-kicking brother step to the plate?*

Briggs shook his shoulders loose; he couldn't believe he had just thought something so disrespectful. That was *not* okay. The mind really was a battlefield. He got into his car before he did something stupid, like approach her.

He would come back to finish paying his respects to Reverend Gregory later.

***

Esther sat at the grave and gently patted fresh potting soil in the clay pots that sat at the end of the bronze plaque. She stood back and admired the flowers bursting with color, knowing that her beloved Lawton would enjoy them. The patter of small footsteps gave way to the arrival of her best achievements.

"Mama, these are pretty," Ruth said as she bent and sniffed a flower.

"Has anyone seen the plant food?" David asked as he approached the two.

Esther stood and stretched, as she motioned David over to her green garden caddy. She looked at her two six-year-olds, who were always together.

Ruth and David were a vivid likeness of her and Lawton. David resembled her, and Ruth was the spitting image of her father. Ruth was the real princess in the household, and was every bit aware of it.

Esther would have liked Lawton to be here to experience the joy of their children, but he had been gone for over two years. One night they lay down, cuddled, and the following morning, only she awakened. The doctors reported that Lawton had an aneurysm, something that may have remained dormant after the car accident he had been in years before, or something totally new; no one knew.

Lawton had left her two beautiful children, and the ability to love without reserve. He had done that for her, and she would forever love him for that and so many other stellar qualities. He had turned out to be her good thing, and he claimed she was his. She had mourned his passing and so had the children, but they had learned to remember the good times; there just weren't that many bad ones.

Her family and her spiritual mentor, Mother Reed, helped her struggle through the rough times. Mother Reed had recently told her, "Sweetie, a new season is coming; be patient. Only God can open or close a door. Stay aware; look for the open door."

Mother Reed—prophetess, surrogate grandmother, and wise oracle. Esther didn't know how she would have endured any trial without her. When things became unbearable and Esther wanted to kill something, Mother Reed was always able to coax her off the cliff and back to God.

She shivered; time wasn't on their side. Mother was approaching ninety years old. They had promised to have a blowout celebration when her ninetieth birthday came. A parade wasn't out of the question.

"What do you think, honey?" Esther said, speaking to Lawton as she sprayed the plaque and wiped it clean. David and Ruth looked on.

"Should we give Mother Reed a parade? You know she hates us making a fuss, but I want to do it big."

The children were used to their mother having a conversation with their father. It didn't scare them, and contrary to what their friends in first grade thought, the cemetery wasn't creepy.

David sprinkled plant food in the pots.

"David, I think you've given those flowers enough food. Say good-bye to your dad; it's time to go home."

They packed up their gardening tools and headed to the car. Esther grinned as they got into her new Infiniti SUV; lately life had been good.

She pulled onto the street heading out of the cemetery. David leaned forward. "Mom, can we go by Love Zion? I left my cap."

"David, can't that wait?" she said, glancing into her rearview mirror.

"No, ma'am. It's my favorite. Please, Mom?" he whee-dled.

Esther sighed and switched lanes. She headed to the church, hitting her Bluetooth when her phone rang.

"Hello?"

Her sister Phyllis started right in when she heard Esther's voice.

"Stop by the ice cream store and bring over some snapping turtle."

"And hello to you too, Ms. Phyllis—"

Ruth interrupted her mother, "Ooh, Auntie, let me speak to Miracle."

Phyllis called out, "She's not here, Ruth. She went to the skating rink for a classmate's birthday party, but she'll be here when you guys come over tonight."

Ruth answered in a screech that filtered over her mother's shoulder and through her ear. "Goodie, Auntie!"

Holding her ear Esther said, "I'm swinging by the church, and then home to change. I'll pick up the ice cream on my way there."

Phyllis cleared her throat. "Do you look cute?"

Uh-oh. For the last year Phyllis had been trying to matchmake for her. Even Lawton's family had introduced her to men they thought she would be interested in. They needed to stop. She had no intention of marrying again. Twice was enough; divorced, and then widowed. Three times wasn't a charm. To her it was just sad.

She exhaled noisily into the phone. "Why do I need to look cute, Phyllis?"

"Because you're going somewhere. What if someone saw you in those horrible jogging outfits you choose to wear?"

Esther took the next exit, frustrated with the fashion discussion. "I'm in jeans today. Not cute designer jeans, but old, beat-up, sagging—Farmer-in-the-Dell, where's-your-straw-hat-at jeans. But, dear Fashionista Sister, cheer up. They are not jogging pants. Bye!"

She pulled up to the church and watched as David ran inside. Shortly after, Ruth saw a friend and deserted her to walk over and speak. Esther tapped on her radio and nodded her head to the music. As her eyes nearly closed, a shadow covered her driver's window.

"Hello, Miss. You look very familiar to me. Do I know you?" a handsome distinguished-looking man asked in amusement.

Esther squealed, jumping out of the car. "Briggs Stokes! How are you? Oh my goodness. What are you doing here? How long are you staying? Where is Monica, and how many children do you guys have now?"

A wide grin on his face, Briggs held up his hand. "Whoa, Esther. Please take a breath. Let me see if I can answer those questions in order. I'm fine. I'm the new pastor of Love Zion, again! Therefore, I'm staying for a very long time."

He stepped back, and Esther's eyes catalogued his athletic stance, the shiny waves in his closely cropped haircut, and her favorite feature, the cleft in his chin. Her finger itched to make its home there, to see if it was still a perfect fit. She had to look up, due to his height, to capture all of him. Before she could catch herself, she gave an inward sigh in satisfaction. *No coveting.*

Briggs had asked her to slow down, but he spoke as though any minute he would be interrupted. "Monica left me over three years ago for a guy named Randall out of Atlanta. We have a son, Briggs Jr. He's seven years old. Due to her current situation, I have custody."

Startled by the news he was sharing, Esther couldn't help continuing her examination. She made a mental checklist of what he looked like the last time she saw him, and compared it to any downgrades she needed to make due to his age, wear and tear, and status of availability. He was ringing in at 100 percent improvement on all fronts. And, she was having a hard time concentrating on his words.

Blinking, she reined in her imagination. Briggs was still hurtling information at her faster than she could absorb it. "We tried to make it work. We went to counseling, and we both worked hard at it. But she was miserable, and it was only after she left me that I could admit, so was I."

Esther stood stunned. "Briggs, I'm so sorry to hear all of that. You've had a lot going on."

Briggs saw her expression and chuckled. "The divorce happened almost three years ago. I'm well over it. I just needed to be as upfront as possible as fast as possible." Briggs stepped closer and lowered his voice. "I hope we both have learned lessons from our past. Over seven years ago we caused rumors to fly that we were having an affair. It wasn't true, but we had enough chemistry to spark a forest fire."

Esther shook her head to stop Briggs from continuing, but he barreled ahead.

"Please, let me finish. I wasn't up front with the entire congregation, not telling them, or you, I was married. I excused my omission by telling myself that it was because my wife was once a tabloid-hounded ex-supermodel and I wanted my congregation to know me, for me. Having a famous televangelist father and infamous wife had left me insecure in my own accomplishments. They both cast some pretty big shadows. When my excuse sounded weak even to my own ears, I justified my behavior by reasoning that her stubbornness, refusal, and then postponement in joining me in Detroit, because she didn't like my new assignment, would make me look bad as a pastor. Who would want to follow a man who couldn't keep his wife by his side?"

The caramel of Esther's face slowly darkened to red. "Briggs, you don't have to tell me all of this. We made peace seven years ago. Let it go." Esther shuffled backward, creating more space between them.

Briggs closed the gap she had created by leaning forward. "No, what I never should have done was let you go the first time. But I was a young, cocky college student. You don't believe that you'll meet, 'the one' at that time in your life. You have no idea how rare love is. The second time we met, I was a pastor in an unhappy marriage. And this may be too much, too soon, but except for evil, I'm through running from anything in my life. I'm only running to it."

As he spoke, Esther watched his mouth move, and she quivered. Lawton had been gone two years. Two years was a long time to go without a man's love and affection, especially when you were used to regular doses. Her finger was twitching again to know the feel of the groove in his chin.

His voice caressed her as though he was stroking her soul. It didn't matter what he was saying, she was enthralled that he was standing before her talking at all.

"Monica is the mother of my son, and I forgave her a long time ago. She preferred to move on with Randall, and there were catastrophic consequences for their actions. I won't go into it all today, but it's not pretty."

Esther rubbed her hand against her thigh putting friction on her finger. She needed to pay attention. She was saddened by Briggs's disclosure. Whenever she had thought of him, it was with the understanding that he was somewhere as happy and content as she was. "Life is not always easy to navigate. We've all had our pitfalls."

"Yes, and like David, I have lain before God and repented of my shortcomings and been forgiven in return," Briggs said. "I had spent the last two and a half years resolved to making my life all about the church. Then I received a letter from Mother Reed that changed everything. Your Lawton had died peacefully in his sleep and left you with two children."

Briggs picked up her hand and his thumb slowly stroked back and forth.

"I am sorry about your loss. He was a good man, and I heard you had a wonderful marriage. I made the mistake of holding back from you last time. If nothing else, I'm a man who learns from his mistakes. My life is an open book. Care to read it?" Briggs asked as he inched closer.

Esther hopped back, snatching her hand away and hitting her backside against the car door. She frowned at his smile. "What?"

"Same old Esther; I'm glad I can still make you nervous. It shows you're not immune to me . . . to us," he said, placing his hand on his chest.

She knew Briggs could see she was blushing. He moved slightly away, giving her some space. "It hurt when I heard he had passed because I knew you were hurting. Mother Reed is a woman of wisdom. She didn't let me know until six months ago that you were a widow. Timing is everything, I might have jumped the gun and come to you right away. She was smart to hold that information back in her letters to me."

Esther's eyes widened. "I didn't know you kept in touch with Mother Reed."

"Oh, yes. The only letters I still write. She's been my eyes and ears to everyone's life here. Let's see, you have two children: Ruth and David, twins. Charles and Phyllis have one child, a girl. They named her Miracle. Mother Reed's long lost son Joshua married Sister Essie, and your parents are still in good health, although I understand your aunt Gert went on to glory; again, my condolences. During Reverend Gregory's illness, Mother

Reed's son, Joshua, has held the interim pastor position, but he doesn't want it permanently and it was Reverend's desire that I take over the shepherd's role here."

Briggs stopped, thought, and then continued. "Oh, yes, and Sister Abigail with all her past mudslinging and backbiting, proved to be no match for Joshua's wife, the shy and humble, First Lady Essie."

Esther fanned her hand in front of her face.

"Can you believe it? Essie took to the position like she had been in training. She came in and cleaned house like she was Ms. Clean and the Dirt Busters wrapped into one. Girlfriend worked it," Esther said and snapped her fingers in the air. Stopping, she studied him. "Briggs, you've managed to surprise me. This is a lot to process."

Leaning over her, he placed both hands on the top of the car, pinning her in-between. She was stuck with nowhere to run. "I'm way past playing childhood games, and it's a sad fact that my last real and satisfying romance was in college. Six months ago, I received two letters; one was from Reverend Gregory, the other, Mother Reed. Both opened the door for my return. It took me six months to get here. I now know, I needed to wait for God's appointed time."

Esther stared at Briggs as her eyes filled with unshed tears. Her descent onto the car seat was gradual as she tried to take it all in.

He crouched down to look into her eyes. "I am here. And I don't know how long this courtship will take, but I do know the outcome. I plan to cherish you, and your children. Whatever time I have left on this earth, I plan to spend it with you. Seventeen years we've waited to be together again. We can do this."

Briggs stepped back, and Esther was mortified to see him stare at her mouth hanging open. She knew it wasn't pretty, but she was shocked. But he had always been a smart man, and she was relieved when he veered the conversation onto safer ground. "You need to go home and get all prettied up. While you look good in anything to me, Phyllis will have a fit if she sees you in those nineteen sixty-nine Goodwill jeans." He smiled, reached down, tapped her nose affectionately, and slipped his hands nonchalantly into his pockets. "By the way, we have a surprise dinner date later at her house."

Esther tightened her previously gaping mouth. Realizing the conversation had her so engrossed that she had failed to check on her children, she glanced around and saw them watching with curious expressions. She composed herself, signaled them over, and introduced everyone.

Esther watched as Briggs captivated her children. He was good with them, bending down to their level, but never talking down to them. He joked and asked questions that he wanted answers to. Both of her children were clever enough to understand that he was interested in them, not just their mother.

Esther gasped when she told them it was time to go and Ruth leaped into Briggs's arms hugging him around his neck. She watched his face mold into one of peace and affection, and she closed her eyes to the openness in Ruth's adoration for a man she had just met. *Does she miss her daddy that much?*

As soon as they got in the car, David started teasing from the backseat. "I liked the new pastor, Mom. He looked like he be liking you. Maybe y'all will get married and live happily ever after."

Ruth had a fit of giggles. Esther groaned. As much as her heart beat furiously from her encounter with Briggs, she knew she had no intention of ever loving him again. They already had two strikeouts. Why get up to the mound and bat again?

***

The malevolent presence that had oozed itself around Esther's car watched as her taillights disappeared in the distance. Its tail slithered back and forth like a dog who was happy for a new treat. It was pleased with the results of the waves of self-doubt it sent to Esther's mind. Darkness needed to keep her chained to fear, for those who were bound lived purposeless lives. When fear had you, you couldn't get a breakthrough. Many became imprisoned by their shame. They didn't know that the One Who Rules had a greater opinion. The spirit of Doubt scrutinized the church parking lot. He looked longingly at the church, but was mindful that he could not enter.

Years before when the Briggs human left town, his pregnant wife in tow, The Leader let them all have a field day inside the church. Doubt gasped remembering the deliciousness and thrill of wreaking havoc among the members. He had even sat with the other spirits in the sanctuary, steering the service into feeble, feel-good sermons, ones that failed to feed the Word to the congregation's spirit. As a result, the people weakened, and foulness of their souls began to creep in.

"Fools!" he screeched into the wind.

He wondered how he knew more than them, for no Word equaled no weapon. What a grand time they all had. Imps whispered accusing words into susceptible ears, demented spirits danced with open abandonment; it was their nirvana. Weekly they all came back to see the disintegration of what was once a force they could not penetrate. The human, Reverend Gregory, was ill off and on and his deacons were not strong enough to hold any of them at bay. Their most formidable opponent was Mother Reed. No matter what they threw at her, she threw it back . . . and then some. But she was one, and they were more than 50,000 strong. She could not chase all of them.

Thus, they broke up marriages, caused pride and jealousy to fester in members, and used the spirit of insecurity to breed anger and discord. The carnage had been high. People hadn't just left the church; they had left Him Who Rules. It was one of Doubt's busiest seasons. Doubt was used when Mother Reed would visit and give a strong Word to a person. When Mother Reed left, Doubt would enter and soon, the person would return to their downtrodden condition. Mother Reed was so faithful, he almost failed to keep up with the old lady.

He did keep up, though, and the fallible humans had him rolling in supreme glee. Abuse ran rapid, lying was common, divorce attorneys were on speed dial, and abortion was a quick fix. Didn't they know that last step would follow them much longer than the act itself? Foolish, foolish, foolish. What they hate, they do. And their pain? It was so euphoric, even now shivers ran up his spine in pure delight when he thought of it.

A hissing sound rustled in Doubt's ear. He was no longer alone. The Leader and an imp approached.

Turning, he bowed submissively. He watched in horror as the imp spoke.

"Leader, magnificent one, what about the angels? They have been spotted as recently as this morning. They are the guardians of this bunch. Do you have a plan for their defeat?"

The Leader rose to his height of sixteen feet of pure evil. He looked over at the spirit of Doubt, who had been called in on special assignment to Esther. His fangs dripped with acidic mucus. His eyes were steely in their silent regard. Doubt gulped, backed away, and twirled into nothingness.

The Leader was livid that the imp was still staring at him as though expecting an answer. Ever since, years before, he had failed in his quest to destroy Briggs, Esther, and their respective families, he was disrespected.

"Imp, did you speak and give an opinion without my asking for it?" The Leader spoke in clear, concise, even tones. Yet, the fire underneath earth's surface glowed red at the timbre.

"I—I—I . . ." the imp winced, his features broadcasting his confusion. He knew no way out of the present dilemma, his loose tongue had walked him into.

"Now you hold your tongue, you insignificant miscreant," The Leader barked in disbelief. An imp questioned him. "What! Do not speak to me of angels. Who do you think we serve? Our leader once graced the heavens. And He whose name we do not speak looked upon him with affection. Then the fall came, and afterward we were expelled to this land, but we no longer had value. And when He created man, once again we were forced into the dust. It is a taboo subject. So . . . Do not question me about angels!"

The imp gulped, shaking in his despair. The other imps had misinformed him. They said The Leader was washed up, he had failed too many times to be powerful in their realm. He thought that this would be an easy time of it. As usual, the imps lied. He had forgotten the golden rule in their world. Lie, lie well, lie often, and never get caught. Now what?

The imp bowed low before The Leader. "You have my respect, you who have weathered the great fall, yet fights the eternal war. I am unworthy to grovel at your feet. Do with me as you will."

The Leader was impressed by the imp's will to survive. He was not stupid enough to fall for his act, but he tired of killing imps on a daily basis. They only got replaced with the likes of the imp who groveled before him. Maybe this one would last the week.

"You have a reprieve, imp. I need you to make a trip to the city that never sleeps. We named it the Big Apple because it reminded our ruler of mankind's fall from grace. Just like that bite of the apple, when people take a bite out of New York, it bites back. It's time to shake up all my old friends, again—starting with Briggs."

Chapter Four

Monica sat at the vanity in her borrowed bedroom, arranging an infinity scarf around her neck. She struggled to place the scarf just right to cover the scars from her attack and subsequent surgeries. Distressed, she squinted at her now-flawed image. She was supposed to die when that knife pierced her skin. But somewhere between crying out to God and asking Him silently to forgive her, she woke up in the hospital. Now, six months later, she had to figure out how she and her child would survive.

Randall's children were contesting her child's share of their inheritance. The Harlem brownstone had been confiscated by their high-power attorneys, and she was only surviving through the kindness of strangers. New York was still home, but her new address was a far cry from the luxury she had become accustomed to.

It was late evening. She was restless and playing dress up like some adolescent. She would need to figure out her life, just not tonight; her mind couldn't wrap around it all, and she was exhausted from trying.

The door abruptly opened, and a startled Monica's head swung in response.

"Monica, when will you get these baby items out of my living room?" Pamela paused and Monica knew what was coming. "You know, darling, I don't do children. Have you found a place to go? Little Fifi is a cutie, but she doesn't necessarily fit into my style of living."

Pamela leaned into her room and arched her eyebrow.

It was eight o'clock in the evening, and Monica's friend from her modeling days was dressed to draw admirers and benefactors. Her finely arched brow indicated the seriousness of her complaint.

"Sis, I do appreciate you letting me live here. I'm working hard to figure it all out. And, my baby's name is Fiona, not Fifi." Monica was irritated, but determined to sound pleasant. She'd used the *sis* term to draw Pam's memory of how far back they went, and how close they used to be.

"Monnie, I know I've said it before, but what kind of name is that for your little girl?" Pamela placed her hands on her hips, making her dress rise even higher to the top of her toned thighs. "I know you told me it means fair and the chile is real light. But dang, girl. Fiona? Now mind you, I ain't ever felt a person should up and call their child by the name of something crazy, like liquor. You know when a résumé says, Asti Spumante Jones ain't nothing gon' happen. Kiss that job good-bye, because your mama was too ignorant to find you a decent name. And then, there are folks calling their babies by some car's name. I mean, Infiniti, Lexus, and Seville? Girl, they've even stopped making that last one. Where they living? A house or a garage? You know they gon' end up as the groupie to some second string basketball star. Now here you come—"

Agitated, Monica twisted the scarf tight around her neck. "Watch yourself, Pam." She whispered.

"Or what, Monnie?" she challenged, her eyes sparks of cold granite.

Monica scowled, and then her expression closed. "Please do not call me Monnie. I haven't been that girl in a long time."

"That girl was fun. She knew how to get what she wanted," Pamela said, stretching her neck back and forth.

Monica loosened her hold on the scarf. Her expression haunted, she stared at her reflection in the mirror. "That girl is gone. She was selfish and spiteful. I'm working hard to be a better person. My child's name is Fiona because she is the good in me—the fair in me. She's the child of light that my mother never let me be, not because I was dark-skinned, but because she made my beauty my weapon and it blackened my soul."

Pamela huffed and crossed her arms at her revelation.

Monica ignored her attitude. "By the way, so you won't get it twisted that I'm into some kind of denial of who she is, Fiona's middle name is Branwenn. It means dark and pure. Randall and I named her together. He never had a say in his other children's names. I wanted him to know that Fiona was ours."

"Okay, I can't pronounce the middle name, but I like what it means. But Fiona? Child, please. She light, but she ain't white. And her hair screams, Natbush, city limits."

"Randall loved her and her name," Monica said, her voice taking on a faraway quality.

"Yeah, well that and fifty cent won't even get you a subway ride. The man is gone, and you here sleeping in my spare bedroom. Monnie would have landed on her feet," Pamela chuckled, and then sucked her tongue loudly, scrunching her face in thought.

"So what are your plans to get you out of here?" She then snapped her fingers. "I know! What about your ex? Isn't he the son of a mega televangelist, and don't they have crazy money? Can't you boo up with him again? You know them Christians big on forgiving people."

Frustrated, Monica yanked the scarf off. She then abruptly turned her back to the mirror. "I was a different person when I first hooked up with Briggs. I didn't care who I hurt, or how I hurt them. Now, I just want my Randall back."

Pamela clucked her teeth. "Well, my dear, unless Jesus comes back and raises him like Lazarus, your boy is done. So it's time to get yourself back in gear. I don't take care of grown folks, especially no woman with a kid named Fifi."

Monica watched Pamela stomp away, and she couldn't even muster indignation. She used to be Pamela. Until life had taken such a toll on her that she had come to the conclusion that God was her only answer. She just wasn't sure how to find her way back to Him.

She had learned a lot about God when she and Briggs first decided to make their marriage work. Her desertion to Randall had made her feel too ashamed to continue that relationship. As a pastor's wife, she had actually read the Bible every day and prayed without ceasing. Then Randall started his pursuit of her, and every day she read a little less, prayed fewer prayers, until at the end . . . nothing.

Contrary to other's opinion, Randall's first foray back into her life was met with resistance. She knew people thought when he came calling, she'd just caved in. The truth was he called for months before she fell back under his bewitching spell. During those months, sleepless nights thinking about what could be, added to wordless days of having nothing to say to Briggs, equaled selfish choices. She felt so guilty when she left Briggs that she left her son behind. Her penance.

Those were hard years while Randall sought a divorce. Then she became pregnant. At that point, Randall went ninja. He fought his wife with everything he had. For three years, Randall sought freedom, only to end up eternally damned one month later.

Monica tucked her lips tightly together, enduring a spasm of pain ricocheting through her chest, a reminder of all she had lost. Some days were just too much. They beckoned her to old coping skills. She fought that Jezebel spirit—the one who manipulated and controlled all that was around her . . . however . . . whomever.

"Lord, give me strength. I'm trying. Don't let nothing else send me over the edge," she breathed into the still night.

The crackle of Fiona's babbling came through the child monitor speakers. Her little girl was up, and it was time for Monica to think about someone other than herself.

Chapter Five

The atmosphere was festive. Charles and Phyllis's house was a decorator's dream, and Phyllis played hostess as the dream maker. This was a celebration. Old friends were together again. Esther sat at the dinner table, almost mesmerized by Briggs and all of his beauty. Almost, because she understood her sister, the dream maker, was weaving her spell once again. Transfixed, her eyes settled, catlike and golden, on the man who once held her heart.

My goodness, there is nothing about him that is not beautiful.

Earlier, her concern bubbled over like lava when she walked in the room and her heart did a rumba dance. There was Briggs sitting with her sister's husband, Charles. He looked as though he belonged there, with her, with her family, in her life.

Now, they sat across from each other at the table. Esther strained to tone down her interest. She was wary. Would they do this tango all over again, only to end up apart as always? How long would her heart let her linger in a place that she fit, but never got to reside in?

She looked at the perfect little replica sitting next to him; his son. His eyes were wise beyond his seven years. He was what the elders would call an old soul. Where Miracle, Ruth, and David couldn't stop chattering, BJ was silent. Yet, he tugged at her core. This child once could have been hers . . . if they had thrown caution to the wind, if they had defied everything they had ever been taught. What was greater? The act or the intent? Sometimes she didn't know. Her eyes were drawn once more to the child who could easily capture her heart.

"BJ, you okay over there?" Esther asked softly.

Eyes framed with heavy eyelashes searched hers. "Yes, Ms. Esther, I'm fine. The food is real good."

Esther placed her finger against her lips. "Shush . . . Wait until you taste the ice cream. I think it might be tonight's highlight."

She was answered by the sun shining bright out of the row of perfect miniature white teeth BJ displayed. Esther gaped at his beauty. This was a heartbreaker, not in the making, but now.

Like father, like son. Lord, I'm in so much trouble.

Briggs sat back and enjoyed the interplay between Esther and Briggs Jr. His son was the best of him and Monica, and if he had to go back and do it all over again . . . What? The loneliness, the pain of rejection, and abandonment, and BJ was the result? He'd skip, run, and jump right into it again. This child was imprinted on his being.

"Briggs, my man, when we going to the hoop? I need to show you how it's done, son," Charles boasted from down the table, rubbing his silver-tinted goatee.

Briggs sat back, throwing his arm over the back of his chair. "You an old daddy now, Charles. You sure I'm not going to put you into traction trying to do a layup?"

Esther fell out laughing. "Both of you guys are fronting. When's the last time either of you have been on a court?"

"Unless you count the children's portable basketball unit he bought for David, it hasn't happened. Don't you go throwing your back out again, Charles," Phyllis scolded.

Both men protested loudly, while the kids looked on baffled at how growing old could be funny.

Esther observed it all, her heart running before her. She was free-falling with no net in sight.

It had grown late and the September night air was chilled, but not uncomfortable. Esther held Ruth, while Briggs carried David to her car. He placed them both on the backseat.

Briggs turned to Esther and held out his hand to help her up into the SUV. When she shyly placed her hand in his, he pulled her to him with a gentle tug. He locked eyes with those that soulfully searched his, as though looking for a hidden meaning in his touch. Devotedly he cupped her cheek, his voice as intense as his caress.

"Please let me hold you. These arms have been so empty. I crave you, woman."

Esther groaned in response, goose bumps scattering across her skin. He knew he wasn't playing fair. Charles had told him earlier that she hadn't dated since she became a widow. He counted that as a little over two years ago. He watched her chest rise rapidly under her lightweight coat.

As the evening became night, the kids' make-believe raft morphed into beds. Now, he needed to get back inside and pick up a sleeping BJ. But he was loathe to leave Esther.

"Esther, may I kiss you?"

"Oh . . . Briggs, I—" her eyes answered, when they flickered close in invitation.

"Just one little taste?" Briggs was already pulling her forward as he met her more than halfway. He held her face and explored her mouth as though he was a blind man and he could learn her from the crevices of her sweet flavor. He slowly pulled away, kissing her forehead as he leaned his head against hers. "Thank you."

Esther didn't speak. She stood still, her eyes remained closed as her fingers brushed her lips.

Briggs hugged her lightly. "Please wait here while I get BJ settled in my car, and I'll follow you home. I'll be right back."

Esther nodded absently, then stepped up into her SUV. Shaking his head, Briggs backed up, observing her blank stare. He knew she was thinking too much already; planning her exit strategy. Maybe he had tipped his hand too soon. He hurried into the house, hoping she wouldn't pull off.

In less than five minutes, Briggs came out carrying BJ in his arms. The kids had all gotten along really well, and BJ had opened up a little tonight. In a moment of quiet discussion between him and Esther, Briggs shared more about Monica in the role of BJ's mother. He spoke of how, ever since Monica was attacked and Randall was killed, his son had been solemn and withdrawn. The counselor said it would take time, and a stable environment to correct the problem. He and Monica agreed that he would be the better choice because of the upheaval in her life, and that before it all happened, BJ had lived with him as the primary custodial parent. He ended by telling her something straight from his heart—he prayed for Monica all the time. He prayed that at the end of the day her life would find some normalcy.

Esther had looked at him in awe then, as though he had spoken some sort of hocus-pocus that melted her heart. The rest of the night she stole glances at him when she thought he wasn't looking.

Briggs approached the car with BJ asleep on his shoulder.

"You okay?" He looked at Esther hoping his inability to wait on her touch hadn't put him behind in his pursuit of her. To put her at ease he acted nonchalant. Her silent nod gave him no indication if he was winning or losing in his efforts to win her heart. "Thanks for waiting.

Although you weren't privy to this being a date, I always see my date home."

Esther turned to him, her expression guarded. "I'm used to seeing my own way, Briggs."

He grimaced in defeat.

"But I appreciate your gallantry and accept," she added softly.

His face lit into a smile, and the moon couldn't compete. She gave a tentative grin in return and beaming from ear to ear, he hurried back to his car.

Soon after, Esther pulled off with Briggs in her rearview mirror. It was a short drive. He saw her hit the console in her mirror, and her garage door rose slowly. At the same time, he saw David's small head pop up. He watched from the driveway as David sleepily staggered into the house and Esther carried Ruth inside. She waved and the garage door closed.

Briggs backed out and watched as she closed her front window blinds. Deep in thought, he sat in front of her home, car idling. She blinked her lights; and then the house went dark.

He remained staring at the house, wondering what life behind those walls had been like over the years.

He imagined that Esther was peeking through the blinds right now, just like when he came to visit her seven years ago. That had been one of his hardest days ever. After revealing to the love of his life that he was, in fact, married, he sat as he did now, in front of her house. His heart bruised, their flirtation ended. In those days, they had so many sparks flying between them, but the flame was not theirs to burn.

Briggs licked his lips, savoring the after taste sweetness of Esther's lips—lips he hadn't sampled since college. Tonight, she had definitely kissed him back.

Back when he first moved to Detroit, he never thought he would stumble into his college sweetheart's life.

If it had been up to him, he and Esther would have never parted during those college years. But after Esther's best friend, Sheri, had committed suicide, she had withdrawn from him, from everyone.

When she dropped out of school, the bottom dropped out of his life. He became king of the party, and his father's prodigal son.

He met Monica and her stardom blinded him to her character. He sucked up what she was offering on a platter; and then his greed had him going back for seconds and thirds. The indigestion lasted far more years than the memory of the satisfying meal.

When she dropped the pregnancy bomb on him, he walked out, only to have guilt make him return and do the honorable thing and marry her, even though she had told him she had gotten an abortion. It was the "preacher's kid" complex—acting wrong, and then sacrificing to make it right.

With his car idling, Briggs watched an upstairs light come on. He wondered what room it was in Esther's house. Was it the bathroom, one of the kids' rooms, or as the rush in his system indicated; Esther's bedroom? He exhaled. It wouldn't be good for his thoughts to travel down that road.

Still, his thoughts did travel back a little more than seven years. To Esther's beautiful face, crumpled in shock, when he admitted he was married. But his admittance was too late to stop the rumors from flying about him and Esther having an affair. They both knew they had impure thoughts and the rumors were shadows of their sin. Sister Abigail, the chief church gossip, made them miserable for weeks before things got straightened out.

In the end, Esther had found Lawton; Monica had come back after her first affair with Randall had ended, and he had decided that it was his Christian duty to make his marriage work. It was only later when he found out that if God had not sanctioned the marriage, why would He sanction the sacrifice? Briggs had acted as Cain, pressing to make his sacrifice God's first choice—when he didn't seek God before he made it.

Briggs turned when he heard BJ murmuring. He put the car in gear and smoothly rode off. He was going to marry the woman God had placed in his heart over seventeen years ago. It was time; it was ordained. Anything less would be an abomination.

Chapter Six

Monica lay across her bed after getting seven-month-old Fiona to lie down for the second time that night. She wanted to take a luxurious midnight bath, but Pamela had male company and she didn't want to disturb them. She could hear their laughter, Pamela tittering at some inane remark he made. Her laughter was always greater than the value of the comment. As usual, Pamela was baiting her hook. Monica remembered the moves; she had mastered them.

She closed her eyes and thought of strong, virile hands stroking her skin, calling her name lovingly, kissing her neck, and caressing her into the night. Randall was her equal in every way; his appetite for her was as strong as hers for him. If it wasn't for Fiona, she would have willingly followed him into the abyss that some call death. BJ would have Briggs, but who would Fiona have?

Fat tears formed and dropped like stones onto the scratchy cover that lay over the lumpy bed. She ruminated on how to scratch her way out of the ditch she was in. She had hospital bills, she had to feed and clothe Fiona, and she needed a place to live. Her head hurt from the circles it was spinning in.

In hopeless exhaustion, she was drifting off to sleep when she heard the crackle of her stuffed monkey baby monitor go live.

"Hey, pretty girl. You're a pretty little thing, aren't you? So innocent and pure. Umm . . . soft and silky skin. You . . .

smell good enough . . . to . . . eat whole." Spastic breaths panted through the speakers. "Yes . . . that's a sweet . . . girl, uh, uh, uh. Right here, little Fifi, come to Papa," the masculine voice whispered through the intercom. With urgency it traveled along the airwaves. It was a desire, criminal in its intent.

Monica rolled to her feet, grabbing her perfume off the vanity and her last good Louboutin spiked heel. *I will kill a fool.*

She rushed down the hall and dashed into her baby's room, to find a finely dressed African American man in his thirties reaching his hand into Fiona's diaper. His other hand was hidden down the front of his pants.

"What the . . .! Get off my baby! Are you crazy?" Monica raised her arm and sprayed him in the face with her perfume, and then swung her shoe, hitting him squarely in the neck. "Don't . . . you . . . ever . . . put . . . your . . . hands . . . on my child!" she screamed punctuating her words with fresh swings of her shoe.

"Girl, get that shoe off of him! Have you gon' insane?" Pamela shrieked as she ran into the room to rescue her guest.

Monica grabbed Fiona and hugged her to her body. She then got in Pamela's face with eyes of fire. "I will break this pervert's neck and stomp on him like the bug he is. He was hurting my baby." She then pulled Fiona back from her chest, pulled her diaper away from her body, and examined her. There was no sign of blood or trauma.

The stranger patted his face, neck, and shoulder. He bled from multiple places and looked ready to kill. "I'll press charges, Pamela, look at my face. She's a nutcase!"

Pamela stood squarely between the two.

"I heard you on the monitor, you freak! Get outta this house," Monica hollered.

Fiona woke up, bawling at the top of her miniature lungs, her pale complexion splotchy with patches of red.

Pamela turned to Monica enraged. "Now hold on. You don't order people out of *my* home. You need to check yourself. *I* run this."

Monica shook her head, stroking Fiona and jiggling her to calm her down. She headed toward her chest of drawers and raised her shoe, its heel bloodstained, until the man jumped out of her way. Quickly, she flung open the drawers, pulled out Fiona's clothes and necessities, packed her diapers, and put her favorite items in her diaper bag, all while holding her shoe up as a weapon and crooning to Fiona who was lying on the bed.

Backing out, she fled to her room with her child in her arms. She reached under her bed and with one hand and began to pack her Louis Vuitton bag.

Pamela followed silently, standing at her door watching. She waved her hand in the air dismissively. "Where you going, Monica? If you had somewhere you could go, you would have already been there. Calm down and put the drama on hold. You making my head spin unnecessarily."

"Uh-uh. Your head needs to be rotating, fooling with that devil." Monica kissed Fiona and laid her in the middle of the bed. She placed her hand on her hip and shook her shoe threateningly at Pamela. "Girl, why would a grown man be in my child's room this late at night? Whispering! Touching! Salivating! Let me school you: If it looks like a duck, quacks like a duck, and walks like a duck, shoot it out of the air, put it on the table, and call it dinner." She then heaved a heavy sigh. "I oughta kick your butt for standing here defending that monster. So, if I have to sleep on a park bench, then I will. You don't get a second chance to do me right, after you're proved to do me wrong. I don't do do-overs. I'm out!"

Monica called for a cab on her cell. She carried her baby in one arm, and placed the shoulder strap of her diaper bag and suitcase over her other shoulder. She staggered under the weight, but kept the shoe sticking out of the diaper bag where she could easily grab it.

She passed Pamela, who stood there seething; she was staring at the man who had now decided silence was his best option. As Monica buzzed the elevator, she heard Pamela shouting and swearing all the way down the hall.

Monica pushed the button for the lobby, when a crash came from her old apartment. *I hope she castrates him.* She sweet-talked Fiona who had started to whimper. "I'm sorry, sweetie. It's going to be all right." Monica sobbed into her daughter's tiny shoulder. "Whatever it takes, things will get better. I lay on that floor in a pool of blood, and I promised God that if He saved me and let me live to be your mother, I would change. But, Fiona, I can't do this alone. I think it's time for us to go visit family."

Anxious, Monica hiked Fiona up in her arms, struggling under her load. She looked around, hoping the darkness of the night didn't hold any nearby predators. She wasn't sure she could fight off another animal. Not feeling safe enough to wait for the cab, she called out raising her arm at a passing taxi.

Please. Please. Please stop.

She breathed a sigh of relief when it slowed. She felt grateful—grateful she heard a predator before he could complete his wickedness, and grateful that this cab with the Jamaican flag on the dashboard stopped. The cabdriver watched as she piled in with Fiona and their baggage.

She inhaled deeply, breathing in the curried goat and incense that permeated the air. She loved it; it reminded her of her old Uncle Aric's cab back in Kingston.

"Where to, Miss?" The rough beard that covered half his face and unruly locks that spread over an army fatigue jacket's shoulders spoke of hardship. But his eyes screamed compassion and home.

Monica leaned forward, Fiona resting against her shoulder. "Tek mi to di bus station."

The cabdriver whooped, "Yuh a hometown girl. Speaking mi language, I gat you."

Monica fell back. Things were finally feeling right. Perhaps she just needed to trust her intuition. Her Jamaican grandmother used to always say, "Leggo, an' Leggod." Or as she had repeated so many times this week alone, "Let go, and let God."

The bus terminal was busy, and even in the dead of night, people strolled in and out.

"Yuh gwine be okay?" the cabdriver asked as he pulled open her door. "Yuh gat trouble?"

Monica looked at him with a question in her eyes.

"Yuh running wid baby an baggage, middle of di night. Nah a good look fah a pretty girl."

Monica shook her head. "I run to something, nah fram it."

The cabdriver acknowledged her statement with a smile. "Den fly free, pretty bird, fly free."

Monica scrambled to pull money from her purse, but was touched when the cabdriver held up his hand in a mock salute, got into his cab, and pulled away.

Monica saluted the back of his cab and hoisted up all her belongings, including Fiona. "Briggs, I hope you're ready, 'cause no matter what, we're coming home."

Chapter Seven

"This is Magic, 106.3, Columbus, Ohio, playing your oldies but goodies. Sit back and enjoy while we hit you up with a little 'Hot Fun in the Summertime,' by Sly and The Family Stone."

The weekend was over, and Esther rocked her body to the sound of the old jams. *Ah, yeah. This takes me back.* She nodded to the beat and drifted back to games of tag, stick ball, and hide-and-go-get-'em. She bounced her shoulders and smiled as she remembered her pigtails flying in the wind. She remembered Sheri's barrettes clasped to too little hair, and Deborah's beads clacking around her head as her braids swung against each other while she double-dutch roped like her Chuck Taylor's were on fire.

Deborah was badddd between those jump ropes. Esther pantomimed a fast two-step jumping motion pumping her legs up and down inside imaginary ropes. Two minutes later she was lying across her bed, panting like the police were after her.

Dang, I'm a need to call the girls, Jenny Craig, and Jillian Michaels. Sistah gotta lay off the hamburgers, french fries, pizza . . . shoot, now I'm hungry.

She lay back with her hands behind her head and memories of sweet times with summer smells, raucous laughter, and three friends who moved in sync to each other's heartbeats.

Esther, Sheri, and Deborah were the tenacious three. She and her girls were always bigger and better together. She still missed them.

Esther never saw the change coming. The world tilted on its axis, and all she could do was hang on. One minute they were all away in college partying and carefree. Then, Sheri did the unthinkable—she stopped her own heart from beating. A broken doll, swinging in chipped plaster; cold, still, vacant . . . gone.

You shoulda fought those demons, Sheri. I fight 'em every day.

Esther lifted off the bed, agitated by the sound of housekeeping carts rolling down the hallway of the luxurious hotel where she was staying. She wasn't sure why that song triggered those memories this morning. She was in Columbus, Ohio, to speak at the Black Enterprise conference, where she would be facilitating the round table on creating social enterprises for nonprofits.

It was better to reminisce about them than her sleepless nights thinking about Briggs. And that mind-blowing, succulent, ready-to-throw-caution-to-the-wind kiss.

Yesterday's church service had been difficult, watching Briggs watch her as he sat behind the pulpit. He hadn't officially taken over the role as pastor, but he was working overtime to take over her heart.

Esther sat in her teal-blue designer pantsuit with a towel around her neck. She was doing her makeup when the phone rang. Holding her eye shadow brush in one hand and eye color pallet in the other, she hit her cell's speaker.

"Hey, Mama. How's my babies?" she squinted, her lids half-closed, applying her eye shadow.

"Hi, lovey. All my grandbabies are beautiful and smart as a whip. Phyllis dropped Miracle over here too. They're all on the computer playing games."

"Make sure they do something else too. Ever since Phyllis bought Miracle a computer and a tablet, she's been obsessed with it, and she has my kids begging for one. That's not happening. They can use mine or none at all. At seven years old, I'm not sure Miracle needs all that either, Mama."

"You know your sister. She thought she would never have children, so she indulges her way too much. I've told her, and then at the risk of being told off, I told her again, no good can come of all this technology at so young an age. Devil be busy."

"Mama, everything is not the devil. Some things are just common sense. Too much of anything is too much!" Esther said, flicking blush across her cheeks.

"Uh-oh. I hear some bickering going on in the other room. Time to put my Judge Judy robe on and get them in order. You slay them at your conference, honey."

Esther surveyed her work, and in satisfaction removed the towel from around her neck. "Thanks, I will. And just because they have a day away from me today, don't let them run you ragged. Make them go sit somewhere and read a book."

"Now, you're talking. Don't forget to call me when you get on the road to come back."

"I will, Mama. Bye now."

Clasping the multicolored necklace closed as a finishing touch, Esther grabbed her purse, tote, and wheeled her overnight bag out of the room. She made a practice of not leaving her children for more than one night, so she was getting on the road at the end of her day.

Woolgathering, a housekeeper rolled her cart past. As the woman walked by, Esther stopped in her tracks, her mouth open in shock.

"Deborah?"

The woman looked up and worn, stricken eyes searched Esther's youthful face, and then expensive clothes. "No, you must have me confused with someone else." Her rough-hewn hands, pulled at her ill-fitting uniform as she looked around. "Excuse me, I forgot something."

The woman hurried down the hallway, leaving her cart behind. Esther followed, calling out behind her, "Deborah! Why are you . . .?"

Ignoring Esther's cry, Deborah sprinted to a room and disappeared inside. Esther chased her, bewildered that her childhood best friend would lie to her face. *I know her, and I know her voice.*

Tears gushed to the surface when Esther stood there in shock and listened as someone inside the room said, "Deborah, you okay?"

Spitting fire and tears, Esther banged on the door. She heard a "shush" on the other side, and then silence. She then kicked it, this time yelling for Deborah to come to the door.

Instead, a door opened across the hall and a tousled man peered out. "Can I get some sleep? It's seven thirty in the morning, for Pete's sake."

Esther held up her hands in surrender. In a sleepwalk trance she went to the elevator. It wouldn't look good for her business for her to be late. But the mystery that just occurred was not over; she would find out where Deborah had been for the last seventeen years and why she had just played her.

Chapter Eight

The sun streamed through miniblinds, allowing the office's lone occupant to forgo lights. Briggs sat, his collar unbuttoned, and sleeves rolled up, reviewing the church's various ministries and their functions.

Glancing at his watch, he arched his back, rolled his neck, and stood. He had been at it since seven that morning. It was time to take a break; he would be having visitors soon.

Yesterday, Briggs had sat back and listened to Joshua preach as he surveyed the congregation. He was still getting settled in and he had asked Joshua to work with him as they transitioned a changing of leadership.

He saw old and new faces as he allowed the sharing of God's Word to penetrate his heart. Scanning the sanctuary, he saw Esther with her family, and he was amused by her obvious refusal to look his way. When he spied the large orange hat and brown feathered plume, he grinned. Mother Reed was a balm to a weary soul, pirate's hat and all. He had hugged her, but their time was limited since she had a previous engagement. He promised himself they would make up for lost time.

Briggs rolled down his sleeves and pulled on his sport coat. He paused, remembering how he entered the office that morning, pulling off his coat and being led to kneel in prayer. He prayed that this new season would be different from the missteps of his time as interim pastor. It had been his first church, and he had made some bad choices.

He had come to town to prove that he was a man of God, and ended up proving he was just a man.

God was so good though. He was able to repent and to receive restoration. He now felt free to pursue Esther, because he had been obedient and he had kept the faith. Wasn't she his reward?

His desk phone buzzed, and Naomi crackled through the antiquated sound system. "Pastor, the Prison Prophet is out here with Mother Reed, the Saint."

Briggs's hand rubbed down his face. "Naomi, that is not how we introduce our guests. That was shameful."

The air crackled as Naomi answered, "Oh, they can't hear me, Pastor. They don' put this new door in with all the glass. At first, I hated it because everybody could see me. Then I realized I could see them first. Mother Reed is old, Pastor. They ain't even halfway up the hallway yet. But they coming."

Briggs huffed. "Naomi, please refrain from calling people out to me by their past. It's so unseemly. Earlier today, you said, 'Here come Mudslinging Sister Go Tell It Abigail.' That's just not Christian."

The air crackled as her voice burst through. "My Bible say the truth will make you free. I was just—hi, Mother Reed. Pastor is waiting on you. Please go right in. You too, uh, Pri—I mean Prop—Deacon Joshua."

Furrowing his brow, Briggs hurried to escort in both his guests. Holding out a chair for Mother Reed, he observed the look of admiration she had for her son. He then wondered about the dynamics between a mother and son that had missed forty years of intimacy that comes with time together.

Mother Reed's first husband's abuse, and his callous act of throwing her into the street when Joshua was a toddler, resulted in years of them being separated. The vengeful man made sure neither knew where the other one was. They all found out later, an abusive childhood led to Joshua ending up in prison. Briggs and Monica had already left town when Joshua was released and through a merciful God he was reunited with his mother.

After Mother Reed sat, Briggs turned to Joshua with a hearty handshake that was open and welcoming. "Man, I know I told you yesterday, but that was a powerful word from God."

Joshua clasped Briggs's hand in return. "I appreciate the accolades, but all the glory goes to God. I'm just glad we can work together so I can turn this all over to you, and soon."

Briggs went around to his desk.

"Yes, I've been reviewing some of the paperwork, requests, community needs, outreach to the sick and shut-ins, etc."

Joshua gave a sympathetic grin. "You have to be called to this position. I'm glad to turn it over and go back to providing outreach through our housing, food pantry, and prison ministries."

Mother Reed chimed in with the voice of a proud parent, "He also owns a lot of real estate and has small businesses all over town. Sometimes I think he's trying to revive Detroit all by himself."

Joshua looked at Briggs as though to say, "She's my mama, what else is she going to say?"

Joshua put his foot on a chair's railing and propped his arm across his thigh. "Mama, reconnecting with you these last years has given me so much. I'd like to give some of that back. Love will anchor you. It will call you to a place of such peace that you can survive what you thought would kill you. And you can let go of what you thought would forever hold you."

Waving her hand in agreement, Mother Reed's smile crumbled and a look of fierceness crossed her face. She leaned forward. "Joshua, sweetheart, concentrate, get in the spirit. Did you feel the sudden shift in the wind? Something is coming." She turned to Briggs with urgency in her voice. "I was hoping this new season would be without the drama, but ill winds blow. You get ready! Stay prayed up. Put on your full armor of God. We gon' win the battle, but that don't mean we won't get a little tussled in the tempest."

Briggs watched Joshua stretch to his full height of six feet four inches and an illumination glowed from his being. He then looked at the diminutive Mother Reed with power flowing from her like water from a faucet. The two were in full spiritual mode.

Joshua hung his head. When he lifted it back up, his eyes were ablaze and he spoke from the depth of his soul. "The gates of hell are rattling. But they are empty boasts. God will not be mocked. Grace and mercy are available. So saith the Lord."

Mother Reed nodded in agreement and got up from her chair. She stopped, turned, and anchored her hand on her hip. "I'm sorry, Briggs. I hear God clearly; I need some time with Joshua in the sanctuary alone. He's a great prayer warrior. He's one to have on your side in a fight. We've learned to flow together; you're welcome to come."

Joshua held the door open, dipping his head at Briggs. "Just waiting on you, Mama."

Briggs felt her invitation was a courtesy. He declined and promised to be there when they returned. He had his own praying to do.

Awhile later, Mother Reed returned, her clothes slightly rumpled, her stockings sagging at the knees.

She hitched up her skirt and smiled with relief as she sat. "That was some good Jesus prayer, Briggs. Some things got settled."

"I know it did, because I felt the power of the anointing all through this church. God bless you," Briggs said and grabbed her and held on tight.

It had been a week since he had gotten to Detroit, each day a new challenge. He was so happy to see this woman whom he loved like a grandmother. He then turned to Joshua, who stood by his mother's side. "Deacon Joshua, Mother Reed's beloved son. Man, I'm glad we finally get a chance to spend some time together. Today is my official first day at the church. Thank you for having me sit with you in the pulpit yesterday."

Joshua smiled. "I was sorry to miss you here last week, but I had to check out some property in the Lansing area. As you know from our many phone calls, I'm glad to have you. Our almost daily talks pretty much have you up to date. Anything else you need, please let me know. I never used this office so everything is the way Reverend Gregory left it."

"I've appreciated our conversations they have helped. I've reviewed a lot of the paperwork, and I have just a few questions," Briggs said as he opened a folder.

Joshua nodded, cleared his throat, then took a seat. Briggs took his measure and determined he was a man who wanted to know where he stood right away.

His thoughts were validated when Joshua stretched forward and dove right in. "Well, there are a few ministries that struggled under my leadership," he said rubbing his forehead, as though pushing back unpleasant memories.

"The government finally tells you, you can go. You've paid your debt to society. The only thing is . . . Nobody believes it. And if you get your salvation in prison, nobody wants to believe that's real either. I have been out for seven years. God knows my heart."

Briggs saw Mother Reed in his peripheral vision. Hands folded in her lap, she sat quietly and waited. He knew this woman of wisdom; her posture spoke volumes. *Set this straight, Briggs.*

As a result, Briggs took his time answering. A quick denial wasn't needed—a real answer was. "I know what you mean. God says that we are to forgive seven times seventy in one day. I don't know anyone who has ever achieved that status. Joshua, I forgive you. It's right for us to work together to bring the best to this church and to this community. Detroit has problems with the mayor, the economy, and crime. It has a fight on its hand to make a comeback. What better city for us to be in, than God's own comeback city?"

Joshua grinned. "Pastor, I'm happy for your forgiveness, but I never did anything to you for you to give it. My sins were more directed to hurt myself than others. My drug and alcohol usage destroyed my life. Your life looks fine from where I'm sitting. But I'm glad to know we can move forward. My wife Essie was ready to storm the church if you answered differently."

"I stand corrected. Behind the prison walls you got free. Then you helped others find liberty too. He's a life-changing God," Briggs said and stretched his fist out. Joshua gave him a pound.

Briggs grinned at the new connection. "Your time in the pit always prepares you for the palace. Man, you bad. You got radical and started your own prison ministry. And you experienced a double blessing; reuniting with your mother, and you're a married man too." Briggs chuckled. "How did you ever separate Sister Essie from her twin? I remember when I was here they were never apart. They even spoke in unison."

Joshua gave a mischievous grin. "Oh, they still talk every day, and they are closer than ever. But what God has joined together, let no man put asunder, including a twin sister. You can bet my Essie stays close to this brother, real close. She's singing her duets with me now."

Mother Reed chimed in. "Joshua?" When she had his attention, she shook her index finger. "Now you bragging." She then included both in her line of vision. "Gentlemen, Mother can't be with you all day. What's the plan?"

Briggs pulled out his notebook and reviewed his plans. "Mother Reed, as head of the mothers of the church, I'd like to start a Love Fest ministry. We're losing too many young people to the clubs and the streets. When I stopped by the church I spoke to a few candidly, and I heard an earful. Young women hurt by people in the church who are bringing condemnation, not conviction. You can't lower the hems of their skirts until you lower their defenses around their hearts. Young men have sagging pants because they have sagging spirits. My Word says we are to draw them with love. I can't be everywhere, but it's my job to make sure that those who are acting in leadership have a heart for the people."

"I like that, Briggs. Love Fest. We do have some mothers preaching hellfire and brimstone. And they're not wrong, just their approach. Love is needed. Correction without relationship breeds rebellion. I can't tell you anything if I don't have a relationship with you. Too many think their position gives them carte blanche to run rampant over other people's feelings. This is going to be a doozy! I'm with cha," Mother Reed said and nodded her head enthusiastically.

"Good. Mother, with you on board, the battle is half done."

Briggs clasped his hands in anticipation. "Joshua. I really want to get our young men's group back on track. I understand after I left it fell apart."

Joshua's mouth tightened. "Yes. I wanted to keep it, but most of the mothers didn't want their sons taking instruction from a felon."

Mother Reed hit the table with her hand. "I understood, but having someone who's been down the wrong path can many times help others not make the same errors. What'd you learn the lesson for if nobody but you was going to learn from it? My God is a God of multiplication not just addition. You know in the last book of our Good News, it says in Revelation, chapter twelve, verse eleven: 'And they overcame him by the blood of the Lamb, and by the word of their testimony; and they loved not their lives unto the death.'"

Briggs flew right in. "Yes, ma'am. And in that passage the enemy had moved from serpent stature to one of a dragon. That devil had stayed before the throne of God, day and night, accusing the brethren. You better know, he may have spoken of my trials, but he never spoke of my triumphs."

"Well," said Joshua standing, "if he could have foretold your victorious comeback, he would have never started. But he's not all-powerful or all-knowing. And when we finish drawing these boys and girls back to Him who is worthy, many will be led to Christ."

Mother Reed got up and did a slow shuffle to the left and right with her hand in the air. "Ah, sookie sookie, now!"

Joshua jumped next to his mother and two-stepped his version of his holy dance. Briggs, not to be outdone, joined in, and together they danced for joy. They were of one accord, and heaven help the man or woman who got in their way.

Chapter Nine

The meeting over, Briggs watched as Mother Reed fanned herself. Joshua exited to bring the car around to the back entrance so she wouldn't have to walk as far. While he was doing that, she'd asked to have a quiet one-on-one with Briggs.

She pinned him with her laser stare. "You gon' sit there and watch me fan myself dry, or you gon' give an ol' woman the nine-one-one?"

"It's four-one-one, Mother," Briggs said with a lopsided grin.

Mother Reed waved her hankie. "Nah, that's the number of information. This here is an emergency 'cause if you don't tell me what's going on, I'm gon' hit you upside your head, boy. This c'here not pastor to church mother. This c'here surrogate mother to son. Tell me!"

Briggs breathed slowly, and then folded his hands in a steeple posture. "She's skittish. Our time together has been minimal, and she's playing the friend role."

Mother Reed's head tilted, her eyes half-closed. "I get that. You been gone a long time, and what she had with Lawton was awful good. I tell you that man was so sweet to her. You could tell she glowed from within. And the twins? Dem golden babies, so manageable and kind." Mother Reed shambled into Briggs's personal space. She wanted to make sure he understood her clearly. "But that season is over. And I didn't see her climb in that there casket behind him. . . . So?"

Briggs perked up. "Esther ain't dead yet? Or my chances?"

She pointed at his head. "Humph, I guess that degree ain't all paper and there is a brain in there. When it comes to you and your relationships, I wasn't sure." Mother Reed stepped back to leave.

"Joshua will be outside waiting on me. When will I get to meet BJ? I don't take my tomorrows for granted."

Briggs looked down at his calendar.

"How about first thing tomorrow? I've told him all about you. He's a good kid, but a little withdrawn. After Monica's hospital stay that's to be expected. I'm so glad he was with me when her attack happened. It could have easily been far worse."

Mother shifted, her face pinched in memory.

"I don't desire bad to happen to anyone. When you called me in tears about that woman leaving you for that rich man, I knew it was the best thing that could have ever happened to you. But her stabbing made even my heart soften toward her. BJ will be okay. He's got a father who loves him, and from what you tell me, his mother loves him too."

"Yes, that's one thing I would never do—tear him from his mother. She has always put his best interest at heart. And even though she is living in New York, she left him with me so he wouldn't be traumatized more as she pulls her life together. I must admit I admire that her motherhood trumps her wanting to be with him," Briggs said, his regard for his ex showing.

Mother Reed moved toward the door. "I agree with that, but you mind that those rose-colored glasses you are wearing about her don't make you miss what's in front of you in black and white. Zebras rarely change their stripes. That would take an act of God."

Briggs nodded. "And I have a front-row seat to His miracles every day."

He hugged her close. "Come on. I'll walk my favorite girl out. You're looking good. I'm glad the mild heart attack you had when I was pastor here seems to be long gone."

Mother Reed skipped a little for Briggs, then laughed. "I'm eating right and staying active. God's a healer."

The imps danced in glee as they listened in through the window on the conversation taking place in Briggs's office.

"He softens toward her, Master. She will easily seduce him. It will all come to pass," Imp One broadcasted.

The Leader was down below listening to the imp through their link. "Is the old woman well?"

The imp ran around to the back of the church and watched Mother Reed skip, then step spritely into the car. "Yes, she moves well."

"Ouch!" The imp held his ear which burned red from the blast of fire licking against it. "I only told what I saw. I didn't create her good health," he said cheekily.

"Ouch ouch ouch! Stop that!" The imp held his face, touched his scaly chest, and bounced up and down on his clawed feet as fire jumped around his body, scalding him at each landing.

The Leader didn't suffer back talk, or even attempts to show him his own errors.

Imp One looked at his scorched body, curls of smoke rising into his eyes. His thoughts were of malicious intent. Ooh, I hate him. He will do well to watch how he treats me. The taste of revenge is becoming sweet on my tongue.

The Leader interrupted his thoughts. "Imp!"

"Yes, Beloved Leader, what can I do for you? I await your command," he sniveled, sticking his finger mockingly down his throat since he knew The Leader could not see him.

"What are you doing?" The Leader screamed.

Imp One jumped clawing into the air. He looked around, then under, and above his seat. Could The Leader see him? No, impossible!

"Nothing, I am thinking of ways to make you greater, O Remarkable One."

"Then find a way to destroy these people. And do it soon."

"Yes, yes, destroy," Imp One lisped.

The Leader's foul intent was clear in his next statement. "And Imp? Stay loyal, Little Dunghill. I would hate to have to kill you. I would take my time, pulling you limb from limb, allowing Abaddon's locust to come and devour you a bite at a time. It will be delicious."

Imp One staggered under his new found fear. If The Leader could hear his thoughts, he was doomed.

Chapter Ten

Deborah was back from the dead. Resurrected. Or at least in Esther's mind, she had pulled a Lazarus. She wondered how much stank she had on her. Her welcoming attitude was sure rank.

Lord, forgive me; that's my pain talking.

Esther pulled into her sister's driveway. She had traveled for three and a half hours trying to piece together why Deborah would turn from her like she owed her money. Perhaps Phyllis could shed some light on it. Either way, she had some words of caution to give her sister, and she needed a shoulder to lean on. The paradox of sisters: nemesis and confidante all within the same conversation.

After entering Phyllis's house, instead of speaking her mind, Esther was thrown by Phyllis's news: Roger was getting out of prison.

In a panic dance, Esther paced back and forth. She'd stop to speak, shake her head, and then continued her silent frenzy.

"Girl, if you walk past me one more time, I'm going to throw something at you." Phyllis's arms were folded protectively as she watched her sister fall apart.

Her own arms folded, Esther turned to Phyllis with a petulant glare. Smirking, Phyllis unfolded her arms and sat with her legs crossed at the knee, a perfect picture of composure. Esther's only clue that Phyllis was not as calm as she tried to make out was the swinging of her right foot, a continual up and down, over her stationed left leg.

"Tell me again. When did you get the notification that my no-good, cowardly, ex-husband Roger was getting out of prison?" Esther harped.

Wincing, Phyllis said, "A letter came in the mail today. Since Charles and I were his victims, the state wanted to let us know he was being released. We were so busy with Miracle, we missed his parole hearing. We thought it would be okay. I mean, it's been seven years."

Esther stopped and yelled out her frustration. "I was married to the man, divorced him, and after two years apart he was stalking me. Does that *sound* like someone who lets go easily? If you and Charles hadn't been there instead of me that night, I'd be dead. What is it with seven years that you all think that it's the end of something?"

Phyllis stopped swinging her foot and looked at Esther as though she was slow. "Well, you know Reverend Gregory taught us that it is the number of completion."

Esther tapped her foot in frustration. "No, this is the start of some mess. Do *you* want Roger around?"

Phyllis recoiled. "No, Esther. You know I don't. But the night he broke into your house, you weren't home. Charles and I were there, and Charles did beat him down. Roger's not trying to go there again. And look at the good that came out of it. Once in prison, Roger met Joshua, and he put two and two together when Joshua talked about trying to find his mother. All that money Joshua's father left him, and he couldn't find Mother Reed. When God is in the mix, things get fixed!" Phyllis raised her hands in triumph.

Esther rolled her eyes and wagged her finger to punctu-ate her words. "Okay, I love Mother Reed, and I am glad she and Joshua finally found each other after years of searching. But I don't care if Roger saved the eight track,

Myspace, and the dodo bird from extinction, I don't want him living here."

Phyllis waved her comments away. "This is too much drama. Besides, Joshua talks to Roger all the time. He says he's changed."

Esther spouted with indignation. "With all due respect, he wasn't obsessed with Joshua. And just because he and Joshua were locked up together doesn't mean that he is like him. We all now know Joshua was innocent. And you best believe we know Roger was guilty as charged."

Esther stopped, and then started pacing again.

"That's another thing. If Joshua is the one he keeps in touch with, doesn't it stand to reason that Joshua is the one he's coming to see when he gets out?"

"Joshua runs the prison outreach ministry. All the inmates keep in touch with him. Roger remembers Mother Reed, and he knows she won't stand for any foolishness," Phyllis countered.

"Joshua doesn't live with Mother Reed. He lives with I-finally-got-a-man Essie. She loves his dirty drawers. If he says let's move a pig in, Essie will go buy the trough. Before you know it, you'll hear her in the front yard talking 'bout 'skewee!'"

Phyllis fell out laughing, then stopped at the look on Esther's face. "That was cold—true, but cold. Charles thinks it will all be fine."

Esther sighed heavily. "I have my children to think about. I'm by myself."

"You have Daddy. You know he's not going to tolerate anybody hurting you. You need to pray about this. If Reverend Gregory was still living, you'd go to him. Why don't you go see Briggs, I mean Pastor Stokes? Get you some peace on the matter."

Esther's mouth gaped open. "Because Reverend Gregory wasn't trying to get with me, and you know it.

You couldn't be more transparent. And now that you bring it up, that's one of the reasons I initially came by today. Please stop pushing Briggs and me together."

Phyllis's eyes narrowed. "Stop running from the inevitable. My niece and nephew have a birthday coming up, and they'll be seven. In eleven years they'll be gone away to school, and you know that kids never really come home after college. You'll still be young, and you'll be alone. Lawton wouldn't want that for you; he loved you too much."

Phyllis got up to hug her sister. Esther shrugged away, still fussing.

"Please, what is your definition of young? Eleven years from now, I'll be forty-eight, and that is not my teen years. I'll be fine; my life is full. I didn't miss you changing the subject from Roger, but since we aren't on the same wavelength concerning his release, I'll keep my own counsel on it." Feeling exhausted, Esther said, "I wish someone had warned me how toxic love gone bad could be. If I had known, I would have planted orange cones around Roger, and declared him a disaster area."

Phyllis heaved a loud sigh. "Girl, you can be so dramatic. I don't know what else you want me to say. They are going to release him, no matter how we feel about it."

"I can hear your concern," Esther said dryly. Phyllis shook her head.

"I *am* concerned, but not about Roger. Don't stubbornly refuse a chance at happiness. Your life is full because of Ruth and David. Just think about your future, Sis, that's all I'm saying. Now I'm changing the subject. How was the conference?"

Esther felt a smile break through. "It went well. I'm getting better at public speaking, and I'm feeling more confident."

Phyllis nodded. "Good, I know how new it is. Consulting and troubleshooting with nonprofits is right up your alley, after working for them for over fourteen years."

"I love teaching what I know. We've got a lot of contracts right now. My plate of craziness is filling up fast," Esther said, with a gleam in her eye.

Phyllis stood back and eyeballed her baby sister. "You look good. Lawton did that for you, and his death should not erase it. You move confidently; you're dressed for success, at least during business hours, and you're passionate about the right things."

"Thanks! I needed to hear that. There are a lot of days that my time runs out before I accomplish the list of things I needed to get done. Single parenting is rough."

Phyllis put her arms around her sister and gave her a firm hug. "Don't worry. Roger is your past. Don't place him on your agenda for the future. It's impossible to stumble over your past if you're moving forward."

Esther patted her sister's arm, then stared off. "Before I leave, I want to tell you about something disturbing that occurred in Columbus."

Esther's head dropped, her voice dripped with misery. "I saw Deborah."

"Deborah, who?" Phyllis asked as she removed her arm and sat.

Esther gritted her teeth in exasperation. "Really? *My* Deborah. Disappeared-ran away-left college Deborah."

Phyllis scooted forward. "*Shut your mouth*. In Columbus?"

"Yes, and I'm telling you she looked right through me. Tried to act like it wasn't her and ran away." Esther's voice shook as the scene replayed in her mind.

Phyllis paused, thinking. "Doesn't sound like the Deborah I remember. That girl wasn't scared of anything. Maybe it *wasn't* her."

Sad, Esther shook her head. "'She's changed. She looked haggard, like she had been through some things, but it was her."

"Where were you?" Phyllis asked.

"In my hotel. She was in a housekeeping uniform. I think I'm going to call the hotel and ask for her."

Phyllis's nose scrunched up. "A housekeeper? Child, that's rough."

"Nothing wrong with her job, Phyllis. Stop being bougie," Esther snorted, knowing her sister was disconnected to how most people survived in the world, being married to a department head of engineering at General Motors.

Phyllis rolled her eyes. "Whatever. Nobody wants to clean up after other people."

"So says the housewife," Esther said defiantly.

Phyllis stood and stepped away. "Oh no, you didn't. I'm a wife *and* mother."

"And there's nothing wrong with that, or being a housekeeper," Esther said as she grabbed her sister's hand and pulled her back down on the couch.

"Well, if I was Deborah, and I looked bad, and I was working at a hotel and you last saw me in college, I'd act like I didn't know you too."

"Oh my goodness. That's it!" Esther hugged her sister. "It's not me, *she's* embarrassed. That makes sense. Now, if Roger is never heard from again, and you will stop meddling in my affairs all will be well."

"Roger is a dead issue. As for me meddling? Let me school you, Sis. You protest too much. You know you want that man." Phyllis stood, bent over, and shuffled a little to the side.

"Mother Reed might say it like this, 'Baby, it's y'alls season.' You know Mother Reed don't lie." Phyllis straightened up, and then dropped her finger from pointing at Esther.

Annoyed, Esther huffed, "First of all, Mother Reed doesn't walk like that. And, Phyllis, when God talks to me, I'll listen. And when it comes to love, I've been there, missed it a couple of times, and then hit it real good. I'm grateful for what I had, so back off. Tend to your own home."

"You *are* my home," Phyllis said, and stomped her foot in frustration, a family trait. "You've been stubborn all your life. Maybe that's why you married that loser, Roger. You smiled your fake smile, hiding your pain, all the while he was abusing you emotionally, mentally, financially, and finally, physically. I've always wondered if somebody hadn't reported him attacking you in the church parking lot if you would have continued acting as though you guys were good."

Esther's skin flushed, and her neck stiffened, its veins tight against her skin. "Sometimes you go too far. Your mouth is like a free-flowing river without a dam."

Phyllis shrugged, and then a small grin formed. "Did you just curse me on the sly?"

Esther knew when her sister was sending out an olive branch, and she accepted it with a frustrated shake of her head. "Oh my goodness, you are hopeless. I'm going to pick up my kids. Mom is probably frazzled having all three kids all night."

Phyllis sank into the couch, pulling her stocking-clad feet under her. "Miracle left about an hour ago. Charles took her to the mall to get her nails done and for some new jeans she wanted."

Esther's voice wavered. "Sis, do you think it's a good idea to give her so much? She's only seven years old. She'll be just eight next month. Maybe you want to—"

Her eyes narrowing, Phyllis flung out her hand. "Mind your own business. I've had this conversation with Mama. Charles and I know what we're doing. She's a good student, and she deserves to be given something nice."

Fingering the hair on the nape of her neck, Esther pressed on. "She's supposed to get good grades. But I can see you are not up to my opinion so I'll take it with me and leave."

Phyllis's smile was hard, brittle like sandpaper. "Yep, still my smart little sister. She knows when to tighten that lip."

Esther let herself out. There were too many things going on to be caught up in trying to tell her sister how to parent. She just hoped that she was wrong and Miracle would turn out fine.

Backing out of the driveway Esther saw her sister standing in the window. Esther smirked; the angel statue Phyllis had in the living room made Phyllis look like angel wings were embracing her.

Ha! We know she's no angel.

Zadkiel stood behind Phyllis as she looked out the window. His wingspan embraced her as though they were in protective mode. "Your charge Phyllis is headstrong. She resists wise council."

"She has a good heart and is always concerned about the welfare of others," the guardian angel protested, desiring to protect Phyllis from herself.

Zadkiel rose into the skies above the home. "See to her, Guardian. Things are not what they appear in this home. Demon tracks come from the child's bedroom. Something is amiss, and you cannot err in being watchful."

"Please, no." The guardian flew around the parameter of the house upset that he had not seen the faint markings of evil. He had been so consumed with watching over Phyllis he had not taken notice of others in the house-

hold. He would speak to his brothers upon their return with their charges. Maybe they had seen something and were on top of it.

Zadkiel ascended higher, moving swiftly to the G. Robert Cotton Correctional Facility in Jackson, Michigan. He wanted to see Roger's progress for himself. Too much was going on to be a coincidence. His Father had only told him so much. Often He allowed free will, when Zadkiel would have made man behave. But he had learned as His Son had, not my will, but thy will be done.

Chapter Eleven

The prison cell was claustrophobic and utilitarian at best. The small desk welded to the wall, and the commode that had a permanent rust ring were commonplace in Roger's vision. He didn't see them anymore. His focus was the unopened letter on the desk. The heavy, unyielding feeling pressing on his chest was an indication that he may be in for a huge disappointment. Fear had him.

He was Moses—minus the entourage—in the desert waiting on a sign from God that he could move to the Promised Land. Roger wanted to scratch this analogy when he thought further and remembered Moses never made it to his destination.

I'm making myself crazy.

The letter held the key to his future, and he didn't have a Plan B. The large groan he expelled and the worrying he was doing wasn't going to open the letter any sooner.

Can I trust Joshua's word?

The last person he trusted had let him down badly. Esther had wronged him. He knew he wasn't a good husband. But he had never seen what that looked like. Ralph Kramden on *The Honeymooners* didn't qualify as a role model. There had been no husbands in his environment—not that stayed. And the few times he met some that might fit the bill, they moved their families away from his hood as soon as they could afford it.

No, he hadn't observed anyone growing up that he could relate to on how to be a good man, let alone a good husband. Never heard one man in his life tell him that his woman was his gift from a God who does all things well.

As a result, when Esther began to rise in her job, his insecurities rose at home. Then the ribbing came, first from close friends, then guys on the job constantly asking him if Esther gave him lunch money. His damaged pride made him go home every night seething with indignation when he spotted some new item she had purchased for his enjoyment. The new flat-screen TV mocked him, and the expensive tool set jeered him. All the while, she explained with hurt in her eyes at his sneering rejection that she just wanted to see him smile.

He now understood that she couldn't comprehend him, because there was no reference in her life that related to his brokenness. The men in her life were whole. She'd been graced with a good childhood, not one stained with the pain of unfulfilled dreams and unrequited love. He couldn't tell her, and she couldn't see. Mute and blind, both of them, their entire marriage.

Yeah, she had let him down. And he had stayed there.

A clang against his cell bars alerted him that he had company. The square-shouldered, gray-haired man walked into his cell and stood before him.

The old man gave him the universal brother nod. "What'sup?"

Roger motioned to the letter and remained sitting.

The old man noted the envelope on the desk. He picked it up and brought it over. "For real? Man, you gotta open it. Prophet is a straight-up dude. He ain't gon' play you wrong."

Roger nervously tapped his fingers on the desk. "Yeah? What if he do? He been out a minute, man. He still be in contact, but that don't mean he gon' help a brother out. He probably don't want to upset his ol' lady."

"His wife?"

Roger's head tipped back, and he looked skyward. "Nah, man. His *real* ol' lady. His mama. She ain't never liked me, man."

The old man pushed his sleeves up his arms and planted his feet. "You acking like a little girl. Grow some. Read the letter, fool."

Roger had learned to come back hard in this steel-plated home, even with those who were friends. It was the price you paid to fit in and never stand out. "Who house, dis?"

"Dis your house," the old man said, chest pushed out, his chin jutted.

Roger sucked his teeth. "I come to your house talking smack?"

The old man's chest deflated. "No, son, you don't. But—"

"Ain't no buts. I been saved a long time. They cut me, and I didn't curse. They denied my parole three times, and I didn't curse. And here you 'posed to be my boy, and you 'bout to make me cuss you out."

"I hear you. I'm done. Let me know when you let me know." The old man pimped out of the cell, throwing the letter back on the desk as he left. He stopped outside in the hallway. "Some new cat in Secure Level One keep asking 'bout you."

Roger tilted his head. "Secure Level One? What dat be about?"

The old man shrugged his lean shoulders. "How I know?"

Eyes narrowing, he asked. "You squash it?"

He nodded. Once again, his shoulders rounded back. "Me and Brother Do Right shut it down."

Roger glanced up, his head cocked to the side. "Brother Do Right didn't get down, did he? You know how he do. And he ain't been saved that long. Changing his name from Do Dirty, to Do Right don't necessarily change him."

The old man gave a cocky grin, looked around and came back into the room. "Nah, I was with 'em. We just had a little talk wit' the cat. Tol' 'em mind his own. But wasn't you the one who taught us what was in a name? Didn't God change the name of men when they nature changed?"

"Yes, but that was after they walked in the change," Roger said, his eyes still on the unopened letter.

"Not always. He called Simon, Peter. Told him he would be the rock he would build his house on before he changed. His name change was an act of faith."

Roger gave the old man his full attention. "You right. You the teacher now, eh?"

"Aww, man. Just flexing a little knowledge."

Roger rose from his bed and approached his friend. "I'm proud of you. When the teacher gets taught by the student, 'it's time for the student to teach on his own. You still doubt you ready to lead these men?" Roger affectionately shoulder bumped him.

Eyes glistening, the older man they once called Wiley Coyote, now known as Wise Will, swallowed deeply. "You been a light, son. And I mean to soak up as much of you as I can in this next week. I'ma miss ya like fish miss grease."

Roger fell out laughing. "Old man, that's what I'm going to miss. Nobody says the stuff you do. You watch out for everybody, hear me?"

"Yeah, I do. These young hotheads can get in more trouble due to pride than any other thing. I keep praying for the Spirit of humbleness to abide in me so I can be an example. But if I can get Brother Do Right to show it, that's going to really set some brothers free. I'm an old man, but he young and tough, and his fists once ruled this whole section."

Roger pulled back his short sleeve and pointed to his upper arm. It was mottled and scarred. "This arm used to hold the likeness of a serpent, emerging into a dragon. In my pain, I destroyed it the best way I could. Man, I was so disturbed in those days, I used to believe that it was talking to me." Roger visibly shuddered. "The thing started giving me the creeps."

The old man sucked his teeth. "I wouldn't front, acting like it couldn't happen. The devil is sho 'nough crafty."

"That he is. That's why I know that a heart can change, sometimes drastically. God can do it. Prophet planted the seed in Brother Do Dirty before he was released. I watered it until he became Brother Do Right, now all you got to do is guide him into Brother Is Right!"

Wise Will clasped his hands and pointed to the sky. "He can do it!" He then turned to go but hesitated. "You want me to find out why that newcomer be sweating you?"

"Nah, man. I'm out of here end of week. I ain't 'bout to get involved in nothing up in here," Roger said, waving him off.

"What is, is. I check you out later. And have a little faith. Read your letter."

Roger called to him as he left. "A'ighhht."

He lowered his head and took a deep breath. He squared his shoulders and leaned over and grabbed the thin envelope. Didn't good news or acceptance come in thick envelopes? He had heard that somewhere. This envelope was slim, like his hope.

He opened it. The letter was like Prophet, straight to the point.

Dear Roger,

I promised that I would always be here for you. Someone gave me a second chance, and I plan to give you one. I love my mother, but I make my own decisions. I love my wife, but I'm the head of this

*house. I'll be waiting in the parking lot for you on
the day you get out.*

*Word to the wise, stay low. Most don't celebrate
when the crab leaves the barrel.*

Yours in Christ,
Joshua

Roger folded the letter and placed it under his pillow.
He knew for the first time in years it would give him
pleasant dreams. He lay back and stared at the mottled
gray ceiling. He could now focus on a whole new agenda.
It had been a long time coming. Finally he was going
home. Esther, Phyllis, Charles . . . He'd show them all
when he got out. Just wait.

*Perfumed air wafted over jailhouse stench. There
were angels in the house. Zadkiel stood in the corner of
the cell. "You tried, Guardian. Humans can be indifferent
at the worst times. The old man gave him the message
directly. He was even warned by the Prophet."*

*The guardian shook his head in sorrow. "His past is
coming after him, yet he only thinks about his future.
Sometimes you must solve the riddle of who you were
to get to who you were meant to be. Otherwise, the past
may overtake you when you least expect it."*

*"Are you ready for this fight?" Zadkiel watched the
guardian seeing his weariness.*

*The guardian closed his wings around himself. "It
has been a battle raging in here from day one. Once he
became a child of God it became easier to guide him. He
listened to the Holy Spirit, and many times his obedience
to His guidance saved his life."*

"But now?"

"But now, he tastes freedom. Sometimes when something is very close, that is the time it is the farthest away."

Zadkiel nodded. This guardian angel was wise. "Stay by him. And speak to the guardians of the old one they now call Wise Will and the babe in Christ, Brother Do Right. I believe that they both will play an important role in the future."

"It is already done. I also have eyes on Secure Level One. It hosts a large number of men whose criminal sexual acts are abhorred, especially by the men who are in this prison. These men have taken their animalistic needs as rights and polluted the very air we breathe with their insanity of choice." The guardian's inner purity could be heard shrieking in the background of his comments.

Zadkiel felt for his brother, assigned to a mortal who was locked behind walls that held so many human emotions. He could feel them pounding against his very sensibilities. "You and I both know Roger's connection with these men. Perhaps when God is finished, he will truly be free."

Twin bursts of light blew out of the corner of the room as Roger blinked his eyes, checked the lightbulb in his room, and wondered what had just occurred.

Chapter Twelve

He was a murderer.

Esther hit her pillow and tried to find a way to get comfortable. Every hit of her fist upon her pillow was a hit in Roger's face.

She wasn't usually a violent person, but Roger had abused her physically and emotionally. When she walked away she thought she had forgiven him. Moved past the past and forged a new life. She had given him the house in the divorce, and the courts even made her settle a small amount of alimony on him for a year after.

Punk!

It was something she had never told anyone, especially not Phyllis. The judge had admonished her for fighting the payment. He advised that she had kept him while in the marriage, and that she owed him time to get on his feet. If not for her lawyer grabbing her hand in court, she was sure she would have spent time in jail for her choice words to the judge. She cried in relief on the day she made her last payment. It wasn't the money, it was always the principle. She believed her Bible, an able-bodied man ought to work if he wanted to eat.

She had worked hard in her marriage and sought to be the perfect wife. But the man would never talk to her, and he hated when she asked him the introverted man's nightmare question: "What's wrong?" To make up for his lack of communication, she stumbled around in the dark, searching for a way to make it right.

It never worked; everything she did was twisted. If she bought him something, she was flaunting her success. If she didn't buy him anything, she was selfish. Then her weight began to pile on. Every damaging word he uttered in her ears deserved a sugary dollop of dessert to make the pain go down easier. It was her drug of choice.

She got out of the marriage before she imploded.

Then years later, this fool tried to murder her. Instead, he ended up fighting her brother-in-law when he and her sister showed up at her house unannounced. Now he was getting out of prison.

Her angst had her out of bed checking on her children. She avoided the areas on her hallway floor that creaked and slowly opened each door. She had a time putting them down to bed. They had eaten too much sugar at Grandma's.

She returned to her bedroom, but chose to sit in the chair by her window. She gathered her thoughts, remembering some items she needed to get for the twins' class at school.

They went to a great school, and she knew BJ would enjoy going there.

Thinking about the son definitely had her settling her thoughts on the father. Her fingers feathered over her lips.

That kiss.

Esther remembered his college kisses, and there was no reason to lie to herself, the older Briggs had perfected his skill set.

She hugged herself. Briggs had totally changed up the game. He was self-assured, and his pursuit of her transparent and flattering. The question remained, was she interested?

She thought about his bold swagger. She had only seen his walk on a few men . . . Denzel Washington and Barack Obama included in those ranks. Both accomplished men.

Whew, is it getting hot in here?

Esther fanned herself like she was an old southern belle reclining on a chaise lounge under a juniper tree with one too many mint juleps.

She patted her glistening face with a Kleenex and thought once more of Briggs's countenance.

Besides his swagger, he was fit; he could make some jeans sing and a double-breasted suit talk to you.

Lord, help me here.

She twisted her hands in her lap and thought past the man's physique. There were other qualities she admired. He was a man of integrity. When they were younger and in college, all of her friends had horror stories about their boyfriends cheating on them. Briggs never gave her that testimony. When he first moved to Detroit, he may not have told her everything, but he never lied. And, choosing to stay in a committed relationship with his wife, rather than creating a scandal with her was the right thing to do. Roger's abuse, and her later divorce from the scoundrel, had her in need of some male attention. She wasn't really sure what would have happened if Briggs had been a different type of person.

And if they had run away together? It would have been a disaster. If his wife couldn't trust him, why should she? The final and best part of this list, he was a true man of God.

There's nothing sexier than your man praying for you. It will make a body sing, yessss!

Esther shook from the cold seeping through the window. She picked up the throw from the matching ottoman and laid it over her bare legs. Peeking at the phone she wondered if she dared.

I used to be daring. Yeah. Young and dumb.

Esther gave her head a hard shake. She hated when she talked down to herself. Lawton used to remind her to think good thoughts, to surround herself with light.

Making a decision, she pounced on her phone before she could change her mind. Marathon phone calls were one of her and Briggs's old habits started when they were in college. They had middle-of-the-night talks, revealing real feelings without filters.

It wasn't until she had dialed the number that she looked at the clock and saw the 5:20 a.m. beaming iridescent in the dark.

"Hello? Hello?"

Esther came out of her dream state. "Briggs?"

She could hear him clear his throat. He then whispered, as though he was afraid it wasn't really her. "Esther? You okay . . . I mean, is everything all right? Not that you can't call me at any time, but—"

"I'm fine. Not hurt, but just . . . hurting. You know?"

"Yeah. I've been . . . hurting for a while too. I'm hoping that we can make the pain go away. Become anesthesia . . . together."

"How does that work? Does the aching magically disappear, like Lucky Charms? Or . . .?" She didn't finish on purpose.

"Glad you still have a sense of humor." He then spoke in a soft, seductive voice. "Do you believe that God wants the best for us?"

Esther gave a soft gulp. "I don't think you're playing fair."

"Game over. No more playing. There is something about late-night, early-morning calls that get me to a place of openness. Care to be open with me?"

"I called you, and you're messing with the agenda. Can I catch up first? Ask a few questions? Can we do that?" Esther said, pulling the throw up to her chin.

Briggs was silent on the other end, and Esther worried that she may have offended him in some way. Not answering his question was the coward's way out. But once they started talking about their relationship in the context of it being God-ordained it opened the door to other questions. Like if they were ordained, then what was her marriage to Lawton, the father of her children? She had five wonderful, love-filled years with him. She would never say her union with Lawton was not orchestrated by God.

Lost once again in her thoughts, Esther jumped when Briggs spoke.

"Ask away," he said so softly she had to strain to hear him.

Esther hesitated, but she needed this answer. "Why me?"

He answered without pause. "Because you're everything I dreamed of before I knew what to dream."

Esther's heart beat faster, and her stomach clenched. "Explain."

"Now who's being intense on a brother?"

"Uh-uh, go ahead."

She curled her legs under her and her head fell back against the chair. She could hear Briggs moving around; and then he inhaled and exhaled loudly.

"I remember watching my mom and dad when I was young. They didn't hear me come up on them because I was tiptoeing. I had planned to jump in the room and surprise them—"

Esther heard his uncertainty. "Please, go on."

"As I tiptoed into the room, I heard my mother's sobs. And then my father said, 'It doesn't matter what the doctors said. You are enough for me. You have always been enough for me. Every morning that I am graced to get up from lying next to you, I give God thanks. You gave me Briggs, and if you hadn't given me him you *still* would be enough.'"

"Oh!" Esther whispered into the dark room. She clutched the phone and waited for him to finish.

"Dad, the honorable, three-piece-wearing Bishop Stokes, then got down on both knees, lay his head in my mama's lap and wept. My mother joined him on the floor, and with both of them on their knees, they exchanged the most passionate kiss I had ever witnessed. Even when I sneaked to watch R-rated movies, nothing matched that kiss. I tiptoed my twelve-year-old silly self out of there quick and in a hurry."

Esther was now breathing shallow. "And then?"

"And then, Esther, I began to dream about creating my own version of that kiss. And I did. The kiss that we gave each other the first night we ever said I love you to each other, which, by the way, was long after we felt it."

Lord have mercy.

"That's absolutely the most wonderful thing I've ever heard," Esther gasped. "The story about your parents, I mean."

"It's all true. So, I'll ask you again. Do you believe that God wants His best for you?"

"Yes, Briggs. I believe that God wants His best for me." Esther paused and said what she felt was right to say in her heart. "I believe He did that for me, Briggs. He gave me His best."

"Mo' better, Esther," he murmured.

"Huh?" Esther's toes dug into the end of the seat.

"I believe that our God goes from glory to glory. He doesn't stop at best when He can go one better. How amazing is it that He would be a God who keeps blessing you?"

Esther understood the four types of love. Agape, love of God. Phila, love of your fellow Christian. Storge, love of family. And, Eros, love between a man and a woman. She had been willing to embrace the three, and had made peace with the absence of the one.

She would need to recalibrate her thoughts. The door to Eros once sealed over her heart creaked open on hinges somewhat rusty, but contrary to her earlier vows, it was opening.

It was like Briggs was in tune to her and knew when it was time to cool down their conversation. He smoothly brought up times and mutual friends in their past, and together, they talked into daybreak. She mentioned her encounter with Deborah, and he commiserated with their failure to connect. Every sentence brought her closer to remembering the chemistry she had with Briggs, and the synergy that used to surround their union.

"Mom, what time is it?"

Esther swung around, and a sleep-rumpled David stood there wiping his eyes. She looked over to the clock and saw that it was now six thirty.

I could talk to him another hour.

It was time to get her children up and ready for school.

Esther placed her hand over the phone. "It's time to take your shower. Can you do that, honey?"

David nodded and stumbled back down the hallway to his own bathroom.

Briggs spoke before she could. "I guess it's time for us to shift from grown folks' business to parent duty."

Esther felt lighthearted. "What you talking 'bout, Willis? This *is* grown folks' business. Good morning, Briggs."

"Good morning, Esther. Thank you for brightening my day."

Esther clicked off the phone and sat quietly wondering where she ever got the nerve to make the call in the first place.

Her smile was blinding.

Mo' better? Humph!

***

The scent of frankincense drifted around the room. Zadkiel sat in the corner of Esther's bed, eying her with interest. He looked at her guardian angel, who had done an outstanding job countering the thoughts of the enemy that preyed to stay on her mind. As a result, maybe, just maybe, she wouldn't get in her own way.

The guardian angel stood behind her blowing gentle breezes through her mind. It was the guardian angel who continued to send thoughts of the many satisfying phone calls she and Briggs had had in the past, countering satan's imp's attempts to derail her from making the phone call, and therefore hindering any progress with Briggs.

Zadkiel knew the guardian understood he could not directly interfere unless he was given permission, but this angel had learned to stay within the Trinity's good graces by being vigilant over what he could perform.

Zadkiel's Cheshire grin spoke of his fondness for this one. He knew he should not have favorites. But didn't Jesus have the Sons of Thunder—James and John? He was closest to them, with Peter being the third one, although He did love all the disciples, even Judas who later betrayed Him with a kiss. Maybe that's where the humans got it from, loving someone who had betrayed you? Birthing forgiveness from deceit.

"You know you skate very close to the edge of impudence?" Zadkiel needed to make sure that the guardian knew he saw his edging toward effrontery, even if he had not stopped it.

"Yes, and I thank you for being lenient with me. Esther is a godly woman, and she has many challenges coming her way. Do you not agree that it is easier to handle pain when it is carried by two?"

Zadkiel floated above the bed and watched as Esther got to her knees for her morning prayer. He then illuminated a soft glow and disappeared.

The guardian knelt next to Esther as she prayed, listening to her requests and recording them in his memory to take with him when he ascended. He needed to go. Daybreak was opening the heavens and pouring out his brethren.

Chapter Thirteen

Who holds the ruler to measure progress?

Briggs pondered that thought as he rewound the early-morning conversation he had with Esther. He prayed he had made some headway with her and that she was open to a relationship where the only boundary would be heaven's. This courtship might be unorthodox because he was not going to go slow, and to some, unseemly because he was a divorced pastor, but he was counting on grace and mercy to lead the way.

Did people see their pastors in need of human love and intimacy? He had learned in the past they didn't. He had also learned not to let people's opinions be higher than God's.

He pulled into the circular drive of the elementary school's parent drop-off point.

"You sure you don't want me to come in with you?"

"Uh-huh," BJ said.

"Use your words, son."

"No, sir. You already did. I'm a big boy."

"That was registration; this is school. I don't want you to feel lost. Do you know where your classroom is?" Briggs said, adjusting his son's backpack straps.

"Uh-huh. I mean, yes. And I know where I'm going. I'm a big boy, Daddy."

Briggs smiled. "So you keep saying, little man. Handle your business today. Listen, be respectful and learn something new to teach me, okay?"

"Sure will. Bye, Daddy." BJ scooted his small body along the seat to get out when his car door was snatched open.

A feminine hand, slender with manicured nails, held the door and pulled BJ into a stand. A pink wool tailored coat bent through the door. The voice sugary sweet in its false gaiety drifted to Briggs before he ever saw the face.

"Hi, Pastor Briggs! I have him, and I'll make sure that he gets to his class. If you want I can meet you at the end of the day and walk him to your car. I really don't mind. We wouldn't want little JB to get lost, would we?"

Briggs combed the rolodex in his mind to place the woman. An image of her being introduced at the church popped into his head, along with her name. "Sister Melanie, how are you this morning? Thank you for your assistance, but BJ has assured me that he knows where his class is and he can get there unassisted."

Briggs's eyebrow rose at the keen, determined eyes and the seductive smile. Sister Melanie was a new member if he remembered Prison Proph . . . uh, Joshua's comments about her when she came into the office unexpectedly the day before. Joshua joked that she looked at Briggs like he was carnival candy, and she was a sweet toothed kid who loved the circus.

At the risk of being conceited, Briggs thought, *is she following me?*

"Sister Melanie, I was unaware that you worked here?"

She simpered, "Oh yes, I'm the assistant principal. So you see, I'm qualified and certified to care for JJ. I really don't mind, and—"

Briggs looked in his rearview mirror and saw a line of cars forming behind him. "Sister Melanie, thank you, but Sister Naomi will be picking BJ up; it's all arranged." Briggs nodded for BJ to go. "Have a nice day, son. Bye now."

BJ stopped his antsy dance apparently impatient to get to class. "Bye, Daddy. I'm going this time." He stared hard at the lady who grinned hard for his daddy, but failed to know his name.

Melanie blossomed red in embarrassment, "Oh, yes. Come, CJ, let's go."

"Help me, Father," Briggs whispered as she swished away, swinging her nonexistent hips hard enough to make a milk shake. "How hard is it to learn initials? It's BJ." He swiveled his head from side to side as he eased away from the curb and into traffic.

Later, Briggs stepped into his suite of offices and greeted Naomi with a cheerful hello and a warning. "No more descriptive titles for people, Naomi. I'm even slipping and thinking of people by those names instead of what their good mamas and papas named them. So government names from now on, okay?"

Naomi gave a small sly smile. "Well, then, I guess you don't want to know the descriptive name of your caller right before you came in."

"No, I don't. Who was it?"

"Esther Redding," Naomi said in a matter-of-fact tone. She peeked at Briggs from over her granny reading glasses and pumped a small amount of lotion from the dispenser on her desk, rubbing her hands together.

"Oh?" he said, biting his lip.

"Yes. I would have called her . . . oops, sorry. It almost slipped out." She pulled the keyboard back into place.

Briggs hesitated, then leaned on her desk. "Well, if you must, get it out. Maybe you can say it just one more time. Ease you into the change versus going cold turkey."

Naomi pushed the keyboard back, removed her glasses, and stared at Briggs. "If that helps you," she said sarcastically.

Briggs held onto his laughter. "Well?"

"The Widow Redding, soon-to-be put-a-ring-on-it, First Lady Stokes, who can ring your bell in more than one way, phoned you, Pastor."

A full-bellied laugh roared through the room. Briggs's swaggering stride was pronounced as he strolled into his office. As he closed his door, he shouted, "As my Uncle June Bug used to say, 'Sho you right!'"

Briggs sailed into his plush leather chair, hit number one for the speed dial on his phone, and waited for the sun to come out in his office.

"Hello?"

"Esther? It's Briggs returning your call," he said, grinning widely.

"Pastor Stokes, I was wondering if I could schedule a counseling session," Esther said, her tone flat.

"So, we're back to formalities?"

She cleared her throat. "That's part of what I want to talk about. I would like to clear the air on several things."

"Esther, this doesn't sound like a session I'm going to enjoy," Briggs rubbed the vein pulsing over his eyes.

"A lot is happening at work. So, I can't make it today."

"I can understand that. I'm working on getting up to snuff here myself." Briggs pulled his calendar close.

Esther filled the silence with chatter as Briggs reviewed his calendar. "So, today was BJ's first day of school. Grace Academy has an excellent curriculum. The twins are doing great there. Phyllis feels Miracle is doing really well in her accelerated program too."

"She would have been in BJ's class if she wasn't ahead of her age group. He would have liked that." Briggs said, as he flipped through his filled calendar. "How about you tell me when would be a good time for you?"

"I can do the day after tomorrow on Wednesday. Is that okay?"

Briggs looked down and crossed out the deacons' all-afternoon meeting. "I'm good. But could you do me a favor? Could we meet at my house? I need to be there that day."

"Hmmm, is that a good idea? I mean, considering all that we've discussed. Perhaps, uh, you know?" Esther faltered when he failed to jump in to help her.

"We'll be fine. It's not like I would be inappropriate and kiss you or anything," Briggs teased.

She huffed. "Really, Briggs? You going *there?*"

"Sorry, I feel good today in spite of someone trying to mess up this natural high. A wonderful birdie woke me up, and I'm all in. So please forgive me. I promise to keep my hands to myself."

Not my lips, though.

"All right, Pastor. Can you text me your address, and I'll be there at . . . say one?"

"One is fine. See you then." Briggs hung up the phone playing Naomi's game in his head. *The Widow Redding, soon-to-be-put-a-ring-on-it, First Lady Stokes, who can ring my bell in more than one way.*

Briggs hit his intercom. "Naomi, please reschedule the deacons meeting on Wednesday to morning instead of afternoon. And apologize for the short notice."

My future is at stake.

"Yes, sir. I'll call tiptoe-inching, toupee-slipping Deacon Clement. He'll be okay. They all retirees except Atta Boy Bow Wow—"

"Naomi!"

"Pastor, you said I didn't have to go cold turkey. And Deacon Clement tiptoes around here like he's scared of his own shadow, constantly fixing that toupee. Deacon Williams goes with three young women in the church, not committing to any of them. The men see him and say, 'Atta boy'; the church gossip mill sees him and says,

'Bow wow.' So, I am weaning myself, Pastor. I'm trying. But you asked me to call the deacons, and they the best renaming I've done. Baby steps, sir, baby steps."

Chapter Fourteen

Monica looked around. The small hotel was no-star at best.

My, how the mighty have fallen.

She rocked a fitful Fiona into a restful sleep. Seemed like even her baby knew they were slumming.

She stared at her reflection in the cracked mirror and worked out in her head her game plan to surprise Briggs. She'd gotten an attack of nerves leaving the bus station, and instead of barging in on him, she'd stayed in a hotel room. She couldn't afford it for long. She was living off jewelry she was pawning as needed.

At thirty-nine dollars per night, they ought to be paying me to sleep here.

It had taken her one day to stop shaking. It was Tuesday, and today she would pamper her skin, do her hair, and refine her approach. She needed a surefire way to get her Mrs. Briggs Stokes title back.

She wrung her hands together hoping that Briggs had softened toward her. He was so compassionate after that whack job tried to murder her. It was the only reason she felt she had a chance.

I'm sorry, Lord. I shouldn't speak ill of the dead. So thank you, Father. I'm so glad she's just that—good and dead!

Monica remembered the tears in Briggs's eyes as he sat next to her in the hospital and willed her to live. Once stable, she had taken a turn for the worse.

The hospital room had been dark only because she could not see more than outlines through the heavy gauze bandages surrounding her head. The hammering in her skull was never-ending and everything that was being said was filtered through the consistent pounding.

She could feel a familiar touch on her hand, its strength willing her to get better. Soon, wetness joined the pressure, and she knew it was someone's tears. *How could so much wetness be produced out of one person?* she thought. The murkiness in her head eluded clarity. She couldn't pinpoint who gripped her hand so securely.

Something had happened, something that was so vile, her mind would not let her focus. It was an innate ability honed from years of having to survive on her own, this sense of wrongness.

Out of her shadows, he spoke, *"You must fight. We need you. BJ loves you so much. Fighting is part of your nature. You don't give up. Don't give up now. Stay here, among the living for both your children. Fiona needs to know her mother."*

The mention of her one-month-old child triggered it all. The knife, the wild, deranged, sneer on her attacker's face. Then . . . Randall's body, mutilated and lifeless.

She screamed through lungs that burned like fire. Then howled from a chest that reverberated from the pain of her wounds. Strong arms gathered her and held on. They rode the wave together, until she came up from the hole of unrestrained agony.

Monica rolled her shoulders, her flashback making her queasy. She would visit him tomorrow. Her ram in the bush. She closed her eyes to pray.

"Holy Spirit, Briggs has to feel something for me."

He's a pastor.

But, it wasn't a pastor's tears, it was more than that.

He's the father of your child.

Monica pointed at the mirror and screamed, "Whose side are you on?"

God's side. You promised Him.

"I promised Him what?"

Not what. You promised Him, who. You promised Him, you.

"I was dying! How are you going to hold me to that?" she screeched.

Monica waited, but there was silence. She had won the argument, but her pleased smile warped into a frown. She didn't like the silence. To her it spoke of condemnation. She cried out to the quiet. "I'll be a good wife. I was for a while, a good wife and mother. It was only after Randall came back that I lost my way. And I was working on being a better person. I was working on pleasing you. Lord, please remember all I used to do for the church. Tell me it'll be okay."

A small mewing sound came from the middle of the bed. Monica looked on as Fiona tried answering her with small perfectly pink bow lips and bright bluish green eyes.

Remorseful, she shook her head. She had to quit talking to herself. She'd woken Fiona after finally getting her to sleep. "You understand Mama, don't you, baby? We need a daddy. And that's exactly what you're going to get. No sense in looking for a brand-new one. The one your brother has is already broken in."

She bent over and rubbed her nose against Fiona's tiny button one and placed her slender pinky finger in her tiny fist. Monica rubbed back and forth as she spoke in a teeny baby voice. "BJ just loves sharing with his baby sister, yes, he does."

All Fiona could do was gurgle her appreciation and contentment for her mother's love.

***

Sulfur spewed from fire-ringed stones. The Leader was worn-out. His tail rested in his lap, and he rubbed it, pleasuring himself after such a daunting errand. Pushing his skills against Zadkiel's was always an arduous task. Every time the human, Monica, heard God's message, he replayed into her ear her own desires. Her own needs. He whispered into her conscience all that she wanted to hear.

He was the accuser of the brethren, the mighty fallen. He was a part of the royal court of darkness, and Monica was theirs. She had made promises to Him whose name is not spoken. So what? All the disposables did that; and then they reneged. They were simple, self-serving creatures. The lot of them weren't worth the last fall from grace his kind had endured.

And now, Zadkiel was in the mix. His nemesis, the one he loathed. He never appeared the last time he had visited this lot, but his signature was in Mother Reed's healing, Briggs's forgiveness of Monica and their reconciliation, Esther's meeting and marrying Lawton, and that doggone Prophet Joshua getting out of prison. Only Zadkiel could counter his evil chess moves with a holy checkmate. But, he had a rook move to make, straight-ahead.

The perfumed atmosphere should have put the guardian angel at ease. Yet, he sat in silent despair. Monica was falling back into her old ways. He tried holding her to her vows to God, but he had begun to fade in his efforts when Zadkiel showed up. Even then it was too late. She was already placing herself into the justification system. It was the system humans used to tell themselves that they were justified in their misconduct. They were, after all, going through something" and not expected to follow

His teachings when the road became crooked. They spoke to their own needs, and asked God for help, but did not provide the faith or works for Him to move on their behalf. Second Corinthians 4:10 states, for the weapons of our warfare are not carnal, but mighty through God for the pulling down of strongholds.

"Are you sulking, Guardian?"

"No, Zadkiel. I am going over my steps and wondering where I went wrong. She's slipping into darkness. I cannot seem to stop it."

"They have—" Zadkiel began to say.

"No disrespect, but please do not tell me about their free will. What about grace? Mercy? Favor? Father can move at any time and make a crooked road straight. I abhor going back to the dark places she once lived. It was horrible. I need light, the Son shining down on me."

"Silence! The Son shines down on you wherever you are. David spoke of it in Psalm 139:8; if man knows this, how can you not?" Zadkiel's voice rang all the way through the tips of his wings. "If I ascend up into heaven, thou art there: if I make my bed in hell, behold, thou art there.' He is God!"

Zadkiel shot into the air leaving a chastened guardian angel behind.

He fell to his face and joined the cherubim in his cries of holy. He was an angel of light, he was a messenger of hope, not just a voyeur of despair. He rose and sailed through the heavens, more determined than ever to help Monica win.

Chapter Fifteen

Mother Reed smiled at the film of food around BJ's mouth. He hummed as he ate, and with every forkful, his humming heightened.

Briggs smiled fondly. "Sorry, Mother. I'm not the cook you are, so BJ considers this a feast." He took his napkin and wiped BJ's chin. "Don't you, son?"

BJ's grin was lopsided, his jaws full of food. "Uh-huh," BJ said, shoveling another forkful in his mouth.

"I sho' do love the sound of that humming. It's music to these old ears," Mother Reed said and gave BJ an affectionate tap on his chipmunk-full cheek. "You save room for dessert, all right little one?"

BJ perked up at the sound of that. He nodded as he continued to shovel in his food.

Mother Reed and Briggs smiled. Neither of them had the heart to tell him to slow down. He was enjoying it too much. Mother Reed's smothered chicken, rice, and collard greens were the best in town, and Briggs was enjoying himself too.

Briggs shook his fork in the air. "This is some mighty tasty cooking. Glad to see you haven't given up one of God's gifts to you. You could make shoe leather scrumptious."

"You sure you ain't been feeding dis c'here baby shoe leather the way he putting down his dinner?" she chortled.

"I try, but its plain fare. Poor BJ. Monica wasn't much better," Briggs said.

BJ stopped eating, and his bottom lip quivered. Briggs wanted to cut out his tongue. Mother Reed sized up the situation and smoothly changed the subject.

"BJ, sho' is a good school you going to. You been to the fishing hole yet?"

BJ's eyes got large. He grabbed his napkin and wiped his mouth. "No, ma'am. What's a fishing hole?"

Mother Reed stood and dramatically pantomimed reeling in a very big fish. "It's a small body of water with fish in it."

Briggs jumped next to Mother Reed and illustrated fish slipping out of his hands. "And, the fish sometimes jump, and are slippery as well."

"Why does the school have a fishing hole, Daddy?" BJ leaned forward interested in something he had never seen at a school before.

Briggs smiled, happy to add to BJ's knowledge. "Well, I asked you to teach me something new today that you learned. But I'll lead by example. It's a Christian school, Christians are fishers of men. Therefore, it's a place where you learn to fish. When you leave school, everywhere you look you'll see men, or as we just explained, fish. Our job is to give them God's Word to reel them into the Kingdom."

BJ's eyes became large as he sat back and studied his father. "Well, then, you must be a head fisherman, Daddy. Because you fish everywhere we go."

Puzzled, Briggs looked at Mother Reed, who just grinned and nodded for him to continue his lesson. "How so, son?"

In thought, BJ placed his chin in his hand, as his father had a habit of doing. "You told that lady at the market that God loves her. And then, at the gas station you gave that man some money and told him that God was his strength. And then, you invited him to the church. That's the fishing you talking about, right?"

Mother Reed clapped her hands in glee. "This is a fine boy you have here. He sees and hears."

She grabbed 'Briggs's hand. "Son, this little one will rise high in the Kingdom, leading more men to Christ than you and your father together. He is the culmination of yours and your father's prayers. Guard him well. Keep a hedge of protection around him."

Briggs looked up in alarm. He knew his son was special, every parent thought so. But, this was Mother Reed, and she was rarely wrong about such things. He turned to BJ. The boy continued to shovel food into his mouth, having lost interest in the adult conversation.

Mother Reed tugged on Briggs's hand. "He is not too young to learn protective scriptures. Teach him now, Briggs. Don't tarry on this. Can you not see the storms gathering? Place the watchmen on the towers, call out the intercessors of the church to begin to pray. We cannot keep walking around unaware. A war is raging. We must do our part to victory."

BJ took that moment to look up.

Alarmed, Briggs thought he may have heard Mother Reed's dire warnings.

"Do you need something, son?"

BJ looked askance at his father, as if he were timid to speak up.

Briggs nodded to BJ. "Speak up. Mother Reed is your surrogate grandmother. What do you want?"

BJ's voice croaked, "Cake."

Mother Reed and Briggs laughed in relief as she rose from her chair at the kitchen table and sliced him some of her famous cream cheese pound cake.

BJ winked at Mother Reed. "Thank you, I may need another soon. I'm a growing boy."

Mother Reed laughed in delight. "Briggs, this boy is pure joy with his mannish self!"

Afterward, BJ played in Mother Reed's spare room as Briggs and Mother Reed enjoyed after-dinner coffee.

Mother Reed sipped. "I sure do love it when I get to have real coffee. I miss other food though, food I used to eat so readily. You think sin is like that to people, Briggs? It ain't good for 'em, but they miss it when they stop doing it."

"I expect so, Mother. But, if you stay in front of God long enough, you'll lose the appetite for it. He says, 'Oh taste and see that the Lord is good.' It's just that most give up too soon. They give up before change can come," Briggs said, cradling his mug between his hands.

Mother Reed got up and put her coffee cup in the sink. "Is it a fear thing? Is it the fear of change? I get so tired of seeing the spirit of fear operate in people's lives. The only fear we should have is the fear of God Almighty!"

"I counsel men and women every day about how fear has played a huge role in their issues. They get fear mixed up with danger. They're not synonymous. Danger is when you cross the street in oncoming traffic and your body screams no. But fear is a product of your imagination. It is the anticipation of bad coming, when good could very well be present. For instance, being afraid to try love again."

Briggs stood and placed his empty cup into the sink. Mother Reed nailed him with a penetrating stare.

"So, you think that Esther is afraid to love again? Or to love you again?"

Briggs turned and leaned against the sink. "That's the question I can't answer. I see her wavering in a relationship with me; and then she falls back into her safety zone, where she tells herself she has already had the great love of her life."

With practiced ease, Mother Reed untied her apron and laid it on the counter.

"Esther is my heart, and I'm vested in that child's happiness. We'll continue to pray on it. Just keep moving forward, even if it's only a step or two. You don't always have to have thunder for there to be rain."

Briggs smiled. "Where should I leave your offering?"

"Ha! Go get that baby and take him home. He's too quiet; he may be back there asleep after all he ate."

Briggs came out of the room, carrying BJ. Leaving, he stepped out on the porch and breathed deeply. He had high hopes for his and Esther's talk the next day. It was time to make like a superhero and rescue his damsel in distress. Only he refused to wear flashy metallic spandex briefs, and any kind of cape was a pimp's move at best.

Meanwhile, miles away, Esther's ideas to find Deborah were falling like dominos. The hotel wouldn't give her much information or call Deborah to the phone. Seemed there was a special number for employees' emergency calls. Using her fine Sherlock Holmes skills, Esther had ferreted out that Deborah worked part-time before the desk clerk got suspicious and clammed up. Esther hung up feeling defeated.

She only had one option; she had to go back to Columbus, Ohio. Esther would have to hunt Deborah down like she was the police and she had stolen something from her . . . which she had—her heart.

Chapter Sixteen

The cement around the walls was cracking, and the aluminum tables and benches were bolted to the ground to deter anyone from using them as weapons. Roger stood in the chow line. He heard the cursing and loud-mouthed boasting that was the usual appetizer before the meal.

He was immune to it, especially since he was counting the hours until he was able to leave this place. He wanted a real bed, real toilet paper for his chafed butt, and to sit next to a beautiful woman in a real church. She had to be sweet-smelling, and if she could sing during praise and worship that would be a plus.

He was jostled out of his daydream, and he turned to give the offender "the stare." The one that said, "Mess with me, and you'll be dealt with." He only used it on a person once. Then, he prayed over the guy after he knocked him out.

Sorry, God. But these fiends will kill you unless you show them that you are stronger than them. Three more days and I'm out of here, and doing things your way.

A guy he didn't know was all up in his personal space. "I know you, fool?" Roger asked.

A pug-nosed, pocked-marked man leered. "You don't need to know me. We got mutual friends."

Roger looked at the guy and didn't like the way he stressed the word, "friends."

The guy licked his lips deliberately. "Yea, we got 'friends.'"

Roger stepped back. He could hit him, but with all these witnesses it could mean trouble. As in, *you don't get to go home* trouble.

The guy rubbed his own chest up and down, then in circles suggestively. "I'm gon' make sure we get to know each other better."

Roger went tense, then he went cold, and his fists clenched. It looked like he was going to have to deal with this punk when all he wanted to do was eat. Only Satan himself could have orchestrated this confrontation.

A shadow fell over the duo. Roger glanced up to see Brother Do Right, all six feet seven inches of him.

Brother Do Right draped his heavily muscled arm over the interloper's smaller shoulder. "We good here?"

The unwanted man stumbled as he looked up into a face that was chiseled like stone. "I ain't got beef with you, man."

"Who you got beef wit' then?" Brother Do Right asked as he pulled on the other man's shirt lapels. He looked at the young man hard. "You new, boy? What's with all the lip licking and touching yourself? That was real gay." He gripped the collar of his shirt harder, squeezing his neck in the process. "What you in for?"

"I ain't got to tell you nothing. You . . . have no right—" The man jerked away and began to back up, only to back directly into Roger.

Roger was angry, angrier than he had been in a while. He had three days, and this was the kind of thing that could catch him more time. He didn't know why this man was bothering him, but he knew that no weapon formed against him would prosper. "Back up off me. Go back the way you came. I—don't know you—don't *want* to know you."

The man turned and walked away, and then spun around. "Duncan said to tell you, full moon coming soon."

Roger's eyes bulged. Sweat broke out over his forehead, and his hands trembled. A despondency settled in the center of his gut. Brother Do Right grabbed his arm and pulled him out of the line and over to a corner in the room. The guards were watching closely and both tried to look unconcerned.

"You good? You lookin' sick."

"Yeah, yeah, man." Roger's voice sounded weak, and his hands wouldn't stop shaking. He jammed them in his pocket.

Brother Do Right pulled him into the hallway. "I don't know why these new bloods be tryin' us, 'cause they think as Christians we can't go upside they heads. That ish ain't right."

Roger saw him peer over his shoulder, checking things out.

"Man, I know you only got three more days here. But you gon' have to put a hurting on that dude. Sometin' real slimy 'bout him. You can't let them see you weak. Peoples already don't like that you out of here. Give them a reason to prey on you, and the action will never end. You know this!"

Roger looked up and gave Brother Do Right some dap. "Good looking out. But you said the key words, three more days. I can't jeopardize that for some yard rule I ain't made," he said kneading his face in frustration, his usual rich brown color now ash and pale. "I'm going to go to my cell. I need to think on this. Besides, I think I'm coming down with something."

"Awwright, den. Peace."

Roger rushed to his cell, his long legs eating up the distance as he hurried along. He was going to be sick. He dashed into his cell and threw up in his toilet bowl. Eyes still shut, he groped around until he found a washcloth to pat his face.

Sitting on his bed, he held out his hand and noted he had the shakes like an alcoholic at a bar's last call. He knew a struggle was coming, and the thought of it had his gut flip flopping. He covered his face with his hands and a soft sob escaped his quivering lips.

After twenty-three years, how had Duncan found him?

Chapter Seventeen

Good morning, heartache.

Esther stretched and leaped out of bed. It was time to get her children moving, and then run to the office before she met Briggs. She had dreamed about Lawton, but she couldn't make out his face. Every time she tried to get a better look at him in her dream, he disappeared.

How could that be? It's only been a little more than two years.

She stood in the bathroom and ran her shower. As she stepped in, she began her morning prayer.

She yelped when the curtain was jerked back. "Mama, David said I stink. Make him stop making skunk noises at me."

Esther squinted through a soap-filled gaze. "Ruth, if you don't close this curtain, you will regret it."

"Sorrrry, Mama." Ruth's eyes were bug-eyed glued to Esther's nude body. "Am I going to get big boobies one day too?"

"Ruth Renee Redding if you don't get out of this bathroom, right this minute!"

"Yes, ma'am."

Esther laughed. Her life was never dull. Minutes later, she was stepping out of the shower when she heard the screaming between her adorable, saved, perfect children.

"Skunk, skunk, skunk, skunk."

"I am not a skunk, David, You are a stupid boy, and you are ugly too. I don't love you anymore, David!"

Esther heard absolute silence after Ruth's last statement. She dried off as she leaned forward and flicked the intercom on the wall to listen. Her whole house was wired, courtesy of being married to a lieutenant on the Detroit police force.

David's small voice sounded broken. "You—don't—love—me—no—more? I was only playing, Ruth."

"You was being mean. I don't stink," Ruth said through her sniffles.

"Well, maybe a little," David started to say, until Ruth's sobs got louder. "No, I was just playing, Ruth. You smell just fine."

Esther smiled. They were at peace again. And she had a feeling if she checked Ruth's bed, she would fine a urine stain, where she had an accident during the night. *Pee does stink.*

About an hour later, Esther dropped the children off at school and headed to her office. She needed to work on a few projects with her assistant, Simone.

Esther was proud of her recent accomplishments. When she first started her consulting business, she was only getting a contract here and there. But positive word traveled, and she soon had to move out of her home office and into a small space so she could have meetings and sometimes get away from the work.

She was happy to see Simone unlocking the front door, and she jogged to catch up with her. "Girl, hold up."

"Hey, good morning." Simone allowed her to catch the door as she glanced down at her watch. She entered, laid down her purse, strolled to the coffee cart, and switched on the Keurig.

"You're early."

"Yes, instead of returning home after I dropped the kids off, I came straight here. I have to cut out early for an appointment."

Simone sat at her desk in the reception area, booted up her computer, and pulled up Esther's calendar. "Well, your appointment is not work-related. You finally going to get a little afternoon delight? Hint, hint."

Esther waved her hand at Simone as though she was a gnat. "See, you take five steps forward into maturity, and ten steps back into nonsense. I am not you. I thought your attending Love Zion would help you with all that. You have the hormones of a sixteen-year-old boy."

"Thank you, Esther, O pyramid of virtue. You crabby 'cause you need to let yourself go sometimes. Now I heard from a little birdy that a new . . ." Simone rose pumping her hand in the air, "Brad Pitt can't touch this, Morris Chestnut can't compete with this, and Boris Kodjoe want to be this brother who will be leading Love Zion ministry from now on." Simone peeked at Esther's stoic stance and noted her tightly folded arms. "And if you don't want to make a play for the A-team, I'ma take one for the team."

Esther went over to the Keurig machine, popped in her green tea, and turned to Simone. "Sometimes when you talk like this, I wonder why I hired you. I could use someone who is so much more stable."

Simone rolled her eyes. "Before you go on, the Stanhope contract has been negotiated and signed. I switched your workshop on Friday from the morning to the afternoon to give you more time to get the kids to school. And I called the property manager about the toilet running and the sink clogging in the bathroom. He promises to have it fixed by midday."

Simone then walked over to Esther, picked up a prong, bent over, and took slices of lemon out of the minifridge, placed them and a small Danish on a plate, and handed it to Esther before she returned to her seat. "I'll e-mail you the new logos that the design team completed. Right now, I like number three."

With her plate and her tea, Esther went into her office, where with her door open she could still see Simone. She sat down and nodded. "Yes, that is why I bribed you to come with me when I left the Helping Heart agency. Thanks, girl."

Simone smirked, flounced to her chair, and turned away from Esther's door. "You're welcome. And I was the same person there as I am here. So unless I typed you a memo to tell you I've changed . . . I haven't!"

Esther grinned sheepishly. She had been put firmly in her place.

Sometime after lunch, Esther could hear Simone flirting with the building's plumber.

"Ooh, you do that so well. How long have you been a plumber?"

Esther couldn't see the man. The bathroom was next to the front door, but she could hear him, and the deep rumble of his response. "About six years. It's a good gig. It's nice pay, and I get to meet some really nice people."

Esther could see Simone as she leaned into the bathroom. "*I'm* nice."

"Yeah, you seem to be real nice. How nice are you?"

Simone leaned further in. "The nicest."

"Well, let me holler at you a minute."

Esther moved swiftly to the outer office before she was witness to any more insanity. "Hi, I'm Esther, and I own this business. I appreciate the service. How much longer?"

The young man stood from his crouched position, and Esther caught her breath. He wasn't very tall, but he made up for it in build and looks. Esther knew right then that Simone was not going to let this one get away.

Wiping his hands on a cloth, he said, "Yes, ma'am, about another fifteen minutes should do it. It doesn't take long to put in a new washer. Listen, there was a lot of hair glue and strands of hair stuck in your pipes. I snaked it out, but would suggest whoever is doing her hair in here, make sure she's putting her trash in the trash can, not the toilet. And, ladies, weave glue is the worst culprit of all."

Both he and Esther turned to Simone, whose cheeks turned crimson in embarrassment. Her weave lay across her shoulders in waves as she tried to push it behind her neck.

Sheepishly she asked, "What?"

The plumber stepped forward. "I won't tell the building manager because knowing it's your office's fault could make him charge you. He can be like that sometimes."

"I knew you were a good guy. What's your name?" Simone asked softly.

His reply was husky. "Lee. Yours?"

"Simone," she said wetting her lips.

Esther watched the two stand there with lust stamped over their faces. Turning from one to the other, she coughed to break the moment. "Well, I have an appointment." She motioned Simone into her office and said in an undertone, "Will you be okay here alone with him? You don't know that man."

Simone whispered back, "No, but I plan to get to know him. He may be the one. And if he is, I'm going to give him that plunger for his scepter and label him my porcelain prince. Shoot, I could keep him forever."

Esther raised her eyes heavenward. "Aren't you getting ahead of yourself?"

"Maybe. But I'm not afraid of the scrapes and bumps life gives you. All we can do is have faith that things will get better. Wasn't it you who dragged me into church where I heard, all things work together?"

"I can't believe it. You're quoting scripture?" Esther said, incredulous.

"Makes you wonder who the real believer is, *huh,* Esther?" Simone walked out of the office and once again leaned against the bathroom door.

Esther was flustered hearing Simone operate. The boy didn't have a chance. That girl always went after what she wanted. If she put truth on the table, she could use some of her boldness.

Later, she held her head down as she walked by the besotted couple. When she got to the door, her hand on the knob, Simone called out softly, "Keep your head up, Esther. The sky's the limit if you're brave enough to grab hold of it."

Esther strode out the door, murmuring as she went.

The last thing I need is advice from the one-night-stand queen.

Chapter Eighteen

Esther sat in her car ruminating on her circumstances and staring at Briggs's front door. He was home, his MKT sat in the driveway. She rubbed her head, ruffling her sideswept bangs, then pulled down the visor and fingered her hair back into place. She was the queen of stall tactics.

She looked at her reflection in the mirror again. Her pixie cut shined, and her makeup was subtle and enhanced her eyes and cheekbones. She was wearing her good jeans, a lime-green shell with a crochet short summer sweater and comfortable peep-toe sandals. She wondered if there was a fashion category titled "sensibly sexy."

It was an unseasonably warm September day, and she was taking advantage of it. There was nothing left to do but go into the lion's den. She peered at the front door again.

Suddenly, the door opened, and there he stood. Somehow as she stared at this grown sophisticated brother, he morphed into the twenty-one-year-old college senior she had left behind. The waves of his low fade haircut gleamed in the light of his foyer. She could see the cleft in his chin that fit her finger just so. And the place between his shoulder and neck, her place—home. She closed her eyes, holding on to the sweet memory of a less complicated time, a time when he was hers alone.

Briggs stepped down the stairs and came to a stop in front of her car. "Everything okay?"

Esther scurried to gather her purse and cell phone. "I was trying to decide if I should make a call. But I'm fine. I'll do it later," she said, as she got out of the car and came around to the sidewalk.

Briggs held out his arm.

She shook her head. "Don't be silly, Pastor Stokes. This is not a social call."

Briggs put his arm down and waved her chivalrously ahead.

"After you then," he said.

Esther went up the stairs putting a little sway in her hip action; if he was going to walk behind her, she wanted the view to be a good one. Yes, she was saved, but she was still a woman walking in front of a virile man.

She regarded his living space with open curiosity. When he lived in Detroit before he lived in Reverend Gregory's place. This was her first glance at a grown Briggs personal living space.

There were boxes still left to be unpacked, but he had done pretty well so far.

She smiled, remembering his dorm room with posters on his walls, a stereo bigger than his dorm-assigned twin bed, and his funky gym socks. Here, there were pictures on the wall and burgundy, chocolate and mustard striped throw pillows on his mustard leather furniture. There were even a few knickknacks around the room. "Not bad, Pastor."

"You thought there would be clothes on the floor and funky gym socks?" he laughed.

Esther clapped her hands in delight. "You are not going to believe that I just had those exact thoughts. How'd you do that?"

"What? Know you so well? Understand you and what makes you tick? Besides, you used to always get so angry when I chased you around the room with those socks."

Esther scrunched up her nose. "Who wants to be hit in the face with sweaty, smelly socks? That was so gross."

Briggs leaned in wiggling his head. "Well, if you hadn't been so cute running from me, I wouldn't have had to borrow other dudes' socks to torture you!"

"You didn't! *Did* you?" Esther paused and looked at Briggs with a gleam in her eyes.

Briggs began to back up, his laughter sputtering up as he moved. "I couldn't help it. You would get so red; and then your skin would glow, and your eyes would spark . . ." Briggs stopped moving and stretched out his hand, reaching for and fingering the swoop of her bangs. "Just like they're sparking now."

He laid her hair against her forehead. "It still feels like silk in my hand."

The way he stared into her eyes, Esther couldn't breathe.

Briggs's eyes glowed; his voice curled around her, cloaking her body in warmth.

"Do you know how lovely you are?"

Esther had no great comeback, no snippy volley of words to deflect his mood. No quip to shift the atmosphere. This conversation was out of her control, and she had no idea how to rein it in. She didn't know if she was ready to commit to trying to build a relationship with Briggs—to start again—this time with both of their children involved.

She gave a timid smile and on weakened legs, she walked to the fireplace mantel and picked up a picture of Briggs holding a tiny BJ in his arms. She placed the picture in Briggs's hands. "From what I can see, you're making a great home for you both here."

Briggs cradled the picture in his palm as though he was actually holding his son; he gently returned it to the mantle. "I've got a son to raise. Normalizing his surroundings as soon as possible is a necessary step."

"What about your pursuit of this relationship with me? How does that classify as normalizing BJ's life?" Esther asked, her voice cracking low and unsteady.

"It allows him to see his father happy. It provides him an up close view of a loving relationship." Briggs motioned for her to sit. "You're worried about BJ or your children?"

Esther sat and leaned back, resting her back against the sofa cushions. "You know, I'm tempted to just throw out any doubts and say let's do this. Let's take a walk on the wild side." She then grabbed a throw pillow and hugged it to her chest. "But I have responsibilities. Two children who count on me making decisions that include their well-being."

The burgundy cloth chair was regal in its appearance, and Briggs sat as though he was its reigning monarch. "Sweetheart, what I wouldn't give to be that pillow. To be the person who anchors you when things go rough. To help you raise your children and for you to help me with BJ."

He rose, reached over, and grabbed the pillow from her hands.

"Woman, I know what I want. And I don't mean to be insensitive, but you need to stop being a martyr. In other words, get down from the cross; somebody needs the wood."

Esther attempted to grab another pillow, but Briggs slid over to the couch and moved it to his vacated chair. She crossed her arms in defiance and said, "I know from past experiences that when you think only about yourself bad things happen."

Chagrined, he placed the pillows back on the couch and gave a loud, exasperated grunt.

"Your frustration with me is unfair. When we were in college I was this carefree, self-absorbed person. It was all about me, then the unmentionable happened."

Wincing, Briggs said, "it's funny how none of us talk about it. How come we can't just talk about it?"

Esther's face was pinched as she pulled her legs under her. So gripped by their conversation, she couldn't even remember when she kicked off her shoes. "It changed so many lives. Sheri's act was a 9.0 Richter scale earthquake in our lives. Her one deed destroyed everything in its wake, and the aftershocks are still echoing even now."

Briggs held his breath as though he was afraid to continue. He then leaned forward, anxious, but with a determined air. "I felt like I was the first casualty."

"I was shattered. I couldn't see beyond my own suffering," Esther said, looking intently into his eyes. She wondered how she could take him back to such a difficult time in their lives. But if she could, maybe then they could both move on. "In those days all I could see was you. I had to force myself to go to class. You were my . . . passion."

Esther heard Briggs's increased breathing. "And, Esther, you were mine. I thought we had forever."

Both were quiet, caught in faraway thoughts. Briggs was the first to seek more clarification. "What made you turn away from me?"

Esther flinched. "How can I help you understand? Shame is a horrible spirit. It's conniving because it seeks to destroy your purpose. It comes at you in your vulnerable places. It whispers your secret fears, and taunts you with your past transgressions."

She once again grabbed the pillow to her, clutching it for support. "I was tormented by my shortcomings. I hadn't been there for Deborah or Sheri. I did what I see women do even now; they fall in love, and then pretty much check out of every other relationship."

Esther looked over Briggs's shoulder off into space. "Men don't do that. But we do. And when we do? We later pay the price."

Briggs looked puzzled. "How's that?"

Ardent, Esther perched on the edge of the cushion. "There's not a woman out there who hasn't experienced what I'm talking about. When the party is over, or a relationship dies down, it's like we come out of a fog. When the air clears we realize we haven't returned calls, failed to keep lunch dates, or nurture any of our other relationships. Men, however, still went to the basketball games with their boys, hung out at the fight party while we used that alone time to prepare for when we would see him again. We did the nail thing, and hair thing, and every other thing that entices and excites."

Briggs cupped his chin. "I never saw it that way. You felt that's what you did with me?"

With hands on both knees, Esther nodded. "Yes, and when my neglect let both my friends down, I felt like I was a failure. There were times I could have been there for my girls, but I put you first." She reached over and took his hand, this release in her chest was a relief and she needed to take it all the way to its conclusion.

"Later, I couldn't express my pain to you because it was all connected to my love for you. Like a ball of knotted twine, I couldn't untangle it or make it go right. So I bailed. I knew it wasn't fair. My intellect bargained with my heart, and in the end they both lost."

Briggs squeezed her hand, covering it with his other. He absent-mindedly stroked her.

Esther faltered at his touch, but she pushed forward. She wanted him to finally understand.

"When I got home, I tried to make amends to family and friends I neglected. But I'd missed important gatherings and failed to support them during trying times so it wasn't the same. When you are separated from family, it makes you feel like the outsider. Getting back home and in tune with those you've ignored, mentally and emotionally, was harder than walking through the door and placing suitcases in your old room. It took all my focus and energy. I didn't have anything left over for you."

Briggs shook his head. "I didn't realize. You were always where I needed you to be, and I didn't think of the cost to you. In my mind you were perfect, and when you left I acted out. My youthful transgressions became my adult burdens. When the mist cleared, Monica stood as a reminder of my folly."

Esther placed her hand over his. "Yes, and BJ became your testimony that we still serve a merciful God. Many times our folly and His mercy go hand in hand."

"Just like love and pain. It's the ebb and flow of life. You can't run from it, Esther. The path of getting through the pain can allow you the freedom to pursue the promise."

Esther threaded her fingers through Briggs's. "I remember Mother Reed telling me that Ishmael would make an appearance before Isaac. Ishmael represented man's impatience and his inclination to settle, Isaac God's promise, and His desire for us to have His best."

Rising, she pulled Briggs up. She took a cleansing breath, her eyes downcast as she gathered her courage and faced him square on. Their hands still joined, she squeezed his gently.

"I identify with the impatient Sarah. She wanted God's Word to come forth, so she pulled a 'Lord, let me fix that for you.' But in the end, she caused more damage."

Esther reached up and stroked Briggs's face. "Our impatience and desperation can derail us from God's perfect gifts. I learned the hard way that when Ishmael is dispatched, Isaac is already on his way. But when we get tired of waiting, we feel we need to help God get it done. We need to hold out for the promise. God's best for us."

"Yes, Monica was my Ishmael," Briggs said, his forehead pressed to hers.

Esther backed away alarmed at the direction of their conversation. "No, no, I'm not your Isaac, Briggs. How could I be your Isaac when Lawton was mine? That man healed me!" Esther cried out as she clasped her hands in front of her.

Briggs wrapped his arm around her and directed her to the mirror over his fireplace. "Look at yourself! By the word of everyone who knew him, Lawton was a godly man. But he didn't heal you, God did! I believe that he was your ram in the bush, honey. And the ram was a representation of Isaac, but he wasn't the promise. He was the sacrifice. You will never convince me that I'm not your Isaac."

Esther turned toward the mirror, inspecting her reflection; she wiped the tears from her cheeks and gave a shaky smile. "We'll see, Briggs. We'll see. What I do know was that Roger was my nightmare."

"I think that's something we can both agree on."

Briggs stepped away from her and started down the hall into the kitchen.

"Let me bring you something to drink. Lemonade, right?"

Esther called out yes and he quickly returned, handing her the drink.

"And you were a good friend. To Sheri, Deborah, and me," he said.

Esther tipped her crystal glass and sipped.

"No, I was selfish. But I've come to some acceptance of that young girl. She was stupid in love, doodling Mrs. Briggs Stokes on her notebooks like she was a high school freshman."

"You were human, and not alone. I had my own ribbing from the fellas. I preferred a chick flick with you than a game of spades with them."

Agitated by his unwillingness to see the depths of her past transgressions, Esther slammed down her glass. She remembered just how far she had been willing to go. "I almost gave you my virginity, Briggs! Something sacred I was holding for my husband."

Briggs spoke in a soothing tone. "Something I held sacred. Instead, it went to your ex-husband, your Ishmael—someone who could never cherish it like I would have."

Softly, Esther started to cry in earnest until she began to sob out all of her misery for the last two and a half years. Through salty tears, she saw Briggs rush to her side and without any fanfare take her into his arms.

"Go 'head, get it all out. I'm here. You can't move me again. I've set my will for you. Cry it all out."

Strong arms held her against the tide of life that flowed through her, crushing against her senses, lapping against her wounded heart. She clutched his shirt, bunching it against his chest.

"Kiss me, Briggs. Kiss me like you did the first time you told me you loved me at the Delta's spring fling."

Briggs placed both his hands around her face and looked deeply into liquid pools of longing. "You sure?" he asked.

She understood his hesitation; she had contradicted herself since she first walked into his house. She had exhausted her own self. He was right. She needed to get down from the cross. Jesus had already made the sacrifice.

She placed her hand on his chest and lifted her face. He lowered his head as she closed her eyes. Softly he kissed her lips.

"You're my future." He then took her lower lip between both his full ones. "All that I will ever want."

He kissed her full on the mouth, both of them caught up in a desire that had traveled through the years to culminate in this moment.

"I love you."

When Esther opened her eyes, she saw the trace of her tears on Briggs's cheek. She wiped them away with her finger. "This may be too much for me, too fast—"

Briggs cut her off with a finger to her lips.

"Please don't do this. Don't take me to a place of hope, and then pitch fear on it. We can take it a day at a time. But we will not go back," he said and hugged her. "Agreed?"

Esther hugged him back. "Maybe we should talk about why I came here. First, I came to talk about us—actually to tell you I'm not interested in a relationship."

Esther noted his smug look and hit him playfully. "So much for knowing my own mind right now. But the other thing I came to talk to you about was my ex-husband, Roger."

"Go on." Briggs sat, moving over, giving her some space to think.

She sat, then bit her bottom lip. "He's getting out on parole this week. I'm really uncomfortable about it, I'm sure he's coming to see Joshua, his mentor and friend."

Brigg's eyes narrowed. "Why would you think that?"

"When we were married, Roger had no friends to speak of, just people he ran the streets with. Joshua has mentioned on more than one occasion that Roger is doing a great job with the prison ministry he gives his money to. Joshua still goes up to Jackson once a month."

Rubbing his chin, he asked, "Roger and Joshua did time together?"

"That's right, but I don't care if he has changed. I don't want him around. I live alone with two young children," she said, hugging her knees.

"Well, you may live alone, but you're not alone," Briggs said with a wink. "I'll have a talk with Joshua and share how it's in everyone's best interest that Roger doesn't plan to hang anywhere around us or the church."

Esther placed her hand on her chest, breathing lighter. "Will you, Briggs—truly?"

"Absolutely! As matter of fact, I'll text Joshua and have him meet me in my office first thing in the morning." He then gathered her in his arms. "You okay?"

Esther leaned up and placed her finger in the indent of the cleft in his chin. "Whew! My finger missed doing that."

Briggs pulled her back and gave her a sweet kiss on the lips. "My lips missed doing that."

"We have a lot to discuss before all of this can be good," Esther reminded him, sliding back.

He placed his arms around her, pulling her into his chest. "No, it's already good. We have a lot to discuss so that we are in sync with each other—so that we can trust each other, have faith in the relationship, and understand who we are as a couple, and then as a family."

Esther reluctantly pulled out of his arms. "This is a lot."

Briggs pulled her right back, took her finger, and placed it back in the groove of his chin. "We'll get through it. This is real life, and it won't be solved like some romance book. We will put the work in, and we will reap the benefits."

Esther laughed freely as she tapped his chin. Having settled on the couch together, he was moving in for another kiss when the doorbell rang.

Esther sat up and adjusted her clothes. "You expecting anyone?"

Briggs got off of the couch and headed to answer the door. "No. But I'll make this real quick."

He swung open the door, and two brown arms entwined around his neck. As he pulled away, a baby carrier sat on the porch, with two tiny arms swinging in the air.

"Monica?"

"Yes, Briggs. I'm home!"

Monica pushed her way into Briggs's home. She dragged Fiona's carrier over the threshold. "Is BJ in school?"

"Hi, Monica," Esther said, arms crossed.

Monica looked up and there she was—her stumbling block. Esther. She wanted to scream, pull out her hair. And then the good and bad sides of her conscience went to work on her, turning her against herself. It was all Esther's fault this internal battle against good and evil.

Clasping the carrier, Monica muttered. "Not *this* time. She will not get in my way. I won him last time. I can do it again."

But, he was married to you, then. You left him.

Placing the carrier on the floor, she continued her muttering. "But I'm back now."

You're back for you, not for him.

Monica lowered her head her lips moving incessantly. "I can make him happy."

You never made him happy, only complacent. You weren't happy either.

Monica batted the air in front of her as though something unseen battled her.

Briggs lightly gripped her arm. "Are you all right? Why didn't you call and say you were coming?"

Monica threw herself in his arms and sobbed. She felt Briggs's hesitant pat on her back, but was encouraged when she noted Esther's bewilderment.

"Briggs, I should leave," Esther said, picking up her purse.

Briggs disengaged from Monica. "I'll walk you to the door."

Monica chose that time to throw herself into his arms again. But Briggs pulled her away, turned to Esther, and held out his hand. Monica watched Esther take it and then Briggs walk her to the door, whispering as they moved together.

Monica was a grade-A spy who had fine-tuned her hearing. Even though they whispered, she heard their hurried mummers.

"I'm so sorry, please don't let this upset you," Briggs pleaded.

"Your arms must be tired from holding all of us damsels in distress," Esther fired back.

Briggs lovingly pulled her face to his. "Esther, I'm not playing with you. We will not go back. I don't know why Monica is here, but she's the mother of my son, and I need to hear her out. She's had a rough time of it."

"We'll see, Briggs. We'll see. I'm going out of town tomorrow, a one-day trip. We'll talk when I get back."

Esther swiftly walked down the steps, and Briggs stood watching her.

Monica wanted to clap her hands in glee. She now had her next plan.

On a whiff of heaven's scent, the guardian flew back into the room after engaging the imp in a battle of wits. At each blow, he knocked him farther and farther outside of Briggs's house. It was a tiresome game, the imp planting thoughts in Monica, and him countering them. He was proud that this time he had the last say without the dominion Zadkiel's help.

He spun when he heard, "Yes, you did well, Guardian. But do not become prideful. Your charge, Monica is planning to do evil. Have you thought about how to guide her back to the light?"

The guardian should have known Zadkiel was close. He remained silent. Wisdom was in the room. He hadn't figured it all out. But he knew that he couldn't protect Monica if she kept doing such counterproductive things. She had already played a part in the destruction of several lives. The murder-suicide wasn't her fault, but she wasn't the innocent bystander she pretended to be.

"She has been given another chance. I pray she chooses her next steps wisely," the guardian said.

Zadkiel glowed bright. "Pray it well, and I will stand with you in agreement. We will lose her to the darkness if things do not turn around."

The guardian looked at Monica as she began to weave her lies and manipulation on Briggs. "And if we do . . . She will perish."

Chapter Nineteen

Esther slipped under the bathwater, immersing her hair along with her entire head. She wondered how long she could stay under without coming up.

Okay, God, I gave it a really good try.

She scowled as she bobbed up and began to scrub her feet vigorously. Her thoughts were elsewhere—at Briggs's house. Monica was back, and Monica never played fair.

Shoot, I'm from the Motor City. Maybe I should just give her an old-fashioned beat down. Her little skinny self, she'd be too light to fight, too thin to win.

Esther looked at her curves sloshing the water around the tub. She grinned mischievously as she imagined she had Monica in the boxing ring. She in a beautiful peach-colored boxing outfit, Monica in her red witch's costume, sans broom. They circled each other, boxing gloves up, heads low.

Esther mimicked her thoughts by putting up her dukes in the tub. She feigned left, then right, jabbing like an expert. In her mind's eye, she saw her opening, took aim—and *bam*. She knocked Monica flat on her assets. She danced around her fallen opponent, hearing the count down. *One, two, three . . . ten.*

Ho down, Ho down.

Esther cupped her hands around her mouth and echoed her triumph with a soft roar. Then reality made its appearance by way of a squeaky, childish voice.

"Mama, you still in there? Mama, what's that sound? Is you playing a game? It sounds like a crowd roaring, Mama," David said from the other side of the closed bathroom door.

Esther "spurned girlfriend" slipped down under the water for five precious seconds, then popped up again—Supermom!

"David, sweetie. Can you do Mama a favor and get away from my door? I'll be out shortly."

"Okay, Mama. Were you roaring, Mama?" David giggled.

"No, David. I may have been talking a little to myself, but I was not roaring."

Yes, Mama, you were right, little pitchers have big ears.

Esther grabbed a towel and wrapped it around her body. Her short reprieve of time alone was fleeting at best. As she bent to dry her legs, she pressed the intercom to remind David to clean up his room.

Instead, she heard her children whispering to each other in her bedroom. The only words she could make out were "computer" and "password." She crept to her bathroom door and pressed her ear to the surface trying to decipher the rest of their conversation.

She remembered she and Lawton discussing how as the children got older, the twin link would get stronger and that they would inevitably be left out of the children's conversations. Wasn't that why God designed siblings? To be there for each other. Didn't Aaron hold up Moses' arms when they got too tired to stay up on their own? And wasn't that another of Cain's sin? The breaking of a covenant between bloodlines designed to provide nurturing and love beyond the womb?

David and Ruth would grow up and grow away into their own lives.

So maybe you need to actually start working on your life.

"Guys? Are you trying to get into my computer? You don't have my password," Esther called through the door.

She heard feet scampering away and low giggles as the stairs squeaked on their rapid climb down. Esther knew she had to have another conversation with Phyllis about Miracle and her computer addiction. That little girl was influencing her cousins to think that social media was a daily necessity. They were too young to be so consumed. At her age, how was she getting on these sites?

Esther huffed; life always handed you multiple issues. As she pulled on her pajama bottoms, her mind rambled trying to figure out over the myriad of things she needed to plot through. The children's well-being was always upper most in her mind. Trying to locate Deborah was a priority. She really needed to know what had happened to her. Then, Roger getting out of prison any day, that frightened her.

Her head pounded, reminding her that so much change at one time could result in too much stress. And, Briggs's pursuit in the face of Monica's return could result in a mother lode of drama. She had an aversion to drama.

Trying to find the humor in her situation, she held her chest and staggered Fred Sanford-style. *I'm coming to you, Lawton. And I'm carrying a boatload of worry.*

Overwhelmed, Esther wilted onto the bed, in a practiced move she slid her pajama top. over her head. It was time for her to give it all a rest and to go to the King's throne. She reached for her bible, and a prayer.

"Lord, you are not the author of confusion. But you are mighty and powerful. Send your angels of goodness and mercy. Direct me away from disaster. Place a hedge of protection around me and my children. It is by your stripes that we are healed. Cover me as I go into the unknown to search for Deborah. Exchange fear for love, Lord. And like Solomon, give me the wisdom to know how to begin again with Briggs. Show me how to make peace with Monica. Take jealousy out of my heart. Make your way my way. Help me, Father. I need you now more than ever. Show me, Lord. Show me . . ."

Zadkiel flew above Esther's home. He heard her in the throes of fervent prayer as he moved to join the other angels in shifting the atmosphere. Her prayers had begun the work; he was here to complete it. It was His Father's decree that he and his kind assist the humans so that they could be directed and protected when needed. It was a job wherein they neither slept nor slumbered.

"Ahhhh," he said as his eyes beheld the shadow of a demon moving away from Esther. It staggered as she moved more authoritatively into her prayer. Esther then rolled into her heavenly language, and he could see the demon tumble back into her hallway; then it crept into her bathroom sanctuary. This cursed being was so obvious, the putrid residue from its attempts to make Esther feel overwhelmed still streaked across its aura, curdling into spoiled waste.

For a lesser angel it may have been a cause for speculation, but Zadkiel smiled and shook his head at the antics of his late brother Lucifer's minion. Didn't he know not to send a fledging demon to do a grown-up's job? This little fellow (for it was only ten feet in height, not even half of one of his wingspans) was about to be blown out of the water. Zadkiel reasoned he might as well have some fun while he did it.

"Psst . . .," Zadkiel blew into the fledging's direction. The fledging fainted.

"Nooooo," it said when it woke, its voice distant and hollow. It crawled away, using its tail for traction.

Zadkiel followed him for the sport of it. He hated the little devils and treated them like humans treated cockroaches. You never let them get away, because if you saw one, there were others. Sure enough, he found him, miles away, groveling and reporting back to a full-fledged demon. The condemned building's roof they stood on was littered with gang graffiti, used condoms, broken needles, and soiled furniture crusted with dirt and grime and disgusting body fluids. Humans sat nodding in corners and puking in their clothes. One young woman, skin and bones, crouched on her knees in front of a demon-possessed young man. It was heart wrenching the things they were doing to themselves and each other.

Zadkiel telepathically sent out a distress call to the angels of lost souls. They would need to come and find out if any of the humans who inhabited the squalor had tender hearts. It was always a day of tears when a heart had turned to stone, encircled by the poison of demon accusations.

Zadkiel swung down with pinpoint precision and pulled his sword of truth. "JESUS!" he cried as his voice bellowed through the angelic skies.

The demon's eyes rolled back, his body trembled, and he lost his balance and see-sawed in a fallen swoop off the roof. The fledging drew into a ball refusing to look at Zadkiel.

As Zadkiel looked at the pitiful sight, he waved his wing over the quivering ball of fungus and dispelled it into thin air.

He returned to Esther's and found her prostrate on her bedroom floor. Her tears were cleansing, and her faith that God would restore her unshakable. He watched her as she basked in God's afterglow as he allowed his body to float to the top of the room. He stretched out and would stay until the changing of the guardians at daybreak. He hummed as he fell into restful meditation. "We are climbing Jacob's ladder, ladder. We are climbing Jacob's ladder, ladder."

Chapter Twenty

"I can't believe I let you talk me into this duck, duck, goose chase," Phyllis lamented as she fiddled with the radio in Esther's car.

Esther switched lanes as her car barreled down I-75 south. Her speedometer hitting seventy-five miles an hour, she checked her rearview mirror several times, loathed to be pulled over.

"I think you mean talking you into a wild goose chase," Esther said.

Phyllis pulled down the visor mirror and checked her lipstick. "Yeah, that too if it means you have me out here at seven in the morning, before God and country. Child, you trying to find your long lost best friend who you have not seen in seventeen years. This is straight-up stupid."

Esther silently said a scripture in her head, when what she wanted to do was curse Phyllis out. "Being my sister don't make you immune from getting put out on the side of the road."

"I wish you would!" Phyllis said. "You remember who used to beat your little butt when you were little? I don't want to have to give you a flashback. Mama's not here for you to run to crying."

"Are you serious? I was five years old, and you were a big bully," Esther said, peeved at the thought of all the times Phyllis had hit her when they were children.

"Awwwh, is the baby of the family getting mad?" Phyllis said in a singsong, baby voice. "You were so spoiled, got your way all the time."

"You know I've never liked that term *spoiled*. Not when it means that someone was given a lot of love and affection. We certainly didn't have any money. I couldn't go to a store and say, 'Give me that,' because Mama and Daddy didn't have it. But I could always get a hug, a kiss, or some attention. When did you want to deprive me of that, Phyllis?"

"You want to deprive Miracle of it," Phyllis retorted, her jaw rigid with indignation.

Esther pressed her steering wheel's control panel and put the car's music on mute.

"What I want to deprive Miracle of is thinking that the world owes her something. I want her to have all the love, kisses, and the affection she can handle. But I don't want her to become a mean little brat."

Red crept up Phyllis's neck, and the tendons swelled, visibly throbbing. "Let me tell you something—"

"No, let me finish. A month ago, I took all of the children to the skating rink. Miracle asked me for one of those ropey things that light up. I had already told Ruth no in front of her, but she asked—no—demanded—I buy her one. When I told her no, she stormed away, yanked off her skates, and had a tantrum right there for the whole world to view."

"She hadn't had much sleep the night before, and when she's tired she gets cranky," Phyllis rushed to explain.

"That's some crap, and we both know it. I've caught her pinching and jabbing Ruth and telling her that she's a baby who doesn't know anything. She has my child thinking she's all-knowing—the ruler she has to measure up to." Hissing through her teeth, Esther continued. "Two weeks ago, when she stayed over, there was more acting out. I asked her to turn off her tablet and to grab a book instead. She rolled her eyes at me, sucked her teeth, and kept playing her game. When I took the tablet from her, she called me a name under her breath and tried to grab the tablet out of my hands."

Phyllis gasped. "No, she didn't."

Esther focused on driving, and Phyllis asked in a panic, "Esther, what did you do?"

"The same thing that would have been done to us. I spanked her rear end. I'm not surprised she didn't tell you," Esther said, noting Phyllis's murderous glare.

"Oh, relax. It was just a tap. But she was so stunned the child was quiet for the rest of the night."

"Esther, we don't spank," Phyllis punctuated her words with her finger.

"Yeah, I know. But I did. And you're welcome."

Phyllis flinched, her shoulders tight. "I didn't thank you. Miracle can be reasoned with and communicated to. *Talk* to her next time."

"I did, and since she acted as though she couldn't hear me, I did some sign language. Ask her butt what my hand said."

"Not funny," Phyllis said through her gritted teeth.

"Not laughing. I love you both, but when a terrorist enters my house, I do like the good ol' U S of A, and I don't reason, communicate, or negotiate with them. I use blunt force, preferably before things get out of control," Esther said firmly. It was her opinion that if her sister didn't like it, Miracle was welcome to stay at someone else's house when they needed a babysitter.

"Let's agree to disagree. However, don't spank my child again. You might want to worry about your own daughter. The way she was in Miracle's room asking about female anatomy, she has a need to know you aren't fulfilling."

Esther veered slightly out of her lane.

"Watch out, Sis. Doesn't feel so good when the shoe is pushed onto your foot, does it?" Phyllis asked.

Esther blinked, trying to calculate when she first started wondering about such things. "Isn't six years old a little early for that conversation?"

"No. Besides, they turn seven in five months. Miracle will be eight next month. The children they go to school with are no angels. They hear and see way more than we want them to."

Esther took cleansing breaths. "What was she asking?"

"Breast size, and why our lower female anatomy looks different than theirs. She and Miracle were pulling up their clothes, comparing. I very casually answered their questions and then had them put their clothes back on," Phyllis said, all of the sudden preoccupied with her nails.

Esther fanned herself vigorously. "I'm not ready for this conversation. SSShhould ssshe be ready? And why are you just now telling me?"

"Okay, Daffy, stop stuttering. She doesn't need to know it all, just enough to answer her basic questions. And I didn't tell you right away because you can be a bit of a prude. Look how you're freaking out now!" Phyllis said on the verge of laughing.

"That's not true," Esther protested loudly. "But her asking about ta-tas, and her pocketbook? I was hoping this conversation was sometime in the future."

Any semblance of laughter left Phyllis's face. "Esther, what is this?" she held up her hand.

"Duh, your hand," Esther said.

"And this?" Phyllis asked taping her own nose.

"Not following this, but it's your nose."

"Then what in the natural and supernatural kingdom are ta-tas and a pocketbook?"

Esther turned crimson. "You know, Phyllis, our breasts, and our . . . you know what."

Phyllis closed her eyes in exasperation. "I know if you can't give body parts their real names instead of creating some alias like the parts were dirty, then you definitely can't give David and Ruth healthy attitudes toward their own bodies."

"Yes, I can. I'm a trained social worker. It's just that—"

"That curiosity didn't kill the cat, lack of knowledge did!" Phyllis said, her jaw clenched.

Esther swallowed her defensive reply when the GPS announced they needed to get off the interstate and turn left at the light. As she followed its instructions, the hotel loomed large in front of them.

Phyllis craned her neck to look for a parking space. "Just think about what I said. There's a spot over there." As Esther pulled in, Phyllis reclined her seat. "I can't believe that you are going to stake out this hotel looking for Deborah."

"Yes, well, you agreed to come. So zip it up. It's eleven o'clock so it shouldn't be that much longer. I did get out of the woman I talked to that she works part-time. I figure she should be getting off anytime between noon and one."

"I'm taking a nap," Phyllis said and pulled a throw from the backseat and covered herself.

Esther began to wonder about their earlier conversation. "You think it's abnormal at her age to want to know about the size of breasts and, uh, uh, other lady parts? She saw me in the shower the other day, and she just kept staring."

"Humph," Phyllis grunted, burrowing under the throw.

Esther's body rose abruptly from her seat. "Oh my goodness, Phyllis, do you think she's going to end up being oversexed?"

Phyllis sat up. "Esther, she is normally inquisitive. Relax and watch for your long lost buddy."

Thirty minutes later, Esther had almost fallen asleep when she saw Deborah leaving the side entrance of the hotel. Jumping out of the car, she ran to catch her before she got on a small blue and white bus.

"Deborah! Hey, wait up!"

Deborah's eyes widened, and she scrambled up the stairs of the bus, pulling a tote behind her.

Esther had driven three and a half hours. This was not how she envisioned their meeting. She had dressed down in her old, comfortable jeans, tennis shoes, and had purposely pissed Phyllis off by not having on any makeup or a fresh hairdo. According to Phyllis, "You don't cross state lines po' looking."

Esther climbed up the bus steps right behind her.

"Hey, lady, I don't have you on my roster," the bus driver shouted.

Esther was puzzled. "Roster? You have to be on a list to ride the bus in Ohio?"

"To ride the mainstream bus you do. This is for special-needs customers, preordered, so sign up, and for right now, get off."

Esther looked back at Deborah who was sliding down into a seat. "Deborah Ridgeway don't you make me show my tail. You come out here and talk to me."

The bus driver intervened. "She gets off this bus, she gets left."

Esther folded her arms. "That's okay, I'll take her home."

The bus driver looked at Deborah through the large mirror hanging over his seat. "You getting off or staying? Make up your mind, please."

An aggravated Deborah slowly walked up the aisle and silently passed Esther as she descended the stairs. Esther followed her off, and they stood staring, neither saying a word.

The bus pulled off, and Deborah glared as she watched it leave. "You made me miss my bus," she griped sullenly.

Closing her eyes briefly to find her composure, Esther spoke with calm. "I promise I'll take you home. I'm just so glad to see you." Esther held out her arms to hug her, but Deborah shrank back. *Okayyyyyy.*

"Seeing you last week was unbelievable," Esther said, determined to break through. "I had to come back and try to find you. Try to reconnect. You know?"

"No," Deborah said with finality.

"You don't want to know me again? As close as we were?"

Deborah looked all around. She appeared to have spotted Phyllis sitting in Esther's car. "Is that Phyllis?"

Turning to look, Esther nodded.

"She still looks good. Ms. Fashion Queen. She still a witch?"

Esther laughed. "Card carrying and cauldron brewing."

Deborah's eyes flickered with remembrance. "I remember the girl could burn. She made the best fried chicken wings ever, and she always had the latest music."

"And you always knew the latest dances. Nobody could keep up with you," Esther said, and to loosen Deborah up, Esther did the Running Man dance.

Deborah turned slightly away in an effort to conceal her burgeoning smile.

"You never could dance," Deborah said, her words muffled under her hand that now covered her grin.

Placing her hand on her hips, Esther jutted out her chin. "I'll have you know that I could dance, just not next to you. You could have been on television with your moves."

A grimace crossed Deborah's face, and she looked at her watch. "I need to go. Can you drop me?"

"Sure, come on."

Esther led the way to the car, and they both got in, Deborah sitting stiffly in the back.

"Hey, Deborah, what you know good girl?" Phyllis rose from under the throw with over-the-top gaiety.

"Nothing," Deborah pointedly ignored her.

"Esther, go out to your left and get back on the freeway," Deborah directed.

Esther forced herself to be cheerful. Looking up at her visor mirror, she said, "Sure, where do you live?"

"I'm not going home. I have an appointment." Deborah said, and stared out the window.

The car was uncomfortably quiet.

"How's your mom and dad?" Phyllis asked, turning in her seat.

"Fine," Deborah glowered.

"The hotel is nice, have you been there long?" Esther asked.

"No," Deborah's answers were terse and revealing as little as possible.

On the sly, Phyllis tapped Esther's thigh as though to say, *Now what?*

"Get off at the next exit," Deborah ordered.

Esther got off and made the next few turns following Deborah's succinct commands. They soon came to a nondescript building with a small sign in bold letters in the window that read Central Mental Health Services.

"Pull up right here. Thanks," Deborah said as she leaned across the seat and placed a card in the ashtray. "So now you know. My number's on the card." She then added sarcastically, "In case you still want to catch up on old times."

Deborah climbed out of the car. She slammed the door, stooped down, and faced Esther through the window. "And since you are too polite to ask, I'm schizophrenic. Have been since that night seventeen years ago. Have a nice life."

Deborah trotted into the building never looking back.

"Dang!" Phyllis said.

Esther picked up the card and read *transitional housing* across the front. She tapped it on the dashboard and wondered if she would have the guts to call.

Shoot! More drama.

Chapter Twenty-one

How do you watch your back without tripping over your past? Roger looked out his cell

Roger had not had to deal with this kind of thing in several years. Prison was no joke; he got jumped when he first got there, and had even had to fight someone off of him sexually that first year. But meeting Prophet and getting with the G squad had given him protection, and he had learned the ways of life behind these walls.

But the changing of leadership from him to Wise Will was causing others to forget that they were Gangsters for Jesus. And while they were down for God, that did not make them sniveling weak brothers. In fact, they were just the opposite. They did not seek to harm, but to do good. They protected the weak and stood on the Word to provide them a guide to handle life's issues. However, every once in a while they had to seek Old Testament wisdom to meet a new-day situation.

When one new brother wanted to make his rep by bullying them they prayed and spoke to the young man several times. But even though they approached him in love, they were not received. So they had to shake the dust off of their feet and provide him with a real-life lesson. Young brother still couldn't hold his head up after being found in his cell, diapered with a bottle nipple in his mouth and a bonnet on his head.

They were on lockdown, and the memory brought needed laughter. Roger laughed out loud, drawing the attention of a fellow inmate coming down the hall pushing a cleaning cart.

He passed and growled real low, "Stay alert, bro. There are snakes in the grass."

Roger gave a slight nod to indicate he heard the man's warning. The whole thing was done so slick that anyone watching would have never seen the other man's lips move.

Roger didn't know how Duncan had found him. Or why after all these years he was still looking for him. But Duncan had always been a single-minded individual, prone to obsessions and paybacks. Back in the day, he prided himself on being judge and jury. No one crossed him, at least no one crossed him more than once.

A cell door clanked open and multiple footsteps could be heard advancing swiftly up the hall. Roger held his mirror out and saw three dudes coming up the hallway who were known to be for hire. They were in for assault, rape, and kidnapping. Tweedle Dee, Tweedle Dum, and Just Dumb were fiercely loyal to anyone who could put a little something-something on their books.

Roger leaped and crouched on top of his bed. He picked up his pillowcase that held his hardest prison-issued shoes filled with rocks he and his friends had brought inside from the yard. He heard the electronic click of his cell being unlocked. His last coherent thought, *Who has Duncan paid off?*

As soon as they rushed his cell, he swung, knocking the first one upside his head and following up with a left hand uppercut that landed him out of the way.

Just Dum—down.

He then threw his body forward, catching Tweedle Dum by surprise. Tweedle Dum expected a defensive move, but Roger gave him a let's-get-it-on roundhouse kick to his chest.

Roger then barreled over him and landed on top of Tweedle Dee. He had dropped the pillowcase, and he was putting Tweedle Dee in a stranglehold, when hands from behind grabbed him by his throat and cut off his airway. He hadn't kicked him hard enough; Tweedle Dum was back. The three-way struggle continued with grunts and short punches, but no one was letting go.

With Tweedle Dum's grip on his neck tightening, Roger was losing his vision. Tweedle Dum was determined, but Roger refused to lose Tweedle Dee. They would go out together. He could feel Tweedle Dee weakening, his breathing sporadic, and hollow. Roger's breaths were similar. Sweat poured into his burning eyes. In mere seconds he knew he would go under.

Jesus he silently pleaded, and Tweedle Dee went limp.

Then abruptly Tweedle Dum's grip around his neck loosened, and he was free. Roger stayed on his knees—his arm still hooked around his opponent's neck—gulping large amounts of air. He looked down finally releasing the dead weight of Tweedle Dee from his clutches.

Tweedle Dee—out for the count.

Iron hands pulled him up and patted his back. "You good, dawg?"

Roger looked around. The G squad had handled Tweedle Dum. He stepped over his adversary's prone legs.

"No man, I'm not okay. This thing could cause me to end up rotting in this place. I can't stay here, man. I can't," Roger said, desperation oozing from his pores.

Wise Will nodded to the four men who had entered the cell with him. "Get it done, fellas."

The men picked up the bodies and between them, they placed two in a nearby cleaning cart, and two of them walked the other down the hall like they were all long lost buddies. A closer eye would have seen the middle person's feet never touched the ground, his arms limp around their shoulders.

Roger sat in front of Wise Will and cradled his throat. Hoarse, he said, "It's been harder here in this last week than it was when I was a newbie coming in the door attempting to cover my flank. Man, I ain't feeling this –ish. "

"Hold up, youngun. Respect the Father at all times. Your foul mouth and thoughts gon' cash a check your life ain't ready to pay. You have led well; you've been a pillar for others to lean on. Don't fall off now. I can smell the panic on you, and it clings, like stank on day-old chitterlings."

"Ha! Long as I'm stinking in a bed in Detroit this time twenty-four hours from now, I'm good with that. Just call it Chitterlings Eau De."

"You going to make the haters' word good? They say we only following Christ 'cause we locked up. Can't get nothing, so we hedging our bets and pretending God is the head of our lives, when in reality, we on our backs like anyone else in trouble."

Roger responded in a calm and determined voice. "I'm saved. I might be a little rough around the edges this week, but a low tide don't mean there ain't depth to the water."

"What? Man, you been reading them philosophy books that Prophet sent you and you don' fooled around and got deep. I don't know what you just said. But if it meant you been off your game this week, and you gon' spend tonight repenting, then the low tide in the ocean can wave all day long," Wise Will said.

Roger exploded in laughter. "All right, old man. You messed that all up. But I hear you," Roger said, rubbing his neck wearily.

Wise Will did his usual cool daddy gait and spoke a little wisdom of his own before he moseyed out the door. "You know whoever this Duncan is, he got clout and some big ends. He don' covered the cameras, the guards on the cameras, and the terrors for hire just to get a chance at you. You be glad we got our own people too. Your enemy ain't no lightweight."

"Naw, but God still holds the world record and champion's title. We need some powerful prayers to be going out tonight. We need the kind of prayers that stops the devil in his tracks and places his minions in the chains that they meant for me. Can y'all pray without ceasing?"

"Now, that is something we can do. I'll send the word out. At exactly nine tonight we all get to praying. Let this corporate prayer shake these prison walls like they shook in the days of Peter and Paul. Shoot, man, I might just walk out of here with you!"

Roger gave him pound, and then backed into his bed. He couldn't wait until nine o'clock. He stared out into the now-darkened hall. The way Duncan was coming after him, he needed those prayers right now.

A shiver ran down his spine and settled in the pit of his swirling stomach. Roger shook his head denouncing the old myth that popped in his head. *Ain't no devil walking over my grave. If I go, I'm heaven-bound.*

Monica sat in the chair next to BJ's bed and rubbed his shoulder, tousled his little curls, and kissed his face over and over. She had missed him so much. She lay her head on the pillow next to him and noted that it was now dark outside.

Her plan was working. She'd been here since yesterday, on the promise that she just wanted more time with her son, and Briggs let her stay. He didn't want her to take BJ anywhere, so she played on that knowledge.

Speak of the angel.

Briggs popped his head into the room. "Is he still sleeping?"

"Yes, he is. I'm surprised, though. As much as I have rubbed and kissed on him, he has slept through it all." Monica looked at Briggs through heavily lashed eyes, a vulnerable countenance on her face. "Thank you for letting me stay and allowing me to spend some time with my son."

Monica looked down at BJ and rubbed his face softly. "We did good, didn't we?"

Briggs came into the room and adjusted the covers over BJ's shoulders. "Yes, we did." Clearly uncomfortable, he then cleared his throat. "Umm, did you want me to drive you and Fiona to your hotel?"

Monica twisted her hands, her eyes pleading. "We couldn't afford to stay another night there. It was a bug-biting, roach-infested motel. Talking 'bout no tell, motel, shouldn't nobody ever tell anybody 'bout that place."

Briggs grimaced at Monica's description. "What about the money Randall left Fiona? She *is* his child," he said and nodded toward the sleeping baby.

Monica's face clouded. "Randall's children have been absolutely awful. And while I fight their allegations, all the money is being kept in escrow. They hate Fiona."

Briggs's face hardened at the mention of the mistreatment of a child. "Regardless, that's Fiona's father. How could they do that?"

"Rich people have their own rules," Monica snorted. She spoke with acidic bitterness flavoring her tone. "It doesn't have to be right. It just has to have a price. And everything has a price."

Briggs laid his hand on her shoulder. "The greatest price was already paid for you. The blood of Jesus is priceless. If you get caught up in the game, you'll get caught up in the rules. Jesus broke the rules, and because of Him, redemption reigns. Don't let bitterness be your calling card. You'll end up like the Merediths of this world."

Before he could move his hand, Monica caught hold of it and placed a kiss in his palm. She was flustered when he pulled away like she had scalded him.

"Really, Briggs? I've seen you naked, and you panic at a simple gesture of affection?"

Briggs stood by the doorway. "You and I both know you don't do simple. You do complicated, you do mind games—you do damage. But, sweetheart, you've never done simple."

Monica purred as she rose and moved with practiced seduction. "Why, honey, I didn't know you knew me so well." She stood on tiptoes just a breath away from Briggs's mouth that was closing into a defiant frown.

She touched his lips with the tips of her fingers, and he stumbled against the doorjamb. "Ooh . . . I'm moving you like that?"

He grabbed her fingers when she attempted to touch him again. "What is wrong with you, girl? Do you want me to put you out of my house?" Briggs breathed, clearly not in tune with her plans to entice him.

Plan B.

Monica kicked out her small foot and gave an exaggerated pout. "You wouldn't do that, would you, Brigzee?"

Briggs's eyebrow arched, and he threw up his hands as he marched out the door. "When you get like this, I can't deal with you. I would love to throw you out of my house on your derrière, but you're BJ's mother, and you were once my wife. You're looking to use that to your advantage." He strode back into her personal space, but not like she had wanted.

"But heed my warning. I am going to have a life with Esther. You will *not* get in the way. And you will *not* use old tricks and habits to get your way."

Briggs spun and headed out of the room. Monica was even more frustrated when he never turned back around, but instead simply said over his shoulder, "Are we clear?"

He continued with his back to her and without waiting for a response.

"You and Fiona can sleep in here again tonight with your son."

Monica looked down at the trundle pulled out from under BJ's bed where Fiona slept soundly. Her sweet little angelic baby girl cooed even in her sleep.

She was moving toward the door to get the rest of her things when Briggs appeared depositing them inside the doorway. He pulled the door shut and walked away, all without saying one more word.

Okay, Plan C.

Chapter Twenty-two

The next day, Monica had Plan C primed and loaded. She arrived at Briggs's place of business, his church. She once was in charge there as the first lady. Four hundred active members was not her idea of a megachurch, but she surprised herself by being good at it.

She could see Naomi sitting behind the desk as she entered the office. At one time she had this woman under her control.

"Naomi, darling, how are you?" Monica placed air kisses near her cheek.

Naomi snuffled as though something smelled bad. "Pastor is busy. Do you have an appointment?" She then looked down at her calendar. "Oh no, you don't."

"He'll see me. Call him."

Monica could see Naomi had switched sides and now would have to be handled like the enemy.

"No, thank you," Naomi said and turned to her computer, ignoring Monica.

Monica headed to Briggs's door. Fuming, Naomi threw out her arm to block her.

"Get out of my way!" Monica yelled.

"I don't work for you," Naomi shouted back. "Come in here like you running things. Let me help you with something. I'm allergic to kissing butt. It gives me a rash in my self-esteem, and a dry itch in my sense of self. So, Ms. Thang, I'm going to take two-get-outta-my-face antidepressants, and how 'bout I *don't* call you in the morning!"

Monica opened and closed her mouth. Eyes ablaze, she placed both hands flat on Naomi's desk. "That was real cute. You're only cute, Ms. Plain-Jane. Oh wait, you hear that?" Monica cocked her ear as though listening. "It's the fashion police coming to get you. Your parole has been revoked, under the 'too tacky to be wandering the streets of Detroit' law."

Naomi shoved her sleeves up her arms. "I'd rather be tacky, than wacky. You demented to come back here trying to revive what you destroyed. You like the morning-after pill; you abort what you too selfish to carry."

Monica's hand trembled with the effort it took to restrain herself from slapping Naomi. "Just get Briggs."

Naomi smirked. "Can't. He's downtown in a meeting."

Monica glared at her and stormed out. She could hear Naomi's laughter long after she left the building.

Home is where you can kick off your shoes, even when there were holes in the toes of your socks. Esther looked around the familiar kitchen, and she was totally at ease. This was the heart of Mother Reed's domain. The large wooden spoon was her sword, the checkered gingham scarf tied around her head, her crown of glory. Anyone invited into this room knew they were on sacred ground.

This was the place where she ran as fast as her little girl feet could carry her when she was a child. Always searching for goodies that only seemed to come out of this kitchen. As an adult, she was still searching for the goodies that emanated from this room. Only the goodies had changed from sweet cookies and cakes, to sweet words of encouragement and wisdom.

She sighed, looking around in contentment. "It's always so comforting just to be able to sit with you like this."

"I like it too, girl. Ain't nothing better than spending time with my little Esther. But you came in here looking a little put out. You gon' share, or am I supposed to use my magical powers to figure out what 'cha thinking 'bout?"

"No, just trying to visit a little before I get into anything heavy."

Mother Reed got up when the tea kettle whistled.

Esther smiled in remembrance of the many times that whistle signaled a good old wisdom-laced conversation.

"I'm going to get you one of those new Keurig machines. They make drinking any kind of tea a snap." Esther illustrated by snapping her fingers.

Mother Reed continued fussing over her and Esther's tea, and then brought her bounty to her table and delicately placed Esther's in front of her. "Watch your mouth, it's hot." She sat down and picked up her cup, showing it to Esther. "Child, I'm in no hurry. This is a perfect cup of tea. My tea kettle is just fine, thank you. Where am I going that my tea need to be made quick?"

Mother Reed placed her hands together resting her chin on top. "I put my thinking cap on here. It's in the kettle hissing, the slow deliberate slicing of the lemon, and spooning of the honey that my thoughts line up, all ready to reveal something special. Nope, I don't need no quick, in-a-hurry contraption."

Esther nodded in agreement. "That makes more sense than you know. Everything is 'hurry up, get it, get it.' David and Ruth don't want to read about it unless it's on a computer screen. What happened to the feel of paper under your fingers?"

Mother Reed took a delicate sip of her tea. "They on that there computer everybody got? Ain't they too young?"

"I thought so too, Mother, and it concerns me. I've placed all the safeguards on my system, so I know they can't go where they shouldn't, but . . ."

"That devil's in the details!" Mother Reed announced.

"On the positive side, surfing the Web can be very informational, and I use it for my business all the time. I don't want you to think having a computer is bad. Matter of fact, we were all talking about getting you one. It will keep your mind sharp. You can play games and send out e-mails to those you want to keep in contact with. You just have to learn more about it, that's all."

Mother Reed put down her tea cup and wiped her mouth with her flowered cloth napkin. "You think I don't know nothing, huh? An old woman you need to school? I reads, little girl. So let me hip ya," Mother Reed said as she rose and placed her hands on her slight hips.

"I don't do no cloud because my Bible tells me Satan is the prince of the air. Now hear me well, child, if you wanna holla at me, hashtag—write a letter; hashtag—pick up the phone; hashtag—walk across the street; hashtag—knock on my door. I try to stay away from anything on the computer that starts with an *e*. I don't do no e-mails because I don't want no evil. I don't do no Evites because I don't court no enemies. So leave me be talking about some Internet."

Mother Reed lowered into the chair and picked up her tea cup again. Sipping, she said. "Close your mouth, child. That is mighty unattractive."

Esther snapped her mouth shut. She couldn't believe that Mother Reed knew what a hashtag was or that there was a Web-based cloud.

"You never cease to amaze me," Esther said.

Mother Reed gave a small smile of triumph. "Well, I cheated a little. I was watching one of them shows on PBS, and they did a series on the computer. Scared me silly. Too much information available 'bout folk can't be a good thing. You wanna know something 'bout me, ask me."

"Right. It's made small people big. They sit in the dark and make themselves feel good by tearing down what others have taken painstaking time to build up."

"Haters?" Mother Reed asked.

Esther placed her tea cup down. "Oh my goodness, Mother. How do you know that term?"

Mother Reed smacked her lips. "Doggone it, Esther, I ain't dead! Little bitty boy up the street got mad when I told him to pull up his pants. Tol' me I was hatin'. I told him to quit shopping at Thugs 'R' Us. Then I had to let the little knucklehead know I loved him enough to help him stop looking foolish. Looked like he was carrying a load back there."

Esther fell out laughing. "Right! David tried to pull his down a little, and I tanned that little bottom. We ain't even starting that."

Mother Reed raised her hand and waved it around. "Girl, get ready. If it ain't this, it will be that."

Esther cracked up. She loved it when Mother Reed shared a story with her. "So, I can look forward to more incidents with David?"

"Baby, you can add Ruth in too." Mother Reed looked pensive. "Be glad, baby. I don't have those memories with Joshua. And if I could go back, I would gladly go through the headaches of raising a hard-headed boy."

Esther took Mother Reed's hand from across the kitchen table. It was a worn hand, wrinkled from time, scarred from life. She loved the texture of it and loved the history of her holding it. "You are so right. Sometimes I want them to be perfect, so life can be perfect for them."

"Ha! Good luck with that."

Esther reached in her purse, pulled out a small bottle of lotion, and began to massage the thick liquid into Mother Reed's hands. As she smoothed the lotion in a back-and-forth motion, she casually brought up what had been in the back of her mind all morning.

Did Monica stay at Briggs's last night?

"Monica's back," Esther said.

Mother Reed cocked her head. "How you feel about that?"

Esther sighed. "How should I feel?"

"Well, you shouldn't be running scared."

Esther let go of Mother Reed's hand. "*That's* what you think? I'm *scared* of Monica? Maybe I just don't want the drama that will be involved if she is involved."

Mother Reed harrumphed. "What you think BJ was? A goldfish they once shared? She was always going to be involved."

Esther didn't like it, but her voice came out as a whine. "I didn't think about that. She was living in another state. I don't know, maybe I was hoping she'd disappear."

"Well, God loves you enough to drag you out of the river of denial and provide you with a front-door view of real life, one-zero-one. Get the lesson so the little yellow bus doesn't have to keep pulling up to your house," Mother Reed said with spunk.

Esther grunted. "Gee, tell me what you really think."

Mother Reed grabbed Esther's chin, tilting her face up. "I think you have always found a way to run from difficult, when it's difficult that makes a thing worthwhile. Difficult cultivated your next level. Difficult provided you with the skill set to be your best self."

Esther interrupted. "Difficult can sometimes mean that it wasn't meant to be."

Mother Reed smacked her hands together in frustration. "Work with me here, chile. What does the Bible say? Job went through trial after trial, but at the end of his difficulties, God said, 'After these things.' Uh-huh. And what about David? He served in the shepherd's field before he reigned on the throne."

Mother Reed stood up. "I love ya like peanut butter love jelly, but when you close yourself up to the promises of life, I get tired. Get up and fight! You think Jesus didn't want to bypass His difficulties? Whew! The man sat in the garden of Gethsemane questioning. But at the end, He proclaimed, 'Nevertheless.' What's your nevertheless?"

Esther moaned. "Mother, she wants him back."

"Ha! Good for you! Don't nobody want anybody nobody else wants. She don' already been there and don' that. Guess what? She didn't do it well. It's dead, baby. She can't come back to the scene of the crime because there is yellow caution tape around his heart. There is a chalk outline warning him that part of their relationship is dead. And although she may be on parole because of Briggs's ability to forgive, she's still down in his record book as having committed a felony of the most grievous kind. She murdered their marriage."

Mother Reed picked her cup up and defying her advanced age moved between the kitchen table and door in record time. "You sit here awhile and think on this, Esther. The reward only comes at the end of the battle."

Esther lay her head down on her arms. Between her less than successful road trip and Monica's return she had not slept well. She knew she had better get a little shut-eye. She never fought well when she was tired.

Chapter Twenty-three

The intercom crackled in Briggs's office. "Yes?"

"Pastor, Deacon Joshua is here," Naomi said in a dull voice.

"Thank you. You see how easy that was? How respect-ful?"

"All I know is that the Prison Prophet is almost at the door. And I'm not having half the fun I used to."

Briggs clicked off the intercom and got up to open his door. He had promised Esther he would fix this problem, so he needed to concentrate on that, not on fixing Naomi. She continued to be a work in progress.

Joshua looked spiffy in a Polo cardigan and well-tai-lored pants.

"Come on in. Thanks for meeting with me," Briggs said.

"Sorry I couldn't get here yesterday when you first asked for the meeting." Joshua looked around the room.

"No problem. I ended up with an unexpected houseg-uest so it all worked out," Briggs said as he motioned for Joshua to sit. "Can we talk for a minute about Sister Esther Redding?"

"Sure, everything all right?" Joshua asked.

He shook his head. "No, man, it isn't. I understand one of your prison ministry's felons, Roger, is getting out of prison, and Esther is terrified he's coming here."

"Well, you can put your mind at rest." Joshua waved his hand in dismissal.

Briggs clasped his hands together in satisfaction. For once things were going to be settled quickly. "Good, good. I told her you would never let him come here."

Joshua raised his arm and laid it across the arm of the chair. His movements were laid-back, but his eyes narrowed and appeared harsh in the office light. "Oh, he's coming here. I promised him that he could." Joshua then allowed his ire at being questioned come through to Briggs loud and clear. "Now, I do respect wise counsel. But I'm not sure why *my* business is suddenly *your* business, Pastor. I know a lot of people believe that their pastor should run their lives. But for a long time, I just had me, my Bible, and my relationship with the good Lord to count on. So, forgive me if I sound irreverent. I'm just seeing you as a person who stepped out of their lane, smack in the middle of mine."

Briggs inhaled and curbed the desire to speak before he understood what his next words would mean for his future relationship with Joshua. He had Mother Reed to consider, and his promise to Esther.

Joshua continued, "He's not coming to bother her. He's changed. But regardless, he'll be here tomorrow."

Briggs saw red; he and Joshua were about to have a problem. Because if it came to getting along with his deacon or protecting Esther, it was a no-brainer. "The man attacked people in this congregation. You don't think people have a right to be concerned?"

Joshua spoke in a deliberate and exact tone. "The man paid his debt."

Briggs stood. "To whom? The city, the state? He has a victim who is still afraid of him."

Joshua fingered the Fedora in his hand in an agitated manner. The cool composure he had shown Briggs crumbled. His skin flushed crimson, and a sheen of perspiration dotted his forehead. "How long should he

stay away? A year more? How about five more years? Is
that good enough? When will it be okay for him to live
again? Breathe the same air as other good law-abiding,
godly, forgiving folk? Huh, Pastor? Give me a number
that would satisfy y'all."

A light flicked on in the cavern of Briggs's closed mind.
He heard truth, and he felt convicted. He struggled to
stay with his first commitment, protect Esther. "Help me
here, man. I have to be mindful of others' needs too."

"Not if their needs cancel out the need of the one. My
Bible says, do this for the least among us. God likened us
to His sheep and said it was the lost one that He searched
for."

"That He did." Eyes at half-mast, Briggs sighed. "You
make some valid points. Can you promise me that Roger
won't be a danger to any of the people here?"

"This man is coming to me because I am the only
person who is offering him a job, a place to live, and
some hope for the future. He's not coming for anything
else. I hope that everyone respects that, and if they can't
respect that, please respect my right to have who I want
in my home." Joshua slapped his hand on his chest.

Briggs stood and moved to the window. It was an overcast day, and he thought rain might be in the forecast.

"This church is a place for the broken to be made
whole, and the weak to be restored. You've made me
rethink my stance on this, and I pray that I'm not making
a mistake in stating that as long as Roger respects others'
feelings, and he stays out of trouble, I won't make this a
church issue. I just hope I can do as good a job as you at
convincing people that the man is not a threat."

Joshua had a smirk on his face. "People . . . or Sister
Esther?" Briggs nodded at Joshua. "Pastor, you sure
you shouldn't be speaking to Brother Charles and Sister
Phyllis? They're the ones who were attacked."

Briggs looked out and saw clouds rolling in. "Yes, and they have each other. But Sister Esther was his intended victim. So we want to make sure that as a widow with two small children she feels safe."

Joshua slapped his hat on his head and stood. "I'm not going around this mulberry bush again. She'll be fine. If Roger doesn't do right, he'll answer to me."

The two men once again took each other's measure. Both gave slight nods to indicate they saw men of honor in their collective visions.

Briggs clasped Joshua's hand. "Thanks, Deacon. I'm going to believe that as a man of your word, everything will be good, because if it isn't, it won't be me as a pastor you're dealing with; it will be me the man."

Joshua headed out of the door leaving his reply in his wake. "Wouldn't have it any other way."

Chapter Twenty-four

The door to his office slammed shut. Briggs closed his eyes briefly and hoped that was the only door he heard closing. He had barely touched the surface of a relationship with Esther, and now he would have to disappoint her by telling her he spoke too soon on the issue of Roger coming to town.

Briggs picked up his cell phone and tapped her name.

"Hello, Briggs."

Briggs swallowed before speaking. "I'm glad I'm already programmed in your phone; gives a man hope. How was your trip?"

"I'm not sure. I went to find Deborah, but ended up thinking maybe the Deborah I knew can't be found. But that's not a topic for today. I didn't hear from you last night. It got my mind to racing. Are you over there playing house?" Esther said airily.

Briggs muffled the coughing fit her saccharine-sweet reply garnered. He couldn't believe that with all the focus he had placed on his conversation with Joshua that he had totally forgotten about Monica. She really wasn't a fixture in his heart anymore.

"I'm not playing at all. My son's mother is in a jam. I'm helping her out *temporarily*," Briggs emphasized. "I was up and out of the house bright and early both mornings. I haven't spent much time with her at all. She's there for BJ."

He heard a catch in Esther's voice. "So, Monica *did* stay the night at your house? Wait. No, she stayed *two* nights at your home? No rooms available at the inn?"

Esther's voice had moved from a catch to an all-out growl. Briggs rubbed his forehead, not having to wonder where the slight throbbing of his head came from. Were they always going to be at cross purposes? To never build trust? "I told you, she stayed with her son—in his room."

Silence. Briggs could have said more, but he didn't feel it was right to share Monica's woes about being financially strapped. She had nowhere else to go, and BJ wanted his mother to stay with them. So he was giving them time together. He knew he would need to help her go somewhere else; she could not keep staying with him.

Briggs's voice took on a teasing quality. "You wouldn't be jealous now, *would you?*"

"Ah, no, I wouldn't."

"Just a little, *teeny* bit?" Briggs said, a grin building on his face.

"No."

Briggs sank back in his chair. "Good, because you are the only one I'm doing my best to interest. Would you like to go out with me tomorrow night?"

"Hmmm, let me think. I guess I could be persuaded to hang out with you a little . . . as friends."

Briggs placed his feet up on his desk. "It's how every relationship should start; friends. Speaking of friends, you actually went to find Deborah?"

"I get these ideas, and then I can't let go. I talked Phyllis into going with me."

Briggs was confused as to why she would need to drive there. "I remember you telling me about this on our early-morning call. Why not talk to her on the phone?"

"I kept hitting dead ends. Her job wouldn't tell me anything, except that she worked part time. I figured working in housekeeping, morning was the logical time to try. I just want to know what happened all those years ago," Esther said.

"Did you get your answers?"

"Some . . . She's schizophrenic and almost *dared* me to keep in touch."

Briggs's feet landed on the floor. "She's carrying a heavy load. I'm surprised she shared that with you."

"I got the feeling that she told me as a means to get rid of me."

He leaned into the phone. "Did it work?"

"I don't know. Still waiting to get some time with God to talk about it."

Briggs's fist pumped in the air. "Best answer ever. Gold star, honey."

"I'll keep you posted." She then said in a saucy manner, "About this date, what time should I be ready?"

"Dress casually and be ready at seven."

"See you then."

Gazing off, he wondered when he would get up the nerve to tell her about Roger. It would definitely be after their date.

The overcast day was showing signs of a rainy evening. Briggs was avoiding going home. He hadn't decided how to handle Monica's homeless situation. He had prayed, but the best solution still hadn't come to him. He was glad, though, that Monica was spending some long-needed time with BJ, and that BJ was also getting to spend some time with his little sister.

He'd called Monica earlier to let her know Naomi was picking up and bringing BJ home from school. She was amiable, and he was relieved when she didn't flirt. She'd complained about Naomi. Something he would have to handle. Naomi had to do better.

He closed his eyes and ran his hand over his clean-shaven face. He felt his grandfather's indentation on his chin and smiled. He had named it Esther's Ridge. Silly? Yeah, and he had never told anybody about it. From the time they were in college she had claimed it as her own.

Did she have any idea how hard it had been over the years for him to shave each morning without thinking about her? Dreaming about her and her lips pressed against his chin?

Tingles covered his body, and he blinked to relieve the tension. He flipped the pages in his study Bible. He had been pulling together his outline for his Saturday morning men's class when he noticed Naomi standing at his door.

"I'm leaving, Pastor. See you, tomorrow."

"Okay. Thanks again for getting BJ. Be sure to tell Jerome to walk you to your car." Distracted, he turned a page.

Naomi placed her purse in the crook of her arm. "Pastor, Jerome so old I need to be walking him to his bed. By the time he could walk me to my car, I could be home with my own children, checked their homework, and had my bath."

Eyes widening, Briggs's mouth tightened around his words. "Naomi, do you always have to be so mean?"

Briggs saw Naomi chew on her bottom lip. Her opaque tights were run, and her ill-fitting skirt was slightly wrinkled. She pushed her glasses up her narrow nose, and as her hand came down to her side it trembled. "I'm not mean, Pastor. Jerome *is* old, and he should be at home, not still working at this church as a security guard. But no one has seen past his always being here to realize he should really be at home resting. He used to gamble before he got saved and came to this church. He doesn't have any money. His Social Security is not enough for him to live on. So he keeps coming in here every day, wheezing and sneezing. Walking me to my car would be a chore. How come I'm mean because I say what you should be seeing?"

Briggs's startled look met with Naomi's defiant glare. She didn't back down, and Briggs saw her slight homeliness transform into one of attractive dignity right before his eyes.

Briggs placed his hand on his desk and stood. "I stand corrected, Naomi. It's dark out. Let me walk you out."

Naomi shook her head. "How about you watch me through your office window? The parking lot lights are bright, and my car is right outside the door. There are advantages to being the first one here in the morning."

Briggs nodded. "I appreciate that about you. But I do have a problem with you not treating our guests well. Monica told me you had a few words this morning."

Naomi pointedly looked at her watch. "I like Esther Redding. I don't like 'Boom Shaka Laka Monica.' It's my opinion that all is fair in love and war. The Geneva Convention would outlaw her as a toxin so hazardous she would be labeled as biological warfare under the articles of war. Pastor, you under terrorist attack. You been Monica'd. Now I have to get on home."

Briggs promised himself he was going to figure out how to have a conversation with Naomi without wanting to go into spasms of laughter. As he held his laugh, he knew this would not be that evening. "Have a good night, and say hello to the children for me."

"Will do."

Briggs understood that having custody of her younger brother and sister, Naomi tried to get home on time most days. She moved at a brisk pace, and Briggs heard when the heavy door to his area of the church closed.

He went over to his window and watched her getting into an older model car, and then her lights flashed, indicating she was good.

He sat back down in his large leather chair, tilting it back and putting his hands behind his head. He thought of Jerome.

Lord, I'm missing a lot around here. As your shepherd for your flock, I need to see and hear better. I feel as though I am failing in tasks I didn't even know I am assigned to. Like Solomon, Lord, I pray for wisdom. Help me to bridge gaps and to understand, lest I perish.

Briggs felt led to turn to Proverbs chapter four, verse seven. He read it and emblazoned it on his heart. "Wisdom is the principal thing; therefore get wisdom: and with all thy getting get understanding."

He loved him some Esther, but he also loved the people of the Kingdom, and he had to be there for all of them. The Jeromes who were living right under his nose, the Rogers struggling to make a new life, and the Monicas who had no idea what the next step should be.

Lord, I'm going to need your help.

Chapter Twenty-five

"Do it, girl, show me what you working with."

Esther panted as she kept up with the dance figure on the video game playing on Phyllis's eighty-inch flat-screen television. They were in her family room, and Esther had been goaded into proving she still had it. The kids were cheering her on, and she felt like a grenade was about to explode in her chest. It was only Phyllis's earlier challenge that had her trying to finish the song.

She could see Phyllis laughing at her, and if the kids weren't all sitting there she'd smack her. Right now, she was tempted to stagger down the hallway to one of the guest bedrooms and collapse. Or maybe she should moonwalk back into Phyllis's gold brocade chaise lounge and just . . . well . . . lounge.

Got me up here, sweating and getting funky for nothing. Humph, I worked a full eight-hour day.

Esther pumped it up on the last bar of the song, and then danced around in glee. "Yes! Who's bad? Mama's bad."

All the kids fell on the floor laughing. Phyllis threw her a hand towel, and then a bottle of water. "Now you don't have to hit a gym."

"Does it look like I was planning to visit a gym?" Esther motioned running her hands down her curvy hips. Contrary to her self-effacing comments, her black wool slacks were slimming and hugged her just right. Her sequined socks looked stylish, poking beneath her

pants hem. Her fitted top showcased her small waist and
screamed that she was working her look.

Phyllis's nose flared. "How come you sound angry? You
didn't have to dance to the song."

Esther mopped her face and pulled on her boots. "Oh,
so you can be the only cool adult in my kids' life? No, no,
not this time, sister."

Phyllis's eyes returned to a twinkle before she grabbed
the remote, chose a song, and threw her back into jam-
ming to the dance moves. When the dance choreography
caused her to turn around, she winked at Esther as she
effortlessly danced three levels higher than the level
Esther had almost expired on.

David yelled at his aunt, "You doing it, Auntie."

Esther rolled her eyes as Phyllis twirled around again,
and Phyllis shook her finger at her. Esther stuck out her
tongue.

Ruth cried out when she spied Esther's antics with
her sister. "Ooh, Mama. You told me I couldn't stick my
tongue out at people. 'Member? You said it wasn't nice."

Esther's ears turned red when Phyllis crowed in
delight. "That's right, baby. Help your mama stay right."

Esther gave a fake smile. "Why don't you guys go in the
kitchen and get a snack?"

Miracle placed her hand on her hip. "Auntie, we already
had a snack. We don't want to eat too much 'cause we
don't want to be fat. You eat too much, Auntie."

Esther gasped as David and Ruth both flew to her
defense, each calling out in anger, "You take that back . . .
Don't you call my mama fat."

Esther looked at Miracle, and then at Phyllis and
waited for her sister to put her grown-butt child in check.
When she said nothing Esther addressed her children.

"Sweeties, Miracle didn't mean it. Aunt Phyllis and I
are going in the other room to have a nice chat. You guys
behave while I'm gone, okay?"

David and Ruth both had their arms folded, and their faces set in determined lines. It was times like this that their similarities as twins could best be acknowledged. Twin flames of anger were never good.

Little Ms. Perfect, Ms. Miracle, looked down at her crimson nails and shrugged her petite shoulders. "I was gon' show y'all something on my computer. But if you mad at me . . ."

As Esther left the room, she heard her defenders cave in, both clamoring to see what Miracle had. In the back of her mind, she felt like she should check it out too, but she needed to have this talk with Phyllis.

It was a short walk to Phyllis's luxurious, all-white with the exception of deep purple accents, formal living room. Esther smirked, knowing Phyllis disliked using the room for anything other than showing off. When she strode in the room, Phyllis went on the offensive.

"She didn't mean anything by it, Esther. She's going to those advance classes, and she's learning about nutrition and obesity. I couldn't reprimand her for saying what she learned."

Esther looked at her sister as though she had lost her mind. "I don't care what she learned. It is never acceptable for her to knowingly hurt anyone's feelings, and you know you're wrong for not addressing it with her."

As though cold, Phyllis rubbed her arms. "No, she wasn't doing that. Miracle is not mean."

Esther gave a sarcastic snort.

"We've had this conversation. The kids told me this morning that you've been called up to the school because of Miracle's mouth."

"No, those other children are jealous. She has nice clothes, and she's a beautiful little girl inside and out," Phyllis said hugging her body.

Esther snapped her fingers in front of Phyllis's face. "Wake up before this goes *very* bad. You know we were taught pretty is not what you look like, but what you act like. Your child has ugly ways."

Phyllis grabbed Esther's snapping fingers. "Take that back."

Esther snatched her hand from Phyllis. "What are you, five?"

They stood there huffing and puffing.

Esther gave in first. She marched out of the room. "David and Ruth, say good-bye to your cousin, we're leaving," she yelled down the hall.

She grabbed her coat and gathered her children as they hightailed it to the door.

She was yanking it open when Phyllis called out, "You want me to pick them up from school tomorrow and just bring them here? They can spend the night since it's the weekend."

"Ooh, can we, Mama?" Ruth said.

Esther thought about her date tomorrow with Briggs. "Yes, thank you," Esther said, as the children clapped, and she guided them to their car.

Shoot, I had planned to stay angry at her.

"Move to the left and follow through on your swing," Briggs said. He was on his knees abreast with BJ, both facing the bowling game on the Wii.

"I want to make a strike, like you, Daddy."

"You will, son."

Briggs watched BJ's face creased in concentration. His large curls bounced with each thrust of his little body. "Smoothly, son. Jerking your body stops the follow-through and it's causing the split in your pens."

"Okay," BJ said. He stuck his tongue out as he took another swing. All but one pen fell down.

BJ pumped his fist in the air, and Briggs gave him a high five.

BJ handed him the game control and said, "Your turn."

Briggs put his feet together, and as he took steps forward and pulled his arm back, he nonchalantly asked BJ, "Did you have a good time with your mother?"

BJ's smile was wide and effortless. "Yes, we talked, and she went over my homework. She made me the best Reuben sandwich for dinner. She left you one too, Daddy."

"I'll thank her. How do you feel about spending time with your little sister?"

BJ sat down Indian-style and looked up at his father. "I felt funny—like—how could I be there for her? What is a big brother supposed to do? How come I never felt any of that before, Daddy?"

Briggs sat down across from his son, crossing his legs in front of him too. He was proud of BJ. "You didn't get a chance to really be around her much. When I stayed in New York for a month, helping your mother, you were only around her for a few days. When your grandmother helped me to contract with a nanny, they were able to leave and take you back home. Fiona was only a month old. Spending time with her makes a difference, especially now that she's seven months old."

"Oh." BJ looked down as though he felt bad that he had never really connected with his sister. "I always thought Fiona was a part of Mama's other life. Maybe I was jealous?"

"Your mother loves you, son. She didn't leave you with me because she didn't care; she left you because of how much she did care."

BJ nodded and ran his hand over the floor in a mind-less pattern.

Briggs's day had been filled with his shortcomings and he felt like this was another one of them. He thought he had made BJ feel secure in his mother's and his love. Yet, he had watched him grow more and more silent in the years after Monica left. In the months following Monica's attack he became more withdrawn, and then sullen. This move to Detroit was the first sign of him opening up.

"Dad?" His small face was pinched.

"Oh, Dad, is it? This must be important."

"It kinda is. I was wondering. Can Mama and Fiona just stay here? She doesn't have a place yet, and it would be so nice to have her here, wouldn't it?"

Briggs felt the sweat roll down his back and his jaw clench. When Monica had gotten out of the hospital, he had made a very hard decision in not offering her the option to come back to Atlanta and stay with them. He had heard in times of life and death a person should save themselves first. He had. Getting caught up with Monica again was something he did not want to do.

Briggs had told BJ they could stay for a few days. Now BJ wanted her to stay period. Was Monica playing manipulative games? "Did your mother ask you to ask me that?"

"Nuh-uh," BJ said but avoided looking in his father's direction.

Briggs snapped at BJ in frustration. "Use your words."

BJ gulped, his eyes now searching his dad's.

"No, sir, she didn't. But I heard her crying, and she was holding Fiona and telling her they had no place to go. She didn't know I heard her."

Of course she did.

Briggs sighed, pulling his son into his arms. "Son, your mother and I are not together any more. She left me, even though she didn't leave you. What we have in common now is that we both love you to pieces."

BJ's bottom lip quivered. "But, Daddy, you said I'm supposed to care for those weaker than me. Mama's awful weak right now, and I'm little. But you can do it for me. Please, Daddy!"

Briggs mumbled under his breath. He had no doubt that Monica had engineered BJ's little eavesdropping scenario.

"Can we agree on this, BJ? I'll let your mother stay here while I find her other accommodations. And you have to understand that this doesn't mean your mother and I are going to be together as a couple again, but we will always be a family."

BJ frowned. "Why not, Daddy? You don't have anybody else."

Briggs tapped BJ on his nose. "What? I have plenty of people: you, Pa Pa, Grandma, and maybe real soon someone else very special."

BJ's head hung. "Ms. Esther?"

Briggs rolled back, unfurling his long legs. "Did your mother tell you that?"

"No. You sound real happy when you talk to her. And you stare at her when you think no one else is looking," BJ said, looking up.

"What do you think about all of that?" Briggs asked, cupping his chin.

"I'm not sure. I been studying on it."

"That's fair enough. I plan to spend some time with her tomorrow night. Your mother tells me she's going out to some type of function where she can take Fiona. So I've asked Mother Reed to spend some time with you. I want you guys to get to know each other better. You good with that?"

BJ didn't sound happy. "She's really old, Daddy. Can I take my video games with me?"

"Yes, but don't be rude. Only pull them out if she says it's okay. And, BJ, there are all kinds of people in the world. They all bring something that we can learn from; older people bring even more. They know a lot. Do you want to know what year she was born?" Briggs said, firm but composed.

"Yes. She's so old, I bet it was nineteen ninety-nine."

"Young man, I was born before nineteen ninety-nine."

BJ's eyes widened. "For real?"

Briggs hid his smile. "She was born in nineteen nineteen."

"Wow!"

Briggs hid his smile again. "She was born before the first robot. Before the first television. Before frozen pizza!"

"Will she tell me all about it?" BJ scooted over to him.

"I'm sure she'll tell you about a lot of things."

"Will she have more cake?"

Briggs stood and grabbed BJ around his middle and hoisted him in the air. "I don't know, but she's known for her cakes." He turned with BJ squealing. As BJ sailed through the air, he dropped him on the couch. "Man, you almost too big for that! What have you been eating, your Wheaties? Let's call it a night. You can go upstairs and find your mother and sister and tell them good night."

Briggs bent down and hugged BJ, then turned and saw a shadow moving up the stairs at a run. A few seconds later, he heard a door quietly snap shut.

He wanted to call up the stairs and tell Monica to mind her business. But BJ was more important than letting her know he was on to her.

You ain't slick, Monica.

Chapter Twenty-six

Briggs waited a half hour before he went in BJ's room to wish him good night. Monica sat on the edge of the bed reading a book.

Turning a page she drawled. "He's already asleep. He was tired."

"Being manipulated will do that to a person," Briggs whispered, his face a storm of anger.

Monica groaned. Then in a low monotone she scathed. "Here we go with the 'big bad Monica' routine." Leaning forward, she then shimmied her shoulders with a leer on her face. "She's *soooo* dangerous."

Their eyes were locked in a test of wills when her leer slowly morphed into sadness. "He's my son, Briggs; he loves me. He wants to take care of me, you taught him that. He wants to grow up and be you."

Not being drawn into Monica's mind games, Briggs snarled. "Yeah, well, as long as he doesn't want to be you."

Monica drew back as though Briggs had slapped her.

Briggs took a calming breath. "I apologize, that was not called for, but if I'm going to let you stay here for the time being, we have to set some ground rules."

Monica stood and walked out of the room; Briggs followed.

She went into the living room and sat down. Her pose was formal and direct. "I know you think I wanted him to hear me talking to Fiona, but that's a habit I picked up, because it's only been me and her. I really didn't know he was listening."

Briggs stared at her in disbelief.

Monica raised her hands in surrender. "Not that I mind the results. Your place beats the streets."

Briggs thought about the ramifications of her living with him. While it couldn't be helped, he longed for another solution. "Are you at least job hunting?"

Monica got up and went to his end table. She then showed him a newspaper, with ads circled. "Now that I have an address I can put down, I can get out there and look."

Briggs exhaled. "Good. The sooner, the better."

Monica stood adjusting her gown. "I get it, Briggs. You don't want me here, you need me to make other arrangements as soon as possible. Should I move my things to the other bedroom now?"

Briggs shook his head. "You'll bunk with BJ—"

"Why? You have two other bedrooms in this big house," Monica pouted.

Briggs smirked. "Keeping you in BJ's room will keep you honest. The portable crib I purchased for Fiona will fit anywhere. You don't need a bedroom to yourself. Take this time and bond with your son."

Monica stomped off mumbling and fussing under her breath. She had totally switched over to her Jamaican language of patois. He had to grin because she had cursed him out in patois before.

He grimaced when he heard her say very clearly, "I not beggy. Yuh too baddasum, kiss mi back side and galang."

Briggs knew enough after being married to her to know she had said something about her not having to resort to begging, and that he was bothersome, and he could kiss her rear end and go away. Grinning ruefully, he thought, *How did I get all that, but never understood her when I was married to her?*

***

The Leader screeched throughout the dugout. He was unhappy, and an unhappy leader was dangerous. "Imp, report to me how this is falling apart."

Imp One backed away. "No, no, O Great One. She's in the house."

The Leader's tail stood straight up, and all the other imps fell back. "But not his bed."

"She is one step away from completing our plan, Master. All we need is one night. These humans make all types of mistakes for the sake of just one night. It is their legacy."

"He wants the other one, stupid. He is obsessed. It will take more than a night." The Leader stopped and jabbed his tail in the air like a sword as he remembered his ace in the hole. "What of the little girl? Blessing?"

"Her name is Miracle," Imp One corrected.

"I will slash your throat. Her name doesn't concern me. How is the work on her heart going? Is it hardening? Do you still have imps assigned to speaking into her pride? Are they accusing those around her of being jealous of her beauty? Are they telling her she is smarter than everyone else? That rules are dumb and not made for her? Speak!" The Leader barked.

A short squeak came out, and the imp cleared his throat. "Yeeesss. It is as you say. She is becoming more and more disconnected with those around her. We play on every arrogant bone in her little body. Already she hears us and obliges."

The Leader's tail dropped some inches. "And the angel activity?"

Four imps fell on their faces, leaving Imp One clearly in the line of fire. "The activity continues, O Great One. Is there not something you can do? Can't you take care of them?"

The Leader's tail swept over the imp and wiped out all four of Imp One's brothers who were cringing in the back. As ash settled over him, The Leader's tail wrapped around his chest and squeezed. "If I have to do that, what do I need you for?"

Imp One stood rigid. "Indeed, O Great One. Indeed."

The Leader released him and watched him slither away. He looked after him thoughtfully, and his eyes glazed over as he rose to his full height.

"If you want something done right, get it don' yourself—then kill everybody you knew who failed you."

Chapter Twenty-seven

Stale pee and bleach.

Roger sauntered through the corridors of the dank hall. He swore to himself he never ever wanted to inhale those combinations of smells again. Not ever. If he was old and he peed on himself, they would have to use Lysol, Formula 409, or Mr. Clean, 'cause if they even approached him with some Clorox he would definitely go kaboom.

He approached the counter and took his property bag from the guard who was releasing him from captivity. He looked inside and snickered. Was anyone still carrying a flip phone? He then rummaged inside and fingered the torn matinee movie ticket for *Big Momma's House*. He vaguely remembered going to the matinee movies in the summer to keep cool, the winter to stay warm, and no matter the weather, to sleep in peace. Survival skills one o' one. For a couple of dollars, he could stay all day, eat leftover popcorn until he puked, and go from theater to theater. Young kids who worked there ended up being easily intimated by his hard looks if they ever approached him with some foolishness.

Memories he had purposely pushed to the back of his mind assailed him. In this hole of Satan, you couldn't keep the past too close or depression could catch you. Once depression got your location and it combined with the oppression that already reigned there, it became the slippery slope many slid down. Before you knew it, you were giving lap dances to anger, fueling its frenzy. That kind of hopeless anger could get a person killed—or have them commit murder.

Some just gave up, and they sipped at the poisonous fountain of bad advice, easy street myths, and the world owed them some fairy tales. On the day they were released, every lie they told their mamas, girlfriends, and children concerning getting their lives straight was flushed down the toilet. Only a chosen few were strong enough to walk away, never to return. The rest left with corrupted souls, believing that their lives were over. Hopelessness was not a badge for fruitful living. As a result, they fell prey to the belief that the next scam was the best scam.

Roger had invested in a God who was the giver of second chances. He had coped by keeping God in front of him and the past behind him. What-ifs were useless in a place like this. What a man needed was the dreams of what would be.

Fearful thoughts of being caught behind prison walls assaulted him. His hands shook, propelling him faster and faster, as small tense voices pleaded with him not to look back. It was irrational, his fear that at any moment the prison officials would change their minds and tell him a mistake had been made. He would wake up in his cell, choking on his imprisonment, the bars that encompassed and strangled him at every angle.

The guard that accompanied him shoved him forward . . . As though he was not already running to get out. No matter. He could see daylight up ahead. The outdoors was filtering into his last cemented section of wilderness. Soon he would be free.

His mouth salivated, and tears sprang to his eyes. He was never coming back. He would chew off his foot and drag himself into the bush to die before he ever let a metal door clang shut behind him again.

The guard nodded to the camera hanging from the upper corner and the door slid open.

"Get out," he grunted, and turned away murmuring, "See you next time."

Roger was immediately convicted when he shot him his middle finger as he sprinted out. "Yes!" he screamed as he stood in the parking lot, dancing in between cars.

"You need a ride?"

Roger looked up, and there was Prophet. He seemed taller, even though Roger saw him every month when Prophet came to visit. But out here for some reason, he looked taller.

Maybe he looked taller too. Roger hoped so. He hoped his stature had changed when he walked out of the prison. And Roger prayed that a merciful God magnified the goodness he had worked hard to obtain, versus the enemy magnifying his mistakes.

"You bet I need a ride. This you?" Roger pointed at the Mercedes SUV.

"Nah, bought it for the wife. Then I got a new one, and she never wants to drive this one now."

Roger slipped into the car, leaned his head against the headrest, and inhaled a sweet smell. "Bro, you even got this ride smelling good. You have been so blessed to have come out and had all that money waiting on you."

Joshua pulled the car out into traffic before he turned to Roger. "I pray you never have to go through what I went through to become heir to this money. To lose your mother at such a young age because of a sadistic father. To be beaten on a daily basis because she was no longer there to take your place." He put on his blinkers, looked into his rearview mirror, switched lanes, and accelerated.

Roger adjusted the vent, breathing in deeply. "Yeah, your story ain't that different from every other brother I just left behind. Forgive me if I'm not crying a river for you because at least at the end of the day, you had the money."

"At what cost?"

Roger slapped his hands together and rubbed them. "The same price the rest of us paid to poor sadistic men and women who were charged to protect, and instead, destroyed us. None of us got a payout. Most just left wanting a payback."

Joshua chuckled. "So, I can't get no help crying a river?"

"Shoot, man. Every tear I have is for the brothers we left behind."

Joshua nodded his head in agreement.

"Remind me sometime to tell you all about Duncan," Roger said.

"Somebody you used to know?"

"No, a nightmare I used to have."

Joshua pulled up to a traffic stop and looked askance at Roger, but he was busy looking at the large stately homes in the upscale neighborhood.

"Shoot, man, I feel like Florence on *The Jeffersons*. How come nobody told me we had moved on up?"

Chapter Twenty-eight

Briggs swung in and parked in front of Mother Reed's house. He didn't have to look to know that she was sitting in her favorite chair, her curtains clutched in her hand pulled back from the window checking out his approach.

He wore a perpetual grin as he ran briskly up her steps, almost having BJ airborne as he mounted them two at a time.

Yep, I got it bad.

His exuberance nearly took the front door off its hinges as he dove through, slamming it in his wake.

"Mother Reed, why is your front door open?" Briggs barged into her living room, pulling BJ's coat off, and snatching his hat off his head. "It's unseasonably cold, and it's Detroit. You can't be leaving your door open for any Tom, Dick, or Harry."

"Humph, hello, Harry. You might greet a person before you start in on them. I saw you pull up, so I opened the door for you. Being old don't mean you foolish, son," Mother Reed said, getting out of her lounger, her print caftan vibrant with colors.

Mother Reed then turned to BJ. "How you like flying Stokes Airline?"

"Huh?" BJ said, hesitating as he worked his backpack off.

Briggs chuckled. "That's just her way of being funny. You got everything? Your games and your book?"

Briggs tapped his hand against his thigh while BJ opened his backpack and slowly went through it. Briggs then grabbed the sack and peered into it himself. "Yea, you're good. So . . . I love you. Be good for Mother Reed and I'll see you later on tonight, okay?" Briggs started stepping backward.

BJ looked at his father as though he didn't know what to make of him. Mother Reed shook her head and motioned for Briggs to bend down so she could whisper to him.

"This ain't your first rodeo. And if you jump on a mare too quick, she'll get skittish and bail on you. But if you take your time and woo her just right . . . well, now!" She reached up and patted his cheek. "Men will make a mess of the simplest things. And a man in love forgets almost everything but the promise of his heart's ease. You've never left your son for a date before. Set this up right so he doesn't get the spirit of offense against Esther later on."

Mother Reed then took BJ's hand in hers and smiled reassuringly. "We gon' be just fine. I bet if we look real hard in my kitchen we can find some cake with BJ's name on it."

Briggs had prayed the day before about seeing and hearing around him better. He would slow down and make sure his son was settled. "Doesn't that sound good, BJ? And since you had your dinner, a slice of cake is a fitting close to your Friday."

BJ's smile was as wide as his father's as he grabbed Briggs's hand and led him into the kitchen. "Let's go, Daddy. You can have some cake with me."

Briggs surreptitiously glanced at his watch. "How about I just sit with you while you have yours."

Mother Reed got down two plates. "I can have just a piece of a slice, BJ, but I would be so honored to nibble on it with you."

"Yes, ma'am. May I have some soda too?" BJ gave a quick glance to his dad.

Briggs shook his head. "You may have some milk."

BJ's face clouded for only a moment before he smiled again. "Then may I have some chocolate in my milk?"

"He's got coping smarts, Briggs," Mother Reed rifled through her cabinets for some cocoa mix.

"Yes, he keeps me on my toes."

Mother Reed exclaimed in triumph, "Found it." As she held the box of chocolate in the air, she pulled out the cabinet drawer; then she spooned the mix into the milk, stirred, and handed it to a smiling BJ.

He slurped his milk and chewed pieces of cake while swinging his legs back and forth.

"You taking Esther somewhere nice?" Mother Reed said low.

Briggs looked down at his crisp blue jeans and his thick Polo sweater. "That your way of asking me if I'm doing right by your girl?"

"Well, Pastor, the spirit of excellence in all thangs is mighty important. And since you mean business, your actions got ta reflect your intentions."

"Well said. And I promise you that my actions will be just fine."

Eating a small nibble of cake, she said. "So, I can't get the four-one-one?"

"No, ma'am. But you can get the live at eleven after our date," Briggs laughed.

"I like that, so I'll just wait until you or Esther report back to me. All the little details, like a small peck here and there, can be left out. Unless you feel the need to unburden yourself."

Briggs stood up, shaking his finger at Mother Reed. "BJ, Daddy is getting ready to leave. Can you hold up your cell phone and show me my number on it?"

BJ did as he was told.

"Now, press the number one." Briggs then answered his phone when it rang. "If you need anything, you only have to tap the number one. Okay?"

BJ smiled and placed his phone in his sweater pocket. "Okay."

"I really appreciate this, you keeping BJ tonight. He shouldn't be any trouble," Briggs said as he began to back out of the room, sputtering. "I can't keep a lady waiting."

Mother Reed waved her hand for him to go. "Boy, get on outta here."

He nodded to Mother Reed, tipping his head and flourishing his hand as though he was bowing with an imaginary hat. "Mother."

Briggs's heart was beating a little faster as he pulled off. Esther didn't live too far away, so he needed to slow down. His timing needed to be on point—not late, but not close enough that he looked pressed. What had Mother Reed said? Woo her slow?

Was seventeen years too fast?

Briggs turned down his Sirius radio; he loved to listen to the Gospel stations. But for tonight, he would be switching to the oldies station, for some old-fashioned romantic songs. They had a little ride ahead of them. Right now, he needed to think, compose himself.

Even though he'd turned down the radio, he could still hear some of the commentator's talk. Then he frowned; as a matter of fact, the DJ sounded a lot like Mother Reed.

Briggs turned the dial to the far left again and noted that it had already been at the lowest setting.

He heard the voices again, and then Mother Reed laughed out loud. "Let me set this alarm system, BJ. Your Daddy think I'm lax. But we good and safe. You want some more cocoa in your milk?"

"Uh-huh."

Use your words, son.

Briggs pulled his phone out of his pocket and noted that BJ had never cut his off. He had an inside radio transmission of his son and Mother Reed's conversation.

I'll just call her on her landline and tell her to shut BJ's phone off.

"BJ, you a miniature picture of your daddy. I wonder who you'll take after. Well, God will reveal it in time. I read somewhere that a child's personality is set by the age of four. By my calculation and rusty math, your personality was formed during some of the most turbulent times in your parents' life."

Okay, Lord. What is Mother Reed saying to BJ?

"BJ, can you take them earplugs off your ears for a minute? Unfold your arms and look at me. Sweetie, why is your jaw sat in defiance? Your little body is swallowed up in my Anthony's big ol' chair. He was six foot and a brawny man."

"Did they name the paper towel after him? What does brawny mean?"

"He speaks! No, they didn't. It means he was big and strong."

Briggs imagined her holding her hands out wide to illustrate. He heard her sigh. Was she smoothing down her sweater, an old habit he had witnessed again, and again?

"You hurting, child?" Briggs could hear her moving around.

"This a mighty big chair. Can I share it with you? Maybe we can read together? Of if you like, we can just . . . talk."

Briggs heard the snapping of fingers. "I know what. Let's play a game. But first you gotta loosen up a little. Your small body is so tight, you gon' get a headache right where your forehead is scrunched up."

"I don't want a headache," BJ said in a small voice.

"Me either, but sometimes we get one when we think too hard about something."

Briggs silently spoke to his son, urging him to talk.

Humming Mother Reed whispered, "Talk to Mother."

"You're not my mother!" BJ cried.

Briggs imagined his son, his mouth poked out and quivering.

"Well, now, I guess that would be true. You do have a mother."

"Sometimes I hate her!"

Briggs slammed on his brakes to miss hitting the car in front of him that had stopped for a red light.

What did BJ say? He loved Monica. Begged me to let her stay.

"I'm not going to tell you you don't hate her. I'm just wondering when she had the time to rile you so. I remember your daddy telling me about her getting hurt. And then she was in the hospital for a long time. Then when she got out, she was too weak to hold you and unable to care for you. She did the hardest thing by continuing to let you live with your daddy, so you would be okay."

Briggs heard BJ sniffle. Was he wiping his nose on his cardigan sleeve?

"It wasn't hard."

Briggs could almost hear Mother Reed's brain rushing to find the truth. "It wasn't too hard to take care of you? Or . . . It wasn't too hard to let you go?"

"Daddy said that when you love someone, you take care of them. You do the hard stuff so that they grow big and strong because you love them. She stopped taking care of me a long time ago. I hate her."

Briggs hoped Mother Reed knew he would never badmouth his ex-wife. "When did your daddy say all this?"

Briggs pulled up in front of Esther's house, but even though he was now going to be late, he didn't get out of the car.

Yes, BJ, when did I say all of this?

"When I ate all the white stuff out of the Oreos, and then put them back. When Daddy found out, he threw them away. Later, he bought some more and made me watch him eat them." Briggs heard BJ hesitate as though he was still pained about that lesson he gave.

"I couldn't have not a one, and he ate them so slow. The middle first, then the cookie." BJ stopped his tale, as though he could taste the missed treat. "When I cried, Daddy said it was a hard job, but he loved me enough to teach me a lesson. Now, I share my Oreos. And I'm not sneaky."

"Now, BJ—"

"She don't love me! She could have taken care of me tonight. She took Fiona with her, but not me. Hate, hate, *hate* her."

Briggs felt tears on his cheeks. As much as he hated to do it, he needed to break this date with Esther and go see about his son.

He was startled when the door to his car opened and a perfumed Esther slid in. Before she could speak, he put a finger to his lips and had her listen. He had already placed the phone on mute on his end.

Mother Reed's voice was solemn, and Esther's eyes questioned him when she heard it. But he just motioned to the phone.

"Shush, baby. You don't ever want to give hate your address. Once you invite it in, it gets right comfortable going from room to room. It'll visit your heart, your mind, and your will."

"Huh?"

"It's like this, hate is rude—"

"Sometimes Ms. Naomi is rude. She has funny names for people. Daddy doesn't like it, but he laughs 'cause he said he can't help it."

"No, not that kind of rude, BJ . . ."

Esther looked at Briggs as though she wanted to know what kind of names. She smiled when Mother Reed said, "Funny name for who?" Then they heard her muttering to herself, "Jesus, stay on subject, old gal. Never mind, BJ. What do they call your body in Sunday School?"

"Ummm, my temple?"

"An A-plus, young man. A temple is like a house, right?"

"Uh-huh."

Briggs closed his eyes. *Use your words . . . Oh, never mind.*

"You start off hating your mama. Now hate is in your house." The phone screeched with static. "See how I have my hand on your chest? You can feel it, right? It's real. When hate moves into your heart, you can feel it too."

Esther took Briggs's hand into hers and squeezed it.

Mother Reed continued. "It's a heavy feeling. So heavy that some days it can make it hard to put one foot in front of the other. You won't want to laugh or play because those are things that are light. When you choose hate, you choose heaviness."

They heard a tiny whine. "Your hand is heavy. I don't like it."

Mother Reed spoke. "I'm sorry, but better to not like it now than to carry it forever."

They could hear BJ's little sobs filling the car. Briggs pulled the phone up to his ear to interrupt and tell his son he was coming back.

"Monica is your mama. It's easy to hate, BJ. It's the loving that gets a might hard sometime." Mother Reed's voice dropped to one of soft urging. "She's your mama, baby."

Briggs heard the muffled sound of movement. He looked at Esther with a raised eyebrow. She shook her head and mouthed, "I have no idea what's going on."

Mother Reed said, "Blow your nose, baby. You want more tissue?"

BJ could be heard blowing his nose.

"My mama left me, and she had Fiona take my place. Sometimes I think she doesn't want me. Then when she comes to see me, I forget I'm mad, and when I'm away from her or she leaves again, it comes back. That's why I don't want my daddy to make her go away, again."

A tearful Mother Reed said, "Oh, BJ, sometimes we forget what our actions look like to other people. How can I explain? Let's say your stomach was hurting real bad, and David and Ruth asked you to come out and play. But you told them no. And maybe you didn't say it real nice 'cause you got that pain, right here in your stomach. Later on, you see David and Ruth at school and you want to play, 'cause you finally feeling better and they're your friends. But they're mad at you because you hurt their feelings. But you didn't mean to, you were just hurting too much to play."

Briggs's face creased in consternation during the prolonged silence.

Then BJ's tentative voice crackled over the cell phone waves, "Mama didn't mean to hurt me? She was just feeling bad?"

"I'm sure of it, BJ. Your mother loves you."

Then a small sigh. "Okay." There was more silence, and then a cajoling whine. "Can I have some more cake now, and maybe a little soda?"

Esther put her other hand over the hand she was holding with Briggs. "Call her," Esther whispered. "If she says come, we can do this another night."

Briggs nodded and took mute off the phone. He called out to Mother Reed from BJ's pocket.

A startled BJ answered. "Hello?"

"Hi, son. You all right?"

"Uh . . . Yes, Daddy. I'm eating cake."

"Good. Can you put Mother Reed on the phone?"

Mother Reed answered, her voice strained. "Hold on a minute, Briggs. BJ, I'm stepping out of the room for a second. Turn on that little gadget you got there till I get back, and cut it up so I can hear it."

"Okay."

Briggs heard the sounds of a computer game dinging. "I'm back, Briggs. Did you use one of them spy cams on me, boy? You know I don't 'preciate being spied on."

"Whoa, slow down. BJ never turned the phone off, and I can't say I'm sorry to have a real-time glimpse into my son's pain. Should I come back and talk to him?"

"No, not tonight. He got a lot out, but he's drained. Talk to him later. Or speak to him and lessen his fears without him knowing you heard everything. It might be better. But that's just my opinion."

Esther gave her two cents. "And mine."

"Two opinions I value." He lifted Esther's hand and rubbed it against his cheek.

"I've never heard my son speak of hate," he said to Mother Reed.

"That's why Mother keeps her curses for the enemy. Hurt and anger has called forth the spirit of hate in that child. In a young body, hate can fill it so full, it can come bursting out at the seams. Then the child begins to act out. The overflow can cause tantrums and bullying. Nobody likes or wants to be around a bully. So, now, 'dere's the emotional damage to self-esteem and self-worth."

"Did we catch it in time?" Briggs asked, his shoulders tense.

"I 'lieve so. We need love to serve hate eviction papers." Esther leaned over and stroked Briggs's shoulder until the tension eased as they listened. "Precious Lord, let love serve a warrant for hurt and pain to appear in the court of forgiveness. I think that your Love Fest idea is right on time. BJ is just one child of many who is hurting. We can't keep letting the streets claim them as family, when they have perfectly good ones in the Kingdom."

"Thank you, Mother. God directed our steps for him to be with you tonight."

"Well, I appreciate that. I can't fix everything, but this here delicious cake is a temporary fix for a young boy with a sweet tooth. Y'all have a good time tonight. This child is already smiling and on to the next thing. Give him time, but now that you know . . ."

Briggs and Esther both called out good-bye.

Briggs looked over at Esther, *really* looked this time. Her face shined with compassion, and she was right there with him during the phone conversation, present in the moment.

My Mo' Betta.

Chapter Twenty-nine

Esther's left foot skated over what felt like a pebble and she was soon falling over her right foot. Large hands tightened around her waist bringing her back on balance. Well, as much balance as could be expected when one was walking and couldn't see a thing.

"I got you."

Esther waved her hand in front of her. "That was a forty-five minute ride, Briggs. And twenty minutes in a blindfold? Really?"

It hadn't seemed like forty-five minutes. They'd discussed BJ and her children, declaring once they got out of the car it would be all about them. But now, she was stumbling in her stiletto shoes. She knew he said dress comfortable, but the heels made her legs look amazing in her designer jeans.

There was a "please be patient" squeeze around her waist when she heard a door open, and then the faint strains of a saxophone playing an instrumental version of LTD's "Love Ballad."

Slowly her blindfold was untied, and she stood before the wall-size window in Toledo's Zoo Aquarium. There was a table set for two with place settings and a centerpiece, cushioned high-backed chairs, and a heater blowing warm air throughout the alcove. When she looked around, there were other heaters sitting in strategic areas on the parameters of the room, and in a corner on a rectangular table sat covered dishes sitting on assorted

warming trays. Somehow, the ceiling had been illuminated with twinkling stars and a clear crescent moon. It
was too magical for words, only deeds.

Esther turned, and with glistening eyes, she gave
Briggs a kiss that had her dizzy with pleasure; parting,
they rubbed their cheeks together and sighed as one.

Briggs took her hand in his, swaying to the music as
his hand on her waist directed her around the room. She
closed her eyes and inhaled his special brand of cologne.
And she knew years from now, this memory would still be
entwined with that smell. When he spun her, she didn't
even open her eyes, she just went with the flow.

Esther wanted to ask her Heavenly Father to stop
time—right now—right away. Just let everything sit and
simmer in this perfect moment.

"We should eat now," Briggs said in a hushed tone.

Esther strained to hear him, but she didn't mind; his
soft-spoken timbre fit the mood.

She moved to the chair and sat after he pulled it out
and gently guided her into the seat. She felt so good and
was tingling right down to her sanctified toes. Her head
rested against the high back of the chair, and the thick
cushion she sat on spoke of lush extravagance. She waited
as Briggs brought her a plate he removed from a warming
tray in the corner.

Esther accepted the plate and looked down in appreciation. "You surprise me, you know."

Briggs sat across from her and pulled his napkin off his
place setting. Shaking it loose and placing it in his lap,
he held out his hand. Esther placed hers in his, and he
bowed his head and gave the blessing.

"I'm not sure why you're surprised," he said after saying grace. "The right kind of incentive can make any man
be a man of many talents. And you are my inspiration."

She smiled demurely and self-consciously took her first bite of her crab cake. "Yum! So tasty." Looking around, she patted her mouth with her cloth napkin. "I didn't know you could rent something like this."

Briggs put his napkin over his mouth when he coughed. "Well . . . You can't necessarily *rent* it. You can kind of, if you know the right people . . . *borrow* it for an hour or two."

Esther looked at Briggs with new eyes. "Resourceful, are you?"

Briggs's tongue-in-cheek grin was one of devilish delight. "I can make a little bit of something happen when I need to."

Esther took another fork full of food. The strands of "Always and Forever" filled the air and she rose, holding out her hand. "May I please have this dance?"

Briggs placed his hand in hers. "I would love to dance with you." He spun her around, dipped her, and then pulled her into his chest. "But I lead."

Swaying in his arms, she said, "Show off."

Briggs did an intricate move that Esther couldn't believe she could follow. She was an okay dancer, but Lawton had been the fancy foot worker in their household. Esther remembered that when she was in college she was pretty good, but unless someone wanted her to break out into the worm or the cabbage patch, her limited skills were rusty, at best.

Briggs rolled her out of his arms, and then pulled her back. "You're a good dancer," he said.

Esther lay her head on his chest and breathed in. "Not usually. But you are so smooth that I'm trying to rack my brain to see if you used to have these moves back in the day. Wouldn't I have remembered?"

The song switched into "Lost without You" by Robin Thicke, the only new song Briggs had on his playlist.

Briggs segued them into a cha-cha move, and then had her moving along in rhythm to the upbeat tempo.

"I love this song." She did a little dip with her next volley of cha-cha moves. "Ha, I got this!"

Briggs laughed and spun her again. "You asked me if I always danced like this. The answer is no. During my wilder years, I had a fling with a dancer. So these moves are courtesy of her."

Esther stopped to think how she would answer that. Yes, she felt the sting of jealousy. But it wasn't a big deal. "Well, give me her address 'cause baby girl has a thank-you card coming," Esther said as she moved to the rhythm.

The dust from sulfur ash floated in the air. Imps scampered. Some yipping and yapping, tearing at their tuffs of hair on top of their elongated snouts. The lot was in panic mode. In the center of it all were Imp One and Imp Two.

"Did you see that? The sweet kisses, the longing looks—you are so done for!" Imp Two said as he shook Imp One in terror. "I do not want to move up and take your place. You must fix this."

Imp One stared vacantly out into space.

Imp Two sneered at Imp One's catatonic state. He used the scales on his belly to rapidly push backward, and then jackknifed himself forward, knocking Imp One on his backside, and landing heavily on top of his head.

"Ouch! You dare? I am number one!" Imp One said holding his snout.

"You are history, that's what your sad tail is. You are next week's ash for some poor sap making soap in the old country," Imp Two hissed, as he reared his head back and shouted, "Fire!"

"Fire . . . fire . . . fire," the other imps echoed with tears and jeers.

Imp One hung his head. "I didn't want this job." He attempted to plead his case to the other imps who backed away from him in a solid wall of pity and fear. "The plan was sound. All of you said so. Who wouldn't break their date to go check on their spoiled kid?"

Imp Two's elongated tail snapped around and smacked Imp One upside his head. "How you gon' plan something around that little holy gal? That old lady been casting us out, rebuking us, and pulling us down as long as she has been on this earth."

Imp Two looked around making sure he was not overheard. "I was told that as a child, she saw visions and spoke authoritatively before she even knew Him whose name cannot be spoken."

Imp One's body's tremors shook the ground they stood on. "Foolish talk. I will not believe that I cannot beat her. I remember when her first husband would punch her with the front window shade up. Neighbors saw, but they never intervened."

He then hissed out his pleasure, "Humans at their best."

"That is because Master knew she would be a formidable ally for the Kingdom. He sent opposition early, but she could not be stopped. Her appointment with her purpose could only be delayed. Now, we are reeling from her meddlesome interventions. You watch, that boy BJ got a mark of divinity on him. This is a mess!"

Imp One paced back and forth, slime trailing in his wake.

Imp Two wailed into the air.

Spooked, Imp One glided away. "What is wrong with you . . . u . . . u?" he rattled.

Imp Two inched close to Imp One and slithered up one side of his body. "It is a small thingggg. I am mourning your death."

"Sss . . . sss," Imp One said, then gave a head butt to Imp Two. When he slid to the ground, Imp One pounded him until tendrils of smoke wafted into the atmosphere.

The cackle and screeches of the other imps was severe. But Imp One slid past them without fanfare. He was going back to the drawing board. And if a sacrifice had to be made for mistakes, Imp Two volunteering his carcass was much appreciated.

Chapter Thirty

He was Dorothy without the ruby shoes, clicking his heels and thankful for home.

The two-level house stretched around the corner. It was white brick and the winding drive to the front door was the yellow brick road to the Emerald City. Roger felt like Prophet was the Wizard of Oz, and he was leading him back to Auntie Em and Uncle Henry. Except it had been a long time since he had anyone waiting on him to return from anywhere.

He knew he could never afford a place like this; he might get caught up again trying to. It was quicksand, and he had to get out as soon as he could. It would be just his luck that the wicked witch and her flying monkeys were waiting to be cued into this scene.

The most I had hoped for was three squares, a cot, and a roof over my head.

Roger was in awe. He hadn't imagined anything like this. Prophet was living larger than any of them realized. The ornate door swung open and a middle-aged woman stepped out on the porch. She was attractive in an understated way, but her significant feature was the look of total adoration she wore for his boy.

She waved as though she had not seen the man in months, even though Roger was sure Prophet had told him earlier he had come to the prison directly from home.

"Joshua, hey, honey. Welcome, welcome," she said, as she ran down the steps clapping her hands in glee.

Roger blinked. Was she for real? He turned to share a "your girl is tripping" smile with Prophet and stopped mid-smirk.

Prophet waved back at her with a besotted grin on his face, and Roger looked on in mystified wonder. This look, on this man, was alien to anything he knew about the man who had led him to Christ. That dude was slow to anger, but also slow to smile. He was the solid, monk type, not this simpering love-struck impostor.

Roger couldn't hold his tongue about this transformation. He covered his mouth and spit out a mocking laugh. "Prophet! Dude, this you?"

The sudden chill in the air had nothing to do with the weather. Roger wanted to call the attitude, if not the words, back. He couldn't afford to bite the only hand that was poised to feed him.

Buying time, Roger stammered, "Uh, yeah—" as his brain worked overtime, trying to think of anything he could say to minimize the effects of what he'd just done.

"No, don't speak," Prophet said. The car door locks he had just popped up now eerily clicked down.

Roger swallowed. An angry Prophet was never good.

Prophet kept staring ahead. "That is the lady in my life. The last, and the most important. When she looks at me, she sees her earthly king, and it makes me walk as though I am who she sees me as."

Roger looked over at the woman standing on the steps waiting for them to exit the car. Her face had a questioning look, but she didn't ask. It was like she trusted Prophet to the point where she would stand right there until he let her know what was going on. And then whatever he chose to do, they would do.

"Prophet, man, I apologize. I wasn't thinking. She looks like the perfect woman for you." Roger didn't see any softening of Prophet's features, and the fear in his chest was hammering out a litany of prayers that he hadn't just lost the roof over his head. He needed to repair this. "Listen, it wasn't her that had my attention, but your response to her. Dude, I have never seen such a look of devotion on anyone's face, especially not you. I mean, it's your 'leading us into prayer' face. It humbled me, and at the same time I felt some envy because I have never had that with anyone but Jesus. I hope that one day someone will look in my heart and call me king. You blessed, man."

Roger saw the rigid line in Prophet's jaw soften, then his neck relaxed, and the hardness of his shoulders rounded out. Had he made amends? "Prophet, she completes you."

Once the corny line left Roger's lips he wanted to pluck it out of the air and stuff it back down his throat. It was too cliché, and Prophet didn't do clichés. He held his breath as he saw shoulders that, a moment ago, were stiff and unyielding, begin to shake. Then he heard a rumble in Prophet's chest, and then a loud guffaw of laughter rang throughout the car.

Prophet banged his hand on the dashboard. "You still crazy. She *completes* me? What y'all do in there all day, watch *Jerry McGuire*?"

Roger woofed his own laughter of relief. "Yeah, man. That movie did come on a lot. All them fools jumping around the cell block, talking 'bout 'show me the money.' Broke as all get-out. My bad."

A small tap on the window alerted Roger that the Mrs. had actually moved from her perch on the walkway. The door locks clicked up, and Roger opened his to get out.

She embraced him, and Roger was shocked at the warmth flowing over him. "Hi, I'm Essie, and I hope you haven't eaten because I have a feast waiting for you."

Roger was surprised at the small sweet voice that greeted him. And he wasn't sure what kind of perfume she was wearing, but it smelled heavenly. He took her soft hand into his. "I'm starving, Ms. Essie. And it would be my honor to escort you inside of this beautiful house." As he tucked her hand under his arm, she took Prophet's arm with her other.

As they entered, Roger was impressed that the three of them were able to walk through the wide doorway abreast of one another. A feeling of safety filled him, and he wanted to shout thanks to a benevolent God. Instead, he looked down at the welcoming face of his benefactor's wife.

"Ms. Essie, you wouldn't happen to sing on the praise and worship team ministry, would you?" Roger said, remembering his vow to sit next to a woman in church who smelled and sang sweet.

Hours later, Roger was in a cottage behind the main house; a jewel of a one-bedroom bungalow. He lay back on the softest bed he could ever remember as he inventoried his new bedroom. He gaped at the gleaming hardwood floors, the large flat-screen TV mounted on the wall, and the personal touch of fresh flowers in a crystal vase that sat on his black walnut nightstand. The fact that he had first passed through a large, airy living room and chef's kitchen gave him pause.

Like a slow rumbling brook, a low wail worked its way through his body, and he wept. He cried for the times he'd had to defend himself, the times he was cold and alone and he felt no one cared. He cried for a God who would lead him away from the great temptation to do harm to those who had harmed him, or to himself. Instead, this God had led him to a person who had seed enough to sow into him.

Roger sat up, wiping his eyes on his sleeve. He shook his head and made his way into the pristine bathroom with granite counters. He grabbed a Kleenex from the tissue box and looked into the mirror.

He needed a haircut, having foregone getting one in prison due to the trouble he had encountered in his last days. He touched the puffiness around his eyes and was glad it wasn't a week before. Puffy eyes would be a sign of weakness, and he wasn't given the leisure of showing soft emotions when he was locked up. He could show anger, hatred, sexual frustration, even lasciviousness 'cause some of them chumps believed in loving the one you're with. But love, compassion, and kindness were frowned on and could get you a target on your back. Roger learned to keep his head down and to not stand out. And if you were blessed, you became invisible.

He had mastered invisible.

Roger's reflection in the mirror picked up the sunken bathtub behind him. He moved as though in a trance and knelt down. He plugged the tub, then from a porcelain jar that sat on the edge, he poured out scented oil. He held his fingers under the force of the water flowing from the gold and silver faucet, then eagerly disrobed and sat in the tub, amazed that his long legs were able to stretch out.

He slipped down under the water and came up in nineteen seventy-five. He no longer saw a luxurious bathroom, but a small tub in an oblong-shaped bathroom, bathed in pink walls and tile.

A feminine hand, splashed water on him. "Hurry up, sleepyhead! Time for school."

A five-year-old Roger splashed back. "Got you, Mommy, got you!"

A beautiful face with rounded cheeks and perfect bow-shaped lips blew him a kiss. "You're my little man. Are you going to be good while I go out of town for a while?"

Wide, slate gray eyes glistened. "I don't want you to go, Mommy. Why can't I go with you?"

"Because you lost too many days from school when you were sick last month. And you need to catch up," she said as she ran the soapy washcloth over his back.

His little lips quivered, and his small face squinted in ire. "I'm not staying!"

A stern masculine voice joined the conversation. "Oh, you're staying, little man, and you're going to stop trying to put a guilt trip on your mother. You got that?"

His small head dropped. "Sorry, Mommy."

Gentle hands pulled his face up, and his brow was tenderly kissed. "That's okay, baby. Two days go really fast. You know Mommy's a nurse to help people. I'll go and take care of Mrs. Burch on her family trip, and then be back."

Roger no longer begged her to stay or to take him. He was quiet. The large man stood ominously over him, watching him like a lion who staked out his prey.

His mother tapped his shoulder. "Come on, honey, you can get out now. The water is getting cold."

Roger folded his arms in defiance and stayed put until his mother pulled him up. She wrapped his small body in a fluffy pink towel and stood him before her, placing kisses all over his face.

She smelled of lavender, and he inhaled deeply, filling his small lungs with her essence. She tweaked his nose and gave him Eskimo kisses. It made him giggle, this joy in being under the protective shelter of her love.

He grabbed hold of her, and his thin arms hugged her as tight as he could.

The man did what he had been doing a lot lately; he stepped between them. "Be a big boy, Roger. Let your mother go. She has somewhere to be and something to do. Just like you do."

He saw his mother take the large calloused hand in hers and tug him back. "He's a baby. He'll grow up soon enough."

The shadowy figure complained, "You baby him too much. And since we're now married, and I adopted him as my own, I have to start teaching him how to be a man."

"A man? He's five years old!" His mother's sweet face was stern in his defense.

"Exactly. Time for him to step up. This world "ain't gon' baby him, that's for sure. He's going to get his pretty tail ate up if he don't man up."

His mother waved the man off. "You're talking nonsense. We've only been married three months. Give him some time to bond with you."

The strong, tall man stooped down and looked at Roger. "Go put on the clothes your mother laid out for you, and I'll drop you at school on the way to Mrs. Burch's house."

Roger ran out of the room, determined not to get yelled at by the big booming voice that was now a constant fixture in their home.

He pouted on his way to school, not answering his mother's questions, ignoring his stepfather's admonishments to stop being a brat. When his mother hugged him good-bye, he didn't hug her back.

Later he regretted not hugging her as hard as he could. It was a regret he carried all these years, and even prayer had not relieved him of the burden.

A reel continued the backward spin in his mind. The color was more vivid, the background more focused.

In his opulent surroundings, the adult Roger splashed water on himself and reached for the large bar of soap sitting in its dish. He rubbed it, and the lavender scent that swirled around him carried a montage of memories that beckoned him once more, back in time.

"Mommy. Mommy," a childish voice rang out from his strong adult vocal cords. Hearing that voice, out of his body, he blinked and fought to control his thoughts.

Roger dipped the washcloth and held it over his face. *Breathe.*

He exhaled to the same place and time. Perhaps God was trying to show him something.

Or the devil.

Water and lavender, triggers to his last recollection of his mother. A faded, tattered whiff of what love smelled like.

That same day, a uniformed officer strolled into his classroom, his face hard, and his voice flat as he called out his name. The kids catcalled and made much of him being escorted out of his classroom by a policeman and his teacher. In his neighborhood, the men in blue weren't a place of safety, but a place to find safety from. Even at his young age he was wary of this cop.

The principal came running down the hall, his nut-brown jowls shaking with anger. "Officer, I asked you to wait while I completed my phone call."

The ruddy-faced policeman ignored him. He flipped open a pad and in robotic affect, read from it. "Roger? Roger Sanders?"

With his hands between his knees and moving from foot to foot, Roger started to shake his head no, until he remembered that was his mother's new last name. Sanders. His head shake changed to a nod. Then remembering his stepfather's training, he squeaked, "Yes, sir."

The officer's eyes glazed over and a sad look rolled across his face before he looked away and gruffly said, "Boy, you need to come with me."

Roger grabbed his teacher's sweater and held on. She patted his narrow back, turning with confusion to the principal.

The principal lifted Roger into his arms. He hugged him and murmured words Roger could not understand.

Finally the police officer had enough. He grabbed Roger out of the principal's arms and stood him on his feet. He knelt down, his ruddy complexion growing redder by the minute. His voice was hoarse as he spoke quickly. "Look, kid, your parents died in a car crash first thing this morning. It is our understanding that only your stepfather—" he glanced at his pad again and corrected himself, "since there was an adoption, your father has relatives. Your uncle is on his way. In the meantime, we have this nice lady who is going to take you with her."

In all of the chaos, Roger never noticed the older woman who stood in the background. She stepped forward and compassionately took his hand. "It will be all right, little one," she said with a lilting Polish accent. "You are one of the lucky ones. Someone is coming for you."

She gave him a smile that showcased a crooked tooth and overbite. Funny, he remembered that, but he wondered if that was why he had never dated anyone who didn't have perfect teeth. The woman was probably being nice, but there was no easy way to deliver such news, and no easier way to haul a child away from everything he had ever known. He never even saw his bedroom again, or the pink-tiled bathroom where happy memories were created.

He sat for hours in the foster care worker's office, dry-eyed. Roger had not cried, because he did not believe. His mother could not be dead. In two days she would come and take him away from these people.

In two days he waited by the door of his foster home. And as he told himself would happen . . . He was taken away.

It was the first time Duncan had found him.

Finally he cried.

Back in the present, Roger stood in the center of his bedroom, a towel wrapped around his middle. No one was behind him waiting to use anything or looking for him to move out of the way. He didn't need to move with eyes behind his head. Therefore, the incessant shaking of his limbs could not be explained, nor the rapid beating of his heart. But he had been told enough times that God did not let you get blindsided; you simply had to be still and listen to what He was saying. Women called it intuition. He knew it was God.

That feeling in the pit of his stomach, the one that said . . . something is coming was raging. *Be anxious for nothing.*

He breathed deeply. Only Wise Will knew his whereabouts. He could plan for the future. Roger pressed down on his shaking thigh. His body needed to cooperate. After all, he was safe . . . wasn't he?

Chapter Thirty-one

Roger sauntered up the hallway of Love Zion Church. His walk was open and free. Using up all the space around it, it was making Joshua walk slightly behind. It spoke loudly, his walk, proclaiming its right to just be.

Their arrival was observed through the glass enclosure of Briggs's reception area, and gave a front-room view to Briggs and Naomi.

"Lord, Lord, we being overrun with the felony population. Is this here Love Zion or Jackson Prison Ministries?" Naomi nervously pushed her glasses up her nose.

Briggs glared. "Naomi, please refrain from those kinds of remarks. We need to set the right example for the membership. This new addition to our flock is going to take some finesse."

"I can tell you right now that this gon' be equal to the parting of the Red Sea. Humph, tomorrow, you better bring the Sermon on the Mount. I can bet you that it's going to be like the Philistines turning on Jesus up in here. You just wait—"

Briggs cut her off, ignoring her injured look. "Enough, you've gotten your point across. Now, I'm going to need you to be on one accord with me and give this man the chance he deserves."

"Well, I don't know nothing about him deserving anything. But I can tell you that Esther, 'Put a Ring on It', ain't going to be happy. Uh-uh."

Naomi then smoothly turned her chair just as the door opened and Roger and Joshua entered. "Hello, welcome to Love Zion Ministries." Naomi then turned to Briggs. "Pastor Briggs, would you like me to bring you and your guests something to drink?"

Briggs looked at Naomi and knew that they were going to have to have a way overdue, very long conversation. She had been with Reverend Gregory for eight years, and Briggs had kept her on because she knew a lot about the intimate details of running the church. Naomi even knew when the furnace needed servicing, and the last time the trustees had voted on a new deacon. But her attitude could be over the top, and the way she was able to smoothly transition to a face full of false niceties disturbed him.

"Fellows?" Briggs asked turning to Roger and Joshua.

Joshua looked at Roger who shook his head. "How about two bottled waters with ice, please?"

Naomi's smile froze. Briggs swiped his hand over his mouth to hide his grin; ice meant a walk down to the kitchen.

"Well, I'll be right back then." Naomi stood to leave with an apparent attitude.

Roger looked back and forth between Briggs and Joshua's silent communication. "Oh no, really, I'm fine." It was apparent Roger didn't want to be a bother.

Naomi blustered, then crossed her arms. "I'm going to need y'all to make a decision and stick to it. I can't be jumping up and down like a Jane-in-the-Box. I got other things I can be doing. There's some bottled water in the little refrigerator in Pastor's office. Drink that up, and y'all be good."

Briggs shook his head. "Naomi, our guest requested ice. Please, I need you to be nice and get that ice."

"All right, Pastor, but you don't need to be going rapper on me and rhyming and everything. It just ain"t necessary. How many cubes you want Deacon Joshua?"

Joshua was obviously enjoying the exchange. "Three, no, make that four. Oh, wait. I'll change that to crushed, half a cup."

Naomi clenched her hands and stormed out of the room, and all three men watched her march down the hallway.

Briggs led them into his office, directed them to sit, and then Briggs and Joshua high-fived it while laughing.

"Did I miss something?" Roger asked, his forehead creased in puzzlement.

Joshua held up his hand to Briggs. "Let me explain it to him."

Briggs tilted back in his large leather chair. "Have at it."

"Sister Naomi is a character straight out of the sitcom, *In Living Color*. You know the gossip that sits on the stoop and talks about everyone, and then proclaims, 'you didn't hear that from me.' Man, she even names people. Calls me Prison Prophet."

Briggs's chair tilted straight up. "You know about that?"

Joshua laughed. "Everybody knows about that. She's been doing that as long as I've been here. And according to my mother, it dates back before that. Reverend Gregory used to keep her on a tight leash. But I couldn't hold it that tight when I was the interim here. I kept giving her days off with pay just to have some peace. I think her names for people got worse just so she could get time off."

Both Briggs and Roger whooped at that admission.

Joshua looked sheepish at this disclosure. "We need to talk now before she gets back."

"I will say this on her behalf, she won't tell the general membership what she hears, just the deacons. And even then, she only tells the old-timers like Deacon Clement. She may tease him with those made-up names, but she loves that man. She told me once he reminded her of a relative."

"Women, you can't ever figure them out. Take my ex—" Roger said warming to the men talk.

Briggs's body stiffened. His stare cold. "Let's not," he said out. "Esther will not be the subject in a conversation between you and me. To be frank, she doesn't want you here, and I'm in the business of giving her what she wants. If Joshua had not convinced me you were a changed man, this little meeting would be going very different."

Roger studied Briggs. He opened his mouth, and then shut it. Briggs stared back, daring him to get bad.

Joshua jumped into the conversation. "Pastor, we didn't come here for this, and I thought we had dealt with this issue."

Briggs continued to lock stares with Roger. His answer to Joshua a clear message for Esther's ex. "And we have. Unless he puts Esther's name in his mouth. Then all bets are off. We understand each other?"

Roger crossed his legs. Unhurried, he leaned back and folded his arms, his body language screaming Briggs was not worrying him. "We good. But you telling me not to say it won't take away from the fact that she was once my wife and all that that privilege entails."

Joshua leaped up, his chair clattering to the floor. "Gentlemen, I thought we were going to have a civilized, intelligent, friendly conversation. Instead, I feel like I've walked into a pissing contest, and I'm the only one who knows that the wind is blowing and you both about to come out smelling foul. Can we *not* do this?"

Briggs didn't know how they had gotten so far from the congenial beginning they had; he was not supposed to have his buttons pushed so easily.

"Let's talk." Briggs moved over and picked up the chair. He motioned for Joshua to take his seat.

Gradually, Joshua sat down and glanced at Briggs, then Roger before he nodded and continued. "As you are aware, I have been financially supporting the church's prison ministry, which includes our support of the families they have left behind. I want to place Roger over the ministries outreach."

Briggs's entire body tensed. His shoulders were held back, his chest heaving as he said in a voice filled with disbelief, "You want to place a recently released felon into this type of position and responsibilities? We have young women and youth in that ministry looking for direction. Looking for hope."

Roger placed his hands on his knees. His voice urgent, pleading for a chance. "I can give them that hope. I can provide answers to what goes on behind those bars. I want to work with these families and help them stay connected to those inside." He rose, leaning over the cherry wood desk, right in Briggs's personal space. "Those who stay connected to family, who are sent letters, visited, and provided with love and affection—they are the ones who are most likely to not return. It's that connection that helps them know there is a different life waiting on the outside."

Moving back slightly, Briggs listened, intent on not just what Roger said, but the passion he displayed when he spoke.

Roger continued, this time standing and walking around the room. "All I had was Prophet constantly reminding me that the world outside those bars was better and that I could get a piece of it. Live differently, change my life for the better. That's what let me know that I can do that for someone else, someone who doesn't have anyone."

Briggs's head dropped. "You don't have any family?"

Roger hesitated before answering, "None that matter."

Briggs was facing a door of indecision. He knew he had promised Joshua that Roger wouldn't be bothered. But he didn't know that he wanted the man to literally take an official position at the church. How was this going to look? How was he going to explain to Esther that he not only told Joshua he wouldn't interfere, but that he was also letting the man work for Love Zion? It didn't matter who was paying him, what mattered was the fact that he would be representing the church.

His chair swiveled in Joshua's direction. "Your mother know about this?"

Joshua grinned. "I never had the benefit of asking my mother for permission. However, we are going over there next."

"I want to do what God would have me do," Briggs said, though there was still uncertainty in his tone. "This reminds me, Joshua, of our earlier conversation, where you spoke about the prejudices you encountered when you first got out. I can better see both sides of this dilemma now."

"If it helps any, I understand your hesitation," Roger said, "but I only want to make better decisions and help others do the same. My past choices crippled my future. Although I may be challenged I'm not giving up."

Briggs stretched his neck, rounded his shoulders, and blinked as though he was clearing his mind. "I remember watching a pastor on television, I can't remember his name, but I remember his message. The pastor spoke of a church being in an uproar about a woman who had once been a prostitute wanting to be in ministry. The good folk of the church didn't want her to be in leadership so they called a meeting. Everyone came. They each spoke of all the reasons her past should stop her."

Joshua raised his hand and waved it, "You know I've been there."

Briggs nodded and continued. "The pastor searched the crowd and noticed that the ninety-year-old mother of the church had not spoken. 'What do you say?' he asked her. The mother asked, 'Is she saved?' the pastor, deacon board, and church reluctantly murmured, 'Yes.' The mother then said, 'Then it appears to me that it is not this woman who is on trial, but the blood of Jesus."

Briggs looked at Joshua who was standing and giving thanks. He then turned to Roger who was on his knees worshiping. "I want to take it slow. Initially, there will be no home visits or any kind of family visits outside the church. You will be provided an office at the end of this corridor, and your door will be kept open during all family member meetings. One of the sister's from the outreach ministry will be at all meetings with female members. Joshua will be at all others. After we see how this works out, we can then move forward from there. You're welcome to visit the prison, of course."

Joshua and Roger both stood as Naomi returned with a tray bearing crushed ice and three glasses.

Briggs motioned her to place the tray on his desk. "Thank you, Naomi, but we're finished with our meeting."

She slammed the tray down on the desk. "Oh, no, y'all ain't. Y'all going to open that water, pour it into them glasses with one quarter crushed ice at the bottom, and drink up. Oh yes, you are!" she said tapping her foot. "I don' walked all the way down there. The ice machine was broke, had to crush them cubes with a blender, then put everything back like I found it. And they talking about they finished?" She placed a glass in front of each man. "Not . . . happening. Just like a bunch of men. Rude, plain ole downright rude."

She then grabbed the bottled water herself and poured into each glass. "Drink up!"

Naomi fussed all the way back to her desk. Behind her Roger, Joshua, and Briggs obediently gulped down the ice-cold water without a word.

Chapter Thirty-two

Zadkiel stood on Mother Reed's porch. First impressions could stay with a person long after amends had been made. He was praying that the God in Mother Reed would lead before the mother in her took over. The imminent arrival of Joshua to reintroduce Roger needed a soft touch, lest it go south real fast. Mother loved her some Esther, and when somebody hurt Mama's baby, it was his angelic observation that even the female humans could be downright vicious concerning their offspring. He sometimes wondered what that felt like, this amazing gift God gave His children. It would be unseemly for him to be envious, but there were times he wondered why the angels weren't given His greatest gift—to be able to reproduce in their own image.

What would a miniature Zadkiel be like?

Hearing the soft purr of a luxury engine, Zadkiel noted that Joshua had arrived. It was time for him to send calming thoughts throughout the house and just maybe they would all survive.

Roger didn't think he was ready for this. He sat in the car long after Joshua got out and waited on the sidewalk for him.

He remembered Mother Reed as a powerful woman of God; he used to quake in her presence when she would focus her keen eyes on him and give him the eagle eye.

That's what he secretly called her, Eagle Eye. She seemed to see beyond your words and penetrate your thoughts. Back then, he would be in the street whoring and come home the next morning to Mother Reed sitting in his living room sipping tea with Esther. He would stumble in and pretend he had been at the garage all night fixing cars. She would just stare at him—no, stare *through* him, then fold her napkin in her lap and tell Esther she had to be going.

It scared the heebie-jeebies out of him. Till this day she never approached him.

When she saw him after he had beat Esther, she simply pointed at him and walked away. He would have rather had Esther's gangster cousin, Tony, beat him down than have that spooky finger pointed at him. When he thought about that finger, he wondered if that was the beginning of everything turning wrong in his life.

"You coming, man? She's eighty-eight years old, son. She can't whip you."

Joshua paced, glancing at his watch. Roger got out and heard the beeping of the car being locked. It sounded like the bell ringing for his first round.

And in this corner, weighing one hundred ninety pounds, shaking like a leaf, Roger, the wimp.

Joshua climbed the stairs, and Roger wanted to ask him what the rush was when a small head appeared in the door.

Her bright smile dimmed when she saw who her son was bringing to her home.

With her hand on her hip, Mother Reed stepped back. "Boy, hav' you gon' and lost your ever-lovin' mind?"

Joshua flinched. "No, ma'am," he said, and stepped into the house, Roger bringing up the rear.

She stood straight in the way of Roger stepping inside. She crooked her finger for Joshua to come closer. "You don' made a mess you can't clean up 'cause I see you don' stepped in it this time!"

Joshua looked perplexed. "Mama?"

Roger could see Joshua was surprised. He wasn't. Roger knew this was the Mother Reed who despised him.

"You can't mean this." Joshua looked back and forth between the two, a look of apology on his face for Roger.

Mother Reed shook her head, sorrow etched in the crevasses of her face. "You know I loves you, son. I loves you like a fat girl loves biscuits and gravy. But I'm gonna go postal on you if you don' get that boy off my property."

Joshua stepped back onto the porch and turned to Roger. "It looks like I'm going to need a little one-on-one with my mama. Why don't you wait in the car? I'll be with you in a sec."

He handed Roger the keys. Roger nodded, pocketing the keys as he backed away, afraid to turn his back on Mother Reed. He prayed she didn't point that finger at him again. Instead, she scowled at him and mumbled to herself.

When he got in the car, he cracked the window and hoped that they would have their conversation on the porch. He needed to know what he was up against.

Roger's prayers were answered when Joshua turned to his mother, never leaving the porch. In a no-nonsense tone he spoke through the screen. "That was rude."

Roger could see Mother Reed huffing. "Sho' was, you bringing that boy to my house. Wat's wrong with ya?"

Sounding exasperated Joshua held out his hands. "No, Mama, that was rude of you. How come you don't trust me?"

She laid her palm against the screen. "Oh, I trust you. But I ain't putting that demon in my house. My Word said, if you see the devil you 'posed to flee."

Roger saw Joshua rub the back of his head. "But—"

Mother Reed opened the door so Joshua could see her eyes. "But I'm too old to be running away, so I just make sure he ain't welcome where I abide. That boy beat my Esther. Treated her like the dirt that was under the shoes she bought him. Talked about her so bad until she finally joined him and she started talking about herself. Now you want me to feed him tea and crumpets?"

Joshua's clasped hands gestured in earnest. "Mama, as a Christian—"

"'Cuse me for cutting you off. But people think 'cause we saved we gotta let the world walk over us. You see a doormat on my back, a sign that say kick me? Uh-uh-uh! No siree. Cast that silliness right outta your head. And get that boy from in front of my house 'cause trash pickup ain't till next Monday."

Mother Reed slammed the door in Joshua's face. Roger saw him stand there, his back to him, with his hands in his pockets. When he turned there was still a shocked look on his face.

Roger slowly rolled the cracked window up.

Strike one.

Chapter Thirty-three

Monica sat at the bar in the trendy restaurant. She was morose, her head low as she sipped her drink. She had been at Briggs's house for over a week, and she hadn't made any progress with seducing him. Manipulation, her greatest weapon, was failing her. He was polite, treating her like a sister. She didn't want to be his sister, she wanted him to remember her as the woman he knocked boots with and did the horizontal tango. The woman who could work him like he stole something. Instead, he was stealing her confidence.

In an attempt to regroup, she had asked if he minded watching Fiona while she went out.

When he said he didn't mind in an offhand manner and handed her some money, not even asking where she was headed, she stormed out.

Monica really had to find a better plan. Just what did Esther have that she didn't? On the pro *and* con side, she had Esther beat. First, she was better looking. Yes, Esther was pretty, but Monica had been a supermodel, for goodness' sake. One point, Monica. Her dark chocolate skin was smooth, blemish free, and like velvet. Esther was light-skinned, caramel, if Monica was feeling generous. But chocolate was in. So, two points for Monica. Her figure was slim, but alluring. If she walked up the street you could hear the strands of the Commodores playing to the sway of her hips. Esther wasn't exactly fat, but she was a curvy girl. And if you heard the Barney song when she stepped in a room? Well, it wouldn't be a stretch. Three points, Monica. Esther's hair was a short pixie cut. Monica's was luxurious and flowed down her back like a black waterfall. Monica was the River Niger, strong, vivacious, and deep. Esther was vanilla ice cream, with no topping. Monica was a slam dunk, all the way net—swoosh, a three-pointer at every turn. Yet, Esther had the MVP award, and she wasn't even in play.

Monica swished the ice cubes in her drink around with her finger.

Why isn't Briggs falling back into my arms?

Monica smoothed her fingers along her neck, tracing her scar. Her self-assurance wavered, and she wondered if she was marred by the attack. Was she no longer attractive? Usually by now, three or four fools would be up trying to buy her a drink.

She looked around, pausing at the mirror behind the bar. It was then she noticed a man with honey-dipped skin and close cropped hair that almost resembled baldness. He caught her checking him out, and his smile was wide with beautiful white teeth. He was attractive enough that several passing women slowed up to see if they could catch his eye. Instead, he began a wide-legged walk over to her, providing her with an unobstructed picture of his chiseled form.

She adjusted the scarf around her neck ensuring her scarlet letter stayed hidden. That's what she had begun to see her scar as, a reminder of her sins, a physical status symbol of her home-wrecker position. God's stamp of disapproval.

She watched him come closer. There was something in his walk.

"Hello, beautiful lady. Mind if I sit here while I wait on my table to be ready?"

Monica checked out his clothes. They were well-cut, expensive. The suit was like a milk ad, it did his body good. He was tight in all the right places. She looked at his shoes 'cause every woman knows what the shoes tell her.

"Sure, have a seat. I'm waiting on my table too."

She glanced down, then up and twirled the straw in her glass.

He propped himself on the bar stool, motioning to the bartender. "Can I get you another of what you're drinking?"

"It's just ginger ale," she said.

"You're not much of a drinker?" he said, lifting his glass and signaling the bartender to give him another drink.

Monica gave a slight smirk. "I used to be. Could drink all night and not get sloppy drunk. Could probably drink you under the table if I had a mind to."

He was curious in his response. "So, that's a skill you're bragging on?"

Monica then noticed the intelligence in his keen slate-grey eyes. "Touché. So what are you drinking?"

"Water. I used to have problems with drinking and light recreational drugs. I don't do either any more, I haven't in years." He accepted the water from the bartender and slid him money for the cost of a soda.

His honesty forced her to put her elbow on the bar, her hand on her cheek, and then lean into his words. They were getting comfortable in the easy exchange of their conversation when they were interrupted by the maître d'.

"Madam, your table is ready."

A little disappointed, she reluctantly slid off her stool, pulling her dress back in place.

She then strutted just enough to make the show interesting, before she pivoted and saw that the stranger *was* assessing her. Turning back she followed the maître d'.

In just a few more steps, his presence hovered over her. "Would you mind if I joined you? Keep the stimulating conversation going?"

Gotcha.

Monica remained silent, then they stopped at her table. He held out her chair and waited on her reply. "A beautiful woman like you shouldn't have to eat alone."

"I'm not alone," Monica said as she glided into her seat, her legs crossing. She picked up her napkin, shook it, and placed it in her lap.

He stepped back, moving away. "Oh, well, I wouldn't want to intrude when your guest arrives."

Monica almost giggled. This was fun. "Don't worry about that because I'm dining with you."

He retraced his steps, giving her another glimpse of that confident walk. Next, he sat, commanding the room. She almost gasped when he reached across the table and sweetly placed her swinging hair behind her ear. The move was something Briggs used to do, and she let her wistful sigh escape.

He was a fortune-teller, reading her like yesterday's news. "You wishing I was someone else?"

Monica's eyes widened. "No, wishing I was."

He leaned back and rested his arm over the back of his chair. Silent, he considered her admission. "Tell you what, pretty lady. Tonight, why don't you be whoever you want to be? And I'll do the same."

Monica's face flooded with delight. She loved games, and she especially appreciated this one. Could she for one night be whoever she wanted to be?

"Okay, I like that. Call me Esther."

The gentleman's eyes shot up. "Like the Bible?"

"Yes. I'm sure not talking about Aunt Esther, from *Sanford and Son*. Why? Don't I look like I could be biblical?"

He placed his hand on his heart. "Well, the first time I saw you I said, 'Jesus!'"

Monica covered her mouth when she burst out laughing. "You're funny."

"And you have the prettiest smile. It was absent when I first noticed you. Don't lose it again. Now who should I be?"

Monica swirled her napkin in the air, as though it could make wishes come true. "Who do you want to be?"

"Since Esther was a queen, how about you call me King?" he grinned.

"Oh, you want to be royal?"

"Wasn't it Esther who prepared for a year to spend just one night with the king?" He placed both his elbows on the table and folded his hands as though they were in high-level negotiations.

Monica stalled while she thought through if he could be her king, if even for one night. "You know your Bible?"

"I'm no scholar, but I know a few things," he said.

Monica gave a seductive grin. "Okay . . . King."

They sat, feeling an electric current of awareness flowing between them. The evening evolved into hand holding and a tender caress along Monica's arm gave her the shivers. King listened as though her opinion mattered, and she responded to his ardent attention. She felt that she had been in a drought and he was satisfying her like a tall glass of cool water.

She needed this. She didn't talk about her life after Briggs. It wasn't what people thought. Randall's ex- was so intent on destroying him that their life together had ceased to exist. Everything was lawyers, court, get attacked and counterattack. Randall's friends deserted him, and his business associates snubbed him. He was withdrawing from her.

She got scared, panicked that he might leave her. And she did what she had done in the past. Told a man who was going to leave her that she was pregnant. Only this time it was true, because she stopped taking precautions. She had given up her marriage and lost the closeness to her son. She was determined Randall was not leaving her. So he stayed, but ended up leaving her anyway. His death a reminder to her that she could not cheat fate.

But tonight she was the golden Esther. And queens were loved and revered, and kings controlled their kingdoms. This was heaven.

Time flew, and the lingering they did at the table had to end. The restaurant was closing. They now stood out front.

"Let me have your valet ticket and I'll have them bring your car around," King said, hand stretched out.

Monica waved her cell phone in the air. "Didn't drive. I'm calling a taxi."

King took her phone out of her hand. "I'll take you home."

He gave the valet his ticket, and they waited for his car to pull up. In the meantime, they continued the easy flow of the conversation they'd had inside until a luxury SUV cruised to the curb.

"Nice," Monica pulled her coat collar closer.

He reached over and opened the car door, ushering her inside. "Thanks. Where can I take you?"

Monica didn't say anything, and they sat, King waiting on her to give him directions. She fingered her scarlet letter and touched the scar under the scarf. *Sometimes you played what was dealt,* she thought. "Your place."

He hesitated. "You sure?"

She turned from him and looked out into the night. Stars twinkled, the moon was bright, and the sky clear. She closed her eyes and opened her imagination.

Just for one night. A night with the king.

The neighborhood was affluent. Monica didn't know his occupation, it was not a part of the game of them being other people. She hadn't learned what he did, however, she did learn who he was. She'd discovered over the years, the latter knowledge was better.

The white gleaming brick house sprawled the corner lot. The front door was wide and impressive with engraved cherry doors and beveled glass windows. *The king's castle.*

They drove down a winding drive that ended in the back. There was a fairy-tale cottage attached to the rest of the house. And a four-car garage door went up as they smoothly pulled inside. They pulled next to another brand-new luxury car and her spidery senses tingled.

"You don't have a wife to go with that other car, do you?" Monica's hand hesitated on the door handle.

King got out and came around to her door. He opened it and attentively pulled her out. "No, I promise there is no one in that house that cares that you and I are together."

Monica's smile was shaky with relief. "Good."

He placed his arm around her and held her from going forward. "But I do have houseguests. We can go inside or stay back here in the cottage. I just want you to be comfortable."

Monica considered her options. She made her decision based on her wanting as few people as possible to know she was having a one-night stand. "Your cottage is fine."

It did not go unnoticed by her that he seemed relieved. But, she reasoned that maybe he had as much aversion to having their one-night discovered as her.

He unlocked the door, and she crossed over into what must have been a miniature window into the splendor of his main home.

Running his hand around her shoulder, he slipped the purse from it and threw it on the table. He then untied the scarf, but before he could remove it, her hand caught his and halted his progress.

"No, the scarf stays," she said.

He shook his head and brought her hand to his lips, taking one of her fingers into his mouth, he suckled. He smiled at her intake of breath. "Baby, everything goes."

King sank with her onto the plush couch. Through her dress he ran his fingers back and forth across her back, slow. He traced circles and figure eights that caused her heart to move in synchronization with his fingers.

He worked his way back up to her neck and pulled the scarf loose. Monica opened her mouth to tell him about her scar; instead, her head fell back when he exposed it and drew his tongue along its ridge.

"Everything," he whispered.

The feelings that fanned over her were like a wave of ambrosia. She should stop. She shouldn't have started. This was a locomotive barreling down the track, and if she tried to pull up now she would crash.

Forget this. Monica flipped him over on the wide couch and climbed onto his lap. She grabbed his ears and ground her mouth into his. He pulled at her clothes, and she reciprocated and pulled at his. They were lustful animals, and she was sure one of them growled. Dazed, she looked down at their clothes scattered across the floor as he encircled her body. He was relentless in his pursuit, and driving her insane in the process. She had stopped thinking minutes ago, and now her eyes rolled back into her head at the height of his frenzied kisses.

Standing, he scooped her up and placed her on her feet, all the while smothering her with his affection, leading her into the bedroom, kiss by kiss, step by aching step.

Monica was going blind from the ecstasy rolling through her body. *How is he doing this?*

They staggered across the threshold, entwined in flames of desire. She fell backward into a cloud of cushiony softness that enveloped her as King hovered looking down at her descent.

"Who are you?" Monica asked with wonder.

"Your . . . king," he said, and then he bent and kissed her so deeply that she felt she was surely dying.

"Are you sure?" he said, his voice husky with need.

Monica took his face in her hands, peering into his soul. "No. But I'm still here."

King rolled over and stretched his hand into his nightstand drawer. He held up a condom, like a sought-after prize. "A king protects his lady."

Monica placed her hand over his, her eyes flickering with hesitation. The condom made her choice real. This was no accident. Her breath shallow, she let go of his hand. "If all we have is tonight, let's make it last. Make it blot out all the ugly things and horrible nights that have plagued us."

He tenderly kissed her, running his hands through her cloud of silky hair. He massaged her scalp until her legs felt like jelly. It was her newest happy zone. He turned her around, trailing kisses down her back, and she was done for.

"The lights," she whispered.

Reluctantly, he paused, holding her hand, then he scooted to the end of the bed and extended his arm out, flipping the switch. The room went into total darkness and she purred.

There was nothing left for Monica to do . . . but do. She had already messed up . . . again.

The imps danced across the ceiling, pernicious in their victory stomps. They could always count on Monica to fall into old habits to feel brand-new.

Imp One sat watching Monica and her "King." He liked sitting in the dark; watching. Both humans were closer to him then they had ever been. The sharing of their bodies also meant they were sharing the spirits of everyone they each had ever been intimate with. It was a hodgepodge mixture. He wondered if they knew the more they connected in this way without a holy covenant, the more they diluted their own essence. They were giving themselves away.

It didn't matter, the deed was being done. Imp One reclined. If he was human, popcorn and 3D glasses would be in order. After all, it was a heck of a show.

Monica tiptoed around the room, grabbing up her clothes. It was still dim enough for her to use the dark as a cover for her sins. Inching past it, she looked into the bathroom and stopped. The countertops were granite, the faucets trimmed in eighteen-carat gold. She was hypnotized by the sunken-jetted tub, a guilty pleasure she hadn't had the luxury to indulge in for too long. She slowly pulled open the cabinet, hoping it didn't creak. She was relieved to find it absent of feminine products, but well stocked with toothbrushes, toothpaste, and deodorant. On a counter, she noted the wipes and grabbed a handful. Wiping down, she sneered at her self-loathing thoughts. She knew what kind of bath her sainted Jamaican grandmother would have called this.

Returning to the bedroom, she paused. But she didn't have to worry about disturbing King. He was proving to be a sound sleeper, his snoring loud and consistent.

Opening her purse and pulling out her phone, she gasped. There were three messages, all from Briggs. The first inquired whether she was all right. The next two were increasingly belligerent. Her cell's screen saver flashed four in the morning. She was toast.

I'm grown.

Her grandmother's voice resonated in her ear, a rich mix of patois and English. "De only ting open after four a.m. is legs and de hotel."

Shaking off her self-recriminations, she dialed for a cab using a magazine label to give the address. She was promised it would come in fifteen minutes.

She waited ten, and then slunk around bushes, staying within the shadows of the house. At one point she triggered a motion detector, but the house remained quiet. Her breath evened when she saw the cab approaching.

Her solo ride on the way home was mixed with feelings of satisfaction and embarrassment. She had no idea at the end of the day which would take precedence. She did now understand, though, that it wasn't so bad being Esther.

Chapter Thirty-four

The window's shade was pulled at half-mast. It was an intentional setting, made to prevent the day's sunlight from filtering over her pillow. Monica was hung over, even though she hadn't had a drink. The man she called King had kept her long after she should have been home sleeping in the bed next to Fiona.

When she got home, she had skipped her sinful body into the guest room. She didn't care what Briggs said, she wasn't sleeping next to her children in her present spiritual condition. *What we hate, we do.*

Spreading her body over the bed, she thought back to last night. Whoever King was, he was good. Very good—shoot—boy had her singing at one point. And Monica had a voice like a frog. She didn't hold a note; she croaked it.

She had always considered Randall her number one. Briggs came in second, and the others were just practice to make perfect.

But this King . . . He touched her like her body was braille and he was blind to anything but her.

Monica stretched, wiggled her toes, and released a satisfied grunt. The high thread count of the sheets felt like silk under her body, and she rolled, enjoying the feel of luxury on skin.

A soft tap on the door pulled her from her musings. She frowned. It was the world calling, and the world held problems she didn't want to think about. Not now. Not while she was enjoying replaying her scandalous activities. She sat up and heard in the recesses of her mind: *You should repent.*

Monica pulled her robe tight and clutched her head as though she could strangle her thoughts.

There's time for that later.

Her inner voice was not done, it continued to debate.

Later may never come.

"Monica, are you in there?"

She stood with her back against the door. Briggs's voice irritated her. When she wanted to have a conversation with him, he was either rushing out of the house, or it was a cliff note version of real talk. Now, when she wanted to have some time to herself, he was at her door, talking.

"Of course I'm in here, who else would you be talking to?" she snapped, wanting to hit the door in frustration.

Briggs sounded annoyed as he stressed his words. "Can you please open the door?"

Determined to anger him, she continued speaking through the door. "Are you sure? I'm not dressed. I wouldn't want to embarrass you."

Her time had run out. Briggs was rattling the doorknob. His voice demanding. "Monica!"

Vexed she swung open the door cutting off his next words.

His fist raised to knock again, Briggs stumbled in. They were inches apart, a kiss away. Monica sneered when Briggs stepped back. She wanted to tell him, "Don't nobody want you," but she knew that wasn't true. The best she could do was mug him like a teenager in a high school hallway showdown. It was ineffective, but it made her feel good.

She lifted her hand and studied her fingernails, as though he was of no importance. "What can I do you out of?"

"Do you realize that I agreed to keep Fiona for a couple of hours so you could get out of the house? I even gave you money so you wouldn't spend what little you had left. Now I don't know what time you came in last night, but it was after one in the morning. I know because that's the time I finally went to bed."

Monica turned her hand this way and that, as though the state of her nails was pressing. "And your point is?"

"What? My point is? Are you *joking*?" Briggs's forehead creased with frown lines.

Monica sauntered over to her bed. Her silky gown flowed as she glided to a stop. With bedroom eyes she gazed back at Briggs. She sat on the bed and patted the spot next to her.

Briggs folded his arms. "No, thank you. I'm fine right here."

Monica gave him a sly wink, licking her lips. She scanned her eyes down the length of him ogling as if he was a sweet treat on a candy dish.

Briggs grunted in obvious disgust. "Are you serious? And you wonder why I don't have conversations with you?"

Her hand over her heart, she moved her back and forth to pantomime its beating. "You shouldn't be so good-looking. Make a girl say, oomph!"

Briggs pulled the desk chair near the door and collapsed on it, as though Monica's antics had worn him down. "Lady, you need help." He began ticking off of his fingers as though he were reading to her from an invisible list. "First, I want you to move back into BJ's room and no more late-night carousing. This is a Christian home, and I don't even want to know what you were doing out that late."

"You could ask me, and I might tell you all the juicy details," Monica said and blew him a seductive kiss.

Briggs loosened his tie and cracked his neck.

"I would also like you to attend church this Sunday. Everyone staying in this house attends church."

"Aww, Brigzee want Monnie next to him in the pulpit?" Monica said in a baby voice.

He furrowed his brow, the lines even more pronounced. "No, you will sit in the sanctuary with everyone else. With a dress the appropriate length and your chest decently covered."

"What's the fun in that?" Monica picked at her finger-nails, thought of something, and stopped. "Hey, is my old friend Sister Abigail still at Love Zion? I loved sparring with that old bat. She still getting in everyone's business?"

Briggs ran his hand through his hair. "You know using words like ''old bat' to describe one of our members is unacceptable. Did your time with Randall erase all your sanity?"

"So, I'm a heathen because I speak my truth? You're so predictable, Briggs. Always being right, doing right." She turned her nose up and curled her lip. "Except when you're thinking wrong. How's Esther, Briggs? You still have all those impure thoughts of her running through your head?"

In a soldier's stance, Briggs folded his arms and glared. "When is the last time you spent some time with God, Monica?"

She jumped up and moved swiftly forward. In front of him, she mimicked his stance. "When is the last time you spent some time with the Lord repenting, Briggs? All those lustful, unrequited feelings bottled up inside of you? Boom!" Monica clapped her hands one time loudly. "You gon' explode, sugah. I got the prescription for your ailment, patient." She placed her hands over her chest and panted.

"I'm ignoring you because I can." Briggs opened his wallet and handed her a business card. "I have a friend who is willing to let you look at one of his apartments. It's a nice neighborhood, and for me he's willing to work with you concerning the rent. I'll text you the details later."

Monica took the card, read it, and then tapped it on her hand. "You know, I don't have any money."

"Yes, I know. I'll take care of it. Today's conversation has proven to me that you cannot stay here forever."

Briggs turned to walk away, but slowed when she called out to him.

"Oh, Briggs? Have a nice day," she crowed.

Briggs didn't answer her. A few minutes later she heard the alarm chime when the front door opened and closed.

Monica pulled the shade up. It was time to face her day. Quarreling with Briggs was exhausting and counterproductive. No matter how nice she was to him or how cooperative she tried to be, it wouldn't matter. He wouldn't be her way out.

But she had always been a stubborn woman, stuck on stupid her mother had called her. She would ride this out; she had no other choice. At least for now she had a safe place for her and Fiona to sleep. She planned to check out some high-end retail stores for a job. She was good at that type of thing.

She tilted her face into the morning light. She needed some sun because everything around her right now looked dark.

Chapter Thirty-five

Esther loved a free evening. They didn't come often. David and Ruth were spending time at Phyllis's house with Miracle. They had made a day of it. Two weekends in a row, something for the kids to celebrate.

She needed a day off. She'd had a super busy week. She and Briggs had played phone tag, rarely catching up to each other, and when they did, the calls were rushed.

She could admit it, she missed him. She had allowed the kids to talk her into a night at Phyllis's because she thought she might be with Briggs this evening. She had hoped he would call for a date. He had disappointed her when they did talk, and he shared he had some type of meeting at the church with the deacons. She knew she could at least look forward to seeing him at church in the morning. So she was starting early to get her pretty on.

Esther was going to take a long hot bath, grab her a good book, and put her sore feet up. She thought about Simone and work.

She knew without a doubt that Simone was clogging sinks in their office so that plumber could unclogged the drains. She didn't know how long before the building's supervisor charged her. When that did happen, she had let Simone know, she was deducting it from her paycheck.

Simone gave her a slow wink and proclaimed, "Child, I'll pay it too. I'll just consider it a down payment on my wedding."

She admired Simone in some ways. She went after what she wanted, when she wanted.

Esther had Briggs back in her life, calling on the woman in her. Asking that woman to meet the man in him. On the fringes was Monica running to and fro seeking whom she could devour. And lurking behind all of that was Roger.

She was hoping he didn't make an appearance in town, but she was afraid he would. She would remember to ask Briggs about it when he called, since he told her he'd check in later tonight.

Esther pulled out her favorite foam bath oil and turned her faucets up high. She wanted the bubbles to touch her nose. She was pulling off her socks when her phone rang. The small crystal clock on the shelf over her sink read a little after seven. Her heart sped up. Maybe Briggs got out of his meeting early, and she would get the opportunity to spend the evening with him anyway. It was early enough that they could still go out.

Sitting on the closed commode she answered. "Hello?"

"Uh, Esther? Esther Wiley?"

Esther held her breath, her eyes shining with hope. "Deborah?"

There was a pause. Esther silently urged her on.

"Yes, it's me. My voice changed that much?"

"A little. I'm Esther Redding, now," she said, afraid of saying the wrong thing. Her voice was stilted even to her own ears.

"I always knew you'd finally get your Cinderella ending. You remember that? Dragging me and Sheri down in the freezing cold. Making us go, so you could try on the glass slipper? Fit you too. And they may not have given it to you, but, girl, you wanted it, and you got it. Seven years old, and you knew what you wanted. How'd you do that? Get built that way?"

"I didn't get what I wanted. I didn't want to just fit the slipper, Deborah. I wanted to *be* Cinderella. To be given the tiara and the wand. Have royal subjects and give them my queenly wave. I used to practice that wave in the mirror. It was precise, just so." Realizing Deborah couldn't see her wave, she brought her hand down.

"You're as close to a princess as I've ever seen. It's why Sheri and I always followed you. You had the stuff we wanted and were afraid to get. So we did the next best thing. We rode out our lives on your coattails. Until we dared to get out there on our own and do our own thing. The result of that? Sheri's suicide and my schizophrenia."

Esther squashed down the hurt of Deborah's revelation as she bent over and shut off the faucets. "Is that what happened? You and Sheri felt my triumphs were in the face of your failures?"

Deborah groaned loud and hard. "I can't believe we're having this conversation now, but I guess it's time. None of our problems were about you. It was just easier to deflect our issues on someone else. Why not the golden girl?"

"You know that is some bull, right?" Esther stood in the small room feeling closed in. She was deflating like the bubbles once crowning the top of her tub.

"Several years of therapy later, yeah. But when I left that dorm room, I went on a downward spiral of alcohol, drugs, and sex. Anything to dull the voices, shut out the rage. I tried to go home, but after about a week, I disappeared on my family too. It was too much. They tried to help, but I wouldn't admit I had a problem. To this day my mother is wary of me, and I can't remember doing what they told me I did to place the caution in her eyes."

Barefoot and down to her skimpy camisole and boy cut briefs, Esther left the bathroom and curled up in the wing-back chair in her bedroom. "I'm so sorry, I had no idea. Maybe if I had understood what was happening back then . . ."

"No, you couldn't help me. I resented you. You had it going on. Briggs was the icing on the cake."

Esther felt it was good that Deborah couldn't see her roll her eyes. Jealousy? All these years later, *that's* what it was all about? They felt she had it all, so they couldn't be vulnerable around her? Share their feelings in a no-fault zone?

Deborah continued, "I see you didn't marry Briggs though. Your last name is Redding?"

Is that smugness I detect? Elation that Briggs and I didn't make it?

Esther was now careful in her answers. "Um, yeah. I broke up with Briggs right after you left. We all go through things, Deborah. I've actually been married twice. Once to an abusive man. I divorced him. And another to a really wonderful man, Lawton Redding."

Again, Esther noted some sarcasm in Deborah's response.

"You're his princess, huh?"

Esther reached over to her nightstand and pulled the photograph to her. She then ran her finger down the image of her and Lawton on their wedding day. Nothing but flashing teeth.

"I was. He died two years ago."

Sounding satisfied, Deborah said, "Dang, girl. No happily ever after?"

Esther was beginning to wonder if her and Deborah's season as friends was over. But, Deborah had called, so didn't that indicate she cared? "For a little while. Our two children remind me happily ever after is possible."

Both were quiet. Esther was thinking Deborah might now understand the tough path they both had to navigate. They were both here—now—full circle.

It was a heavy topic for a first conversation. Esther sought to lighten the tone. "So, you still the master at double Dutch jump roping?"

Deborah bayed her laughter. She was always the loud one. "Girl, I would break my neck, and *both* my legs. You saw these hips."

Esther moaned. "You didn't go there, did you? Child, I was a fine size nine."

"Now, you bringing the bling in an eighteen," Deborah screeched.

Esther had forgotten that Deborah had always been the one who pounced on a person's weakness. How had she forgotten? "Hold that down, girl. That's bringing the bling in a *fourteen*." Esther paused than admitted, "Well, a sixteen too, depending on the cut."

Deborah hollered. "Then there must be elves up at night trimming your clothes down. What? You keep getting up in the morning and what fit you yesterday is mysteriously too little?"

"I'm going to ignore you. You know you're crazy!" Esther realized what she said, and she gripped the phone, rubbing her hand nervously up and down her thigh.

Deborah laughed. "Yeah, but I ain't stupid."

Esther chuckled while she still wanted to kick herself for using such a poor choice of words. "Remember when . . . ?"

And the two spent the next thirty minutes reminiscing on the old days: sour grape bubble gum, her favorite. Their college days of Riunite white wine, Deborah's favorite. Neither of them mentioned Sheri's passion for Chocolate Yahoos.

Melancholy dripped from Deborah's words. "I can't believe it, my times up. On Saturday nights we get a little leniency on the phones, but I don't want to push it."

Esther actually felt the loss before they disconnected. The last thirty minutes of their conversation had been bright with memories. Caught up, Esther asked, "Any chance you can come for a visit?" She clamped her hands over her mouth. *What did I just say?*

Deborah's robust voice was now timid and low. "You not scared to have a crazy girl around your children? That I might snap, crackle, and pop?"

Worried she had moved too fast, Esther looked for reassurance from someone who probably couldn't give it. "Will you?"

Esther was glad that Deborah appeared to take her question seriously. "Not as long as I'm on my medication. For years I didn't believe it was necessary. I would take it, and then feel better. But I didn't like feeling like I was dealing with people through a fog. So I'd stop taking it. And for a little while, the medicine that was still in me made me feel okay. Lucid, able to focus. That made me believe that I wasn't sick; that I didn't need any medicine. Then I woke up one morning, and the voices were back, mocking me. Laughing that I thought I could get away from them. Man, it was such a vicious a circle."

"Come home," Esther said and rose from her chair, and moved back into her bathroom. She frowned at her tub previously full of bubbles now totally bubbleless.

"I haven't been home in years. Not since I knocked over the Christmas tree and peed in the tree stand. Not that I remember any of it."

Esther couldn't help it. She laughed hard. "You didn't!"

Deborah chuckled too. "Ha! You know I did."

Esther couldn't seem to stop herself. "Come home. You're on medication now. You're better."

"Maybe. If I come, I won't stay with you. I'll stay at my parents'. They moved back to Detroit years ago. They said they missed it. And they say *I'm* the one on medicine," she joked.

Esther knew that Deborah loved Detroit just like the rest of Detroiters. "You need to stop. Girl, you know those of us born here have factory smoke in our veins. You know the Super Bowl was here last year."

"Yeah, I ain't dead, girl."

Esther turned on the faucets and poured a little more bath oil under the hot running water. She was determined to get her bath. "Sorry, guess that was silly."

Deborah gave a rude snort. "Uh, I'm *not* unaware, Esther. We got a black man running for president."

Esther stuck her toe in the water. "That's happened before, remember—Run, Jessie, Run? You should come home."

"Well, Ms. Broken Record, I'll get back to you about the visit. I promise."

After she hung up, Esther luxuriated in the bath, pleased with her evening. She had spent time talking to her ex-best friend and learning more about her last seventeen years. She would need to do her homework on schizophrenia. Although she dealt with people with the diagnosis, she wasn't an expert. But she knew experts. She'd make some calls.

The specialty shea butter was perfumed and saturated her feet. She ran her hands up and down her rounded thighs blending the cream, watching them gleam with her ministrations. She used her fingertips, massaged her scalp, and fingered her hair. She pulled out an emerald green gown and slipped it over her head. *Home alone bliss.*

Heading downstairs for some fruit, she stepped off the bottom step in front of her foyer when her cell phone rang in her bedroom. She ran back up the steps reaching the top step, when it stopped, and her house phone started ringing. She entered her bedroom and grabbed it before it stopped too.

Breathing heavily, she said. "Hello?"

"Sweetheart, did I catch you at a bad time? You sound winded."

Esther bent over holding her side. "Was that you on my cell?"

"Yes, it was. But when you didn't answer I thought I'd better try the landline. What are you doing?"

"Getting myself a snack. Is there something you'd rather see me doing?" she asked.

"How about answering your door?"

Esther's stomach fluttered. "Yay," she said with a burst of adrenalin. She sprinted down the stairs and to her door.

Before she could crack it wide enough, Briggs was pushing through it. "Nice . . ." he said, at the picture she made standing in her green chiffon gown.

In her excitement, Esther had forgotten what she was wearing. She knew the gown fit like a second skin, so she crossed her arms over her excess cleavage and began to head back up the stairs. At the top, she called down to him. "You're giving me my exercise today."

Briggs nodded, and as she strutted out of his vision, he placed his hands in praying motion and said softly, "I know you've got my heart pumping. I must have lost five pounds just watching you climb those stairs."

He was surprised when he lifted his head and she was smiling down at him from the top of the steps.

Esther said, "You're a naughty man, Pastor Briggs."

Briggs gave her a wicked grin. "Sweetheart, that green gown is the devil."

She giggled like her daughter Ruth. "I just wanted to tell you to make yourself at home."

"Thanks. I'll do that." Briggs walked out of her entryway into her living room.

In a matter of minutes, Esther returned, a robe securely covering herself.

Briggs stood when she entered the room and kissed her on the cheek. "Thank you for keeping this man holy."

"And this woman," Esther said as she spied the bag in Briggs's hand. "That smells so good. What is it?"

Briggs held it out to her. "You still love Chinese food?"

"You know I do."

Esther took the bag and peeked inside. "You had this bag in your hand the whole time?"

"A testament to how good-looking I am that you didn't even notice." Briggs pulled food out of the bag. "We have some spareribs, egg rolls, mixed vegetables, and house fried rice."

"Perfect at this hour of the evening." Esther got up and went to her kitchen. She returned with paper plates and plastic ware and laid it all out on the coffee table. "Sorry, all we have is grape Kool-Aid or bottled water."

Briggs looked at her doubtfully. "I've never thought of you as a Kool-Aid-type of woman."

"You still don't. It's the little people's," Esther said in a matter-of-fact tone. "I let them have it about once a month. They got hooked on it at Phyllis's, one of Miracle's many influences."

Briggs forked out a plate of food and handed it to her. "You sound like you disapprove."

Esther faltered because she loved her niece. "Sometimes." She waved her fork around in the air. "Guess what?"

Taking a forkful of food, he chewed before answering. "I'll bite. What?"

Esther's smile was contagious. "Deborah called me."

Esther knew it was because of the recounting of her trip that he looked surprised. "She did? What's her story?"

Esther related her conversation with Deborah. "I told her to come and visit."

Briggs grimaced. "With schizophrenia?"

Esther nodded. "Yes, but she's on medication, plus she works part-time at the hotel I stayed in. She's doing well." Esther hoped to convince him and herself.

Briggs pushed his plate away. "But why would you invite her to come here? You've only had one real conversation with her. You said she barely spoke to you when you went to Columbus."

Esther's face screwed up. She didn't like Briggs doubting her. This was a good thing. *Right?*

Esther defended herself hotly. "Why are you doing this? I was feeling good about it, especially after the week I had and the fact that Roger got out. I needed something positive to happen."

Briggs glanced away from her. Catching his discomfort, she frowned. "Did you talk to Joshua?"

Briggs fiddled with the carton of spareribs, pulling one out. Casually he said, "You haven't talked to Mother Reed?"

Esther put her plate down. "I've been busy. I normally talk to her. But I've barely talked to you. Now I feel bad. Did I miss something? What's going on?"

Briggs placed his sparerib on the plate. He grabbed a napkin and wiped his hands. "I spoke to Joshua. He was very convincing."

Esther's temperature soared. All she could think about was that Briggs was about to let her down. He was not going to keep his promise. "About what?"

Briggs squinted. "About giving Roger a chance. The same type of chance we all deserve. He has served his time, and when I met with him—"

Esther wrung her hands together. He had been keeping things from her. "You met with Roger?"

Briggs had sweat popping up over his forehead. "Well, I wanted to make absolutely sure he was not a threat to you, and Joshua wanted to speak to me."

Esther slapped her hand on the table in the middle of Briggs's sentence. "When?"

"Last week," he said softly.

Esther froze. "Before or after our dinner date?"

Briggs paused. "Before."

Esther stood and began tossing the cartons of food back into the bag. She grabbed the fork out of his hand, and threw it in the bag along with every other item on the table. She grabbed their bottled waters and drained hers, stuffing them both inside the bag.

Briggs watched her in silence.

She stormed to the door and opened it. "Get out!"

Briggs stayed where he was. "Esther, please understand. I have to be with God on this."

She kept the door open when she asked, "God is with Roger? But not with me? Is that what you're saying?"

Stricken, Briggs said. "No, honey, I didn't mean it like that."

Dejected, Esther came over and pulled Briggs off her couch. "Doesn't matter. This wasn't meant to be. I know that now. I want your first concern to be me, but your first concern is your duty as a pastor. Then you have your son to consider. On top of that, you have Monica your ex-wife living in your house, cohabitating. How's that play to your congregation? Then, Monica's child. Haven't you already babysat for her? Somewhere down that list comes Esther. I can tell you right now, I feel like I'm *way* down that list" She pushed him toward the open door "You should go now."

Briggs tried to put his arms around her, but she shrugged them off. Instead, she was making headway in pushing him out. "You know Monica means nothing to me. But she's BJ's mother, and I can't just throw her out."

Esther swung her hands in the air as though she was done with him. "You're not a poor man. You could have put her up in a hotel room; but instead, she's in your home, trying to get in your bed."

"That'll never happen." Briggs worked to place her hand over his heart, and a tug-of-war ensued.

"Stop it," Esther said. "Did you ever think I didn't *want* her in your home? Are you clueless?"

Briggs was now in the doorframe pleading his case, halfway outside. "I told her earlier that she had to move out, and that I would get her an apartment. I'm trying here, babe."

"Yeah, well . . . too little too late."

Esther motioned him to make the rest of his way out the door. Briggs's countenance began to crumble.

"Don't do this. I'm not a yo-yo. You can't keep bouncing me around. If we have a difference of opinion let's talk it out. Putting me out of your house is rude and unnecessary. The last time you put me out, you were young and impulsive. It's been seventeen years, and here we are again. Grow up!"

Esther stepped back and slammed the door in Briggs's stunned face. She set the alarm and slowly dragged her body up the steps. There seemed to be a lot more stairs this time, and they seemed a lot steeper. Finally, she made it to the top and released her first heart wrenching sob. Inside her bedroom, she threw herself on top of her comforter and wept.

Breathless, she inched across the bed. Her tears had slowed to a trickle. She was tired of crying, tired of the drain and pull on her heart. She had waded through the death of one love affair, she didn't have it in her to do it again.

Chapter Thirty-six

Morning glory. Early-Morning Prayer. A petition.

Briggs knelt next to his bed and prayed for God's presence to fill the room. Tears of repentance streamed down his unshaven face. He made no attempt to dry them, but raised his head to the heavens and let them drip freely. Perhaps, he thought, the wetness would hit his dry places. He should not have made promises before he knew God's heart on the matter. Logic would say that the right thing to do was to forbid Roger from being a part of his church. Then God reminded him, it was not his church, but His. And His doors were always open.

He had learned long ago, his time of worship and praise should always be higher than his petitions. There were times when a man's worship is so pure, that even the angels stood in awe. That's how Briggs felt this morning. He was not conflicted. He wanted to make Esther happy. But his greater need was to be the man God had shaped and formed even in his iniquity. He had paid dearly in the past for being disobedient. He didn't plan to travel a crooked road God had already made straight.

Today was Sunday. A day to celebrate God in His house, among His people. Briggs had a word for them, and he knew that it was coming straight from His throne.

Standing in his double-breasted suit, the pinstripes distinct, the cut perfect, fitting every dip and angular contour of his body with his wing-tipped shoes polished, he wished he felt as good as he knew he looked. His father had once told him, it wasn't bragging if it was true. And if the amount of women in the church who passed him with a flirt-induced smile and a pronounced sway to their strut were any indication, he was rocking the suit.

So many churches had stopped dressing for service. Jeans, jogging suits, and even the occasional shorts were a part of the present-day church scene. And there was definitely something to the adage that God wanted you to come as you are. It was just Briggs's opinion that He didn't mean for you to stay there. Shouldn't an inner change be validated by the outer appearance? If you came in jeans and a T-shirt and you were in jeans and a T-shirt two years later, perhaps you had failed to understand the true essence of God. He was excellence. He pulled you to be your best self, and Briggs just didn't think your best self was jeans and a T-shirt. Even if said jeans sported the logo True Religion, they weren't.

He sat in his office and opened his Bible, reviewing the notes for his sermon. He'd had a hard time concentrating after his argument with Esther. He hoped she didn't think they were through, because they were far from it. He understood her disappointment in him; he was wrong to make a promise he couldn't fulfill. However, she would need to learn to communicate with him and not dismiss what they could have together every time she was upset.

He was a man, not a boy, to be led around by his sleeve and told what to do and when to do it. It was best she understood that now; he was not going to take second seat in their home. He would be the man of their house, and she would learn that while he heard her and her concerns that did not mean he was going to be her lapdog.

His intercom beeped, and he pushed the button to listen. "Yes, Naomi."

"Pastor, Deacon Clement out here and he's ready to escort you into service."

Briggs met Deacon Clement at the door. The short man, with his slightly crooked toupee, had a heart for the church and for the people.

"You look good, Pastor. Is there anything you need before we proceed?" he asked, as he tugged his toupee straight.

Briggs averted his eyes, a half smile on his face. The toupee was still askew. Once again, Deacon Clement had missed his mark. Naomi cleared her throat and tugged her hair to the left to help him out. Deacon Clement, mirrored her movement and nodded his head in an embarrassed thanks.

"No, Deacon. I have everything I need. Let's get started."

Briggs's spirit was full. On a mission, he marched down the hall and the closer he got to the sanctuary, the louder praise and worship sounded. He heard the lead soloist getting what good church folk called, "happy." She was singing as though the angels were sitting right there with her, calling out her name, beckoning her to give her best.

Briggs's voice joined hers as he came up the aisle, his praise resounding through his mic lapel, harmoniously joined with hers. He knew the anointing was on because he sounded good. And as a rule he was not a singer.

Surveying the sanctuary he nodded to Esther's parents, Hickman and Elizabeth Wiley. They smiled as though they were his proud parents. Charles and Phyllis joyfully clapped and swayed near the front. Esther and Mother Reed sat together, both frowning at him, their stiff arms folded. He knew he better get up to the pulpit and bring the house down.

He skipped up the two stairs and placed his Bible on the pulpit. The soloist continued singing while he hummed. He felt a tug on his spirit and lifted his eyes. There in the balcony was Roger sitting to the side all alone. Joshua sat up front with the other deacons.

He grabbed his Bible and as he held it up, there was Monica in the back row. A red dress, high-necked, falling to her knees. He breathed a sigh of relief, glad she had listened and was dressed appropriately . . . until he saw her lean over for a tissue and you could see the entire back was cut out of the dress. She winked at him, and it was his luck that Esther, who was lovely in a deep mauve dress, followed his gaze and saw Monica when she winked.

Esther whispered something in Mother Reed's ear. Mother Reed turned around and gave Monica a glare, then pinned him with a disappointing glower.

Father, help me. Clear up this atmosphere.

"I love the Lord. He heard my cry. Did He hear your cry this morning? I can tell you, He did. He loves you, Church."

A member yelled out, "He's good like that, Pastor!"

Briggs nodded to the member and continued. "When you've made mistakes, He loves you. When you're on your knees crying out for His mercy, He loves you. I'm here to remind you this morning, in case you've forgotten! Maybe it's been a rough week. Your boss has been hard on you. The mortgage is behind. You had a court date, and it didn't go well."

Another member yelled, "The devil's a liar!"

Briggs was now on a roll, pacing back and forth. "Doctor's report brought you to your knees. Well, stay there and worship Him! He . . . loves . . . you."

Briggs shook off his double-breasted jacket, came around from the pulpit, down the steps, and swaggered across the front of the room. He stopped and stared at the congregation. He pinpointed Esther, let his eyes roam over to Mother Reed, glanced at Roger, and fixated on Monica.

He then roared, "My Word tells me, 'For God hath not given us the spirit of fear; but of power, and of love, and of a sound mind." Look it up for yourself, 2 Timothy 1:7. Get it in your spirit, because for some of you, fear has you. That's right! And fear is not a visitation from God. Quit letting it cohabitate with you. That's right! Turn to your neighbor and tell them to tell fear they have to quit shacking up. You've let fear move in. You've given fear squatter's rights! Oh, I know you're saved, sanctified, and Holy Ghost-filled. But I got some news for you. . ."

Briggs froze, the congregation leaned forward as if all of them were saying, "Go on, Pastor." He tiptoed over to the deacon section, bent down, and whispered, "Your salvation doesn't make you devil proof!" He pivoted and urgently ran over to the church mothers' section. He put his hands around his mouth and called out, "It rains on the just and the unjust." He then walked down the center aisle, pausing at Mother Reed and Esther's row. "Beloved, salvation is a gift, but sanctification is an act; it's gon' cost you."

He stood still for a moment, backed up, and sat down on the steps at the altar. One of the deacons came and handed him his handkerchief. He swabbed his brow.

"Listen, the devil is vigilant. He's bombarding you spiritually and naturally to keep you in a stronghold." Briggs's eyes had a fervent glazed cast to them, as though he was listening and repeating directly from the Holy Spirit. "When fear has you, you can't get a breakthrough. And fear has the tendency to usher in other spirits like guilt and shame. God's people, the spirits of fear, guilt, and shame lead us into insecurity, and it is in our insecurity that we fail to recognize our vulnerabilities as strengths. My Word says He makes the weak, strong. It is in our worldly thinking that being weak is a disadvantage. The world teaches us that being vulnerable is a bad thing."

"Can I speak to the men for a moment? You're taught by fathers who were taught that any sign of vulnerability is a sign of weakness so you don't cry. You cover your emotions like an addict protects his last stash."

Several in the congregation chuckled and called out, "Teach, Pastor."

Briggs stood. "We don't want to be naked. Listen, human beings are the only beings God created that cover their nakedness. Everything else He created is naked. It was in the Garden of Eden where Adam and Eve were asked by God, 'Who told you, you were naked?' In other words, 'Why are you corresponding with the enemy?' I know you talked to him, because the covering you have on is an indication of your sinful actions."

Briggs strode down the aisle speaking to each row, punctuating his next words. "What God was saying was before that act . . . Your nakedness! Your vulnerability! Your transparency! These were my gifts not my curses to you. Now you're feeling vulnerable and ashamed because you have allowed the sneaky, lying, two-faced serpent to infiltrate your thoughts. Sin and shame go together like smoke and fire. You see one, you need to get the fire extinguisher. What did the one young man say? It's getting hot in here, so take off all your clothes?"

Briggs heard some gasps from the upright and uptight. "What the singer didn't know is God would say it this way: 'Yes, my child, get transparent with me so I can rebuke fear, cast down your shame, and put your guilt in shackles.' The heat you feel is your sin, and it's burning you up. But get free! What the devil meant for your harm, God can make it your point of elevation."

Mother Reed stood to her feet. "Say that!"

Briggs spoke in a low, soothing tone. "God loves you. The adversary loves our shame. He laps it up with his forked tongue and feeds it so that we stay in bondage to it, and to him. Shame, fear, and guilt are conspirators in a plan to steal your potential, kill your vision, and destroy your purpose. Staying hidden keeps the serpent alive, while he feeds on your problems. Bring them into the light, starve them, and the serpent dies from malnutrition."

Several members called out, crying in earnest.

Briggs stood and motioned for the organist to softly play. "Beloved, it's time to let it all go. Your silence is prohibiting you from getting prayers for your condition. Come to the altar naked and unashamed. Let God handle it. Take it to Him in prayer and supplication."

Many staggered to the altar, hands raised while tears flowed down their cheeks.

"The church doors are open." Briggs motioned for a couple of members from the praise and worship team to sing.

He was inspired by the number of men who came up. He held out his hand and Deacon Clement poured anointed oil into his palm. As he went down to the far end of the line, Mother Reed stepped up, and Briggs's heart overflowed. He dabbed her forehead with oil and prayed.

Chapter Thirty-seven

"Esther, did you not hear any of the sermon today?" Mother Reed said, chiding her with a look of disapproval as she accommodated her request that they move down to the church social hall for punch.

Esther flinched as though she had been pinched. When she was younger and she would giggle and whisper in church, Mother Reed would give her a pinch on her thigh that hurt like fire. Then her grandmother would nod at her, as though she was saying, "The next time, I'm coming down from this choir stand and I will tear your tail up."

Esther flinched but played dumb. "Not sure what you mean, Mother. I'm good."

"You didn't go over to the receiving line with your parents before they left. Then you spent all of your time glaring at Briggs and frowning to let him know you're still angry with him. You wrong, little girl."

They entered an empty hallway that led to the social hall. "How am I wrong?" Esther had attitude dripping from her pores.

Mother Reed grabbed her chin and pulled her face down to hers. She whispered furiously. "Does he go to your job to air your personal issues? This is *his* job, and *his* calling, Esther!"

Esther was taken aback. She had never thought of it like that. Had Briggs tried to explain that to her before, but she wasn't listening? That not only was he a man of God, but church business was his business? And if Roger chose to come to this church, and he was not a danger, then it was his job to forgive him?

The edges around Esther's heart began to thaw. What was she really scared of? Was she scared that Roger would hurt her, or was she scared that her old life, once buried, would rear its ugly face again? Her children didn't even know she had been married before their dad.

Mother Reed took Esther's hand. "What are you really afraid of, child? And how much of a part does shame hold in it?"

They entered the hall where Briggs held court. Their eyes collided, held, and then softened. His eyes proclaimed, "I love you." Hers professed, "I'm sorry." The silent conversation repaired their breach.

"Well, don't stare the man to death. Go on over there and make up," Mother Reed chortled.

Esther squeezed Mother Reed with the hand she was still holding. She kissed her on the cheek and moved toward Briggs. Before she could get there, Monica stepped in front of him and loudly stated, "You were wonderful, sweetheart."

A second later, BJ skipped into the room from children's church and joined them. Monica had picked up Fiona from the nursery, and she placed Fiona in Briggs's arms while she searched in her purse. As she pawed through it, Briggs caught Esther's eye, his facial expression pleaded his need for her patience. He then motioned her over.

Esther received his message. He didn't want Monica's games to stop her. But Esther couldn't do it; she abruptly turned her head and went back to Mother Reed's side.

Mother Reed's entire body screamed frustration. "Don't you let that Jezebel play you."

Esther's mouth fell open. "Jezebel, Mother Reed?"

Mother Reed grasped her long purse strap and waved it at Esther. "Yes. Jezebel! That girl ain't a bit more holy.

She may have tried her hand at church, but she didn't marinade on it when God placed His hand on her. I'm not saying she ain't had her moments. I'm just saying she didn't stay on her knees long 'nough to allow the change to come through."

Esther checked out Monica in her red clinging dress and couldn't believe the cut out in the back. Did the woman even *know* she was in church?

"She is a beautiful woman though. Look at that hair," Esther sighed as if she felt defeated. Monica had been a supermodel. Wouldn't Briggs always be tempted by her? The woman had two children and was still a size six.

"Tsk . . . You all caught up in the outer wrapping. She's like the fig tree Jesus cursed. It looked good, had Him salivating wanting a good taste of that fruit. But when he got there in need of nourishment, it had leaves, but no fruit; it was barren. Now, in my studies I've learned that in that land the fruit appeared on trees before the leaves. You see, Monica had the trappings to lure the man, but lacked the character to keep him. Stop looking at her outside. The girl has no fruit!"

Esther's hand on her chest, she nodded, relieved. "And my Word says, 'You will know them by the fruit that they bear.' Thanks, Mother."

Mother Reed placed her purse strap on her shoulder. "You welcome. Now, sashay over there and claim ya man. I'm going to get some punch and speak to Sister Essie."

Esther retraced her steps. As if she could feel her, Monica turned around and watched her approach. Then Monica slinked closer to Briggs and purred, "Well, darling, I'm going to go fix dinner. I'll see you at home."

Esther's steps did not falter.

Fool me once, shame on me. Fool me twice . . . and get your butt kicked.

Briggs waited alone, his raw power drawing her near, transmitting she was the one for him.

"That was a great sermon, Pastor." Esther wondered if she should apologize for last night now or later.

"Thank you."

Briggs did a quick glance around the social hall. He lowered his voice and said, "I'm glad you came over. Would you like to have dinner with me?"

"I thought you were having dinner with your family?" Esther said, alluding to Monica's dig at her.

Briggs stepped as close as he felt he could in the church social hall. "You're my family. BJ can have dinner with Monica. You and I have unfinished business. Where's David and Ruth?"

Esther's voice was also low, but soothing. "They went on over to my parents'. You know they always do Sunday dinner. Would you like to join us?"

Briggs placed his hands in his pockets and rocked. "I love your parents, but what I would like is for us to have dinner. Let's get this romance on track. Let me get my 'mack' on."

Esther laughed, and the last vestige of anger toward Briggs fell away from her heart.

"I would love to have you practice to perfection your 'mack' moves on me."

He leaned forward and said into her ear, "It's not practice when you're the focus of my intentions."

Making sure they were not being watched, Esther dusted imaginary lint off of his shoulder. She just needed to touch him. She was about to say something when Briggs's body stiffened. He stared at something over her shoulder, and she turned and followed his line of vision.

Cut in an expensive suit, wearing custom-made shoes, clean shaven, with his hair cut low, her past made a striking appearance. There was a buzz from the women in the social hall. The children's assistant principal, Melanie, sauntered over to him, and held out her hand for an introduction. Esther and Melanie had attended a seminar together. She was a pretty, intelligent, educated woman who bought into the media's forecast for a single woman of color's future—loneliness. She wasn't a bad person; she was just desperate for a husband.

Roger took her hand in his and held it too long. Soon the two were laughing over something Melanie had shared.

Esther's chest rose in rapid succession, and she clenched her teeth.

"Don't let this bother you. Shake it off. Focus on us and dinner," Briggs said as he moved in front of her to block her vision.

Esther stood there seething as though she could see right through him. "Can you believe this madness?" she bit out.

"Esther—"

Briggs was talking to an empty space; Esther had already gone around him to confront Roger.

"Oh, Lord," she heard Mother Reed groan.

Roger had panic in his eyes as Melanie stepped aside.

Esther walked around Roger examining him up and down. She saw a question in Melanie's glance, but the woman had enough sense to let the scene play out.

"This the outfit the prison issuing to its parolees now, Roger?" Esther said loudly.

Melanie gasped, backing away.

Roger held out his hand, trying to forestall her next words, but Esther continued.

"I thought stripes, no, orange was the new prison fall colors. But here you are up in church like you deserve to be around decent people."

Speechless, Roger never moved, and after his outstretched hand's silent plea didn't stop her, it seemed like he tuned her out. But still he stood there letting her spew her venom over him.

"That's enough, Esther!"

Dazed, Esther swung around, surprised that it was Mother Reed who called a halt to her diatribe. Dazed, Esther's countenance gradually grew horrified at her own actions. Mother Reed embraced her and murmured while she stroked her back.

"I know, baby, I know. But you can't let him change you. You can't let what he did make you a victim twice. Don't you do that."

Roger walked away robotically, bypassing the small crowd that was left in the social hall. The crowd parted as though he had the plague.

Briggs came over and an embarrassed Esther kept her eyes glued to her feet.

"You canceling dinner?" she whispered.

"No, but it may include a spanking," Briggs said without humor.

"I just saw red. I didn't even think about it. I hate that man," Esther said, shaken by the encounter.

Mother Reed held her peace. Esther could see she wanted to say something, but knew Mother Reed was going to take the high road and just pray for her.

Briggs spoke from his heart. "Esther, let it go."

"He's a no-good, lying, abusive dog." Esther opened her purse and pulled a tissue out, dabbing the perspiration off of her face.

"He's a lot of things. Let it go," Briggs said, still calm.

Briggs spoke to Mother Reed. "I understand from Joshua that you had your own run-in with him earlier in the week."

"Yes, I did, and I owe my son an apology. First time me and him been on different sides of the fence, and I was the one on the wrong side. Your sermon today cleared that up. I was afraid that this one would lose all the progress she had made since he had been locked up," she pointed at Esther. "She was a different person after her divorce. It took her a long time to pick up the pieces. Don't let her slip back into darkness. While I was praying about him, I should have focused my prayers on her."

"I'm still standing here," Esther said. "I can hear you."

"And?" Mother Reed said, placing her hand on her hip.

Briggs glanced at his watch. "Esther, I'll pick you up at four. Mother would you like to go with us?"

Mother Reed smiled. "Bless your heart, you don't nary mean none of that invitation. No, I'm going on home to pray awhile. There is trouble brewin'."

Mindful of watchful eyes, Esther nodded at Briggs and placed her arm around Mother Reed to guide her out as they left.

As they passed a man in a red suit, Esther wondered how she had missed him in the sanctuary. She rubbed her arms at the sudden coldness in the room and pulled her jacket closer as she passed by. Mother Reed hissed, and Esther could hear her urgently praying in her heavenly language.

When they exited the building, Mother Reed turned to her with a dire warning. "You better get that hate out of your heart, and right away. That type of energy opens a door to entities better kept at bay. Child, hate don't even love its owner."

She then pulled Esther away from the door, mumbling and fussing about "the sanctity of holy ground."

Chapter Thirty-eight

Earlier that morning before church, The Leader had stood behind the tall, stately man. Together they fixed the red and blue tie in the mirror. They took their finger and smoothed down their eyebrow. They were one.

"You sho' looking good, Master," Imp One said.

"Yesss . . . s . . . s. This human form will do for now. He's one of my best. Evil is his middle name. I've been with him since he was a child, pulling the wings off of butterflies and then chasing little girls with their mutilated bodies."

"We like, we like," the imps chorused.

"He's what they call, handsome. Huh, Master?" Imp One asked.

"Yes . . . s . . . s . . . s. Was not the mighty Lucifer beauty personified? And good looks are important to the human species. They make much over something they have no control over. Yet, the things that people do have control over, like working hard, being good to each other, they dismiss."

The Leader strutted around the room. "I love it!"

"They major on minor, O Great One."

"Exactly. I'm going to set this place ablaze!" The Leader said in malicious glee.

Imp One danced around. "You going to do an Ohio Players on them; they'll be yelling, 'Fire!'"

The Leader tossed him a dismissive glare. "Do you know what to do next? You have to be cunning and play this thing right. No slipups!"

"Yes, Leader. We're already bombarding Esther with her past failings with Roger. And to make real sure she doesn't falter, I keep replaying the night of her abuse from him over and over. Really, Master, at one point, he slapped her so hard, she should be waking up from her nightmare with whiplash."

The man in red smoothed his mustache. "What about Monica? How's that coming along?"

Imp One slid across the bedroom's laminated floor. "She doesn't know if she's coming or going. She fell back into her old ways like we knew she would. Her mama trained her that her body was her tool and that sexual manipulation equals power. So she powered up, Master."

The Leader forgot he was inside his human avatar, and he reached for his tail to stroke himself. Instead his human hand did it.

The imp's snout wrinkled in disgust. "Uh, Leader, sir?"

"What?" he roared, hating his silent planning was being interrupted.

He gestured to where The Leader's hand rested. "I'm pretty sure you can't do that in public."

The Leader reared back, but again, he could not strike the imp as he wanted. Human force would not even be felt by him.

Imp One's eyes gleamed. "You look good, Master. Maybe you should inhabit this form more often."

The Leader glided over to the mirror, entranced with his image. "I'm in him often enough. We do great things together. He hears, and he obeys."

"Yes, Master," Imp One said, but at the same time he was devising a way to keep The Leader in his human form for as long as possible. He liked the fact that he could not hurt him while possessing a body. A chilling thought came to him: The Leader was not all-powerful, not all-knowing? He needed to be in this human form to act? He was not everywhere? What did this mean? Was there someone more powerful? He was told over and over that there wasn't, but they were all liars. There were too many questions. He needed answers. He would have to study on it.

The man leered at him through the mirror. "What of the little girl? She will be eight years old next week. Is everything ready?"

Imp One slithered to attention. "Oh, it is coming along well. The parents are consistent in their adoration. She is pliable. She sits in church, but it does not sit in her."

"Good, good. Be ready."

"Yes, Master."

"Where are you going now?" Imp One wanted to know The Leader's whereabouts so he could goof off a little. He was beginning to realize that The Leader wasn't as powerful as he always thought.

"To the church," he said, as he began to slither away.

"No! You shall burn," Imp One said. Although in all truth, he really didn't care. But he was finding that he could outsmart this Leader, more than most. So perhaps it was important to protect his interests.

"Burn, burn, burn," the imps chanted.

"Quiet! I will only go as far as the church's social hall. I want to test how far I can go inside of Love Zion. Even in human form, the angels will not allow, I mean, they will fight me for position. And I want to see some of the action up close."

Imp One heard the slip of The Leader's tongue. The angels had the power to not "allow" The Leader in the church? This was news to him.

Continuing to play dumb, Imp One said, "Whew! You scared me for a minute there. I know we plant suicidal thoughts in human's minds, but I was hoping you were not having them. Going into a Word-filled church's sanctuary—ugh! Heavenly prayer-laden perfume kills."

Imp One knew he needed to change the subject. After all, The Leader was not overly stupid. He studied the form The Leader inhabited.

"What is the name of this human?"

The Leader grabbed the hat and placed the car keys in his hand, then he walked through the hotel room noting its luxury. He gave a sinister grin; he treated his human minions well. Imp One was scurrying behind him when The Leader finally answered.

"Duncan. Its name is Duncan."

Zadkiel flew over Love Zion Church. The demon was inside the social hall, and he was not happy. It was too close. When did they get this bold? In the last 1,000 years, the lot of them were bolder than ever. The snake growing steadily into the dragon it had become. But his guardian angels stood ready to stop any demonic activity. What they weren't allowed to do was interfere in the free will of the humans.

Monica and Esther were acting up big time. He wanted a spiritual paddle big enough to give them both a sound spanking. They weren't listening.

The angels had spent time with Briggs in his early-morning worship. Zadkiel was pleased with Briggs's rousing sermon about fear and shame, for it hindered and crippled too many of His Father's people. Yet, those God needed to plant the seed in rebelled.

Monica heard the Word, but failed to let its seed penetrate her heart. And Esther heard it, accepted it, but allowed it to be plucked up by Monica's actions and Roger's appearance. It was not furrowed deep in the soil of her spirit, but was on the surface, resting at soul level.

When would they learn that faith without works is dead?

Chapter Thirty-nine

Roger sat across from Joshua and Essie at the dinner table. Essie's sister, Janie, sat next to him, but continued to turn and stare sullenly at Roger. Joshua gave him an apologetic gesture. The awkwardness was palatable, and Roger was exhausted from it all.

"I'm going to excuse myself from the table. Essie, thank you for a lovely dinner. As usual, it was delicious." Roger was stiff and formal.

Joshua stood with him. "Let me holla at you a minute."

Roger led the way out of the room, and behind him he heard Janie's whispering and Essie shushing her. He went to his own cottage and sat down in the living room.

Following him, Joshua dropped into the plushness of the couch and crossed his leg. He pulled a pack of gum out of his pocket and held it out to Roger.

Roger's eyes drooped as he shook his head. "No, thank you."

Joshua took out a stick, opened it, and then chewed it as though he was savoring the flavor.

"Who was the woman you sneaked into your place like a thief the other night?"

Roger squirmed uncomfortably in his seat.

"Like a thief?" he repeated.

Joshua didn't shy away. "She stole something from you, didn't she?"

Frustrated that Joshua felt he had the right to come at him like this, Roger went on the offense, his voice rising with each question.

"So, you the morality police? You guarding my salvation now? You've gotten out, and now you somebody in the church and you all holier than thou?" Roger used his fingers as quote marks. "You got a lot of nerve. Last time I checked I didn't have a father."

"Wrong. You have a Heavenly Father, and He sees all, Roger, so who you yelling at? Me or Him? 'Cause He's not moving, and me you don't want to move."

Joshua uncrossed his leg and placed his hands on his knees. "I know you been locked up. I know it's been awhile. But repent, brother. Don't start falling back into ungodly habits. One mistake can start an avalanche; you gotta put your soul in check. Don't be caught up in no R. Kelly shenanigans 'cause before you know it, you'll be crying out about her body calling you. But your mind wanna say no."

Roger had to chuckle. "I don't think that's how it goes."

Joshua flicked his hand as though he didn't care how it went. "Whatever. I don't listen to his mess. Last time I paid attention to him, he was singing 'I Believe I Can Fly.' Then the boy fell."

Joshua rose to demonstrate his point.

"He did a Peter. He was walking on the water," Joshua said, and started pacing, placing one foot firmly in front of the other with his arms out. "Then he realized he was doing the 'doggon' thing."

Joshua sped up, again placing one foot in front of the other, but this time, he looked around as he stepped.

"He then took his eyes off God and plummeted into the water," Joshua said and fell back and landed on the couch.

Roger gave him a pound. "You still got it, man; that was deep."

"No, son, that was tragic. R. Kelly had something. Something beyond a bump and grind. But he didn't stay the course. Later, the enemy had him in the court. And he may have gotten a not guilty in the legal system, but he lost a lot in the court of public opinion."

"Yeah, the question of his morality is always going to be second-guessed." Roger hoped to take the spotlight off of his sins by illuminating someone else's.

By the look on Joshua's face, Roger knew he had not succeeded. Joshua was not playing around.

Joshua clapped his hands. "Stay with me, man. But Peter rebounded. Later, he was the one who told Jesus he was the Christ, the son of God. And Jesus told him, flesh and blood did not reveal that to him. You see, Peter was validated by Christ Himself that he was in the spirit. And he still messed up again, only to later have the ability to heal people."

"Yeah, Peter was a cold dude. I can identify," Roger said thoughtfully.

"Identify? Bro, you're a modern-day Peter. The bed was your water test, but you can get up from there. 'Repent ye therefore, and be converted, that your sins may be blotted out, when the times of refreshing shall come from the presence of the Lord.'"

"Acts 3:19," Roger said, beginning to feel remorseful.

"So, you do know your Word," Joshua said in a blunt manner.

"I know a little something," Roger replied.

Joshua looked pained. "Lucifer knows the Word. He was God's chief worshipper. Stayed before Him day and night. I'm not impressed by the knowledge you have, I'm impressed by the knowledge you live by."

Roger was nervous. "You don't want me to leave, do you?"

Joshua ignored his question, and instead said, "Do you know why I didn't come to you with this when it first happened on Friday night?"

"Uh, no, why?" Roger asked.

Joshua shook his head. "I was waiting for you to come to me and ask for some direction. For us to pray together. Confess your sins one to the other. One of the scriptures we learned to live by inside the joint. Remember?"

"Yes, and I'm going back inside to visit others and help them, so I'm going to need to be prayed up. Just getting ready to go back to minister gives me heartburn," Roger rubbed his chest.

Joshua knelt. "So I'm here, and you're here, and I can guarantee you, God is here. Let's pray about it all."

Roger slid onto the floor and onto his face. He hadn't wanted to have this conversation. He had wanted to avoid the appearance of sin, even though he had thoughts of doing it again.

He anxiously pressed his face into the carpet, his wayward thoughts were concerning even to himself. He now came into agreement that what he wanted to justify as something he deserved as his compensation—because he had been locked up for so long—was a lie from the pit of hell. It was a portent of ill choices in the future.

Jesus! Joshua was right, his repentance was necessary.

Briggs had come to Esther's house for the first time in the light of day. It was a beautiful brick colonial. It sported a stained glass window that rested above the top of the mahogany wood door, and the sun glimmered like a prism through the glass.

He stepped to the door, his eyes drawn to a wooden plaque that hung over the doorbell. It was heart-shaped with four blue handprints: Two adults, two children. Written in cursive across the top: The Reddings.

One added touch, and the house instantly turned into a home. The home that love built.

Briggs knew that Esther's story with Lawton was not the same as his with Monica. They had a good life together. Could what he offered her compare?

He pulled out his cell phone and called the one man who always gave it to him straight.

"Hey, Dad."

Bishop Stokes spoke with his usual stamp of authority. "Briggs, it's good to hear from you. How's my boy doing?"

"Oh, BJ is fine."

"I'm not talking about BJ. I'm talking about you. BJ calls me all the time."

"He does?"

"Boy, sometimes you about beat it all. BJ calls me and your mother several times a week, especially when his mother showed up. Don't the two of you confuse my grandson with grown folk nonsense."

"Dad, you saw me after Monica left me. You think I would ever go through that again?" Briggs spoke low; he didn't want Esther to peek out and see him on the phone on her porch. What would he tell her? That he was trying to get some love advice from his seventy-year-old father?

"Yeah, you were tore up, but it was more about your feelings being hurt than the woman who left you. You know that now, right?"

Briggs kicked a pebble into a shrub. "I do. And the woman that I have loved since I was twenty years old is available, and I'm trying to court her seriously. But I'm kind of stumbling at it."

"Well, the only woman I know that you felt that way about was Esther. And I know that you're not trying to break up her marriage, so is she now divorced or a widow?"

"A widow," Briggs said, nervous and jittery on the porch.

"Aha. It was a good marriage?"

Briggs looked at Esther's front windows. "Yes, Dad. So can you help me out here?"

"No."

"No? Why not, Dad?" Briggs was frustrated. He was tired of making mistakes with Esther.

"I don't know the young lady, or where she is in her life. Son, there is no cookie cutter format for a successful relationship. Except to love and respect each other. But what her love language is depends on who she is, and I can't help you with that."

Confused he asked, "Her love language?"

"Yes, there's been a book written on it. But basically you want to know what your partner values. What is important to her? You love BJ and you want him to be happy. So would you buy him a model plane for his birthday?"

Briggs closed his eyes in thought. "No. He doesn't like that kind of thing, but I would buy him a construction set or a video game."

"Exactly, but you loved model airplanes, and you love flying them now."

Briggs listened and thought of the times he did what he thought Esther would want, instead of finding out what she wanted. "And if I bought him one, I'd be giving him what I want him to have versus what he wants?"

"That was all net, boy, all net," his father said, chuckling.

"So, Dad, you're saying listen to her, and then give her what she wants?" Briggs thought about Esther wanting him to get rid of Roger. So was Esther right and he was wrong?

"Not always. Use wisdom. If a woman wants a large house in the hills, and the man knows he makes apartment money, he shouldn't go into debt trying to get her something he can't afford. But if it's in his plans to one day own a house like that too, and he wants a better job, and doesn't mind a large house, then they can work toward it together. A man still has to hear from God. He's the final say-so, including is this the right woman for you or not."

Thanks. I gotta go," Briggs said rushing his father off the phone.

"You not doing something simple like sitting in front of her house, are you?"

"I kinda am," he said. Briggs thought he saw a shadow in her front window and the curtain move. He was praying it was just a breeze. "I'll talk to you later."

"Pitiful," was the last thing Briggs heard as he hung up the phone.

Esther and Briggs watched the ship pass along the river as they sat and enjoyed their meal. They didn't have to fill the empty silence with chatter; contentment filled their quiet.

"You are so beautiful." Briggs watched the candlelight dance off her hair. Thank you," she said, as a becoming blush spread across her cheeks. "I want to apologize for giving you a hard time at church. I have to admit sometimes it's hard to know how to respond to you."

Briggs picked up his fork. "What do you mean?"

Esther's brow puckered. "You're a pastor, so, if I say certain things to you, how does that line up with honoring my man of God?"

"That's just it. All women should honor their husbands like they honor their pastor." Briggs took a bite of his food.

Esther smiled, taking the edge off her question. "Am I stating the obvious when I say you are not my husband?"

Briggs scooped up a forkful of his crème Brûlée cheese cake and held it out to her to taste. She opened her mouth and moaned in delight when the cake touched her tongue. He forked another piece of cake and ate it.

"You may not be married to me now, but you will be. And let's stay on the topic at hand."

"How to treat your pastor boyfriend." he motioned for him to feed her another bite of the cake.

He scooped up a forkful, fed her, and said, "No, how to treat *your* man. If you gave him the same respect you give your pastor, then he would rise to the station you need him to be in."

"Well, in my first marriage, I couldn't treat Roger like I treated my pastor. The man made me mad all the time," Esther said between swallows.

Briggs was not letting her get away with inane answers.

"Now, come on, Esther. Your pastor has made you angry before. How did you handle it?"

"I prayed about it. And then I realized we weren't always going to be on the same page, but I could still respect him as my man of God."

Esther stared at the water, deep in thought.

"And when Roger made you angry?" Briggs saw she was thinking.

Esther exhaled heavily. "I cursed him out. I cried. I yelled. I tried to control the situation."

So, you see, I don't mind if you treat me like you treat your pastor. I just don't want you to think about me as your pastor. Except when we are in that spiritual position with each other. This . . . is . . . not . . . that . . . position." Briggs punctuated his sentence with kisses across her hand.

"And should a pastor be kissing?" she asked coyly.

Briggs stopped and considered her question. He knew they needed to have this conversation. "Some things can be dangerous in the wrong hands; kisses are one of them. What's too much? And as a man of God, how do I lead my flock by example?"

Esther hunched over the table. "Right! I've had those same questions."

She fanned herself. "Your kisses are potent, Briggs. They are the grown-up steroid version of my adolescent experience."

"So we have to master our desires. I'm not a saint. My favorite new pastime is kissing those lips." He slapped his hand to his heart. "Look at you, girl. Can't be nothing better than falling into your gaze. I could drown in it." Loosening his collar, he continued. "But we have to agree that there may be times I'm feeling vulnerable, or you're in that place and we have to call a halt to even holding hands."

Esther slid her hand out of his and into her lap. "I agree because what you said turned me straight up to a ten."

Grabbing their water and gulping it down, they turned to the river, praying a boat would float by.

Chapter Forty

Too many choices. The kitchen was a poster child for a magazine layout. It boasted organic fruit, a freezer full of free-range meat, and enough whole grains to feed a yoga class. The appliances were state-of-the-art, including a subzero refrigerator with multiple self-closing drawers.

It was early in the morning and Roger pulled out the coffee machine, then proceeded to paw through and disregard its various selections in the little plastic cups. Frustrated, he murmured and complained that all he wanted was a plain cup of coffee . . . black, no chasers.

Esther's and Mother Reed's embarrassing tirades the week before had rode him into the early sunrise. Nothing like finding out the people everybody else loved, hated you. Moving like a snail in a snowstorm, he needed additional fortification. Preferably a caffeine shot straight into his veins, and then, he might make it through the day.

He was headed to one of Joshua's buildings to work and get a couple of apartments ready for move in. He had always been mechanical. In prison, he learned some additional skills in the wood shop. As a result, he was quite handy. Courtesy of Joshua, he had brand-new tools. Today, he needed to sand and buff the hardwood floors in one vacancy and do some cabinetry work in another.

He grabbed the top-of-the-line tool kit and added it to his list of "pay back Joshua" items that he kept in his head. He knew the man had money, but it was not an automatic that said money belonged in his boy's pocket.

The fancy clothes, which he accepted so he wouldn't embarrass Joshua when they went out, and the use of any of his vehicles. The list got longer every day.

Joshua had given him a great job. The added bonus was he didn't have to interview for it and be questioned about his seven-year gap in work history. Or watch their eyes grow icy when he told the truth on his application because he checked the little box asking if you were a felon. Right next to it, it should have read, "If you are, you might as well go home and stay there 'cause your no-count tail ain't wanted here."

He knew this for a fact; he had experienced it his second day out. He wanted to find a job on his own, but it went bad real quick. He left the temporary employment agency humiliated. He sat in one of Joshua's cars looking out at nothing for hours. So he was grateful to Joshua; he was just sick of needing his help. Finding out he had skills Joshua needed could only have been God.

When a furnace went out in one of Joshua's apartment buildings, Roger tagged along. Joshua was impressed when Roger spotted the problem and fixed it before his regular guy could be called in. Now, Joshua was giving him more and more responsibility. They were even going to look at an apartment building that had just gone up for sale.

He'd been out a month, and for two weeks he had been playing wingman to Joshua. Roger soaked up everything on the business side he could. He had never been a person who liked to work with his hands. But life changed you. After prison, anything that was an honest day's work was a step in the right direction. In the meantime, he wasn't letting knowledge skate by him; if there was something new to learn, to absorb, he was the sponge. That was the new philosophy he lived by.

Whistling, he left his house and pulled out into traffic. He saw the upscale coffeehouse and parked. He hoped he could get a plain coffee to go.

He was standing at the counter when he heard his name called.

"Roger?"

The hair on his arms stood up, and he gripped the edge of the counter. A cloying sweet musk cologne infused the air. He almost choked on the memories. If the voice had escaped him, the smell was a slap-upside-the-head reminder of terror-filled days. His grip on the counter became so tight that his knuckles turned opaque.

The heart is an organ that is used to pump vital oxygen and nutrients throughout the human body. It was a ridiculous thing to remember at this moment that bit of trivia from his high school anatomy class. But he could understand the reference. He felt like his had stopped working. And if it had, then no oxygen or nutrients could flow. Would it be the death of him?

He swayed. Light-headed and faint, he held his breath and waited. Nothing. Just the inescapable need to breathe.

Still here. Lord, help me.

"Sir, are you okay?"

Roger looked at the perky salesgirl who had just taken his order. He tried to smile, but he couldn't muster the strength. He needed everything in him to remain upright.

"You not gon' turn around and speak to me, boy?"

Roger grimaced at the young girl and gave her a strained smile. "Yes, I'm good. Thank you for your concern."

"I'm talking to you!"

The veins in Roger's arms began to pop out. He was prison strong, and if he had to, he could fight to defend himself. But how do you tell your six-year-old self that? He was back to being a terrified child. He had lived for more than eight months with an uncle he didn't know and all during that time, all he heard about was that he owed him. He owed him for the bed he slept in, the clothes on his body, and the food in his stomach. It was a hellish existence. At the end of the eight months, at the first full moon, the child began to pay his way. The debt was too high.

"You still a crybaby?"

In response to the salesclerk's widening eyes, Roger's head fell forward, his eyes downcast. The barista's cheeks had been flushed, and he could tell that she was uncomfortable.

Roger had started out embarrassed, but as old memories washed over him, his anger swelled. No, not anger; red-hot, molten rage. He was near an explosion. Sweat that trickled down his arms dripped from his hands.

Then it happened. The apparition of evil touched him. Grabbed him by the shoulder to swing him around. Before he could think, he wrenched away and punched him. Knocked him on his back, and then placed his foot on his chest. Dead center. Maybe he could stop *his* heart?

"Duncan. What . . . do . . . you . . . want?" He punctuated his words with applied pressure to his chest from his work boots.

Duncan didn't flinch. This cold, calculated, vicious narcissist grinned. His grin was so evil in its delivery that a shiver ran down Roger's spine.

Roger's eyes flashed a question: *Can't you see I am the dominant one now?*

"No," was the bogeyman's answering grin. *"You're not."*

That grin made him fall back and say a quiet prayer.

Roger hissed. "Stay away from me, Duncan."

Duncan rose from the floor and dusted off his clothes as though being knocked to the ground was an everyday occurrence. He leaned into Roger, his breath tickling his ear. "I've missed you, baby."

Roger convulsed, willing the bile back down his throat. "Don't say that to me. You have no right."

Duncan reached toward him and Roger froze, holding his breath. At the last moment, Duncan smirked, faked to the right and picked up Roger's coffee from the counter. "Your coffee's on me."

Roger knocked his hand away, the lid on the coffee cup preventing it from spilling. "I pay my own way."

He turned to the salesclerk with another apologetic smile and handed her a fifty-dollar bill.

"Here, I'm sorry for the confusion. Thank you for not calling the cops. Keep the change."

Roger stomped out of the shop with Duncan on his heels. Turning the aggressor, he spun, grabbed the lapels of Duncan's jacket, and slammed him on top of the hood of the car. This time, the coffee still clutched in Duncan's hand popped open. The steam from the coffee's heat swirled over Duncan's clothed arm. Yet, Duncan failed to acknowledge it burned.

"Do you want me to kill you?" Roger screamed, shaking him back and forth like a rag doll. The coffee cup flung into the air.

Duncan was a big man, but Roger's strength was in his agony. He had pushed his pain down for years, until it boiled to the surface as a living, breathing thing. It held such loathing for this man that Duncan lifted his head and inhaled, as though this dark abyss was an intoxicating aroma he couldn't get enough of.

Roger stumbled back when Duncan's eyes glazed black, and then became violet with desire. "The gates of hell! What are you?"

Duncan seemed to slither to his feet and glide across the hood to stand inches from Roger.

"Why, I'm your loving uncle, and you've been gone from me too long. I've been searching for you since you were sixteen. Come on, lover, give your ol' uncle a kiss," he said, puckering his lips.

Roger's projectile vomit flew out of his mouth and sprayed all over Duncan. He finally stepped back.

Holding his arms out from his sides, Duncan shook the bile from his body. His voice was like water on a hot surface.

"This is not over. I'll be seeing you."

Hands curved like claws, he pointed at him and said, "Sorry I missed you in church yesterday. So many beautiful people there. Whole families, smiling with lovely children. Remember how you used to help me meet such wonderful families? And now without even knowing it, you're doing it again. Yes, I'm going to like Love Zion."

There was nothing but red haze in Roger's vision. He held his stomach and lurched to the driver's side of the car. "You stay away from my church. You hear me, you stay away!" He jumped in, wiping his mouth on his sleeve. Not checking in any mirror, he peeled off, missing by inches a car already in traffic. He heard the horn blow, but it didn't matter. Duncan was back.

Chapter Forty-one

Esther's laughter could be heard throughout the office. She saw Simone get up and indicate she was closing her door.

Esther held up her finger. "Okay, girl. Yes, I'm looking forward to it. I'll pick you up at the bus station. No, I'm not still late all the time. I'll be there. Bye."

"By that silly grin on your face, I take it that was your childhood friend on the phone." Simone crossed her legs and leaned against the wall.

"It could have been a man, Simone. Or Phyllis," Esther made note that once again Simone's skirt was way too short and too tight.

Simone pushed off the wall and twisted her face. "Uh, no, Chica. When you're speaking to a man, you don't laugh like a donkey giving birth. Hee-haw, hee-haw," she mimicked Esther.

"Whatever! You're not so smart. It could have been Phyllis."

Pensive, Simone bit her lip. "No, something is going on with the two of you lately. She doesn't call as much, and when she does, it's all about the children."

Esther moved papers around her desk, ignoring Simone.

Simone crossed her arms. "Phyllis is bougie and can be a pain, but that's your blood. What's up?"

Esther stilled, and then chewed on her ink pen. "We disagree on how to raise our children."

"Well, since you both have your own, problem solved. You raise yours and let her do the same. See, wisdom has been served," Simone said, and swept her arm in an arch in front of her, and then curtseyed.

"No, problem is not solved. My children spend a lot of time with their cousin—as should be—and they are influenced by her. Every day they are asking for more and more things, because Miracle has them. I am not buying almost seven-year-olds cell phones. Nor are they getting their own computers."

Simone shrugged her shoulders. "You can afford it, Boss Lady."

"I can afford weed and cocaine; they not getting that either," Esther fumed.

Simone laughed. "When you come hard like this, there's no changing your mind. But blood is thicker than the thin line you are both walking on. Talk now, before you have to talk during a tragedy. I hate it when people crying at funerals about something they refused to discuss in life. I want to pimp slap them and say, 'Shut up! They can no longer hear you.'"

Esther rolled her eyes. "Nobody's dying. What's wrong with you?"

Simone shook her finger. "Make up with your sister beyond surface pleasantries. Deborah can't replace her."

"Yeah, well, when I see her, we'll talk."

Esther then remembered what she wanted to say to Simone. "Did I not ask you to stop wearing those—" The office phone rang drowning out Esther's voice.

Simone hurried out of the room, calling to Esther, "Sorry, I better get that."

"Saved by the bell," Esther grunted.

She didn't see the cell phone palmed in Simone's hand with the office's phone number flickering in the light.

***

Roger picked up the bottle and tilted it to his mouth. He allowed the drink to flow down his throat and waited for its numbing effect. He had driven straight to the liquor store after his encounter with Duncan. He just wanted to forget the times that he would scream for anyone to help him, and no one ever came. The nights he went to bed with rough hands tearing at his still-growing body, and he would wake up in the morning with a busted lip . . . and worse.

Roger stood up and staggered. He was glad the drink was taking effect. But he could still see the scenes played out before him. If he could, he would put his own eyes out. Maybe that illogical act would stop the pictures from playing in his head.

He swigged more liquor, swallowing large gulps at a time, rushing to oblivion. When he turned the bottle up again it was empty.

I just need a little more.

He hunted around for the second bottle he knew he had bought, finally finding it in the trash. He didn't remember drinking it. Maybe if he drank one more bottle he would forget it all. He turned over furniture and pulled out groceries from the well-stocked pantry. No liquor, not even cooking sherry.

Roger decided he would go back to the store. Searching for the keys to Joshua's car, he was too inebriated to find them. He then had an Aha! Moment, remembering that Essie, a housewife, was usually at home and he could probably borrow her car. Zigzagging out of the house, he screamed her name.

Hair tussled and with a towel in her hands, Essie came barreling out of the house. "Roger, what's wrong?"

Roger stumbled into the bushes, then started swinging his arms as though he thought the bush was attacking him. "Get off of me."

Twirling around and not seeing anyone, he stopped swinging midair. Blinking, he said, "Need the car, to get what . . . I need, keys . . . now," he slurred.

"You're drunk! Reeking of liquor in the middle of the morning. It's not even ten o'clock yet," she shrieked.

Roger wiped his hands down his shirt attempting to stand up straight. "Sorry 'bout this. Keys, I need—" Roger tripped over a hosta plant and lay sprawled on the ground.

He could hear Essie speaking to someone demanding they come home.

Yes, he thought, *come home and take me to the store.* It then all went black.

Sudden cold water drenched over him. Roger scrambled up, and standing over his prone body was Joshua with a water hose and a murderous look on his face. Essie was nowhere to be seen.

"Get up before I kick you while you're down there," Joshua said, rolling the water hose up. "You are close to being put out on the curb. I can handle your lapses in judgment, but not my wife. You understand me?"

Roger sat in the yard with his head in his hands, nursing a humongous headache. "Everything came down on me at once, man. Your mom, Esther. It won't happen again, and I'll make up the time I missed today and apologize to your wife. I'm really sorry."

Roger waited for Joshua to leave or say something more. Instead, he continued to stare as though he was trying to figure something out. "Look, man, it can be hard out here. You sure nothing else is bothering you?"

Duncan's face swam in his vision. "No. Nothing I can't handle."

Chapter Forty-two

"The Lord's house is overrun with gypsies, tramps, and thieves," Naomi said, alerting Briggs that they had company. Briggs walked out and saw Roger and Joshua coming down the hallway.

His eyes narrowed.

"Naomi, I'm scheduling one-on-one counseling sessions with you. We are going to get to the bottom of that acid tongue of yours. Now, what I see is two men of our church. Please explain your comments."

"Okay, I gotta hurry on account of both dem brothers tall with long limbs. Oh, hold on. They just got stopped by Mudslinging Sister Go Tell It; we good," Naomi said referring to Sister Abigail, once known as the worst church gossip. She then pushed her chair back so she could see Briggs better. "Gypsy is Brother Roger; well, he could be the thief too, I guess. But he don't really have a home. And before he was locked up, he went from place to place after Put-a-Ring-on-It Esther divorced him.

"Joshua is the thief 'cause he got all that money and you can't pay me to believe it's all legit. How much time he do in jail? Long as he was in there, he had to have did some of everything to be locked up like that. And the tramp ain't here, but she just called. Here's her message," Naomi said and handed a pink slip to Briggs.

Briggs took the message and read it out loud. "*Please bring home some milk. Monica.*"

"Boom! Case closed."

Naomi pushed her chair back up just when the door opened and Joshua and Roger entered.

"Gentlemen, glad to see you both. Please, let's go in my office," Briggs said. He escorted them inside and turned back to Naomi. "Sister Naomi, please make yourself available after this meeting. You will not call my son's mother or any other person who visits this office names."

Naomi gave a trembling nod. "Yes, sir."

As Briggs was shutting the door, he heard her say, "Crap!"

"We not doing enough!" Joshua yelled after entering Briggs's office.

Whoa, calm down. You mind letting me in on the beginning of this conversation?" Briggs took a seat on the edge of his desk.

Roger nodded to Joshua. "I'll let him tell you. He was fired up in the car, all the way over here."

"I'm buying an apartment building, and I want to fill it with people who are just getting out of prison, drug rehab, with mental illness, or who were previously homeless. People who need a place to stay. I got all this money my father left me—money he stole from people through his insurance scams—it needs to go to better use. If we could start a program here at the church, it would help those serious about turning their lives around."

Briggs was stunned. "We already have a housing program. You know that."

Joshua fumed. "But only for the folks you deem presentable. More than single mothers and the elderly need help."

"You want me to turn my church into a refuge for felons and the like? Have you lost your mind" Briggs asked.

Joshua stood up. "Now, wait just a minute. Our church is already full of these very people, you just don't know it.

I thought the church was a place for the sick. You judging the ailments now?"

Thunder rolled across Briggs's face, and lightning sat in the rigidness of his spine.

"Don't make me kick you out of my office."

Joshua slowly calmed down. "You said the key word, Pastor."

"Oh, I'm Pastor now?" Briggs said, having stood and now sitting back down.

"Forgive my exuberance. I charged in here, and my urgency became your problem." Joshua's body relaxed. "The key word is refuge. This place is anointed for those who are burdened and heavy-laden. Am I right? What if you decided that all HIV and AIDS patients needed to go somewhere else?"

"I wouldn't do that," Briggs said, offended.

"Because it's wrong," Joshua pounded his fist into his hand. "Many of them had behavior or made choices that caused them to get the disease. But we give mercy. Why have we chosen not to do the same for others with different offenses?"

Briggs didn't understand why Joshua couldn't see the difference.

"Some of those people you mentioned can be violent," he retorted. He was getting tired of being on the losing end of his conversations with Joshua. "I want to help, but I don't want to lose my regular members because 'we're overrun with people of dubious origins.'"

"You just named everyone. We were born in iniquity, Pastor. All our origins are dubious. Yet, a debt was paid to save us all. Listen, I will fetter out the mental health patients who have a history of not taking their medicine, the hard core, dangerous, and the predators. At least hear me out, and let's meet some more," Joshua reasoned.

"I'll agree to that and nothing more," Briggs said. He spoke to Roger. "Man, you haven't said a lot."

Joshua interjected, putting his spin on Roger's silence. "He may still be upset with me about Tuesday."

Briggs looked between both men. He didn't know Roger well, but he was acting uneasy.

"Nah, I'm cool. That was two days ago. I had a setback. You had a right to remind me of the promises I made on how I wanted to live my life when I got out," Roger mumbled.

"Setback? Man, you was filthy drunk. Staggering around the front yard, swinging at imaginary foes. Essie had to call me to come home. You scared her, bro."

Roger folded his hands. Shoving them between his knees, he rocked. "I apologized for that. Essie is a sweet lady. I shouldn't have been drinking."

"Why did you drink?" Briggs asked.

"And why did you never show up for work? We're behind getting that unit ready now," Joshua added.

Roger tipped back his chair in his now frantic rocking. "What, y'all my wardens now?"

Briggs pulled his chair around to that side of the desk and sat. "No, he's your friend. And I'm your pastor. We're both trustworthy. I can look at you and see the pain. Holding it in will only delay the explosion."

Roger jumped up, sending the chair flying against the wall. Immediately, Briggs's intercom buzzed, and he answered it.

"I'm fine, Naomi," he said. "Everything is fine in here. Why don't you take the rest of the day off?"

He wouldn't listen to her prattle but cut her off and told her firmly to leave.

Briggs tried to help by sharing his past. His voice sounded faraway to his own ears, as though he was watching a scene unfold, his past unfurled.

"When I first came to Love Zion, I came as the interim pastor. I was so damaged, and I carried multiple insecurities." He turned to Joshua. "Then I met your mother. On my first visit to her house, she read me plain as day, and she wouldn't let me run from the pain of my past mistakes. I left her house delivered from some things and recognizing the shortcomings I needed to overcome in others. I now know it was a life-changing moment for me."

"You don't know what I carry," Roger said, wrapping his arms around his body, his rocking crazed.

Transfixed, Briggs watched Roger. He saw that he was becoming unglued. "I'm your Pastor. Nothing you say can make me turn my back on you. God orchestrated our meeting in a place where dreams are recovered. Now, I'm here to tell you that they can live again, be again."

Roger's shoulders shook, and he hunched over and howled out his torments. Then he cried out his burdens. And as Joshua left his seat and grabbed Roger in a bear hug, he yelled out his rage.

"So, hard . . . the pain of his hands on my body. The savagery of his taking me again and again. You . . . can't fight someone more than a hundred pounds heavier than you."

"No . . ." Joshua cried out as he wrapped his arms around his friend even tighter, his tears running down Roger's back.

Briggs slid onto his knees calling on God, praying quietly through the confessions of a nightmare. Neither were untutored to the things of the world, but Roger's raw pain was stripping them all bare.

Roger's guttural moans were uttered throughout his disclosure, heightening Joshua and Briggs's horror. "Night after night. Year after year. The steps to my bedroom, the scent of him on my skin, on my pillows."

Roger pulled back from Joshua. Turning away, he rubbed his face back and forth on his sleeve. His eyes were closed, helping him to tell his truth.

He then stared blankly ahead, still not making eye contact. "Then when I was around twelve years old, it changed. One night there was the sound of *two* sets of footsteps. I sat in my room, praying my ears were deceiving me that there weren't going to be two of them."

"Nah, man. Nah!" Joshua cried out. It was obvious he was in pain for his friend as his mucous mixed with his tears.

In a catatonic cadence Roger revealed his childhood. "There was no escape, though over the years, I tried. The door locked from the outside, and the windows were sealed shut, painted black. I wasn't allowed to have any friends. I believe one of my teachers suspected, but she never said anything."

"You never told anyone?" Joshua's face had aged in the last half hour. It seemed to say, "I understand abuse, but nothing like this."

Roger had a fleeting flicker of animation when he spoke of his one friend. "I did. I told the pretty little girl next door with the flyaway pigtails, and the one chipped tooth. We were six years old and we were going to get married when we grew up. Then the abuse started, and I came outside less and less. She was a spunky little girl. Knocked on the door and demanded I come outside. I think she cursed me out. She was bilingual, so I'm not sure. But she was so mad at me, I told her what was going on. I told her, and she ran home and told her mother."

Briggs was still on the floor praying for a way to reach Roger and help him ease his pain. He listened as his heart bled. How many of his parishioners were in this type of distress? And because of the enemy's cunning they were lost and alone? They needed more than one apartment building. They needed a whole village.

It was Joshua who asked the next question. "What happened after that? Did anyone help you?"

"Her dog was found that night dead, hanging from their clothesline," Roger wept. "Until Esther, that little girl was the only person who loved me. And until you, she was the only one I told my story to."

Roger blinked several times, remembering the whole ordeal.

"Her mother had called someone in the police department, but Duncan was well connected. They moved shortly after that because it was just her and her mother. I'm sure their dead dog scared both of them."

He sighed. "That was when I learned that my pain couldn't be shared. He told me that next time, she would be hanging from the clothesline."

"You can let it go, Roger. It's over. You're a different person," Joshua said as Briggs prayed harder. "And you did nothing wrong."

Roger shook his head. "Duncan's back."

Joshua stood, one hand pounding into the palm of the other. "Where is he?"

Roger slumped. "You don't understand. When you see Duncan, you know that the whole network of predators is with him."

"The other set of footsteps?" Briggs sat up from his prayer position.

Roger nodded, numb from the telling. "Yes, from the age of twelve until when I ran away at sixteen he sold me to the highest bidder. Nights of the full moons were the worst."

"My God!" Briggs's knowledge of what to say or do was limited. This was outside anything he had encountered.

"We have to do something. A whole network of pedophiles in Detroit?" Joshua paced the small confines of the office.

"Not necessarily physically. But they have a very sophisticated system. It has to be more so since I ran away."

He then folded his hands and said resigned, "They're here for me."

"For you? Man, you're almost forty years old. How old is this maggot?" Joshua said.

"I don't know. When I saw him on Tuesday, I can tell you that he looked exactly the same. How is that possible?" Roger said, forlorn and lost.

"It's not, not after over twenty years," Briggs said, thinking of the evil that would keep this man youthful.

"What could he possibly have planned for you?" Joshua said. "You're too old to be of interest to him now."

Roger placed his unsteady hands over his face. "It doesn't matter. I got away with two things no one has ever done. I stole his money, and I ran. He intends to make me pay."

"Well, we won't let him. We'll call the police" Briggs grabbed the phone.

"And tell them that a felon who just got out of prison wants a well-dressed, upper-middle-class man to stop trying to get with him? Where they do that at?" Roger asked, pulling his hands down from his face.

Joshua nodded. "Yeah, and just asking the police to help gives me the creeps."

"We have officers who attend this church. They're good brothers," Briggs protested.

Joshua nodded. "You're right. But I can't help my instant reaction to getting them involved."

"So, what? We wait?" Briggs asked. "Then what?"

"He was at church on Sunday," Roger said softly.

"What?" Briggs and Joshua yelled.

Roger nodded. His eyes were now dry, and he was finally thinking on the offensive instead of defensive. "You see? We don't have much time."

All three men looked at each other, knowing that it would take their collective thoughts and prayers to figure out how to bring down Duncan. Joshua rolled his sleeves up. Roger pulled out a paper and pen, and Briggs opened his Bible.

"Let's start with the Word and see where that takes us," Briggs said.

They all knew God had to have a plan.

Chapter Forty-three

Heels click clacked across the linoleum floor, and to Esther's ears they resounded like loud drums, beating out her arrival for anyone to hear. She knew it was petty, but she was glad she was in Columbus, Ohio, where she knew only a few people.

And yes, she was ashamed too. She knew about mental health diagnoses, and understood it was like other diseases. And she worked in the field, but her expertise was poverty not mental health, although many times the two were synonymous. In the last two weeks, she had done her homework and read as much as she could on the subject of schizophrenia. She also spoke to friends who were in the field. They were kind enough to give her concrete advice.

Yet, shaking off the stigma that went hand in hand with being associated with someone living under the shadow of schizophrenia was an exercise in courage and character. How did Deborah's family handle it? They hadn't discussed her parents or her brothers during their several phone conversations. Were they involved in her life?

The Help Desk was circular, and two women sat with identical artificial smiles, welcoming her to their agency. "Hello, I'm Esther Redding. I'm here to see a Dr. Kimbro."

One of the women ran her finger down the screen of the computer. "Yes, Mrs. Redding. She's expecting you. Please have a seat."

Esther had tuned her out right after she said she was expected. She was tired; she had been driving the whole morning. Deborah asking her to pick her up from the bus station had somehow morphed into Esther driving all the way to Columbus to have a session with her and her psychiatrist. Then afterward driving her to Detroit for her weeklong visit.

From what Esther could understand when the doctor had called to schedule the appointment, she and Sheri were a constant theme in Deborah's clinical counseling sessions. This was even before she had run into her at the hotel and tracked her down. Deborah had given the doctor written permission to talk to her and invite her to a session. So, here she was at the mental health facility, because of Deborah's session with her psychiatrist.

Teetering on telling her she couldn't make it, she had talked to Briggs about it. He felt that it was important for her to finally get "closure." She didn't care for that word. It sounded as though people were doors that you could either enter or exit at will. But she had listened and she knew that if she could figure out all that went on back then, she might be able to figure out how she had gotten to where she was today. She knew more than anyone that she had major issues with trust.

She didn't know what she expected, a couch to lay on maybe? But they all sat around in comfortable chairs, and Esther listened. They were discussing the suicide. It always came back to that night. Esther willed herself to hear it all. She needed to know how Deborah's experience differentiated from hers. Somewhere in Deborah's past were her answers.

"Have you ever thought about suicide, Deborah?" Dr. Kimbro swiveled in her leather chair, tapping her pen on her clipboard.

Esther could answer that for her, and she was supposedly normal. Had Esther ever thought about suicide? Yes, when her first husband beat her, and her second husband died on her. She had thought about it, had the flavor of it in her mouth, but the trauma of Sheri's exit left her unwilling to leave that kind of pain behind.

Deborah stared with eyes of molten steel. "Why do you ask me questions you already know the answer to?"

Esther sat forward, hoping the end to Deborah's pain would be a road map to ending hers.

Deborah continued. "The other doctors said her death was a trigger. That Sheri's act summoned an invisible hand that clicked off a switch in my head. It caused this dark, dank, unyielding break in how my brain functions. As a result, I spend too much time wandering through mazes answering voices no one else hears."

Deborah glared at Esther, finally acknowledging that she was in the room. Then her practiced look of blankness appeared. Only a supernatural eye would be able to see beyond the cover.

Suddenly Esther was acknowledged. "Esther, tell her how much fun I was. Who I used to be before the voices took over. I tried to make sense of what they were saying, but they were rude, always talking over each other, screaming to be heard."

"Did you ever figure out what they were saying?" Dr. Kimbro asked.

Deborah looked over at Esther, this time lowering her eyes. "I already told you what they said."

Dr. Kimbro squinted at Deborah. "Esther is here with us today for a reason. So, please, tell us again."

Deborah twisted away from both of them. Her voice was soft, causing the two women to lean in. "They were warning me, protecting me. They told me that smiling faces lie. People like my parents, who secretly plotted against me. People like Esther, who the voices assured me had already killed Sheri. They were the devil. The voices said I would be next, which meant I had to be smarter. I left school, Esther, my family, and all I knew. I couldn't allow them to get me."

Esther gasped, then held her mouth shut, pulling her lips in tight.

"And now? How do you feel now, Deborah?"

She looked over at Esther, saw her crimson cheeks, and her unshed tears.

"My medicine has allowed me to see that the voices lie. My behavior modification program taught me that I can't let them take over my thoughts, I have to fight them."

Dr. Kimbro wrote in her journal. "And you're ready to go to Detroit? After all these years, you feel equipped to handle this kind of pressure?"

"Yeah, Doc. I told you that when you first asked me. I been in this program for five years now. And you've said yourself that the new medication and the strict program has alleviated a lot of my symptoms. I can't afford to think I'm like other people. I have to constantly stay vigilant. When I feel like I'm slipping again, I know what to do." Deborah tapped her feet, and scratched her thighs up and down. I'm now here voluntarily. You can't make me stay."

Dr. Kimbro arched her brow and turned to Esther. Her nod asked Esther to make note of Deborah's sudden fidgeting. "What you are noting is the onset of Deborah having an episode. She is unhappy with my line of questioning, and as a result, if she doesn't do her breathing exercises and reduce her internal stimuli, we could have a problem. Isn't that right, Deborah?"

Esther saw Deborah take charge of her breathing. She stilled her feet and clasped her hands together. Eyes closed, she sat for a moment before speaking. "That wasn't fair."

"No, but I asked Mrs. Redding to come so that she'd understand some of what she's facing."

Deborah leaped up, her chair falling backward. "What you want me to tell her? You want her to know how my brain goes into a fog? How I could see a nothingness inside my head when I closed my eyes and tried to summon a thought"

Deborah had a beautiful head of thick, natural-styled hair. She pulled it apart, and Esther saw a bald patch covered by the thick growth around it. "How about how I pulled my hair out to the follicles in some areas, and it won't grow back?"

She came over and grabbed the arms of Esther's chair, bent over, and murmured into her ear, so close that Esther could feel wet heat as she spoke. "Or that I would open my mouth, and incoherent gibberish would spill out. How I would wait for people to answer me, but instead, watch horrified expressions cross their faces, then pity. Then they would leave as fast as they could. Most never came back."

She stepped back, searching Esther's face. "Kinda the way you're looking right now."

Esther worked to mold her face into its normal visage. She had no idea what to do. Dr. Kimbro motioned for her to sit still.

Deborah stared off into space. "And then there were the times when I literally stank so bad, *I* couldn't stand it. But I could never quite figure out what the smell was. I would check around the two-bit motel where I stayed, and I could never locate the smell. It never dawned on me that if I hadn't bathed in two weeks the smell was me. Is that what you want me to tell her?"

Dr. Kimbro stood up and gently led Deborah back to her seat. "How are you feeling now? Do an inventory, a self-check."

Deborah shook her head. "I'm good. Every time I let off a little steam, it doesn't mean I'll have an episode."

"It also doesn't mean you won't. And yes, I needed her to see the truth about your past, because without that truth, the two of you can't go forward."

Esther didn't want to hear more. She was sorry she had come. This closure was darker than anything she had imagined. She had enough problems without adding Deborah's.

"What truth? The last time the Deborah that Esther knew was present, we were at a homecoming dance in college. At least Esther was at the dance. I had left to go and find our other best friend, Sheri," Deborah said, her voice fading out as though the memory she was having happened to someone else.

Deborah explained that she had one solid memory, of one night only. Everything else during that time had faded into shadows. It was the school icebreaker, and she had left Esther mooning over Briggs.

"I approached the front door to our dorm room, key in hand. I was feeling good, so I called out, 'Sheri, you better not be bent over some book when I get in here.'"

"I was bummed out; couldn't believe I had to leave the party to rouse her from schoolwork. My key easily turned, but I was annoyed when the door wouldn't budge. I started banging on the door.

"Sheri . . . Sheri, open up. Hey, quit playing."

"The whole time, I was pushing, and shoving against the door. Then it started to inch open.

"Finally," I said, and maneuvered my body sideways as I slipped through the sliver of space I had created.

The room was pitch-black so I reached for the light switch, and my heart plummeted. 'Nooooo . . .' I kept blinking, the sight before me was a macabre scene from a Hitchcock movie. Sheri, a broken doll caricature, hung from the living-room light fixture.

"I raced forward grasping Sheri's legs fighting to untangle her from the clothesline noose. She was too short, and the noose too difficult to reach while I struggled to support her body.

"My eyes burned with my tears as I leapt on the desk and pulled at the rope Sheri had made into an instrument of death. I swung her body into the rope to get momentum, pulling with everything I had, when suddenly Sheri, the light fixture, and the ceiling plaster crashed to the floor. Plaster particles covered my hair and clung to my eyelids as I sobbed in terror.

"I knelt beside Sheri's pale, waxy body and shook her. Cold, dark eyes stared vacantly while I desperately searched for a pulse. There was none."

Esther grabbed Deborah by the shoulders and pulled her into a hug. She pressed their bodies together, trying to give her, her light, her love.

She had never gotten this version, the pain, and the trauma of that night. Deborah disconnected after the incident, and she gave monosyllabic answers to everyone's questions. Even hers.

They held each other, crooning words of absolution, rocking back and forth. Seventeen years later . . . closure.

They were in the city. In the three-and-a-half hour drive, Esther learned all about the years they had been separated. It was like the old Deborah was back, and she wanted to share everything. The way they used to do with lip gloss and girlhood secrets. Then she would fall into silence and not say anything for twenty minutes. Esther would become tense, but then Deborah would start speaking again. Sometimes her speech was slow, other times she rushed to get it out.

Her pace was slow as she discussed the doctor's explanation that Sheri's suicide triggered a psychotic break, which brought about her schizophrenia. She stated she was at an age where this type of mental illness manifested. When most young adults were entering their careers, or choosing their life's path, her path of mental illness was chosen for her.

Esther shuddered. Schizophrenia, no matter the technical name for it, was a thief, a robber, and a malevolent force of nature.

"Have you been in Columbus all this time?" Esther said.

"Nah, girl, one city just folded into the other. A bottle of booze, pills, powder, anything that got me high was good. And you don't want to know 'bout all the sweaty bodies in the back of dingy clubs, backseats, and one-hour hotels. They all felt the same in the dark."

"I am so sorry, girl," Esther said, her eyes on the road.

Deborah said, "For what? None of this is your fault . . . Although for a long time my demons told me it was. Then memories started to fade. I could remember bits and pieces, like a thousand-piece puzzle that was never finished, you know? You walk by it, added a new piece, stared at it, and then you got tired of trying to figure it out."

Deborah looked out the window, her face reacting to all the changes in the city that was once her home. Her parents now lived on the Far Eastside, and Esther's GPS was taking them through downtown.

"Hey, what's going on with our city?"

Esther grimaced. "You know us, we're a tough group of people. We helped build this nation; through steel, automobiles, even the music of its soul. Some people try to forget we exist, but we won't lay down. We still here, girl!" Esther said, changing lanes.

Deborah gave her a high five. "Like me, child, like me!"

***

Twenty minutes later, they stood in the foyer of Deborah's parents' home. The aroma of Pine Sol mingled with some form of southern down-home cooking tickled Esther's nose. Esther watched Deborah hesitate, then blow out a frustrated breath. "I hope I'm not exchanging one prison for another."

Esther spoke under her breath, urging Deborah to patience. "Give it a chance. Growing up, your parents gave you more freedom than any of us ever got."

"There is a premental breakdown and postmental breakdown relationship," she whispered back.

Deborah's father rushed out of the kitchen, calling back inside. "Maisie, they here, they here!" Turning toward them his strides were long. "We left the door unlocked for you. Come on in here, baby girl."

Deborah's father lifted her in a bear hug, setting her down with a kiss on the forehead, then he threw an arm around Esther's shoulders. "Yo' mama 'don' outdid herself in this kitchen. Oxtails and rice. You ain't had nothing this good in many a moons—" Eyes widening, he stopped and started again. "I mean, ain't nothing like your mama's cooking," he said, wiping his hands down his apron in a nervous gesture.

Deborah placed her hand on her father's arm, holding him back. "Hey, Pops? Don't tiptoe around my problems. Lay it out there. I can't do this if everyone is jittery around me. I'm paranoid enough."

Deborah's father's eyes raised in anxiety when he heard her mention the word paranoid. "You need something, baby girl? Your medicine? I can get you a glass of water, right now."

Deborah fingered her hair, pulling it at its roots. Esther froze, then exhaled when she saw Deborah catch herself and release her hair quickly. "No, I think I'll go lie down for a minute. Same place as last time?"

"Sure is; your mama fixed it up nice like for you. And it has a big bed in it, give you room to stretch out." He began to move away, but then shook his graying head, inhaled deeply, and swung back around. "Sweet girl, no more running for any of us. I'm going to love you enough to hear you. I hope you'll do the same. We're going to work this out as a family. Your diagnosis doesn't make you unloveable or unhuggable. Your mama and I love you!"

Esther faded into the background as she witnessed Deborah's eyes moistening and her silent lean into the man that Esther knew was once her friend's hero.

Clearing his throat, Mr. Whitaker pulled Deborah under his meaty arm, and spoke to Esther. "Esther, how your folks? They good? Your daddy still at the plant?"

"They're good, Mr. Whitaker. Dad retired last year. I'll tell them that you asked about them. Should I go in the kitchen and pay my respects to Mrs. Whitaker?"

Pulling Deborah along, he stepped in front of Esther as though blocking her path to the kitchen. "Uh, no, no. She always been funny 'bout her kitchen. Was right snappish while I was fixing my banana pudding. You staying for dinner, right?"

Esther gave a regretful frown. "Oh no, sir. I have to get home to my children."

"That's nice, children mean the world to their parents. Love 'em well."

Esther heard his hidden meaning. This front-seat look at her best friend's life was painful. She needed to go.

She hugged Deborah. "Girl, call me tomorrow and we'll get together as soon as you get settled in."

Deborah's smile wavered. "I sure will. I have something else to tell you. So, dinner is on. Okay?"

"Sure." Esther left. However, now she was puzzled. They had just had a counseling session and a three-and-a-half hour ride together. What was possibly left to tell?

***

The imps scattered like dust as Esther walked out of the Whitaker household. They had spent the morning sending the spirit of anxiety over Maisie Whitaker.

The Leader waited at the end of the walkway. "Did you reach her?"

"Yesss, she is afraid for her daughter. Her fear will separate her from the love her daughter needs," they said in unison.

"What of the father? He has familiar spirits. His uncle had schizophrenia, although the family hid it. Locked him away as though he no longer mattered, visited him on Sundays after church. And they call us evil," The Leader sneered. It was what he felt the best part of the human race was, their ability to be hypocritical.

Imp One stepped up to report their failure. He knew the others would never speak up. "He was not receptive, O Great One. Every time they spoke into his ear to accuse, he would sing a line from the hymn "We've Come This Far by Faith.""

The Leader smacked him with his tail. "Did I ask you what he sang? Shut up! I can't stand even to hear the title of that noise."

Imp One staggered back, but he did not fall. He had learned how to take The Leader's abuse.

"Watch him. A man is the head of his house. If he is strong the house will not be divided. Even if we can reach the wife, he has the ability to cover her. Bombard him with lost opportunities. He's older. Bombard him with regrets. Send a young sweet thing his way. Have her shake what goodness has given her, and whisper secret longings in his ear."

"We got you. It will be done," the imps sang.

Imp One stood in silence; he hated fools' errands. He might as well be wearing a court jester's suit. Couldn't

The Leader tell when a human had fixed his heart to Him whose name is not spoken? He could. And this man wasn't budging. He had been praying for his child for so long, that sooner or later the prayers were going to be answered. When a parent doesn't give up, he causes a setup in the heavens.

They had done all they could. He was through fooling with this family. At least for now. He'd continue to focus on the Love Zion members. There were still weak links in that bunch. Deborah's news to Esther would surely help him break Esther all the way down.

Imp One slinked beneath the earth and entered into a rock-encrusted cavern, gleaming with red sulfuric ash. "Master is right. I need that hymn music out of my head. I'll play me some gangsta rap."

Chapter Forty-four

The receiving line in church was dying down. The last spot at the end of the line was Roger, who waited patiently. Even two weeks after their talk, he was still staying out of the way of the main body of Christ.

They had all kept an eye out for Duncan, but there was no sign of the man. They were on high alert.

It was October, and the day was an unseasonably warm sixty-five degrees. The children were outside on the church playground, running and playing. Briggs longed to join them.

Roger came forward, and they shook hands. "Great sermon, Pastor."

"Thanks, God gets the glory. Tell me, are you close to getting that apartment ready for Monica? You hang back so much, and she's the first person out the door. I wanted you two to meet so she could arrange to get the keys."

Briggs was almost desperate to get his house back from Monica land. She had a way of soaking up all his air. He wanted his privacy back.

Roger rubbed his chin concentrating on Briggs's pressing need. "The apartment shouldn't be a problem. It'll be ready this week. I was delayed because I added some sweet upgrades." A look of relief crossed Briggs's face. Roger then added, "And, I hang back from the crowd to minimize confusion."

Briggs nodded, understanding Roger had been given the cold shoulder since Esther confronted him. "Keeping confusion down is good. Esther may not have told you, but she was apologetic after she caused that scene. She has a good heart. It's just an uncomfortable situation that will take time to heal for all involved."

Briggs cleared his throat. He didn't want to be unfeeling concerning Roger's issues with the church members, but he wanted Monica gone yesterday. "I appreciate you getting the apartment ready. It's a miracle this hasn't caused a scandal, but it seems like this is a season where Love Zion is minding its own business."

Roger smirked. "I don't know about that, but I haven't heard anything. Of course, no one really talks to me, either."

Briggs clapped Roger on the back. "That will change; give people time. You're doing a great job with the prison ministry. I understand that the number of inmates committing to Christ has grown."

Roger appeared embarrassed by the praise. "He does all things well."

Ending their conversation, Briggs held out his hand and Roger clasped it. Then Briggs began moving away. "I'm going outside to bring the children in. Sister Greene's granddaughter, Kathy, is today's playground attendant, and she can be a bit inpatient to leave church."

"She's a teenager." Roger scanned the area. The hall was emptying, and most members had left. "Since Joshua's not ready to go, I'll walk with you."

As the two men walked outside, Kathy stood right by the exit door talking animatedly on her cell phone.

In plain sight, the children surrounded a strange man who towered over them, a red scarf flung around his neck. They were excitedly raking their hands over a tablet's screen as he appeared to give the group directions.

In less than forty seconds both men took off running.

Holding her cell out, Kathy called from behind them, "It's just Mr. Easy!"

Roger hollered, "Duncan, you get away from those children!" Pumping his arms with ferocity he picked up speed.

Briggs was slightly behind him as he pulled out his cell and hit three for the deacons of the church, yelling into the phone, "Code 1, playground!"

Startled by the commotion, the children backed away, all except Miracle who stood there indifferently, flicking the screen. Before Briggs could speak, Roger was in Duncan's face.

At the same moment, BJ pulled his father's hand. "It's Mr. Easy, Daddy. He's real nice."

Briggs squeezed BJ's shoulder. "Shush, son."

Duncan raised his hands in surrender. "Whoa there. Hold up. The kids were interested in a game on my tablet. I told Kathy I'd watch them when her phone call came in."

Kathy, who had followed the men, spoke in a shaky voice. "That's right. I'm sorry if I did something wrong, Pastor."

Stone-faced, Briggs said with authority, "Kathy, take all of the children inside. Now."

With a pout, Miracle reluctantly handed Duncan his tablet. Duncan whispered something to her, and she smiled.

"Yes, sir." With tears escaping, Kathy quickly hustled the silent, wide-eyed children away.

Three deacons had approached, and Briggs put up his hand for them to stay slightly back. The air sizzled with tension as Roger refused to give an inch to Duncan. They were so close, Roger leaned slightly back to jam his finger in Duncan's chest.

In a furious whisper, with a crazed look in his eye Roger warned Duncan. "You just changed the game. You come on God's property with your evil and dared to approach our children. You a dead punk walking!"

Duncan, who appeared to be the kind of man that never backed down, stepped back. He brushed off his camel-colored cashmere coat in a nonchalant manner. "There are witnesses to your threats. Maybe I should have you arrested? Send you back to prison."

Briggs stepped forward. "What witnesses?"

Duncan grinned mockingly and said, "And you a man of the cloth." He then said to Briggs, "You should pay more attention to your children. The world is so forward now, and there are a lot of things in it that can go 'boo' in the dark."

"I'm warning you." Roger grabbed him by the collar.

With amazing strength, Duncan pried Roger's hands from him. "You have a thing for grabbing me by the collar. That was your last pass."

Turning back to Briggs, his voice slimy with innuendo, he continued. "Kids are curious little creatures. I was doing you a favor. The young madam was giving the others the wrong information about how their anatomy works. Pity, I thought they taught these things in the schools. But this *is* Detroit."

Briggs stepped forward placing his foot on top of Duncan's. His body blocking his actions to the others, he spoke in a hushed tone. "I know what you are, and what you've done." He applied more pressure through his foot. "Don't ever come around here again. Even better, get out of town." He pressed harder watching Duncan grow pale. "If I even *see* your shadow, I will make it my business to destroy you."

His features drained of color, Duncan held Briggs captive with eyes of chiseled animosity. "You have no idea who you're dealing with. You don't have the power to destroy me, Pastor Briggs Stokes of 1455 Seminole Street,

48214. Son, BJ, ex-wife Monica Hawthorne, newest love interest, the widow Esther Redding—"

Briggs lost it. Leaping forward he was caught by the arm as Roger swung him away from Duncan.

Gripping his arm when Briggs sought to break free, Roger muttered, "There are curious eyes watching. We'll deal with this later."

Duncan gave Briggs an arrogant smirk. "You better listen to your boy. We'll be seeing each other again, I'm *sure* of it." Before Duncan walked away, he gave a last parting shot. "Tell your father, the bishop, that Duncan said hello. After all, I'm one of his biggest supporters."

When he turned more people were in the yard. They held various levels of interest, but the deacons' faces were concerned.

Shoulders tense, Deacon Clement stepped forward. "Pastor, something tells me we have trouble. How can I help?"

Briggs's chest heaved. He exhaled, working to remain calm. "Get me the name of a good security company. Brother Jerome needs help securing this property."

Roger arched his eyebrow but remained quiet as Briggs continued to speak to his deacons. When he was finished, Roger gave his opinion.

"The man is evil personified. You can't wait till he strikes again. We have to go after him. Your interference in his fun has now made you a target."

Briggs shook his head. "No, we became a target when he staked out the children. They knew him, man. That means while we have been watching out for him in the sanctuary, he's been checking out the children's wing. We have a member who works as church security in that area. He must not have picked up on anything."

Roger appeared frustrated with Briggs. "This man is a master. He's been getting away with doing this for more than twenty-five years that I know of."

Briggs's face was drawn. "How is that possible? He looks our age."

Roger had fear stamped all over him. "I don't know how old he is. My stepfather was forty when he and my mother were killed. He was his younger brother. At least that's what I was led to believe. I was six when he got custody of me."

Briggs saw the remaining parents milling around talking. "I've got to go. I need to have a word with all the parents, and then a long talk with BJ." Briggs didn't look forward to the parents peppering him with questions he couldn't answer. Not when he was looking for answers himself.

It was later at her parents' house that Esther took David and Ruth into her old bedroom. It was time they had a talk about their bodies. Briggs had opted to go home, because he wanted to have a similar conversation with BJ. Whoever the man at church was, his actions prompted her to have the talk she had been working her way up to for several weeks. And like Phyllis had said, it would not be about the birds and the bees. Or about storks, or cutesy names for body parts.

When they were younger, David and Ruth had learned about stranger danger, and good touch, bad touch. Now it was time to become more specific about who was a stranger, and what parts on their bodies was theirs alone to govern. Esther had used her time wisely and researched what they could understand at this age, and what could wait for later. Most of all, she needed them to understand they could come to her with anything and she would be there to help with answers. Leaving that information to an almost eight-year-old and some strange man was not an option.

Chapter Forty-five

Filth clung to him like a gold digger to the NBA. Roger couldn't believe he had to inch his way through the building's crawl space to find out how one measly mouse had gotten into the building. But Joshua had insisted. Now he was covered from head to toe in grime.

Things sure do change. When he was in prison, mice were a given. The transition in his mind from stalking mice to his larger rodent problem was smooth.

He thought about the chaos that followed Duncan's visit. Parents demanding to know how some stranger got on the church property. The children trying to tell the adults he was not a stranger. Their continued assurance that he attended their church, and his name was Mr. Easy. None of the children could remember when he first appeared. None could remember how he first approached them. They could only remember he was "nice."

When questioned further, they said he never gave them candy. But he had all the latest games on his tablet. He promised to show them more. He was showing them a new game when they were on the playground. Roger knew Duncan. The games were his candy, and the kids couldn't resist.

Frustrated, he'd wanted to warn the parents, but while Esther was not in attack mode she was still hostile. They wouldn't have listened to him anyway and would have turned his past into his prison. Everybody couldn't handle your testimony.

At the end, Joshua assured the parents that he would be glad to spring for a full state-of-the-art security system, including cameras and a security person to protect the members when on church grounds.

Esther angrily yelled, "About time. It only took nine years for y'all to take security serious around here." She sucked her teeth and rolled her eyes directly at Roger as though reminding him that the last time he had put his hands on her was in the church parking lot.

That was his cue to leave, and he did. Now this morning he was treading through more dirt; he couldn't catch a break.

Roger pulled a white handkerchief out of his pocket, wiping it over his face. It came back soiled. It couldn't be helped. He could either go home and change, which meant he would be extremely late showing the tenant the varnished floors and giving her the keys or he could let her see that they worked hard around the place to make it nice for them.

After the incident at church, he'd needed an outlet. Or, as his prison counselor taught, a way to work through his feelings of aggression, so he came to the apartment building and finished Briggs's ex-wife's unit. He felt like he owed him.

He'd called him at first light and told him she could come by today. Briggs was ecstatic. Then Joshua called about finding the mouse. Couldn't be helped; he'd have to go up and meet the tenant like he was.

He took the elevator to the third floor. He hurried off, noting that a woman was standing at the door, her back to him, tapping her foot. He glanced at his cell, two minutes late.

"I'm sorry, I'm late," he said, before she turned around and he stopped, stunned.

"You!" she said.

"You!" he said.

Roger looked her up, and then down. In the light of a new day, she was still gorgeous, and he still felt used. "Thanks for slinking out of my place without a word. Next time you decide to treat someone like a boy toy, just leave money on the dresser like any other John."

"King, what are you doing here?" she stammered.

"I work here," Roger said, sliding back, indicating his green khaki work uniform.

She turned up her nose and sniffed as though he smelled. "It certainly is a step down from the clothes you had on when we met. I took you for a businessman, and you're nothing but a maintenance man? I don't do laborers."

Roger laughed. "Too late."

Monica stabbed him with her words. "Boy, you better cherish that night, because it is the closest you will ever get to the mountaintop again."

Roger sneered, looking her up and down. "You think pretty highly of yourself, don't you?" He then mimicked a woman's voice in passion. "Ooh, baby. Yes, like that, baby."

Her eyes darted quickly up and down the hallway. She hissed, "Be quiet. A real man never talks about what he does with a lady."

"Well, you're proving you're no lady," he said, his eyes cast down, hiding the hurt of her dismissal.

"You're ignorant!" she shouted.

"You're a stuck-up snob," he yelled.

"Whatever!" she screamed, her hands clenched into fists.

"Yes, well, I'm out." He pivoted, intending to stride down the hallway.

"Out? Fine. Give me my keys and leave. I hope you redid the floors like I requested," she said, holding out her hand.

Roger ignored her outstretched hand. "Your Highness, your castle awaits you."

With a flourish, he opened the door to the apartment. The floor was as smooth as ice, the wood shined like a penny, newly minted. But it was the unexpected crown molding that had Monica doing a happy dance.

"The crowning around the ceiling and the matching chair rails are just what this room needed. How did you know?" Monica said, with a squeal.

Roger's chest swelled. He had taken a chance, putting his own spin on the room. It had paid off.

"I wanted to showcase the floor, and these were the touches I felt would set it all off."

"I like it," she said, walking around. "It's been a long time since I had my own place . . ." She stopped as though she had said too much.

"I know how that feels." Roger couldn't stop his own curiosity. "Why the name Esther?"

Monica's attitude came roaring back with his question. "I told you then why. It's royal."

"You don't lie very well, Monica."

Roger knew that he had just thrown her for a loop.

A panicked look crossed her face. "How do you know my name? Have you been following me?"

Roger put his hands out in a reassuring gesture. "Calm down. Nobody's following you. It was good, but not stalker good. Dang, woman."

"Says who? You? Psssh . . ." Monica scoffed at him.

Roger pulled the ring with three keys on it out of her hand. A tag hung from it with the name Monica Hawthorne and the apartment number typed in bold. "Here, Einstein."

Monica blushed. "Oh." She moved around, running her hand on the new fixtures.

Roger studied her. "So, you're Pastor Stokes's ex-wife. I can't see the connection."

Monica tripped on air. "How do you know that?"

"Unlike you, I can string two and two together and actually get four. Joshua said the apartment was for Pastor Stokes's ex-wife. She was currently staying with him and needed a place. The fact that Pastor Stokes has spoken to me twice this week to make sure the apartment is ready leads me to believe that Ms. High and Mighty doesn't actually have a home. And the one she is currently residing in, she's worn out her welcome. Am I right?"

"Forget you, King," Monica threw her keys at him.

Roger easily dodged the keys and snorted. "My name is not King, it's Roger. And that's real ladylike behavior you're exhibiting."

"What do you know?" Monica asked.

Roger looked at her. She was like a balloon losing its air. Her puffed-up demeanor shrunk and left in its place was someone who was lost.

"Do you know why I went with you that night?" she said.

"No. But I have an idea of why you wanted to be called Esther."

She grunted. "Two plus two?"

"Yeah. But tell me about that night" Roger said, before he pulled the work towel from the bar counter where he had accidentally left it. It was stained, but not dirty. Surprisingly, she didn't fuss when he spread it out. She just hiked up her jeans and sat on it.

"It wasn't the sex. I wanted to be held. To be caressed, like I was cherished. Sometimes for women, we have to go along with the sex to get the affection. My children's hugs and kisses were no longer sufficient."

Roger wanted to dance through the apartment. He had been digging and like a gold miner, he had finally hit the payload. Honesty.

"Can I share something with you?" He continued when he saw her nod. "I wasn't looking for sex either. It was your vulnerability that drew me. Then, when I finally got close enough, it was the smell of lavender in your hair that held me."

"Lavender?"

Roger nodded. "I always associate that smell with my mother."

"You had it in your bathroom. I wondered about that. It wasn't a normal scent a man would use." Monica pulled her feet under her.

"Lost my mama when I was a little boy. You hold on to what you can," he said.

"Did I just detect a southern accent?" Monica teased.

Roger gave her a bashful smile. "Wow. I taught myself to get rid of all southern inflections in my voice."

"I'm from Atlanta. There is nothing wrong with a southern drawl," Monica protested.

Roger called her on her hypocrisy. "Then why don't I hear it?"

"Point made." Monica stared at him, as though trying to figure out something. "So where you from?"

Roger had hidden his past for so long he didn't know what to say. Then he thought about it, and decided honesty deserved honesty. "Macon, Georgia."

Monica clapped. "Ha! Right down the road."

"Yes, even lived in Atlanta for a while. Ran away from there when I was around sixteen years old."

Monica moved around as though the floor was getting hard under her rear end. Roger took off his shirt, leaving him in nothing but his wife beater. Still, he folded his shirt, and she raised up as he slid it under her. His muscles were lean, but rock hard. Monica turned slightly away, and he gave her a knowing smirk, then winked.

"I lived in Decatur," she said, ignoring the wink.

"Me too. It was a really hard time in my life," Roger said and leaned back on his elbows.

Monica's shrug was practiced and deliberate. "It was okay, then it wasn't. My mother moved us away when I was six years old."

Roger picked up on her wistful tone and her expertise in diminishing this time in her life. He wanted to know more. "What happened that it wasn't okay anymore?"

Monica hesitated as though she grappled with disclosing the intimate details of her life. Choosing, she sighed. "Somebody hung my dog, tied him on the clothesline right next to my Raggedy Ann pajamas. Scared me and my mother so bad, we moved by the end of the week."

Roger's breath left his body. He rose off the floor, then knelt before her. "A black-and-white spotted terrier, with half an ear?"

Monica gasped. "How do you know that?"

Roger reached out his hand, fingering the tips of her hair in wonder. "Monnie?"

"How do you know my nickname?" she asked as he cupped her cheek and stroked.

Monica leaned forward noting his light gray eyes and caramel skin. "Wait!" She turned his face, left to right, studying his profile. Her eyes widened. "Raj?"

They stayed there, in that moment, allowing a flood of memories, to reacquaint them. They had been friends, the little boy who had lost his mother and was new to town, and the young girl, too pretty and shy to readily make friends. They had both changed, but in that space of time, they were who they remembered.

He held his arms out, and Monica scooted into his embrace.

Roger whispered into her ear. "You still bilingual?"

Monica burst out laughing. "That was Jamaican patois from my grand 'mere. Yes, I still speak it."

She pulled his hands from around her. "Whatever happened to you? You know, after . . ."

"After I was molested? It went on until I was sixteen, then I ran away." Roger had spoken about it so much in the last weeks that he said it in a matter-of-fact way. He was finally learning that he was not what was done to him.

Monica gripped his arms, digging into him. "For ten more years, Raj? Oh, please, don't tell me that."

Roger placed his arms around her. "I can't believe we are even talking about this. Before two weeks ago, I hadn't told anyone but you. Not even my wife, Esther."

"Please tell me you weren't once married to Esther Redding?" When he nodded, she shook her head. "God must be laughing. This is getting stranger and stranger." She put her head on his shoulder.

"What's the Bible verse that says, 'think it not strange'?"

Monica shrugged her shoulders. "I was a first lady, but I didn't quite have the Bible memorization down."

Roger strained his memory. "Can't think of it. But I do know this, there are no coincidences. God gives us who and what we need, when we're ready."

"Oh my. You're a blue-collar worker," Monica sputtered as though she was in agony.

"Yeah, and you're a high-maintenance, gold digger, who, from what I hear, has as much baggage as I do," Roger said, a faint smile on his lips.

Monica started laughing; she laughed so hard that she fell back on the floor and cackled. Roger joined her.

Monica rolled over. "Oh my goodness. I just thought about something. Didn't you do time for trying to hurt Esther?"

Roger sat Indian-style across from her. "Guilty as charged. I can't change my past. I have been really trying to change who I am, though. And I know my behavior didn't give you a clue, but I'm a Christian. Not perfect, though. And sitting across from you," his eyes slowly traveled over her body, "I'm definitely struggling in some areas."

Monica boldly did the same to him, ending at his lips, and then licking hers. "We can't seriously be contemplating anything . . . Can we?"

Roger spoke in earnest, liking the fact that so far, other than their names, they had been honest with each other. "I know you have two children. And I heard that there was an incident and you were hurt."

He removed her scarf and tenderly stroked her scar.

"I don't have any children. I have a good job, and I'm going to get counseling to deal with my past. I think you need counseling too. Just because you're functioning doesn't mean you're not dysfunctional."

Monica opened her mouth to protest, and Roger placed his fingers over her lips to force her to be quiet. Her eyes bulged at the sight of dirt on his fingers.

"Oops, sorry," he said, as he removed them. "I just need you not to say anything right now. Just think about everything. We can talk later."

Monica stood and gathered her purse, looked around the room, and headed to the door. "The apartment is really beautiful, Roger. Thank you."

He watched her leave, her long legs snug in designer jeans, her long hair swaying across her back. Soon, the hair morphed into two fly-away pigtails, and he heard her girlish laughter.

Roger picked up his shirt and the towel from the floor. "Monnie," he whispered as he left the room.

Chapter Forty-six

The security team was placing cameras in the upper corners of the church. Briggs stood talking to Steve, his new head of security, when Esther walked into the room.

"Hey, sweetheart. Did we have plans?" he asked, taking in her print wraparound dress.

She observed the cameras being installed. "No, but I was in a meeting down the street and thought you might be free for a little talk."

"Sure," he said.

He gave a pat on Steve's back and said to him, "See you in a minute. Any problems come up, let me know."

Steve nodded, but remained focused on the installation of the camera. They walked down to Briggs's office. Naomi nodded a greeting as they went inside.

After sitting down, Briggs grabbed two bottles of water from his miniature fridge. While handing her a bottle, he gave her a soft kiss on her cheek.

Opening his bottle, he asked. "Honey, you wanted to talk?"

"Did Monica finally move out?" Esther asked, setting her bottle on his desk firmly.

"Yes, she did. She left yesterday. And get this—Roger helped her move into her new place."

Briggs watched for Esther's response to this news.

"You're kidding?"

Briggs looked at her like he wanted to laugh.

Then Esther stammered, "The two of them together? Lord, today, the imps must be having a celebration."

"I don't know about the imps, but I think *we* have some celebrating to do," Briggs said, finally letting his laughter spill over. "I had a long talk with Monica about BJ's feelings. She was horrified, and she plans to spend more time with him. He's spending the night over at her apartment tomorrow night. So, would you like to come over for dinner?"

"Hmm, with just the two of us?" Esther's eyes danced with the possibilities.

Briggs took his bottled water and rolled it across his forehead. "When you put it like that, you making a brother's temperature rise."

"Then it's definitely a date," Esther said and lifted her bottle in a mock toast.

Briggs swigged a large mouthful and lifted his bottle in return. "How was your dinner with Deborah last night?"

Esther sighed. "It was good, but her cousin tagged along. When we went to the movies the other day her sister-in-law came. I know they haven't seen her, but we haven't had more than ten minutes alone together since she got here. Her family has had one celebration after the other since she got back. She looked a little frazzled," Esther said and tapped her finger on her bottle thinking out loud. "I'm still puzzled as to what she has to tell me. But she leaves tomorrow. Her dad is taking her back. I asked her when we were on the phone, but she said she wanted to talk in person."

Briggs sympathized. "Now you're really wondering, huh?"

Esther sulked. "Yes, but the good news is she'll be back in two weeks." She then brightened, "The security cameras look like they mean business," she said with approval.

Briggs hadn't told Esther about Roger's molestation. But she was aware that they felt the man Duncan was a predator. They'd used their connections with their law enforcement church members and had the police come to the church the same day as the incident. It didn't help. They were advised that Duncan had not committed a crime by talking to the children. It may have been inappropriate to engage the children without parental consent, however, none of the children reported he had so much as touched even their hand. And the church was considered open to all.

So Briggs vowed to do all he could to protect them himself. Joshua was helping, and Roger was using all his street contacts to comb Detroit for him.

Esther had shared at lunch earlier in the week that she felt the church's security measures had long been out of date. She brokenly spoke to Briggs of Roger's physical attack in the church parking lot when they were married. Her description of that night, and his knowledge of Roger today, had him conflicted.

Sometimes the only way he could work it out in his mind was to remember all the people in the Bible who God had changed. People like Saul transitioning into Paul. Jacob whose name meant trickster, evolving from trying to steal his brother's birthright to becoming a man of honor called Israel.

So Briggs hugged her and told her those days were over. She smiled, snuggling under his arm in the booth they shared, and stole a french fry off his plate.

Now sitting in his office, he looked at this woman that he loved and had vowed to protect. Yes, he would place cameras, alarms, and a moat, if he had to, to keep her and their children safe. *And the gun in my office drawer is added insurance.*

***

The next two weeks were whirlwind days as everyone became engrossed in their own day-to-day living. Esther and Briggs had several dinners together, and when their schedules were too full they learned to make lunch dates a priority. They now included the children in their outings.

Today was a teacher conference day and Esther and Briggs had met with the children's teachers, then they all went bowling.

"Mom, look at the score. Pastor Briggs is beating everybody," David said excitedly.

BJ jumped up and down, "Dad, this is so much better than the Wii. You have to help me knock all my pins down."

Briggs was draped over Ruth, guiding her hand to swing the ball down the lane. When he let go, Ruth went down and slid part of the way forward with the ball.

David and BJ fell back on the cushioned benches, howling with laughter. When Ruth's bottom lip began to tremble, Briggs scooped her up in the air, hugged her, and tickled her until she was laughing too.

Over Ruth's head, Briggs's eyes caught Esther's, switching from lightheartedness to blazed heat, then quickly back to laughter. Esther had a hitch in her breath, then her hands moistened, and her stomach dipped and swirled. Shyly she turned her head.

It was always like this; the pull of one for the other. In church, he would look for her, smile, and at the end of his message, he'd glance again for her nod of approval. At work, she would puzzle over a problem, call him and pick his brain, then find her answer. She was learning they were good together.

Mo Betta'.

Chapter Forty-seven

The month was flying by. October's chill had settled in, and Esther watched Phyllis put the finishing touches on the children's favors for Miracle's party the next day. She had asked Esther to come over and help her, and Esther had been glad to do it.

Esther looked at the silver party bags with yellow piping and large yellow and white butterfly appliqués.

"This is really pretty, Phyllis. She'll love it. You went all out."

Phyllis's eyes narrowed. "Don't start, Esther."

To Esther, this was the time to go all-out on your child's special day. It was just that the party at the museum, with caterers, waiters, and tours—and a DJ—was a bit much for her age.

"No, I'm happy to help. This is going to be a great party. The kids are all excited."

Phyllis blew out a breath as if she was relieved and smiled at her sister. "We'll start at the African American museum where the kids will have a special tour and specially designed treats. Then a sumptuous luncheon will be laid out of all her favorite foods. All twenty-five children will have their names on their place mats, and the boys will have crowns while the girls, tiaras. I got that from when you were that age and you so wanted to be Cinderella. You remember that?"

Esther laughed, remembering how she even had her father paint an old wooden chair gold. "Yes, I do. Even I know I was a mess."

Esther picked up a party favor and fixed its bow. "Then what?"

Phyllis started recounting all the activities she had planned. "Then a car service will take them all to the mall, where they'll go to the movies, and afterward, they'll build a bear. Do you think they're too young for the Build-A-Bear Workshop? Miracle's classmates are a year older." She paused, thinking about it, then shrugged her shoulders as if to say, "It's too late to change it now."

"Then all the little girls will come here for a sleepover and the little boys will go home."

"And David will be picked up by Mom and Dad and stay with them because Briggs and I have a date after we leave the kids at the museum."

"All right now, stay holy. I'm glad you guys are getting along so well, even including the kids on dates." Phyllis gave her a high five. "Ooh, sis, I can't wait till you see what we bought Miracle for a gift."

Esther almost frowned, but caught herself. "The party's not her gift?"

Phyllis grunted, "Girl, no. Can you imagine Miracle's reaction if she didn't get something fabulous?"

Esther's face took on a strained look. "So what did you get her?"

"A custom-made playhouse. All the kids are going to love it. It has curtains and even electricity. Charles didn't want to, because he said she'll only get another few years' use out of it. But she'll have the best clubhouse in her school," Phyllis bragged, completely missing the look on Esther's face.

Keep your mouth shut, Esther, you've made peace.

Before she could talk herself down, Esther's mouth was moving. "Are you *serious?* What's wrong with the large recreation room she already has with every toy and gadget in it you can imagine?"

Phyllis slammed down the favor in her hand. "*Why* do you have a problem with what I do for Miracle? She's a very bright little girl. And she never gives me or Charles any trouble."

"Because you never say no. Don't you feel that one day when someone finally says no, Miracle won't know how to cope?" Esther picked the favor off of the floor and gently set it back on the table.

Phyllis scoffed, turning her back on Esther and moving items around on the table. "That is so ridiculous," she said with a sniff.

Esther stepped to her sister and put her arms around her from behind. "I love you. I shouldn't have opened my big mouth. I just care so much, that's all. One thing we can agree on and that is that we all love each other."

Phyllis sniffled, and then wiped her eyes before she turned around. "So are you going to help me with the rest of this or not?"

"All right, but then I have to leave. I'm having dinner with Deborah. She came in this morning for the weekend."

Phyllis nodded handing Esther a glue gun. "Get to work."

"And before I go, I'll have one of these cake pops," Esther said and snatched it from the table.

Phyllis pointedly looked at Esther's waistline. "I thought you were going out to dinner?"

Esther laughed. "Now who's dipping?"

"I'll have the rib tips, corn on the cob, and baked beans," Deborah said, handing her menu to the waitress.

"I'll have the same, except make mine chicken," Esther said, scanning the crowd.

When the waitress walked away, Esther said, "So, how's it going?"

Deborah's eyes blinked rapidly, and her jaw seemed to be twitching. Esther was further concerned when Deborah's leg then began shaking. "My last visit was good. But today my mom—who I love dearly—is already tripping. She didn't want me to leave, always hovering over me. Dad's trying to keep peace. It's not their fault though they just have no clue how to treat me."

Esther reached out and placed her hand over Deborah's. "Why don't they meet with your doctor? And maybe you should educate them on just what your illness entails. You can't expect them to know something they've never been taught. Open up to them. If you act ashamed, they'll do the same. Girl, tear the roof off the sucker."

Deborah's twitching eased, although her leg continued to shake. "Dad met with my doctor in Columbus, but Mom couldn't make it. She has sciatica. She can't take that car ride. She is much better around me though. So, you're right, if I'm going to be here, I need to figure out how to best educate everyone. I know how much my Mom loves me. I'll talk to Dr. Kimbro next week and get some pointers."

Esther lifted her glass in agreement.

"Speaking of getting things in the open, I have something to tell you," Deborah said.

"Go on," Esther encouraged her, but feeling like what was coming was not going to be something she wanted to know. Perspiration beaded across Deborah's nose.

"Sheri left three letters behind: One for you, one for her mother, and one for me. You once asked to read mine. I didn't let you. I didn't want you to know what was in it." Deborah reached into her purse and pulled out the letter. She unfolded it and spread it out on the table. "I'm going to now read it to you."

"Wait!" Esther yelled, a volley of memories assaulting her senses. She didn't know if she wanted to know. At one time it was all she could think about, but not now. It was then that Esther realized she had already moved on, and Deborah needed to share the truth so she could. Hoping she didn't forever regret her decision, she relented, "Go ahead."

Deborah began to read.

> *Dear Deborah,*
>
> *You were always the keeper of my secrets. You were the one who saw all, but said very little. Thank you. My choices were never your fault. You were the tomboy, the one everyone thought would turn out funny. But I was the one who had feelings for girls. I was the one who tried to fit in, but never felt "in." So I used the excuse to study, to pour myself into my books because I was never able to pour myself into you.*
>
> *You never said or gave me any indication that we were more than best friends so don't feel bad. I never should have touched you that night, never should have gotten mad when you pushed me off of you and said no. You and Esther are my girls. I love you.*
>
> *There have been so many secrets. My mother had them. She had expectations of me to validate her to my dad. The pressure has been tremendous, this attempting perfection.*
>
> *I hope you know this decision is not about you. Don't even go there. I'm just tired. And running from myself is no longer possible.*
>
> *Do me one last favor. Don't tell Esther what you know. It's my last secret. I want her to remember me like I was. That's how I'll remember all of us. The tenacious three.*
>
> *Don't cry for me,*
> *Sheri*

Esther reached out and pulled the letter off the table. For some reason she needed to touch it, read it through again. "Why now?"

Deborah paused, twisting her hair between her fingers. Esther watched but she didn't see her tug on it or pull any out. "Because her secrets were weighing me down. I don't want to hide one more thing. I want to walk out of this restaurant free. I want this weight lifted."

Esther didn't have a reply. She was trying to think back in time for clues, some sign of Sheri's preferences. But she came up blank. Deborah jammed her straw into her drink, but when Esther remained silent she continued.

"I dragged the thought that it was all my fault everywhere I went. Let me tell you something. The truth is as light as air. But the devil's lies are heavier than any one person can carry," Deborah said as she rocked in her seat. Her hands were no longer pulling her hair, and the twitch and perspiration were gone. "I'm free."

Esther wondered how long Deborah would have carried this burden if she had not stumbled on her in that hotel. "You get now it wasn't your fault?"

Deborah scrutinized Esther, searching for what, Esther could not fathom. "The doctors have been telling me that for years. But what the mind considers, the heart knows. It took my heart a long time to make up its mind to let it go."

Esther placed the letter in the ashtray and lit a match to it. They both watched the paper curl into nothingness, leaving just a few ashes in the center of the ashtray. Then she laid her hand across the table, and Deborah took it. "Isaiah 61:3 says that he will give us beauty for our ashes. I believe that. I'm glad we reconnected. Our lives can change whenever we will them to. I believe that great things are in store for us all."

Deborah got up and came around the table. She bent down and hugged Esther. "Thank you for not giving up on me. I'm learning that everyone's path is overrun with obstacles. I thought your life was perfect, and here I find out it was just perfect for you."

Esther was humbled. Deborah's words clicked in her spirit. Her life was perfect for her; she was the one graced to live it.

When the waitress arrived, Esther took Deborah's hand in hers to say grace. They had much to be thankful for.

Chapter Forty-eight

The music was pumping, and the adults were having as much fun as the children. They were in the Charles H. Wright Museum of African American History. Between the exhibits and watching the children enjoy themselves so much, it was a joyous group.

Briggs put his arm around Esther's waist. "You having a good time?"

"I am. Not as much fun as I'm going to have later, though." Esther bumped him playfully with her hip.

"So, we can leave soon?" Briggs made Groucho Marx's eyebrows at her.

"Most definitely," she chuckled at his silly antics. "Let me go see if we're needed for anything else, and then if not, we can go."

Briggs watched her walk away, glad that in a little while he'd have her all to himself. His attention was drawn to BJ laughing with David and he felt at peace. His son was flourishing. His love life was on the right track. Monica was out of his hair, and actually seemed to be working on herself. He knew she was out job hunting every day. He heard from BJ that Mr. Roger was fun. Better still there were no signs of the Duncan character. Even Roger was breathing easier.

He felt a tap on his shoulder and turned. Esther was radiant.

"We can leave. I'm all yours," she smiled.

"Yes, you are," he gathered her close, as they strolled arm in arm out of the room.

Briggs and Esther were stretched out on the couch relaxing. Her feet were in his lap, his were draped over the ottoman. He put the movie on pause and stood. "More juice?" he asked, as headed toward the kitchen at a leisurely pace. Suddenly, his cell phone went off, then Esther's. They looked at each other and scrambled to answer their phones.

"Hello."

Esther's scream drowned out what Charles was saying to Briggs on his phone. He leapt over the chair and grabbed Esther's phone out of her hand. "Hello? What's happening?" he yelled.

All he could hear was a female sobbing. "I'm sorry, I'm sorry. It was only ten minutes tops. Just ten minutes."

Briggs held on to Esther who was collapsing onto the ground while still trying to find out what was happening. "Phyllis? Are the children okay?"

Esther beat on Briggs's chest with her fists. "No! Can't you hear? They lost our babies . . . They lost our babies."

"We're on our way!" Briggs grabbed Esther's hands. "Stop! This is not helping, let's go!"

Esther sat in the car, while Briggs broke every speed limit posted.

"Please, God. Please, God. Please, God." Esther's litany was nonstop.

Briggs reached out and took her hand. "We're both frightened. But we have to trust and believe that God will intervene. Let's pray. Father God . . ."

Esther moaned loudly, hiccupping through her tears. "I can't pray. I want my babies!"

Briggs's hand trembled as he released Esther's and banged his steering wheel. "Prayer changes things. Right now, it's all we have."

Esther howled as she babbled what she knew. "Miracle asked Phyllis if she could go to the restroom. But she didn't want the adults accompanying her, because the other kids would think she was a baby. So Phyllis sent Ruth with her, but I warned David to not let his sister out of his sight. So he and BJ went too. Now they're all missing," Esther sobbed.

Briggs ran a red light, pulling into the mall. His chest tightened when he saw the path of squad cars lined up in front of the entrance to the movie theater. Somehow that made it more real . . . and scarier. To him it said they weren't lost, *they were taken.* Each squad car restricted his breathing a little more. By the time he double-parked the car he was almost hyperventilating.

They both jumped out, holding hands to connect, to calm themselves that they were not alone. They dodged around the gawking crowd, pushing and shoving until they were blocked from proceeding.

Crying out for people to move, Briggs said, "Please. Let us through!"

"Please, please!" Esther cried.

Briggs held tight when he felt Esther slipping behind. He pulled her through the tightest spots, edging them closer. Finally, they made it through the crowd and approached the line of officers blocking the entrance.

A hulking, bald-headed police officer stepped forward cutting off their approach. Before the officer could speak, Briggs implored. "Please, we're the parents of three of the missing children. We have to get inside."

Esther grabbed the officer's uniform sleeve. "Do you know anything? Can you tell us something? Anything at all?" she demanded as she yanked on his arm.

The officer moved the line of policemen aside as they made a path for Briggs and Esther to run through. He turned to them not answering any of their questions, only saying. "Follow me."

As they burst through the doors, Esther saw her sister being held in Charles's arms. When Phyllis saw her, she broke away. Running to Esther, she collapsed in her arms.

Esther's arms encircled her, shaking her for answers. "Talk to us, Phyllis."

Charles walked up, his face ashen. He repeated what they already knew.

Phyllis cried out, "They did what we told them. They all stayed together. All four of them are missing."

"How long now?" Briggs croaked in fear, his mind racing trying to think of what they should be doing. Where were the police in charge?

Charles looked away. If possible, his face looked even more drawn. Then when he made eye contact his were asking them to forgive. "An hour."

Esther screeched, "*An hour* and you're *just* calling us? What is *wrong* with you?"

Phyllis bawled louder. "My child is gone too, Esther. We thought they were playing, lost track of time."

Before anyone knew it, Esther slapped Phyllis so hard her head snapped back. "This is what comes from your constant cuddling and spoiling that child. They should have had adult supervision. Are you mad? There are sick people out here."

Briggs grabbed Esther around her waist and carried her away from Phyllis. Charles held his wife trying to check her face. They were all shouting and hurling accusations at one another.

Briggs could see the police coming over. He pulled out his cell. He knew he would need to hurry while he had a chance. He didn't want to do to Monica what was just done to them. "I have to call Monica."

Esther's hands were over her face when she looked up and said coldly. "No! I don't want to deal with her right now, Briggs."

Briggs took in her disheveled appearance, her red-rimmed eyes, and knew that she was not thinking clearly.

"I love you, Esther, but right now, that is BJ's mother, and I'm calling her."

Esther murmured under her breath, raking her hands through her hair. "Jesus, help me. I'm so sorry, Briggs." In her angst, she squeezed her face, leaving red blotches on her cheeks. "I feel sick."

Briggs spoke for a few seconds into the phone, then he hung up and pulled Esther into his arms. "Breathe. Just take a long, deep breath."

He felt Esther doing as he instructed, and he assured her, "The police are standing behind us. They must be waiting to talk to us. If not, we need to talk to them. We're going to go over there, and then I promise you we are going to find our children." He could feel Esther's breath calming even more, her body not trembling as much. "Baby, I need you. We can get through this together. Help me keep it together, okay?"

Esther burrowed her face deeper into his chest; then she squeezed his hand. "I want to scream, throw some-thing, but I know it won't help. I'm here. We have to find our children . . . together."

They swiftly moved over to the police officer who appeared to be in charge. "Officer, we need to talk," Briggs said and shook the woman's hand. "I'm Briggs Stokes Jr.'s father, and this is Esther Redding, my fiancée. She's the mother of the twins, David and Ruth Redding. What's being done?"

Briggs heard Esther gasp at his announcement that she was his fiancée. He probably should have waited for some place fancy with flowery words, and even for her to say yes. But he meant for this to be the last time they went through anything and they were not standing together as husband and wife.

Esther's answer was in the caressing of his back and the lean she gave into his side as he spoke to the officer in charge. The blond-haired woman in plainclothes stepped forward with a pad in her hand.

"Due to the Amber Alert laws we're on this. We've canvassed the area, and there is no sign of the children. We've sent the other children home. They remained in the theater and had no idea what happened. None of them saw any suspicious people, neither did the other adults in the group."

"What about staff? Surely, some of the ushers, cashiers, *somebody* saw something?" Briggs asked, desperate for information.

"No, not a thing. There is one picture of a man crossing a camera, heading in the direction where the children were last sighted, but he kept his back to the lens."

Phyllis came over to Esther and took her hand. "Sis, I'm so sorry."

"No, I shouldn't have slapped you. Forgive me." Esther clung to her sister.

"In a strange way it made me feel better. Woke me up. I was in shock." Phyllis's voice trailed off, and her face paled. Esther swiveled to follow her line of vision.

A commotion could be heard at the front entrance. Monica came striding in, Roger on her right.

"Heavenly Father, please tell me I'm having a nightmare." Esther clutched Briggs's arm. "Why is that man here?"

Briggs reminded her, "They're seeing each other, remember?"

Coat flying open, Monica barged into the center of the group. "Somebody better tell me where my child is! Briggs!"

It was like Monica carried TNT, and everyone exploded at once.

"You lost my child . . ."

"How dare you come in here yelling!"

"Stop, screaming . . . We're all upset."

The plainclothes officer had clearly had her fill. "Quiet!" she shouted.

The chaos stopped, everyone standing defiantly in their own pain, then turning as one to listen when the officer began to speak.

"I am Detective Lucinda Moore. I will do everything I can to bring all of your children back safely. If you have any pertinent information that can help us, please tell me now."

The officer's blond hair was plastered to her forehead, clinging from her perspiration. A wet line saturated the collar of her crumpled shirt, and her black pants were crisp in comparison. She turned to each adult, intent in her statements.

"It's best if we can bring children home in the first twenty-four hours. The longer they're missing, the worse the outcome. We are circulating a picture of them taken at the party. We have an Amber Alert on. The news cameras are outside, and the media are waiting for one or all of you to speak to them. Your best weapon right now is to be calm and start thinking if anyone you knew could have done this."

Briggs and Roger said in unison, "Duncan."

"Who?" Charles asked, as Esther and Monica similarly chimed in.

Roger ignored them. "Duncan Sanders. If Duncan has them—Lord, have mercy—we've got to do something fast."

Esther jumped in front of Briggs and yelled, "The man on the playground?"

Roger stepped forward. "Officer, Duncan Sanders is a pedophile. He's never been arrested that I know of, and he's highly placed in a syndicate of men and women who prey on children."

Detective Moore wrote furiously in her book. "How did you come by this information?"

Monica stepped forward and placed her hand on Roger's back. Her gesture was not lost on any of them.

"He was my tormentor for ten years," Roger said, grabbing hold of Monica's hand. "You cannot let him leave the state with those children."

Suddenly those gathered heard a thump. Esther was sprawled out on the ground in a dead faint.

Monica fell to her knees and lifted her head up. Holding her head, she fanned her with her clutch purse.

Esther's eyes gradually flickered open. "What? Who . . . Why are you holding me, Monica?"

Monica looked at her, a single tear falling from her eye. "Because we are both mothers, and this is not a time for division. It's going to take all of our prayers to bring our children home safely. I know something of this Duncan, and I'm scared to death," Monica cried.

Esther rose, and she tentatively patted Monica. "We'll find them," she said as her gaze met Briggs's and she added fervently, "We *have* to."

As they moved to the mall bench and sat down, Esther reached over and without saying a word pulled Monica's hand into her own.

Phyllis hiccupped hysterically. "I'm going to be sick."

"Shush," Charles told her as they all gathered around the bench, taking each other's hand while Briggs led them in prayer.

***

It was now pitch-black outside, past midnight, and the temperature had fallen. The group huddled in Briggs's office as phones were being plugged in and the police set up their command center. Now that Roger had updated everyone, the parents all knew that no one was going to ask for a ransom. Duncan wasn't in the business of giving children back he had stolen. But the police were doing business according to protocol. Hence, a phone command center.

Briggs felt a series of shivers run up his back. His head pounded with all the possibilities that could make this all go very wrong. A crazed man like Duncan didn't follow the usual protocol. As a result, he believed they would also need to ditch their usual methods.

He looked at the clock and chewed his bottom lip. The children had officially been gone for four hours. If Detective Moore was right, they had twenty hours to find them before they were out of state. If Roger was right, tomorrow's full moon promised to find Duncan at his worst.

Everyone in the room was quiet, each lost in their own thoughts. They were afraid to say the wrong thing, to dash someone else's hope. Periodically, the door would open and Naomi would advise that more people were arriving at the church to offer support. No one in the room had moved outside to accept it.

Naomi had reported that outside of the police's command center, Love Zion's members had also set up a phone network. Esther's parents had come in and they were leading that team. They wanted those who wouldn't be caught helping the police to know they could call them.

They were also sending search teams out all over the city. Charles's and Lawton's family members were leading those groups. The Stokes were on a plane making their way to the city.

Inside Briggs's office they continued to brainstorm. In an effort to try everything, he pulled up all the footage on the security cameras to see if Duncan had come back on church property.

Her voice quivering, Esther leaned over Briggs's shoulder as he poured over church camera footage. "What can I do to help?"

Taking her hand in his, Briggs looked over at everyone. "Can you guys give me five minutes?"

When the other parents walked out of the room, he explained, "This man was Roger's childhood tormentor. Before Roger ran away from him, he said he would overhear Duncan talking about using new technology to lure children. He had computer geeks in his network, who had him all excited about the possibilities. I know it's a stretch, because I don't allow it for BJ, but do the kids have their own accounts on the computer?"

Esther bit her lip, thinking. "No, they wanted them, but I told them playing games was enough." Esther's eyes narrowed. "But Miracle does, and she has an iPhone, tablet, and PC."

Briggs leaped from his chair and went to the door yelling for Charles, Phyllis, and his security person, Steve. They all came running into the room.

"Steve, Miracle had several social media accounts. Can we check them?" Briggs felt a flicker of hope.

"You bet." Steve jumped in Briggs's chair and pounded away on his laptop. He then looked at Phyllis. "Who's your e-mail server?" When she answered, he typed it in. He then asked. "Your e-mail?" He added that information when Phyllis recited it out loud. Steve flexed his fingers. "What's her user name and password?"

Phyllis wrung her hands. "Her user name is Daddy's Girl. I'm not sure of her password." She looked at Charles, "Honey, do you know it?"

Charles hung his head. "No. I thought you had this kind of thing under control."

Esther interrupted. "Try Princess."

Steve typed in the word, and the screen pulled up Miracle's instant messaging. "Good work. How'd you know?"

Esther smiled. "It was either that or Sleeping Beauty. You know us Cinderella girls have princess fixations."

Steve turned the large screen so they could all see it. He spoke as they each read the message for themselves. "It appears that Duncan and Miracle have been communicating by instant messenger. He's been promising her the newest software that hasn't come out in the market yet. He says here he wants to give it to her on her birthday."

Phyllis slumped down in the chair, her sobs loud and fierce. Charles looked helpless, stooping down next to her, trying to sooth her as his own tears drenched his shirt.

Monica and Roger entered the room, both looking around to see if more news had come in. Briggs held his finger up for them to hold on while Steve finished.

Steve turned the screen back around and clicked more keys. He frowned as he turned to the group. "Her last communication is Duncan telling her he was in the rear of the building by the women's bathroom." Steve looked up at the group. "Unfortunately, it's also right beside the exit door. He must have disabled it and took them out that way."

Roger shook his head. "No, Monica found out by charming one of the young male attendants there that they rigged that door for their smoke breaks."

Briggs looked at everyone. "So now we know how he got them. Can we trace her GPS?"

Detective Moore stepped into the room. "No, you cannot. Her phone was found in the back parking lot of the mall." She then hit her notebook against her hand as she walked around the group, pinpointing each of them with a hard stare. "While I appreciate your feelings, you have to let us do our job. We are on this. Stay out of our way or else you may do something that could jeopardize the case and cause the children to be lost forever."

No one spoke, and she pivoted around and stalked out the door. Briggs then went over to the door and shut it. "Roger, tell them what you told me."

Monica took his hand as Roger cleared his throat. "I didn't have the guts when I was younger, but one guy Duncan held made it to the police and told. Later that week I heard Duncan bragging on the phone that in every state he had the police on lockdown. I never saw the guy again. And I knew he hadn't made it when nobody came for me."

"So we have to decide if we leave this to the police or if we do our best to get our children back ourselves," Briggs said and waited to hear the others' opinions.

Roger came forward. "I think that we have to at least try to find them. I know he has gotten away with this many times and the police weren't able to catch him. I do have an idea that may work, though."

Briggs felt a tug of hope. He wanted Roger to expound, but Mother Reed entered the room at that moment. She shuffled over to Esther, hugging her, and then went straight down the line, even pulling Monica to her bosom.

Mother Reed spoke to the group. "I know y'all busy, and I'm so sorry 'bout this happening. But we need to gather and pray."

She went over to Phyllis and took her ravished face in her hands. "Baby, God has been talking to me, and these children will be fine. Evil has not rested, but neither has the glory of God. Be watchful. The answer is near."

Mother Reed turned and placed her arm around Briggs's waist, squeezing him as she spoke. "Now, Briggs, gather everyone up. We need a powerful corporate prayer to bring down the enemy."

Briggs signaled Esther, hoping she would follow Mother Reed out.

Esther nodded. "I have to do something or I'll go crazy. Many of the people who have come are expecting to have an opportunity to speak to one of us. I'll ask them to move into the sanctuary and before we pray, I'll thank them for coming."

Somber, Phyllis accompanied Esther. When they passed Monica, she turned away, her body language screaming she was staying with the men.

Briggs was proud that Esther failed to react to Monica's snub; she just shrugged and kept going. Her last silent message to him was to keep her informed.

Mother Reed followed, but before they took too many steps, she said, "That's your helpmeet, son."

"Yes, ma'am, I know." Briggs took calming breaths. "We just need our children so we can be a whole family. Would you mind going on ahead? I'll be there shortly."

Mother Reed touched his arm in understanding as she left the room.

Roger closed the door and propped up against it after Mother Reed left. "Right before I got out of prison, Duncan sent a message to me through this new guy. I believe he'll know how to get to him."

"Good, good. We'll contact the warden right away." Briggs pulled out his phone grateful that Love Zion had a relationship with the warden due to their expanding prison ministry.

Roger pushed away from the door and grabbed the phone out of Briggs's hand. "No, we don't go through the warden. That could take forever, and he'll never talk to them anyway. I have to get word to my friends inside. They'll make him talk."

Weary, Briggs rubbed his eyes, contemplating Roger's offer. "I'm not sure this is the right thing to do. But time is getting away from us." Bleak and unsure, Briggs asked, "No one gets hurt?"

Roger sighed. "No one gets killed."

Monica sucked her teeth. "Briggs Stokes, they have our son. I don't care what happens to this man. If he's involved with these monsters, he deserves whatever happens to him."

"I understand your concerns, Briggs. But this is the only thing I know to do." Roger's fist was balled tight. His entire body jumpy. "Nobody came looking for me when I was being abused."

Monica twisted her hands. "Do you think they're still in town?"

Roger pulled her close. "It was a long time ago, but Duncan used to never move at night. I think it was his way to thumb his nose at the system. He would move kids in broad daylight, right under the nose of the authorities looking for them. I told the police there would be male and female partners riding with a child between them. But there's a full moon tomorrow night and Duncan is his most sinister during a full moon."

Charles snorted, kicking a chair. "A werewolf fetish? Mr. and Mrs. All-American transporting kids?"

"It's real. And the police would watch them ride right out of town." Roger began to put the church's number into his phone as Monica collapsed in a chair. "I'll call this number when I'm on my way back."

Roger squatted down in front of her. He took his finger and moved her hair away from her face. "When I find the way to bring back the children, we'll talk."

Monica cupped his face in her slender hand. "Yes, we will. Now go find my son."

Roger stood and swept out of the room. He was going to bring back the children . . . or get killed trying.

Zadkiel sat next to Monica. She was now alone; Briggs's office was her refuge. When her composure broke and she slid out of her chair onto the floor, he followed her to the ground. When a mewling sound came from the pit of her stomach and she stretched out on the floor, he lay next to her.

The guardian's wings expanded. He glowed from the center of his being. A low sound rumbled through the room as he hummed a lullaby from Monica's childhood. It was one her mother stopped singing to her when her father left. A song that had been replaced with bitter tears and items crashing against the wall, nights her mother's pain was too full for her to contain. The guardian was there, in her childhood home, shielding her young ears from the contamination of unbridled venom-filled words.

"She is breaking," the guardian said.

"No," Zadkiel said. "For the first time in a long time, she is bending before she breaks."

"What is different now?" the guardian asked, lifting high over the room, twirling to change the atmosphere of fear.

Zadkiel rested his wing over her. "She understands it is out of her hands. She cannot scheme to achieve it. She cannot manipulate to correct it. It is on God."

"But the Roger human?"

"She understands that he will only win if God says so." Zadkiel sent another wave of peace over her. *"Not even when she lay dying has she felt the total need to surrender to God."*

"Then it is a just thing?" the guardian wanted to know.

"No. The children being kidnapped by a demon-possessed human is not just. The act is evil, the children are a by-product of evil's rule."

The guardian now sat next to Monica, wanting to help, but unable to heal her emotional wounds. *"What is Father saying of the outcome?"*

"He has not spoken. Michael sent me a message earlier that his legion fought the demons into the breaking of dawn. The congregation in the sanctuary praying will fuel our brothers to fight toward victory."

The guardian flew to the door. *"Someone approaches."*

They watched as Esther came in and knelt on the floor. She wiped the wetness from Monica's cheeks and lifted her to her feet. Embracing, she whispered into her ear, and then the two left the room.

"It is a remarkable thing how God can use anything to work together for people's good, is it not, brother?" the guardian said, watching the miracle of the two women bonding through their shared pain.

"Yes, He is God all by Himself. You follow your assignment. I will go to the prison and open doors that man cannot shut."

Chapter Forty-nine

Phyllis approached Esther as she walked back into the sanctuary holding Monica up. She went to the other side of her, and holding hands, the three of them approached the altar. They knelt and began to pray in earnest.

Briggs watched, sitting in a chair behind the podium. He raised his hand to God's orchestration. He closed his eyes wondering if BJ was scared or hungry. Had he been hurt? Did he know that his daddy was doing everything he could to bring him home? To bring all of the children home?

The church doors opened and more people streamed in. They were his members and people Briggs did not know. There were black, white, and even those of the Muslim faith were entering God's house.

Briggs stood and went up to the podium. "Brothers and sisters, for we are all brothers and sisters here today. Evil cannot win. It cannot rule over a land that was created by God. My Word says in Psalm 24:11, 'The earth is the Lord's, and the fullness thereof; the world, and they that dwell therein.' It's all His! Satan is confused. We are not his creation; therefore, he cannot know the inner workings of our hearts. He would love us to speak evil, but we shall not. He would love us to say, there is no hope. But we shall not. Our Lord is strong and mighty. He is mighty in battle. Evil has already lost. Stand up and give praise." Choked up, Briggs paused. He then looked down at the three women who knelt at the altar. His next words were strong and true for them.

"Our children are coming home!" The women's faces returned his regard with reflected hope. Briggs nodded, and said, "We will win this war through prayer and supplication. I can feel the atmosphere shifting already. Is there a psalmist in the house?"

Several people stood, even some who were not members.

"Then come forward and sing songs of worship, usher everyone into His presence. The battle is not ours. Let us sing songs of praise. We shall have our children returned. Church, our camels are coming. Camels indicate provision. In the days of old, camels brought spices, oils, treasures. In Genesis 24:63, Isaac sat in the field in mediation. In meditation, Church. He sat praying! And as he looked up he saw camels approaching. Rebekah, his bride, sat on one of the camels. So we see that camels also transport our greatest treasure . . . people. The camels are coming."

Briggs ran back and forth across the pulpit. "And just like Isaac who sat in that field meditating, we are going to sit here until the camels come. And on those camels will be BJ, Ruth, David, and Miracle."

The church broke out in dance and people prayed in their heavenly languages. Phyllis started running through the sanctuary, and Esther and Monica followed her. Mother Reed's hands were raised as tears dripped from her withered cheeks onto her clothing. Charles lay prostrate before the Lord in front of the altar and Esther's parents both sang God's praises.

The imps scattered to and fro.

The Leader was on a rampage. He could not reach one person in Love Zion's camp to manipulate because they were all in the sanctuary. He did not understand it—not one member was missing. When the Baptist, Church of God in Christ, and the African Methodist Episcopal church members showed up, he killed three imps in a fit of temper.

"Imp One!" The Leader bellowed, angry beyond compare. He had planned this out. The children were hidden. Yet the people sang to Him, when they should have been cursing Him.

"I am here, your lowly servant, a mere shadow of your greatness, a—"

"Do not test me, idiot, I am not in the m . . . o . . . o . . . d," The Leader hissed out.

"Yes, Master."

"Go to the miscreant in the prison. Take care of him. Do not let the human Roger speak to him."

Imp One hurried to leave. Any assignment that took him out of The Leader's presence was a good one. Three imps had been fired today, and he was okay with that; he just didn't care to be one of them.

Roger sat in the visitation room. One of the guards who he had always had an amiable relationship with made an exception and allowed him to see Wise Will before official visitation began. His ministry role at the prison gave validation to the sergeant's leniency. He looked up when he heard a familiar step.

"Everything all right?" Wise Will asked, his clothing even at this hour, crisp and creased.

Roger shook his head as he stood and gave his friend a handshake. "I got real problems. The cat who was stalking me before I left. Can you get to him?"

"I been here twenty years, I can get to anybody. What you need?" Wise Will said, a toothpick hanging out of his mouth.

Roger leaned forward, looked around, and whispered, "I need to know where his pervert-in-arms has taken four children."

Wise Will reared back. "What you say?"

"Snatched 'em up last night at a mall," Roger said, his fist curled tight.

Wise Will rubbed his neck, thinking. "Might take me letting a few of the boys get rough. Hurting people don't sit well with my soul, but a man who will grab babies? That don't sit well with my spirit."

Roger looked ready to beg. "You all I got, man."

"Well, that'll never be true. You got the Lord," Wise Will replied.

"You gon' help?" Roger snapped.

Wise Will stood up. "Who I place the call to when I find out?"

Roger signaled to the guard, "Can I borrow your pen?"

The guard grunted but handed over his pen, and Roger wrote the number on the back of Wise Will's hand. "This is the number to the church; you call it and our pastor will answer. He's forwarded it to his cell."

"Dat be dat." Wise Will gave Roger pound and started his journey back into the cell block when Roger called his name.

Roger knew he had pressed him hard. But the sour feeling in his stomach would not go away. They had to find the kids. "We good?"

"Golden," he said as the cell doors shut behind him.

Chapter Fifty

The fervency of the prayers had not stopped. Instead of grinding down, they were riding higher . . . from glory to glory. The church could no longer hold everyone, and there were hundreds of people in the parking lot. Briggs had continued to pray, preach, and teach for three hours straight.

The Honorable Bishop Stokes had arrived, and he had taken over the pulpit for his son. There were news vans in the parking lot. People ignored the media. They were praying for each other in front of the cameras, ignoring the news reporters' commentaries as they pressed in.

Briggs was once again on his face when his phone vibrated. He grabbed Esther's hand and pulled. She lifted her face, and he held up his phone. Esther leapt to her feet, pulling Phyllis along with her. Immediately Charles, Roger, and Monica followed them out of the sanctuary. Briggs answered his phone as they all ran back to his office.

An urgent voice spoke quickly, as though he might have to hang up any minute. "Pastor, this Will. He say the only place he knows of is one he and a female partner did a pickup for about six months ago. I can tell you that if he had any other information he would've shared it by now. You got a pen?"

"Yes, I have a pen. What's the address?"

"What's he saying?" Charles asked, then he spotted the address Briggs was writing down. "I know that area, that's off West Chicago. There are a lot of abandoned homes over there."

Roger peeked over Charles's shoulder. "Some of my boys used to live over there. Man, seven years ago before I went up, it was a rough neighborhood."

"Rougher still now. Briggs, you have to get our children out of there," Esther said. She knew that side of town wasn't even on the news anymore when a crime occurred it was so prevalent.

"I left New York because some fool tried to touch my baby; now somebody here ain't got good sense. What is happening to this world?" Monica moaned, hugging herself tight.

Phyllis ran to Monica and wrapped her in her arms. "We didn't know. When did the world flip on its axis?"

Esther joined the women, all three clasped together.

Roger spoke urgently, "We got an address; we need to move."

Briggs saw the women were unraveling. "Are we all agreed that we go and call the police once we get there? If what Roger said is true, we don't want anyone tipping Duncan off."

Collectively, everyone agreed, and then began to move to the door when Charles said, "Phyllis, you'll stay here."

"Uh-uh. That's my baby too, Charles. I'm going," Phyllis said with an attitude of desperation.

"Baby, you will allow me to go and bring our child home. No discussion, point-blank. Period," Charles said, giving her a hard stare. "I can't cover you and rescue them."

Phyllis's face calmed and she nodded, her eyes half cast.

Briggs looked over at Esther. "Don't even ask."

Esther said, "You're going for BJ, Charles is going for Miracle. Who's going to make David and Ruth their priority?"

Briggs took Esther by the hand and pulled her over to the side. "*I* will. They will be as much my priority as BJ. I will love them as the Lord loved us, His adopted children. I know I once broke a promise to you, but I will get your children."

Esther's face pleaded for him to not make her stay behind. "But, Briggs, I'll worry."

"No, you'll pray," Mother Reed said, walking into the office with Joshua. "All of you leaving at once meant something big was going down. So I come to find out what it was."

Briggs hurried to the door, and the men filed out behind him. Esther held up her finger to Mother Reed, and then surprised everyone by catching Roger by the arm and pulling him away. Several faces with varying degrees of caution watched the exchange.

"Esther, I know how you feel about me. I'm only going to help—" a nervous Roger said, ready to get going.

Shaking her head, Esther held up a trembling hand. "All these years I was determined to keep you locked up in prison. I now understand it was because my unforgiveness had me bound. I couldn't see who you had become, only who you used to be. You left me in such pain . . ."

Esther couldn't finish as she sobbed. Briggs swiftly moved toward her, but she straightened and said firmly, "I forgive you, Roger. And, just maybe this will free you as it's freeing me. Please bring our children home."

Stunned, Roger stood motionless. Then with a determined air, he led the men out of the office.

Monica followed him out, squeezed by the other men, and slid in beside Roger. "So you think I'm just going to automatically fall in line like those other women?" She trotted beside him as he skirted chairs and quickly headed for the exit.

Roger looked at Briggs and Charles moving away from him. He grabbed Monica and gave her a hard, passionate kiss. "For once, trust somebody. Trust *me*."

Monica fell back as Roger ran to catch up. She turned around only to find Esther, Phyllis, and Mother Reed right behind her, all looking at her with their mouths open.

"What?" she squawked, and flopped down on the nearest chair.

It was a dilapidated house. The windows were boarded up, graffiti was blazed across the front with gang signs. Houses on both sides of it were similar in nature. The men crept along the back, climbing through a crumbling fence to get to the property. They could see an old, beat-up car parked in the abandoned house's garage next door.

Roger tapped Charles and pointed to the car's tires; brand-new, expensive, and high performance. Charles elbowed Briggs, whose eyes scrutinized the tires as well. Nodding, all three moved with defined purpose. There was no sign of anyone. It was like the whole block was silent, and that was preternatural.

Light on his feet, Charles ran and stood with his back against the building. Listening for sounds inside and gesturing for them to come forward, he gripped his crowbar. Keeping low, Briggs ran with a bat in his hands, Roger close behind carrying a tire iron.

"I pray we didn't bring a knife to a gunfight," Roger whispered.

"We didn't." Briggs's hand slowly went under his jacket, and he pulled out a gun.

Roger grabbed Briggs's hand and pulled it down. "Where'd you get a 9 mm? And, do you even *know* how to use it?" he said furiously.

Briggs yanked his hand away, continuing to look around them. "I'm not ignorant. I've been going to the range for a while, ever since I learned someone like Duncan was in the picture. It's licensed, and I'm proficient."

"You're just full of surprises," Roger smirked.

Charles then sheepishly opened his leather jacket, exposing a .380 Magnum. He looked at Roger and said, "Before you ask, I was ROTC. I know how to use it."

Roger was looking down at his little tire iron when Briggs said, "Don't even think about it. You're risking everything just being out here with us. We'll take the heat if something goes wrong."

Charles motioned for Briggs to get on the other side of the door. He pried the crowbar under a loose part of the door and popped the rotting wood off the hinges. Briggs caught it and he and Roger wrenched it the rest of the way off. All three men cringed when their efforts produced a loud, splitting sound slicing through the still night air. They paused, listening for any sounds that would indicate they had been caught.

Briggs released a pent-up breath. *Nothing.*

"You first," Roger said to Charles.

Charles crept into the building. He hesitated at the stairs, not knowing if he should go up or down. Making a last-minute decision he went up. Briggs followed with Roger coming behind and pulling the door closed after him. They shook their heads and pointed to the warped steps. There was no way anyone could get up those stairs without being heard.

Roger whispered to Charles, and he nodded. Charles grabbed Briggs, and they moved back beyond the stairs.

Roger charged up the stairs yelling when a man came out with a gun.

He was muscular and had a slight limp. "Stay right there," he said pointing the gun at Roger.

Roger slowly stepped backward down the stairs, his hands raised.

The man waved his gun in the air. "I said stop."

Roger continued his downward descent. The man advanced, this time aiming his gun at Roger. Roger continued to step down the stairs backward.

Angry that Roger was forcing his hand, he growled, "Boy, if you don't stop, I'm going to put a hole straight through you."

Muffled voices could now be heard coming from behind the man. Both the man and Roger froze. Roger turned and raced down the stairs, the man on his heels.

Charles stepped out, aiming his gun at the man and yelled. "Stop! Don't make me shoot you!"

The man stopped, then saw Roger getting to the bottom step. He took aim and fired. Right after his gun went off, Charles pulled his trigger.

Briggs began running up the stairs when a woman rounded the corner, a gun in her hand. She saw Briggs, spun around, and ran back to the end of the hall. She turned, raised the gun, and shot erratically. Briggs ducked, zigzagged, and prayed as he moved forward. His adrenalin pumped when he heard childlike yelling and screaming.

He hadn't pulled out his gun. He didn't know if he could shoot someone now that it was happening, and he wasn't sure if he could shoot this woman. She looked like a child herself.

Is this what Roger meant by being a lure? Did Duncan use his past victims to lure and keep the others in check? God help us.

When the woman got to the end of the hall, she went around the corner, and he could no longer see her. But he could hear her panicked demands.

"Stay back. I will shoot one of these kids if I don't hear you going down those steps," she shrieked.

Briggs froze. He quickly asked God how he could use this new turn of events to his advantage. "I'm going down. Please don't hurt anyone," he said, making his voice weak and fearful. "I'll talk to you as I go down, so you'll hear my voice as it gets farther away."

The girl now sounded cocky in her demands. "Have your friend call out from downstairs too. I'm not dumb, you know, I know there's two of ya."

Briggs had found his advantage. She didn't know that there were three of them.

"I'm leaving." Briggs motioned to Roger to sneak up the stairs. He mouthed and pantomimed that for every step he took down, Roger would mirror moving up. Roger's steps would be camouflaged by their synchronized movements.

Catching on, Charles then called out, "I'm still downstairs."

Briggs's and Roger's steps were matched landing on the warped boards. "I'm still going down," Briggs called out. His voice purposely fearful.

They continued this way, with Briggs calling out and Charles calling out after, making noise. Roger was now on the floor of the hallway, crawling forward. Briggs and Charles tried to make enough noise calling out to keep her mind busy and her ears full.

"Shut up!" she yelled. "I can't hear myself think."

It was quiet. Roger lay still on the floor. Charles watched over the man he had shot in the thigh. He and Roger had tied him up, stuffing some of his shirt in his mouth to gag him.

Briggs closed his eyes. The children were quiet. There was no screaming or muffled sounds. As if every living soul in the house understood the importance of the next few moments. A door creaked, and then hesitant steps were heard. Briggs could tell she was coming out to make sure that they were both downstairs. He had no idea how she planned to get by them and keep the children hostage.

Her cockiness was gone as she blustered, "I've called for my backup, and they'll be here soon. I'd run if I was you." She then giggled off-key, as though she was losing it.

Sweat dotted Briggs's forehead, and perspiration dripped from his armpits as he tried to determine if she was high or just nervous.

Suddenly pandemonium ensued. The young girl came flying around the corner, the gun waving in her thin hand. Peering down the dark stairs, she failed to see Roger sprawled on the floor before her. When she stepped forward, he grabbed her by the foot and pulled.

Startled and screaming, the girl wildly swung her gun around and fired off a shot. Briggs had run up the stairs right when the gun went off. Before she could aim again, he body slammed her into the wall.

He heard a crack in her back, and then silence. Falling to his knees, heart racing, Briggs wheezed, "She's down for the count, man. Let's get the kids."

When Roger didn't answer him, he turned to see him lying motionless on the rotting wood. His breath caught when he noticed blood spreading out beneath his body.

Feebly, his breath sporadic and short, Roger moaned, "Get going . . . Duncan . . . still a . . . danger."

Briggs crawled to his side, his hands shakily searching for Roger's wounds. "We're good, man. Don't you die on me. If you do, my lady wasted a perfectly good forgiveness speech."

Roger grimaced, his face was blanching, his voice weaker. "Get . . . kids . . . said . . . backup coming."

Shouting, Briggs yelled, "Charles, call 911! Roger's been shot!"

When Briggs called out, BJ began to scream for him. "I'm coming, son, hold on."

Briggs was conflicted, wanting to run to his son, but concerned that blood continued to seep through the jacket he held over the wound on Roger's side. His voice croaking, he swallowed, "Thank you, man. We're going to get you out of here."

Charles came up the steps yelling his daughter's name, "Miracle?"

"I'm here, Daddy! I'm here." Her voice came from around the corner.

Charles ran that way, calling behind him, "I'll get the kids. I called, and the police are on their way."

Briggs heard a siren in the distance. "You hear that? The cavalry is coming. Just hold on, Roger."

Roger's eyes drifted closed. Reluctantly, Briggs stood. He had done all he could for now. He needed to get his kids. He rushed around the corner. In the darkened corridor, his eyes scanned the multiple rooms with shut doors, all with padlocks on them. The smell of urine and feces permeated the air, gagging him. He had to wonder how many children had been kept in this hellhole before they were transported out of state.

He approached Charles who was bent before a door with multiple locks. Charles had his crowbar jammed against one of the padlocks prying it, to no avail. The voices that had once been insistent were quiet.

"BJ, David, Ruth? We're going to get you out," Briggs called.

"Hurry!" they all yelled, some voices weepier than others.

The last lock was not popping off. Briggs took the crowbar from Charles and tried to break it. It wouldn't budge. Charles and Briggs began dropkicking the warped door with their combined weight. Finally, the frame began to crack, and then give way. Briggs was glad that while Duncan had thought to use padlocks, he hadn't ever felt any of the young children were heavy enough to break down a door. These were the original doors, now just old, warped wood. Charles used the crowbar to knock out the splintered door's center enough to pull the children out, one by one.

Each child came out crying and screaming, a prize to hold and hug. Briggs grabbed BJ and David into his arms and stood. Charles did the same with Miracle and Ruth.

Ominously, Briggs heard a creak in the floor behind him. His chest tight, he turned saying a silent prayer. Duncan stood inches from him a gun in his hand. Cautiously, Briggs set both children down, pushing them behind him. Charles did the same.

Waving the gun, Duncan said, "Congratulations. You found your children. It's a pity I hadn't had a chance to play with them yet." He frowned. "I waited, because the full moon was so near. I do love to play in moonlight. Now it is too late."

He bowed as though he had ended a stellar performance. "That hasn't happened before. Maybe as a prize I'll let you live since I see my nephew died a hero. What a shame; he was once my greatest accomplice."

Briggs's face didn't register surprise. He had figured that out when the young girl lying in the hallway first appeared.

Duncan watched Briggs and noted his lack of expression. "You figured that out, I see. How poetic is it. When the victim becomes the abuser; the prey, the hunter. To create someone else's pain to numb your own. Now, the fool, is dead."

Briggs tried to see past him, to see if Roger's wound was fatal. Duncan knowingly blocked his view. "You're scum. The most depraved being I have ever had the misfortune to meet," Briggs snarled.

Duncan roared, inching forward, his gun pointed. The children whimpered, reminding Briggs that he was not alone, and that their presence made him vulnerable. Then the sound of sirens in the yard penetrated the fog of defiance both men were mired in.

"Time's up." Briggs placed his hands behind him and pushed the children farther toward Charles. He then glided in front of Charles. He would keep his promise to Esther; he would protect all of the children.

Locking eyes with Duncan, and praying, he waited for him to pull the trigger and the bullet to pierce his skin.

Instead, Duncan dropped his hand holding the gun. "Willing to die for them? Sweet. I came for Roger, and now he's dead. Pity I couldn't mix a little business and pleasure too, but I'll adjust." He laughed and went through one of the previously padlocked doors, cackling.

The police burst through the front door, and Briggs called out, "He's up here! He's getting away!"

As they stormed up the stairs, Briggs showed them the door Duncan had fled through. At least six officers ran into the room, but they didn't find anyone. A trapdoor in the ceiling was open, and an officer went up, but later came down empty-handed.

The paramedics came, taking Roger out. Concerned for him, Briggs followed them out, picking up the children, placing kisses all over their faces. That's when he noticed David and BJ had black eyes. He silently fumed but whispered words of comfort. He knew they were all still scared. He could hear Ruth sobbing, "I want my mama."

Climbing down the stairs, Briggs could smell the stench from the sewage settled into the room as much a part of the house as the floor and walls. He trembled, thinking how close they came to losing the children. He hugged the boys again, speeding up, almost stepping on the backs of Charles's shoes.

Outside, he breathed the fresh air, pulling it into his lungs greedily. They placed the children in one of the fire department's paramedics vans when Officer Moore stormed over. Her voice was as cold as ice. "This could have been a catastrophe." She saw Briggs staring at the other ambulance as it pulled away and exhaled. "Your friend is on his way to the hospital; the paramedics feel he'll make it. I'll need a statement from all of you, including the children. We'll do it at the hospital."

Agreeing, Briggs's hand shook as he dialed Esther. "Honey, we have them, we have them!" he sobbed as he heard her resounding cry, "Thank you, Lord!" Wiping his eyes, he told her to hand the phone to Monica.

Before she did as he asked, Esther screamed, "Thank you, thank you. I love you, baby!"

Briggs half-laughed through his tears. "I love you too. Tell me that again when I see you." He then repeated his good news to Monica.

In the hospital emergency room, several children's voices floated over curtained sections of exam rooms. The mothers had not arrived yet and Briggs was still on alert. He'd stationed himself between all three children, attentive to their needs.

Assuring himself that all was well, he pulled the curtain next to his back and observed Charles, who held fast to Miracle. He touched her over and over, smoothing her hair as he clutched her close. Briggs knew for Charles more questions would be asked. But after giving a preliminary statement, Charles was being allowed to go to the station in the morning and give a more thorough report.

The news media's coverage stating that they were all heroes kept Detroit's finest from hauling them all out of Henry Ford Hospital down to the precinct . . . that and Detective Moore's intervention. She was angry, but she understood. Both assailants had been unconscious and were somewhere in the hospital being treated under armed guard. But that was a problem to worry about later.

Releasing the curtain and giving Charles and Miracle their privacy, Briggs's face contorted in anger, and his jaw clenched as he noted David and BJ's black eyes.

Putting his arm around Ruth who leaned against her brother, he asked softly, "Boys, who hit you?"

David, always the more talkative one, sat quietly looking over at BJ who sat on the bed across from him to answer.

"It was the tall man, Daddy. He was trying to lift Miracle's dress, and she was crying and kicking." BJ kicked his short legs out to demonstrate. "She got him good too. Right after that he said some bad words and he started limping toward her again. Then David jumped on his back, and I plowed into his stomach and punched him."

Stopping his spiel, BJ tenderly touched his eye. "He was so mad, he punched both of us, calling us nasty names." BJ got up and went over and put a protective arm around David. "He said we would behave soon enough. Is the bad man coming back, Daddy?"

"No, son," Briggs said visibly shaken, going over and hugging both boys, wondering how long it would be before any of them would feel safe again. He was determined that all of them would get counseling, including himself.

Right after that thought, the women burst in the room, yelling and crying simultaneously.

"My babies!" Esther hollered, her arms flung wide open.

Both David and Ruth screamed, jumping off of their beds. "Mama, Mama!"

Interspersed in their cries were loud smacks of lips on miniature cheeks.

You could hear Phyllis run past and the commotion in the next exam room.

But right on Esther's heels was Monica who screamed the loudest, "BJ!"

BJ lifted his head. Monica saw his shiner and raised her eyes in inquiry to Briggs. "Seems we raised a fighter," he said.

Monica nodded. Barreling over, she embraced BJ until his young body relaxed into hers.

"I love you, Mama," BJ said, and Monica whimpered through her tears.

She looked around, but didn't see Roger. "Where's Roger?"

"He was shot," Briggs said as gently as he could. Monica grabbed her chest. Her eyes glazed over, and Briggs rushed to finish his statement. "He's alive. He's here; they took him into surgery as soon as we got here. I'm not sure of his status, but the paramedics believe he'll be all right. I'm sorry I can't tell you more, but I couldn't leave and could only ask the nurses who came to check on the children."

Monica's eyes spilled over with tears as she kissed and murmured words of love to BJ. Briggs shook his head in wonder. "Monica, the man's actions were heroic. You could do worse."

Monica nodded, kissing BJ once more. "I'll go see if I can find out anything."

Later, after all the exams were complete and the parents' questions were answered by the doctor, quiet snuggles and muffled yawns reigned. They were all waiting on their dismissal papers from the hospital.

Stretching the curtain back from his room, Charles said, "Now that all of the children have been declared physically in good shape, we should take them back to the church, let all our supporters see them, and then leave."

Already having pulled back the curtain that separated Briggs's and Esther's exam rooms, Briggs stood. He turned to Esther who had all of the children draped over some area on her body. "If we go, it can only be for a few minutes. I want to take the children home," she said.

Charles nodded, "Has anyone checked on Roger?"

Turning to lift BJ from Esther's leg and placing him on his lap, he said, "I've asked on and off since we first got here. I was only told he had not gotten out of surgery yet. Monica's gone to the nurse's desk twice, and a little while ago she went to check again."

Esther placed her head on Briggs's shoulder. "Y'all did good. He deserves everyone's support."

Happy to see her free from bitterness, Briggs moved BJ to his other knee, and gave her a lingering kiss on her forehead.

BJ and David comically protested that kisses were yucky and both boys slid to the floor Indian style. Not to be outdone, Ruth climb down and sat with the boys, while Miracle remained glued to Phyllis's side.

Esther leaned against Briggs, their arms now entwined when Monica approached the group. "He's out of surgery now and sedated. And because of us all being brought in together, they were okay with telling me it looks good and giving me all of our paperwork."

As Esther smiled at Monica and she warmly smiled back, she straightened and pulled the children up to leave. Elated she squeezed them close.

Briggs grinned. Looking up, he shook his head. God was wondrous. This was the new shape of his family, and he could live with it.

"Monica, do you want to stay? Roger could awaken soon," Briggs asked as he picked up BJ and David.

"No, him waking up to me at his bedside is a huge step. I don't know if I want him to think of me like that," Monica said, her eyes blinking with moisture.

Moving the children forward, Esther studied her. Then as though deciding she would speak her piece she said, "Never thought I'd say this, but the man deserves a second or third look. He's changed."

Silently, Monica nodded, hesitated, then followed them out of the hospital.

The churchyard was packed to capacity. Briggs pulled up to his reserved spot by the back door and the rest followed his lead. They then took the children into the church.

Using the pastor's entrance to the sanctuary the entire group stood on stage. The whole church went up in a roar. It was deafening. People were jumping up and down and hugging and high-fiving their neighbors.

Esther's parents ran to the stage, taking their grand-children in their arms. Bishop Stokes held the mic praising God as he ran back and forth across the stage, celebrating God's goodness. Briggs's mother was on her knees kissing BJ all over his face. And, Mother Reed the pillar for them all, paced with her hands in the air, giving thanks.

Briggs grabbed the mic from his father. "Thank you all for your support. The last thirty-six hours have been fraught with tension. But you prayed on, you hoped on, and you had enough faith to encourage us to hold on. We're going to take the children home now. Take this as a reminder that God is faithful, and prayer changes things." Briggs moved to hand the mic back to his father, and the others all began to file down the stairs.

"Can I get everyone's attention?" Mother Reed yelled, taking the mic out of Briggs's hand before it reached Bishop Stokes. "Before we go home, we must give thanks for what He has already done, and pray for what He is about to do. There is a young man of our church—his name is Roger—he's in the hospital—"

"He's a criminal," someone yelled from the crowd.

"Yeah," another added.

Mother Reed tapped her mic. The feedback echoed throughout the room. "Can y'all hear me?"

Esther yelled, "Yes, Mother, we can hear you."

"Let him who is without sin cast the first stone. And you know I know who should be shutting it up, right now! You betta tell the truth, 'cause the devil won't. He's the accuser of the brethren, and he'll tell you your mistakes were written in ink—irreversible. God is telling you His blood can erase your past for a brighter future."

Mother Reed stopped talking and peered out among the crowd. She then stared at Naomi. "You brand people, call them by what their mistakes have been. You better be glad God doesn't do that. Hey, Liar, Backbiter, Mr. and Mrs. Jealousy, Fornicator!" She mopped her face with her lace hankie.

"You want to label the man a felon, call him a predator. I was guilty of it too. The devil spoke it so loud, I missed God telling me that first he was His child. Y'all love to talk about David in the Bible, yet nobody wants to talk about the facts that he was an adulterer, a murderer. Why? Because he was more than that. There are people here," she looked at Monica, "who are more than that. More than the body they gave away so easily. We can help somebody by first being the change we want to see."

She then looked at Deborah standing in the back with her parents. "You can change the quality of your life by changing the quality of your choices. I take heart medicine so that I can continue to live and love. Just because your struggle is different doesn't devalue your life."

Taking Joshua's hand for leverage Mother Reed stepped down from the stage. "I'm an old woman, and one thing I can tell you for sure, *everything* is subject to change. The person who you raise up today—calling out, 'Hosanna'—the highest praise, you may want to nail him on a cross and crucify him tomorrow. God is love, church."

The crowd grew quiet, some hanging their heads in shame. Mother Reed stopped in front of each of the children and kissed them. "These babies are so precious. So we gon' pray for Brother Roger, who was key in saving these children and who was shot in the process. Amen?"

"Amen," they roared.

Every bone in Briggs's body was tired and achy. He had officially been up for more than forty hours. He could feel his body crashing.

But before he left he had to try one more time to get through to Monica. He saw her grab and rub on BJ's shoulders. She turned to him slightly shaking her head as though she knew his mission was to champion Roger.

She covered BJ's little ears, and then hissed at Briggs, "He ain't got no money." Her tone was ghetto fabulous, her eyes of concern betraying her false bravado. She faltered as she continued softly, "But since he did so much, I'll go up to the hospital to see about him, seeing as he really doesn't have anyone else."

Briggs locked stares with her. "I think that would be good of you." Then he reminded her gently, "Money is good to have. But even when Randall's money comes in, that won't be yours, that's Fiona's. By the way, where is she?"

"Sister Abigail and Sister Janie have several babies back in the nursery. Sister Abigail will keep her for me overnight."

Briggs leaned down and kissed BJ's forehead. "Praise the Lord for faithful saints and changed hearts. Sister Abigail is a reminder that anyone can change."

Esther and the children joined him as he let BJ hug his mother again before they left. Still teary-eyed and punch drunk from lack of sleep, Esther yawned and leaned against him. "You did it. You brought all the children back safely. Thank you," she said as she held on tight to both Ruth and David.

"We all did it, most of all, a merciful God."

Chapter Fifty-one

The church members were happily dispersing. They had prayed for Roger, and quite a few members came up and were led in a prayer of repentance by Bishop Stokes.

Esther saw Deborah and her parents in the crowd, and they all went over to speak with them. Briggs hugged Deborah, reclaiming lost years. With tears in her eyes Esther said, "Thank you so much for coming."

Deborah took her hand causing Esther to release the children. "We're sisters. I will never let you down again."

Esther grinned through glistening eyes. "I promise the same."

As they walked away Briggs knew he needed to get the children home. It was just every time they started to leave, they saw someone else to thank. Esther was now hugging Simone and who he suspected was her new boyfriend, Lee. Looking around, he realized everyone they loved was in this place.

Briggs walked up the stairs to the podium and took the mic off the stand. "May I have everyone's attention, please?"

He walked through the crowd making his way to Esther. "I mean no disrespect to anyone, but I have loved this lady for a very long time. And if it was going to fade, it would have been gone by now." He waved BJ over. "Okay, son, this may not be what we had planned, but do it like we practiced."

Both Briggs and BJ, in sync, dropped to their left knee.

Esther covered her face, and both her children pulled her hands down.

"Will you marry us?"

Briggs watched Esther looking at the smiling faces of her children, her parents clapping, and Phyllis and Charles with their thumbs up. She then looked over at Monica who was back from the nursery, standing near the door, preparing to leave. During the last twenty-four hours he knew the two had made a connection. Was she upset by this announcement?

Briggs saw with relief, Monica mouthed, "Go for it."

"Yes, I will marry you both," Esther said, as whooping and hollering resounded joyfully throughout the sanctuary.

Briggs kissed her then jumped up and down, doing his own Holy Ghost dance.

"Can we go home now?" Esther said, grinning from ear to ear.

Briggs lifted her up, swung her around and shouted, and with the children hanging on, they pranced out of the church. Laughingly the entire crowd followed them out.

"This is Channel Four news with a breaking news report. Duncan Sanders, who has been on the most wanted list since the abduction of four children five nights ago, has been apprehended in a red-light district in New Orleans. He was in possession of child pornography, date rape drugs, and several passports in different aliases."

Monica turned off the television mounted to the wall in the hospital room. She held up the drink for Roger to sip from. "Justice is served."

Tubes running from his arm, Roger gingerly lifted up to sip his drink. "My counselor thinks it would be a great idea for us to have some sessions with her together."

Feeling the beige walls and antiseptic smell closing in on her, Monica pulled the drink back. "I don't know why, we're not a couple."

"You've been here every day for the last five days. So, yes, we are a couple. You said you would marry me." Roger pressed the button, and the hospital bed whined as it rose until he was even with Monica's gaze.

"We were six years old." Her eyes rolled skyward.

Bandaged and reaching for her hand tentatively, Roger said, "Doesn't matter, you promised."

Monica peeked at him under her eyelids. "You're broke."

"You're broken," Roger said in a matter-of-fact manner.

Outraged, Monica jumped up.

Roger frowned at her antics. "Sit down, girl. We will always be honest with each other. I remember a little girl who was innocent and pure. She stood up for me when nobody else cared to. We've both made so many bad choices. We've hurt people because we were hurting. Sweetheart, we deserve each other."

Monica sank down. She picked up the cup and held it to his lips. "We'll see."

Roger smiled, and his eyes lit up his entire face. "Yes, my queen, we will."

Imp One lay at the bottom of the lower region of hell. It was where those who failed were sent. He felt it was unfair. He had done what he was told. He had not let Roger talk to the pedophile. The Leader said nothing about Roger talking to anyone else.

There was an upside to the fire scorching his scales . . . There was no Leader. This was what would make his exile bearable.

Suddenly, a large bang sounded, and flaming rock slid back, revealing an entrance. Through it, The Leader staggered in. There were many cuts and welts covering his body. Scales were missing from his tail, and his back had whip gashes down it.

The Leader spotted him right away. "Good, you are here. Fetch me something for these cuts," The Leader roared.

Imp One looked on in misery. He could not take this, he would not. He turned and walked into the fire's flames. Seconds later, ashes floated in the air.

"Fool!" The Leader yelled, as he looked around for who he could coerce to take his place.

Archangel Michael stood on a majestic mountain. Zadkiel stood next to him. He said, "It was a fierce fight, brother."

Michael shot up into the air, and then floated down. "The end was spoken before the first blow."

"The prayers were fuel for our battle," Zadkiel said.

"Yes, when our people pray, then heaven responds."

Zadkiel watched those in his charge from on high. "There shall be rest for a season. Briggs and Esther will finally have their happily ever after. And Phyllis is taking more care in giving Miracle too much, too soon. The wild card is Monica and Roger a story still unfolding."

"And what of Deborah? Have she and Esther restored their childhood friendship?"

Zadkiel shook his head. "No, brother. They are well acquainted, but much has transpired over the years. They have gone down different roads."

"*Is this a good thing?*" *Michael asked, puzzled as to the relationships humans engaged in as he was of the warrior class.*

"*Yes. Deborah has met several people in her classes here in Detroit. They have common interests and they encourage each other. She is happy. She is with her family, and her mother has learned how to help her and to help educate others too. Her life will be challenged, but full.*"

"*Joshua and Mother Reed are truly fierce prayer warriors. The demons could not distract or tire them in their press.*"

Zadkiel spun. "*I love an unwavering heart. In her twilight years, Mother Reed is as dangerous to the dark ones as those in their youth. Hell absolutely despises her. Yet, her work is not done.*"

"*So, we live to love another day?*" *Michael said.*

"*Yes, we fight on,*" *Zadkiel said as he flew into the heavens, headed home.*

Book Club Study Questions

1. The majority of the characters in the book struggle with their self-image. Why is this such a prevalent problem today?
2. Meredith Hawthorne's refusal to forgive led to her bitterness and heartache. Is there someone(s) you need to forgive?
3. Esther felt she had had her chance at real love. Can you have more than one "real" love in a lifetime?
4. Roger changed over the years, but Esther could not accept it. Is Roger's change realistic? Do people really change?
5. The issue of mental health is explored in this novel. How can you learn to be more accepting of those in our families and communities who struggle with these illnesses?
6. The angels played an important role in this novel. Do you believe in angels?
7. Mother Reed finally has a relationship with her grown son. Is it easy to form a relationship with a once-absent parent?
8. Monica falls back into her old ways of using her body and the spirit of manipulation to try to control those around her. How hard is it to break past destructive habits?
9. Naomi loved to label people. How often do you label people?
10. Miracle was given everything she asked for from her parents. How dangerous is this?

11. The children in the book are curious about their bodies. Esther has problems discussing their anatomy without using "pet" names for their body parts. Do you use nicknames for body parts with your children? Why or why not is this appropriate?

12. How old should children be before they are on social media?

UC HIS GLORY BOOK CLUB!

www.uchisglorybookclub.net

UC His Glory Book Club is the spirit-inspired brain-child of Joylynn Ross, Author and Acquisitions Editor of Urban Christian, and Kendra Norman-Bellamy, Author for Urban Christian. This is an online book club that hosts authors of Urban Christian. We welcome as members all men and women who have a passion for reading Christian-based fiction.

UC His Glory Book Club pledges our commitment to provide support, positive feedback, encouragement, and a forum whereby members can openly discuss and review the literary works of Urban Christian authors.

There is no membership fee associated with UC His Glory Book Club; however, we do ask that you support the authors through purchasing, encouraging, providing book reviews, and of course, your prayers. We also ask that you respect our beliefs and follow the guidelines of the book club. We hope to receive your valuable input, opinions, and reviews that build up, rather than tear down our authors.

What We Believe:

—We believe that Jesus is the Christ, Son of the Living God.

—We believe the Bible is the true, living Word of God.

—We believe all Urban Christian authors should use their God-given writing abilities to honor God and share the message of the written word God has given to each of them uniquely.

—We believe in supporting Urban Christian authors in their literary endeavors by reading, purchasing, and sharing their titles with our online community.

—We believe that in everything we do in our literary arena should be done in a manner that will lead to God being glorified and honored.

We look forward to the online fellowship with you.

Please visit us often at:

www.uchisglorybookclub.net.

Many Blessings to You!

Shelia E. Lipsey,
President, UC His Glory Book Club